Long Isle Iced Tea

Magic & Mixology Mystery Series, Volume 4

Gina LaManna

Published by Gina LaManna Publishing, 2017.

LONG ISLE ICED TEA

First edition. November 2, 2017.

Written by Gina LaManna.

Islanders, this book is for you!

For updates on new releases, please sign up for Gina's newsletter on her website at GinaLaManna.com

Acknowledgments

To the Islanders!

SPECIAL THANKS:

To my fiancé, Alex! 11/11—make a wish! я тебя люблю!

To my family—for always being an inspiration.

To Stacia—for your spreadsheets!

To my fabulous proofreader, Connie!

To my awesome cover designer—Sarah at Sprinkles on Top Studios.

And above all, to my readers. Without you, there wouldn't be a Ranger X or Lily!

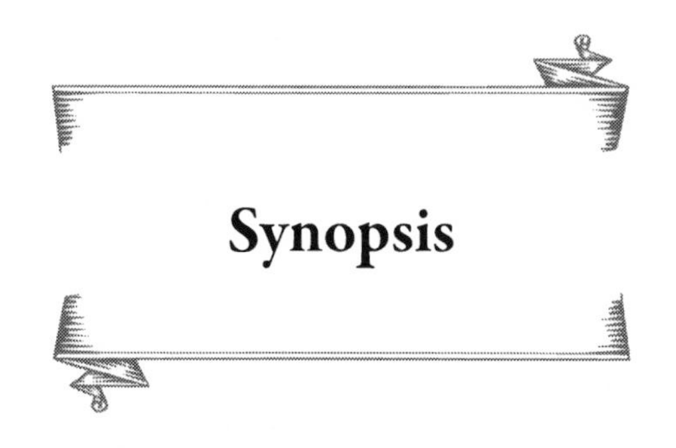

Synopsis

STAR LIGHT, STAR BRIGHT, the first star I see tonight...

A childhood chant turns near deadly for Lily Locke when she's swept into The Faction's latest triumph—the overthrowing of the hidden, magical city of Wishery.

When Ainsley and her team at MAGIC, Inc. beg Lily for her help, she agrees, taking on a load of problems that pile up faster than she can say *Abracadabra.* A new revolution in black magic stumps the island's burgeoning Mixologist, while a haunted house, a surprise birthday party, and rising familial troubles back on The Isle compete for her already-limited time and attention.

Lily's barely hanging on by a thread, juggling life, love, and the pursuit of magic, when islanders start disappearing—one at a time. When a man warns her the next disappearance is imminent, Lily must crack the curse...before she's next.

I wish I may, I wish I might...have the wish I wish tonight.

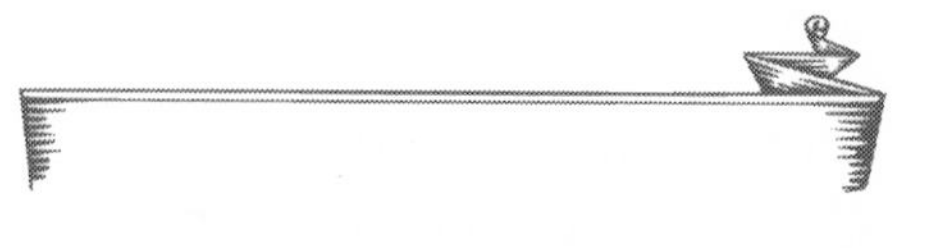

Prologue

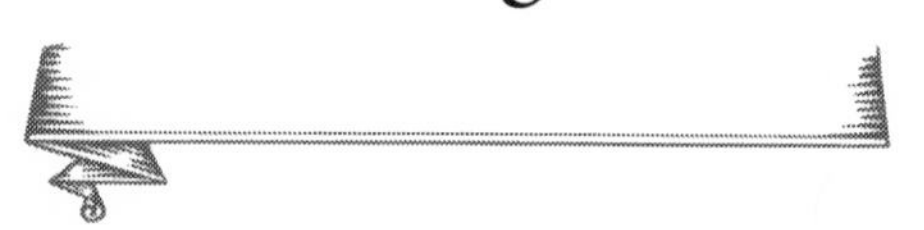

"*Star light, star bright,*

The first star I see tonight.

I wish I may, I wish I might,

Have the wish I wish tonight."

I closed my eyes and made a wish as per the tradition of human children everywhere. I felt Ranger X's grip around me tighten until I opened my eyes and looked at him.

"What'd you just do?" A streak of curiosity flitted through his eyes. "That sounds like a spell."

"Don't be silly. It's just a nursery rhyme."

"Did you make a wish?"

"Of course! Close your eyes," I instructed him. "And make a wish, too. That's the rule."

"What did you wish for?"

I gave him a playful swat to the chest. "I can't tell you *that*. Everyone knows wishes don't come true if you say them aloud."

"But—"

"Just say the chant and make a wish."

X did as I suggested. He closed his eyes, and I watched as his lashes fluttered against his cheeks.

"What'd you wish for?" I asked.

"I wished—"

"Shhh—" I interrupted him by swallowing his words with a kiss. "You must promise you'll never tell."

"But—"

"Do you want your wish to come true?"

He fell into silence. "More than anything."

"Then keep it locked away in here." I tapped his chest. "And let the world work its magic."

"Magic?"

"What else would you call it?"

"Fair enough." He closed his hand over mine, locking it against his chest. "I promise."

Chapter 1

IN A TIME WHERE THE very existence of our Isle had been threatened, the things we'd known and loved broken, and the relationships we'd cultivated shattered—one man had managed to offset all of it. The fear, the danger, the stress of life had been cast aside for one night.

Leaning in, I pressed my lips to his and let the whisper of passion speak for itself. From within me came a longing, a burning need for Ranger X to know this feeling, to understand what this night meant to me.

X deepened the kiss as his hands slid over my waist, pulling my hips closer to him as we curled on the blanket underneath the stars. The evening had begun with a picnic, a surprise meal prepared by him and finished with a shared bottle of wine as the moon sparkled above the waves of Lake Superior that surrounded this enchanted island.

"You are so beautiful, Lily." X whispered against my cheek, following the pause with a press of his lips to my forehead. "I love you more than all of this."

"This?"

"This island, this lifetime, this..." He spread one arm wide and encompassed the weight of the world around us, the sugary sand against the shoreline, the inky blackness of the waters, the milky glow of the constellations above. "This. You are my everything."

My arms circled his neck, and we curled closer in our private, snug hideaway against the side of the volcano. We'd climbed for hours to reach this nook, not far from the Library of Secrets. We'd had lunch with the Witch of the Woods and taken directions from Glinda's fairies before stumbling upon the privacy that would soon be ours.

Here, tucked into the highest point on The Isle, we'd played under the waterfall and eaten fresh fruits and berries before settling down for a light meal of crackers and cheeses, meats and olives. Then we'd sipped wine to the setting sun and rang in the night tucked into a blanket with our limbs entwined.

"This place is magic."

"I thought you might enjoy it." Ranger X pulled himself into a sitting position. "May I?"

Without waiting for a response, he poured the last of the wine into the glass nestled onto a makeshift tree-stump table. As he did so, I took the moment to study his long, stunning physique clothed as always in black from head to toe.

When he caught me looking, I made a big show of sitting up, adjusting my nightshirt, pretending I hadn't been staring. Technically, the shirt belonged to X. The last few months I'd taken to wearing his old button-ups as sleepwear because the material was soft and smelled of him.

When we slept apart, there was something comforting about having his clothes wrapped around me. Plus, I had the added bonus that came when he spied me in an article of his clothing: the satisfied, primal look that took over his face, brimming with possessiveness.

I liked being *his*.

"You're cute." The wine gave me a pleasant sort of buzz, my stomach warm and my heart warmer. I reached out for him, grasping his cheeks between my hands and landing a kiss on his lips.

He chuckled, and then murmured a few suggestions in a low voice, dry and gravelly, that sent shivers over my spine.

I followed his gaze as he glanced at his shirt on me, specifically at the button near the top that'd popped open during our embrace. I moved to close it, but his hand came up and circled around mine instead.

Nestling in, I rested my head on his chest. This whole evening had been planned by X—the food, the hike, the location. An evening getaway, just the two of us with no work and no distractions.

Nothing except for us and the quiet of the world.

One night where, finally, peace settled in, and the darkness stayed away.

At least, until morning.

Chapter 2

"THANK YOU, *so* much." I circled my arms around Ranger X's neck as my bare toes sank into the white sand outside of the bungalow. "I had a wonderful time."

X surveyed the area around us, the morning sun just barely rising. We'd spent the night in the cave wrapped around one another, a warm and delicious cocoon, before he'd woken me in the still-dark hours to make the early morning trek back. He'd claimed the sunrise would be worth it. I argued that sleep would've been *more* worth it.

"I'm sorry we had to get moving so early; if we weren't still on the training schedule—"

"I know, I know. Zin tells me about it every day." I rolled my eyes, smiling at the reference to my cousin, a newly minted Ranger who might very well marry her job. She'd already fallen in love with it. "You're the boss, and you have a job to do. I should get back to work, too."

"Wait, Lily. I have something for you."

I let my hands slide back from around his neck and raised an eyebrow.

X moved from one foot to the next before clasping his hands behind his back. His eyes shifted to look out over the lake, watching the orange glow of the horizon.

"What is it?" I asked. "Is something wrong?"

"No."

"Do you need help?"

"No."

"Are we going to play this game all day?"

"No."

"Just say it then," I said. "Spit it out."

Ranger X sighed, reached into his pocket, and retrieved something small. "I'd like to give you something. I'm not any good at this—sorry."

"*What* is it?"

He grasped my wrist, guided my hand until it flipped palm up, and then pressed something hard and metal into my skin. "Don't take this the wrong way, but I want you to have—"

"A key?!" I retracted my hand enough to expose the small, tarnished metal he'd placed there. "Where does this lead?"

"To my house."

"Your house? Where you live? In The Forest? Where you sleep at night? And shower? And eat?"

A flicker of amusement crossed his face. "That would be my house."

"Well, gee." I flipped the key over again and examined it. "I don't know what to say."

"I told you I'm bad at this. I'm sorry—if it makes you uncomfortable, or if you don't want it, just say the word, but—"

"Are you kidding?" I flung myself at him and let my arms do the rest. "I love it! I'm so touched, X, really. Thank you. I'll use it wisely."

After catching my flying hug, he tugged me closer still. "You're sure it's not too soon? I didn't want you to feel uncomfortable or rushed."

"I'm surprised," I admitted. "With your job and your skills, you're pretty...uh, anal about locking up everywhere—no offense. Are you sure you *want* me to have it?"

"I'm positive." His hand ran through my hair and came to rest on my back. "I had it made for you."

I frowned. "What does that mean?"

"It means you're the only person who's allowed to use it."

"Ah, a spell. But how—"

"Liam has a contact on the mainland. Specializes in complicated locks and defense systems."

"Of course he does," I said with a smile. The key felt warm to the touch, and now that he mentioned it, I could sense the magic sizzling around it. "And if I lose it?"

"If you lose it, it will combust and incinerate everything within fifteen feet."

I gawked at him, then shoved the key toward him. "That's horrible and dangerous! I can't be trusted with this."

His eyes crinkled. "A joke. If it's lost it becomes useless. It's enchanted to only work for you, so if anyone else gets ahold of it, it won't do them any good."

I smiled up at him and let my hand close around the key. "So, what am I supposed to use this for?"

"Whatever you desire. If you ever need a place to stay, and I'm away or at work, you're welcome to let yourself inside. If you need any supplies, you're welcome to help yourself. If you want—"

"—to swing by for no reason and surprise you with one of these?" I leaned onto my tiptoes and pressed a kiss to his lips. "Is that okay, too?"

His arms tightened around my waist as he returned it with a deeper one. "I was hoping you would ask, and I think the answer to that is obvious."

Humming, I practically hopped into the bungalow a few minutes later, once I'd finished my goodbyes with X. Our trip had been nothing short of incredible.

I had fresh air in my lungs, a lightness in my chest, and a key in my pocket. I had an amazing man who loved me, a family that supported me, and a career for which I'd been born.

Absolutely nothing could dampen today. Nothing, except—

"What'd the idiot give you now?"

I pressed a hand to my chest, startled by Gus's growly voice. I'd been so intent on humming my way inside the purple and pink shuttered building that I hadn't noticed him sitting there. The bungalow served as both my place of employment and my place of residence, and Gus came with the package.

"What idiot?" I turned to face Gus with a frown. "You'll have to be more specific."

"That lovesick puppy who had his hands all over you."

"Oh, Gus." I sidled over to my mentor and sat on the bench across from him. "Are you feeling jealous that I spent the night away from here?"

"I used to think that man had manners. Thought Ranger X might be the last soul on this island with any ounce of chivalry, aside from myself."

"He is the most chivalrous person I know, and the least idiotic. What's got you upset?"

"Chivalry ain't sticking his tongue down a woman's throat in public."

"He kissed my cheek!" I fought off a rush of warmth to my face, and I stood up, kicking my bench back. "You need to relax. We're all adults here."

Gus fussed some more, busying his hands as he chopped something that looked like dried lizard's tail into dust. "It's about time you made it back. Mixologists shouldn't be gallivanting around the island without protection."

"Gus, the sun is barely up. Ranger X is more protection than I'll ever need. Plus, it's good to take time off now and again. I need to explore and understand the island that *I'm* supposed to help."

Gus struggled to agree.

"Would it help if I said I brought something back for you?" I reached into my travel belt, a nifty little gadget used to carry first aid vials while traversing The Isle, and removed a baggy full of the bright red flowers that could be found growing only on the sides of a volcano. "I harvested some Fire Birds..."

Gus took one of the Fire Birds and burped it. An impressive flame shot from its petals. I watched as he surveyed the size, shape, and color of the fire. The health of the plant. The sturdiness of the bloom.

Finally, he gave a nod. "Not bad."

"Not bad?! We looked for hours to find the best ones! You have to admit these are prime specimens, and—"

Both Gus and I turned to watch the commotion storming through the front door. Zin, dressed in her leather pants and dark tank top, her severe bob swishing around her chin, stomped into the storeroom.

She glanced up, caught Gus and I watching her, and scowled. "What are you looking at?"

While Gus made himself busy studying row after row of the colorful canisters along the wall, I was stuck matching Zin's gaze and struggling for a response.

"Why are you smiling?" she asked. "What do you have to be happy about?"

"Gee," I murmured to Gus. "She's even crankier than you."

Gus muffled a snort as he studied a tin filled with bright purple leaves. He popped the lid open, sniffed it, and then grimaced. He placed the jar back on the shelf as Zin hurled more questions our way.

"Where were you last night?" Zin asked. "I thought—"

"Hold on," I said, raising my hands in surrender. "What's wrong?"

"Nothing," Zin snapped over a loud exhale. After a pause, she shook her head. "I'm tired. It's nothing."

"Are you sure?" I pressed. "You seem pretty upset for it to be nothing."

"I haven't been sleeping well, *okay*? Leave me alone!"

"Does this have anything to do with Trinket?" I asked. "Did you have another argument with your mom?"

"It's *nothing*. Forget it."

Gus's shoulders stiffened along the back wall, frowning as he swirled a pearl-colored liquid around in a vial. He hated when people brought drama into the store—*it's a place of business*, he'd say. *Not a psychology office.*

I ignored him and eased onto the bench next to the room's center table. "Sit down and tell me what happened."

"Nothing happened." Zin's slight figure shifted as she dropped onto the bench. Her eyes, flecked with gold ever since her first shift into a jaguar, found my face. "Nothing important, anyway. It's stupid."

"Well, I am really good at listening, and my offer still stands. You can always come stay here if you aren't getting along with your mom, and you want a change of scenery. We have plenty of space."

Zin glanced over her shoulder, first at me, then to Gus. "I don't think so. I shouldn't have come here in the first place."

"Zin, wait!" Before I could stop her, however, she jumped up and hurried out the front door, slamming it behind her. I whirled to face Gus. "Look what you did!"

"What?" He looked genuinely confused.

"You stomp around here, frowning all the time. My own cousin doesn't even want to talk to m-e-ee..."

Before I could finish the word, my mind began to swirl, spiral out of control as I tumbled forward and fell into the table. My hands collapsed onto the wood as I attempted to ease myself into the seat. I missed, unable to control my limbs. My insides felt like they were melting, turning to liquid. A sharp pop sounded between my ears, and I remembered nothing more.

Chapter 3

"GET HER UP HERE."

"She's not going to be happy."

"Well, she's waking up, so we can't wait any longer."

"I *told* you not to take her. There are specific procedures we're supposed to use with residents from The Isle—"

"—too late for procedures now, isn't it? Get the boss in here. She'll want to see this."

The voices sounded too efficient to be malicious, but my brain struggled to piece the puzzle together. One male voice and one female, and then *the boss.* Three people at least, one of them not yet here.

I kept my eyes shut tight as my brain, fuzzy at best, struggled for clarity. One of the two people in the room hovered over me. Judging by the faint floral scent of perfume, it was the female.

"I didn't think we hit her so hard," the woman's voice said next to my ear, confirming my theory. "Do you think she's never been Zapped before?"

"I'm sure she has. She's the Mixologist."

I couldn't bear to keep my eyes shut any longer. If these people had taken me for harm, I'd rather find out and figure out a plan. As the female pressed a finger against my throat, possibly checking my pulse, my eyes flashed open.

The woman leapt back, a shriek of surprise flying from her lips as she landed on the other side of the office. "Jiminy Crickets," she said, masking a few obscene words as she recovered. "You scared me, Mixologist. How long have you been awake?"

I eased myself into a sitting position, surprised to find I'd been lying on something that resembled a conference room table. For some reason, I'd expected to find myself in a doctor's office, or a cell. Instead, I was sitting in an office building not unlike the one I'd been fired from at my last marketing job on the mainland.

"How long have I been *awake*?" I rubbed my neck, discovering my muscles were a bit sore. "I want to know how long I've been *out*!"

The woman cast a guilty look at her male counterpart. They wore almost matching ensembles of black pants and white blouses—hers slightly more feminine than the male's.

"Sorry about that," she said. "We were just wondering if you'd ever been Zapped before?"

"I don't know what that means. And I have no clue where I am."

"See?! I told you to wait for permission before you Zapped her!" The woman snapped at her partner. "Why don't you ever listen to me? Ainsley is going to be royally pissed you dragged her here with no prior knowledge."

"Ainsley?" I latched on to the one familiar thread in this web of confusion. "What does Ainsley have to do with any of this?"

"She's currently heading up our cross-functional team," the woman said. "Sorry, but I should introduce myself. I'm Lizzie Beacher, and this here is Zane Donovan."

I glanced between the two, both looking like a mid-level executives in a high-security technology company. "And we are located...where?"

"Oh, right. Sorry," Lizzie apologized. "You are at—"

"What were you *thinking*?" Ainsley stormed into the conference room, took one glance at the situation, and shuddered. "Why is she here already, Lizzie? Zane? You'd better have some answers for me!"

I gave a feeble wave at her. "Hello."

"Hi, Lily. By the way, I'm thrilled to see you, despite the frustration in my voice. That's aimed at these two knuckleheads."

"Great to see you, too."

"Go get her some water at least, will you Zane?" Ainsley gestured with a clipboard under her arm. "Move it! The woman's been Zapped."

"Sorry, but I'm super confused." I raised a finger. "Where are we?"

Ainsley tried to stay calm, but I could see her blood pressure rising from across the room. Her cheeks turned pink as she focused on Lizzie, and her fingers clinched tight. "You haven't even told her where she is?! The poor woman is probably thinking she's kidnapped! I swear, this place is going to hell in a handbasket."

"It's okay, really," I said. "I'm just curious."

"Naturally!" Muttering under her breath, Ainsley wound her way to me, a bright smile on her face as she approached. "Sorry about that. We're in crisis mode around here, but I didn't know that meant people lost their *common sense*!" Then she hesitated and threw her arms wide. "Can I get a hug, boss?"

I grinned and leaned into the embrace. "It's really good to see you again. I'd have shown my excitement better if I wasn't—"

"—confused, I know. Zane was so anxious to get you here he acted without approval. I wanted to come talk to you in person first, like normal people do, so you'd know what to expect."

"So, Zapping is..."

"A legal way for law enforcement to bring outsiders onto the MAGIC, Inc. properties."

"Does that mean I'm at MAGIC, Inc.?"

Ainsley flexed her fingers, casting a scathing glance at Zane, who'd just returned with water. "Yes. They should've informed you that you are safe, you are a guest of the agency's, and we really appreciate your appearance."

"It's not like I had a choice," I said, accepting the glass of water and taking a sip. "Kidding," I added quickly, before she could fire Zane. Thanks to my friendship with Ainsley, I'd heard of MAGIC, Inc before: Magic and Guardian Investigative Committee. Located on the mainland, it was the central governing body for paranormals. "What do you need help with?"

"Lizzie," Ainsley, my former Guardian, instructed. "Start from the beginning."

Lizzie nodded, clearly anxious to redeem herself. "I'm Lizzie Beacher, as I mentioned. I'm head of the Wishery Department at MAGIC, Inc."

"Wishery?" I looked to Ainsley. "Never heard of it."

"That's to be expected," Lizzie said, consulting her notes. "We received your wish at approximately 11:32 yesterday evening."

"What are you talking about?" I thought back to the previous night, but my only memories those of Ranger X. Memories I didn't exactly feel like sharing with strangers. "I'm sorry, I was on a date. I wasn't working on magic, or spells, or—"

"Star light, star bright," Lizzie began. "The first star I see tonight...ringing any bells?"

"That's not a spell," I argued. "It's a nursery rhyme."

"Nope," Ainsley said. "It's actually a spell. And you activated it successfully, which means Lizzie received your wish. Lizzie, care to explain?"

"Right!" Lizzie jumped to attention. "This is an instance where a genuine magical spell somehow worked its way into popular culture as a fairy tale. As you know, most fairy tales have their basis in reality."

"I didn't know that."

"It's true," Ainsley said. "But humans never figure out that Sleeping Beauty was actually a real person who'd been put under a poisonous spell for years. Cinderella was a ditz who lost her shoe—the story doesn't go on to explain that she'd had one too many cocktails at the party. *No,* the humans focus on the *shoe*."

"Are you telling me that wishes are made real?"

Lizzie nodded. "At the moment, I'm the managing director for Wishery, the wish department of MAGIC, Inc."

"You're going to have to clarify. Do you guys actually grant wishes?"

"It's more complicated than that." Lizzie rolled up the sleeves to her blouse and moved toward the other end of the conference room. She murmured a spell under her breath, and the end of her finger turned into a piece of chalk. Immediately, she started writing on the board. "There are three pieces to a wish. Stop me if you've heard this before."

"Uh, nope," I said. "Clueless."

"Great. The first is that the wish must be selfless, or mostly selfless. Wishing for a million bucks for no reason except greed will get you diddly squat."

"Diddly squat," I repeated. "Okay."

"Number two is that your wish can't harm anyone. Wishing for anyone to fall ill will get you...?"

"Diddly squat," I finished. "I had no idea there were stipulations on wishes."

"We don't make it public. If we did, people would manipulate the rules and make our jobs much, much harder. This way, only the purest of wishes land on our desk."

"You said there's a third thing?"

"Ah, yes. My favorite." Lizzie dropped her hand from the board, turned to me, and smiled. "A sense of wonder."

As I sat there watching her, the word ***WONDER*** appeared behind her on the chalkboard. The chalk disintegrated from her finger and the word grew and grew until it took up the entire board.

"A sense of wonder?"

"A person must believe with the utmost certainty in the power of wishes. They must absolutely, wonderfully let go of everything in this world that tells them wishes are a load of crap and believe that it can come true. If all three things are present, a wish is put in our queue to examine for granting."

"How long is your queue?"

"Let's just say we're working a lot of overtime these days." Lizzie sounded a bit cross. "It's a very complicated procedure that we've been perfecting for—"

Ainsley cleared her throat.

"Right," Lizzie corrected. "High level overview—sorry."

"I'm interested!" I said. "Keep going."

"It's not about you," Ainsley said. "If you get Lizzie going, she'll talk about it for days. And I mean that. She's three hundred years old and has been working at Wishery for two hundred and eight of those years."

I gawked at the woman who didn't appear to be a day older than me. "Three hundred years?"

"I have some strong Elfin blood," she said with a shrug. "Anyway, back to the details. There's a queue of wishes, and once they're sorted into different departments, we set to addressing them."

"What do you mean you address them? You grant them? Make them come true?"

Lizzie's fingers flinched again, struggling to keep her responses concise. "Not exactly. It's more complica—"

"More complicated than that, we know," Ainsley said. "Keep moving, Liz."

"Sorry," she huffed again. "Wishes are not always granted for various reasons. Sometimes people wish for one thing, but it's not their true desire. One person might wish to be happier, but what they need isn't to be happier—it's to find a better job. Reconnect with an old friend. Overturn a bit of money to get them through a tight spot.

Things like that. It's nearly impossible for me to grant even the purest of wishes if it's too big—"

"Like happiness?"

"Yes," Lizzie said. "Which is why, oftentimes our job is just to point people in the right direction. The answer is almost always right before their eyes."

I waited for more, fascinated. I almost wished Ainsley hadn't arrived right away so I could've sat and listened to Lizzie talk uninterrupted.

A clap of the hands from Ainsley, however, signaled our time to chat was nearly up. "I really hate to be the bad cop here," Ainsley said. "But we do have a serious problem."

"Yes," Lizzie resumed, the look in her eyes morphing from passion into something darker. Frustration maybe, or anger. "We have a problem, and we need your help."

"I recommended you for the job," Ainsley said. "If anyone can solve our little issue, it's you."

"Gee, no pressure."

"We're severely limited in who we ask for help; the whole beauty of the Wishery program is that it's never been confirmed to exist—you know, nobody knows about it outside of these offices except for you," Lizzie said. "Which reminds me, I'm going to need you to sign some confidentiality papers."

"Sorry," Ainsley agreed, pushing her clipboard toward me. "I told them you were the Mixologist and could be trusted, but it's the standard procedure."

"What is this?" I took the proffered pen in my hand and glanced over the document.

"Standard NDA," Ainsley said. "Basically, it says that you won't tell anybody else about Wishery's existence."

"Not even Gus? Or my cousins?"

"Sorry," Ainsley said. "MAGIC, Inc. is quite clear on it. The whole reason Wishery isn't overloaded with wishes is that most people don't believe it's true. If it was confirmed to exist...all the real wishes would get lost in the noise."

I frowned, reviewed the document and found nothing suspicious, and signed my name. As I swirled the final 'e' in *Locke*, I felt the familiar zing of magic as it ran up my arm, tingled around my elbow, and then warmed me fingers to shoulder.

"A magical contract," I said. "Impossible to break."

"Near impossible," Ainsley corrected. "But yes, of course. This is MAGIC, Inc. What'd you expect, a spell-less sheet of paper?"

"Now that you've signed the document, we must show you the rest," Lizzie said. "Have you ridden before?"

"Ridden?" My face probably looked blank. "In a car? A horse? A train?"

"A broomstick, of course," Lizzie said. "We're going to Wishery."

"Uh, no. Broomsticks aren't allowed on The Isle."

Lizzie stiffened. "I've never understood that rule."

"Come on," Ainsley said. "We'll check one out from the Transportation Department. It's easy."

"It takes weeks to check one out," Lizzie said. "She can ride on mine."

"Nah, Stan owes me a favor." Ainsley moved across the room and threw her arm over my shoulders. "And Lily here wants to try for herself. "

"I don't know," I said. "I should probably just ride on the back of someone else's."

"Nonsense," Ainsley argued. "Once you get a taste of the fresh air and speed, you'll be begging Ranger X to get the rules changed on the island."

"I don't know about that."

"Trust me," Ainsley said, a few minutes later as she handed over a broomstick from Stan. "You will love it. Follow me to the flight deck."

Chapter 4

"I DON'T REALLY LIKE this," I said, gripping the handle for dear life. "It feels like a death wish."

"I would ignore your death wish if it showed up in the Wishery queue," Lizzie said, comfortingly. "Don't worry. It's against policy."

"That doesn't make me feel better."

"Riding on an agency issued broom is one of the safest ways to travel," Ainsley said. "They have to inspect it between each and every flight."

"Except for that one time last year when Stan..." Lizzie trailed off at the look in Ainsley's eyes, then quickly muttered, "Never mind."

"Seriously. Just hold on tight, squeeze everywhere you can, and enjoy the rush of it!" Ainsley clapped a hand on my shoulder and gave me a sympathetic pat. "You will love it, I promise."

"I just don't think that's accurate." I stood at the very top of MAGIC, Inc., an eighty-story skyscraper in downtown Minneapolis. I finally recognized my whereabouts now that I had the entire view of the city before me.

The top forty floors of this building were invisible to the human eye, and the bottom forty floors had been disguised as a bank. This high up, there was absolutely nothing between me and a painful death on the ground except for a flimsy little stick with some straw attached to the end. The thing was meant to sweep floors, not hold my weight when I took a nosedive off the flight deck.

"One, two..." Ainsley took my hand, tugged me to the edge, and on three we all tumbled over the side.

For the first thirty seconds I screamed bloody murder. I shouted until my throat went hoarse. A tear from pure fright might've manifested on my cheek.

"Am I flying?" I glanced at Ainsley, who had muttered a silencing spell to cut down on the noise. I nodded toward the shimmering bubble around us. "Sorry about that."

"No problem. Are you good?" Ainsley held up a hand and, when I nodded, waved the spell away. "Excellent. I hate to use the spell; it blocks fresh air, and you're not really flying until you're one with the clouds."

"You make it sound so poetic."

Lizzie zoomed around to my side. "I got caught outside the Silencing Spell. How are you liking the flight?"

"Once I realized that I wasn't dead, I was fine." I took stock of my surroundings. My hands encircled the thin broomstick, and when I glanced behind me, little wisps of cloud circled behind like an airplane writing messages in the sky.

"She's ready," Ainsley said, beckoning with one hand. "Follow me."

I didn't have time to agree or disagree because the next thing I knew, Ainsley bolted out in front of me. I leaned forward to follow her, and to my surprise, the broomstick leapt into super-speed behind her. The first rush of air in my lungs sent a crisp, raw freshness through my body that had me feeling more alive than ever.

Over the next thirty minutes, Ainsley took us on a tour of the countryside. We dipped through the clouds and skimmed the tops of trees. We raced above barns and loop-de-looped through fields with no company except for the cattle, until finally Ainsley declared me a natural.

"Excellent work," Ainsley said. "And, we're here."

"Where?" I scanned in confusion around us, but there was nothing. Pastures with horses grazing and hay bales stacked halfway to the sky, but no buildings, no humans, no nothing.

"There." Lizzie's finger shook as she pointed toward the distance. "Do you see the cloud?"

I squinted beyond a row of fully grown evergreen trees to where the top of a storm cloud roiled and churned in anger. "Looks like a tornado coming through."

"Beyond those trees, underneath that cloud," Ainsley began, "is the property line for the city of Wishery."

"The storm cloud's not supposed to be there," Lizzie said darkly. "In fact, it's the reason we evacuated. For now, we've set up shop at MAGIC, Inc. headquarters."

"Wishery has its own city?"

"Due to the highly confidential nature of our business, we require a remote location protected from the human eye."

"So, humans can't see anything in the city? Even the cloud?"

Lizzie shook her head. "They can sense some unrest, though. I've been watching the human news and there are stories of things happening that they can't explain."

"Did all of you evacuate?" I asked. "Or are there people still in Wishery?"

"There are people inside," Lizzie said, her eyes darkening. "But they are not Wishery citizens. We managed to evacuate before the worst of the curse hit."

"What sort of a curse?"

"We don't know," Ainsley said, spinning on her broom to face me. "The city was protected by wish magic—a type of magic that can only be used for good. It's supposed to protect against curses, so...the short answer is that we're clueless."

"My people, those of us who work for Wishery, live and breathe our jobs," Lizzie said. "We rarely leave the grounds. Wishery is its own, nearly self-sustaining, community. Or, it was until they ran us out. It started with one cloud. A hint of darkness. By the time the evacuation warnings went out, it was almost too late."

"We don't even know *what* it is," Ainsley said. "There are wizards specializing in cracking curses, and they couldn't touch this one. We have Spell Specialists, and they said the thing—that it wasn't a spell. We don't know *what* sort of magic is being used to block the city."

"Do you know what's happening in there?" I asked.

Ainsley sucked in a breath, glanced at Lizzie, and then focused her stare on the ground. "We imagine it has something to do with The Faction. It's incredibly difficult to create a city masked entirely by magic. The Isle is one, Wishery is another. By taking over this area, The Faction has secured a safe place for them to organize, set up shop...or worse."

"And The Isle is too big and too well protected," Lizzie said. "They'd never be able to take it over. At least, not quietly and not without one heck of a fight."

"Exactly," Ainsley said. She glanced toward Lizzie, and when she spotted a tear pooling in the corner of her eye, she looked away quickly. "The people of Wishery were almost defenseless. Their magic is so focused on bringing good to people that when the cloud struck, they had no choice but to evacuate. There weren't enough witches or wizards skilled in battle magic to fight back."

Lizzie swiped a hand across her cheek.

"Where is everyone staying?" I asked quietly.

"They've been rehomed for now," Ainsley said. "Some have gone to stay with family, and the others have been placed in safe houses around the Twin Cities. My parents took in three families."

"Anyway," Lizzie said, a sniffle ending her display of sadness and frustration. "The Faction obviously saw an opportunity. They put a spell over the city to keep us out, and now they have a safe and protected space to do...whatever it is they plan to do. We have not been able to stick one toe into the city limits."

Ainsley kicked her broom into action. I followed while Lizzie trailed behind us. We moved without speaking, slow and cautious, until the tendrils of black wound their way around one another just inches before our face. I leaned forward, watching, studying as Gus had taught me.

After a few minutes, I shook my head. "I've never seen anything like this before. It's not a spell, and it's not a curse."

"So we've heard," Lizzie said. "Can you help?"

I reached into my travel belt and withdrew a vial. Gus had gotten me into the habit of carrying one or two with me at all times—for moments like this. Moments where a new and unexpected *thing* needed to be gathered and studied.

I uncorked the vial, extended the tip toward the cloud, and murmured a chant to collect the smoke. Ainsley and Lizzie watched from behind me as the first inky finger of black hesitantly dipped its way into the vial. I repeated the words louder this time, and louder again, until the vial filled with enough smoke for me to slam the lid shut.

Pocketing the vial, I turned to Lizzie. "I'm really sorry I can't do more right away, but I promise I'll take it back to the bungalow and study it. If there's anything I can possibly do, I will."

Lizzie nodded and murmured a thank-you. "I'm going to take a lap. I'll be right back," she said, then kicked off and began to sail the outer limits of her city.

"I feel so helpless," I told Ainsley, watching as Lizzy flew high above the city. "I can't believe a whole city was displaced. How many were there?"

"Nine hundred and sixty-four," Ainsley said. "Counting the families, children, and employees."

I shook my head. "Do you think it's really them? The Faction?"

"Who else can work magic like this?" Ainsley asked. "The most terrifying part is that they couldn't have come up with this magic overnight. It's a whole new revolution in the art of magic...or whatever this might be. It would've taken a lot of planning."

I bit my lip. "You know that I'll do everything I can to figure this out, right? But I'm still shocked... I had never intended for my wish to actually be... I don't know, received."

"Don't worry about it," Ainsley said with a smile. "Lizzie's bound by confidentiality to not share specifics, but I haven't seen her this excited about a wish in many months."

"Are you coming back to The Isle anytime soon?"

"They need me here," Ainsley said. "But I'll be sure to check in with you on The Isle. And if you need me, I'll be there in a second."

Lizzie made her way around Wishery and back to us. As she approached, she began to speed up, brushing right past us as she sped toward the cities.

"I guess it's time to get back," I said. "I should get Gus's opinion on this, too. Maybe he'll have a thought, or maybe he'll have seen something like this before."

"I trust you," Ainsley began. "But I have to remind you that you've signed an NDA. You *must* keep Wishery a secret—it's imperative."

"Understood."

"Come on," Ainsely said, spinning her broomstick to face MAGIC, Inc. "We should leave."

"Ainsley, wait," I called as she sped off. She paused, waited for me to catch up. I took a deep breath as I floated next to her. "Why me? I'm nobody special. If your best witches and wizards were stumped...I don't know that I have much of a chance."

"That's where you're wrong, Lil," Ainsley said, offering me a gentle smile. "Like it or not, you're the Mixologist. You have powers that most of us can only dream of."

“But I’m still new, and I’ve never seen this before, and I—”

“—and you’ll figure this out, I guarantee it,” Ainsley said. “I wouldn’t have asked if we didn’t need your help.”

“But there must be someone else.”

“I’m sorry, Lily,” Ainsley said. “Like it or not, you are the only option we have.”

Chapter 5

"WHAT DO YOU FEED THAT thing?" Poppy asked as she stepped through the door of the storeroom. "I've never seen anything like it."

Blinking, I shook my head and rested my hands on the table before me. A familiar table. "Umm..."

"I mean, it's blooming like crazy!" Poppy made her way over to the calla lily I kept potted in the corner. "I didn't think they could bloom so many times. I swear I've seen three different flowers in the last week alone. Unless I'm imagining things?"

The realization that I was back home in the bungalow finally dawned on me, and with it came the slight tingling from being Zapped.

"Where'd you go?" Gus remained standing along the back wall, a jar in his hand as he watched me with curiosity. He said it so quietly that Poppy, still invested in the flower, couldn't hear.

"What?" The last thing I remembered was Ainsley giving me a hug goodbye, a kiss on the cheek, and then a whisper to *hold on tight*.

Glancing down, I found my fingers gripping the table so tightly my knuckles nearly matched the calla lily in the corner, which jolted my attention back to Poppy's question.

"Oh, right—er, uh. I don't do anything special to it," I said. "But this week it has been going crazy, and, uh—"

"Are you feeling okay?" Poppy strode to me and rested her hand against my forehead. "You feel a little warm. Are you catching that bug going around? My mom had it last week. Gus knows."

Gus scowled. It was common knowledge that Gus and Mimsey had been spending more and more time together, but he didn't like to discuss it. Especially not with his girlfriend's daughter. Or me. Or anyone, really.

"No, I'm feeling fine," I said. "Just a little warm outside today. Anyway, what brings you around?"

"I'm looking for Zin. Have you heard if she's started planning my birthday party yet?"

"Sorry," I said, shaking my head. "She just left a few minutes ago, but she didn't mention any plans. Is there something specific you're wanting to do for it?"

Poppy's expression took a dive into disappointment. "Oh, no. I don't really like birthday parties anyway. I was actually just finding her to tell her *not* to plan anything. Nothing fancy at least, and no cake. Definitely not that triple chocolate fudge double decker cake that I love."

"I'll let her know." I felt bad playing along, but it was the only way to keep Poppy's real party a surprise.

Zin, Mimsey, and I had been planning it for months. Poppy loved birthday's—hers, along with everyone else's. She'd been throwing birthday parties for all of us, but nobody had ever given her the surprise party she deserved. This was the year.

We had not one, but two of her favorite cakes lined up for the occasion. Balloons that sang and danced. Even Glinda's fairies were working on a dance routine to perform in the air—they'd write *Happy Birthday, Poppy*! in the sky while we popped champagne below.

I'd been selected to create a potion for each guest to drink when they arrived at the party. Its purpose was to change everyone into the costume they most desired. Poppy would love it. She had a thing for personalized potions. I'd once made her a Glo potion when I'd first moved to the Isle, and she hadn't stopped talking about it since.

As Poppy's lips trembled while she reiterated one more time how much she *didn't* want a party, I curled my fingers into fists to stop myself from reassuring her. The end result would be worth it, but watching her walk around in misery these days was becoming increasingly difficult.

"Maybe I can have a little something here," I offered. "Small cake, and—"

"No, really." Poppy held out a hand. "I don't want anything. And... *there* it goes again! Seriously?"

Before our eyes, the lily grew inch by inch until the petals bloomed into a perfectly white flower. Every time it did this my skin chilled, my heart pounded, and my warning senses went on the fritz.

I suspected the flower was tied to my father. I had reason to believe he'd left it for me as a sign he was coming. A sign that we'd meet. Soon.

I'd also learned recently that my father, Lucian Blackmore, was most likely the leader of The Faction. Trinket had broken the shocking news to me. The more curious part, however, was that my mother had chosen Trinket, above anyone else, as her sole confidant. Unfortunately, that was one mystery that would never be solved.

I had yet to share the news with the others. I owed it to The Core, at least, to pass along the information I'd learned, but I just wasn't ready yet. Some part of me clung to the hope that maybe there'd been a misunderstanding. Maybe it wasn't my father leading this rogue group of witches and wizards in an effort to wipe out the humans. Maybe it was all one giant mistake.

"Leave it alone," I said of the flower. "Maybe it's enchanted."

Poppy frowned at me. "Wouldn't you be able to tell?"

"I...I guess so," I said. As a vampire, Poppy didn't possess the same magic as witches. "It doesn't feel enchanted, but something's not quite right."

"Why don't you get rid of it?"

Because I need to know when he's coming. I didn't dare say it aloud.

"It's too dangerous to get rid of without understanding it," I said instead. "I have to figure out what it means."

"You're braver than I am. I'd throw it as far into The Forest as I could. So anyway, what was Zin doing here?"

"She said she was *tired.* I think her and Trinket are having trouble getting along again. I told her she should move in here if she's so sick of it," I said with an eyeroll. "They're fighting nonstop."

"Forget Zin. What about your offer for me to move in—is it still standing?" Poppy sat at the table opposite me and leaned her arms on the table. "Somebody—I'm not naming names, but he's in this room—has been spending more and more time at our house, and he's a grouch."

"You forget," I said, glancing over at Gus. "He's here more than he's at your mom's house."

Poppy let out a frustrated sigh. "I just can't seem to win these days."

I wanted to wrap my arms around Poppy and tell her to hold on, that things would improve if she could just wait for the surprise on her birthday. Since I couldn't, I smiled instead.

"Seriously, consider moving in here! There's plenty of space, and it would be fun."

"X wouldn't mind?" Poppy asked. "I don't want to interrupt your private space."

"Go on, interrupt it," Gus said. "They're all over each other."

"You should talk," Poppy shot back.

Gus's face turned red as he struggled to prepare a retort. Eventually he gave up, stomping out of the storeroom and over to Magic & Mixology, the outdoor bar attached to the bungalow.

"Well, I should be going," Poppy said. "I'm working dispatch today at Ranger HQ. We're starting to send the trainees out on actual missions. Exciting, huh?"

"Has Zin gone out yet?"

Poppy scrunched her nose. "It's been pretty quiet here on the island. Almost too quiet, if I were a more suspicious person. Her turn hasn't come up yet."

"I'm sure she's disappointed."

"It's a little alarming how ready she is for something to go wrong."

I shook my head. "I wish she'd listen about moving in here. She doesn't need to be stressing over her mom while she's on the new job. You too, Poppy."

"I'll think about it." Poppy took one last glance at the calla lily, then pointed at it with her thumb. "Do me a favor and have Gus take a look at that. It's not natural. I should know with the amount of time I spend in Hettie's gardens. She doesn't have a *thing* like that."

"Sure. I'll ask him—"

Poppy pulled open the door before I finished speaking, and both of us jolted in surprise. There on the porch stood a man three feet tall with a scowl on his face.

"Discrimination!" He pointed a stubby finger at Poppy. "And you call yourself the Mixologist!?"

"Me?" Poppy snorted. "Yeah right. I can barely mix coffee and cream. You're looking for Lily."

I straightened. "Can I help you?"

By now my brain had caught up with my eyes, and I realized the man before us was likely a gnome, or something of the sort. He had beady little eyes and a bulbous nose that looked like a misshapen tomato. Grunting, he swiveled his finger to point in my direction instead.

"I've been trying to reach the doorknob for ten minutes. Not even a stool," he said. "How do you expect the height-challenged folks around here to get inside?"

"I'm, uh, sorry," I said. "I didn't realize—"

"Of course you didn't. Nobody cares about the little people." He scowled around at us. "I have a complaint to file."

"I think maybe you need Poppy?" I raised my eyebrows and nodded in my cousin's direction. "She works for Ranger HQ, and they handle most complaints."

"I tried that," he growled. "Nobody listened. I can't get anybody to listen. You're my last resort."

"Wow, thanks," I said. "What an honor."

"There's a house near the edge of The Forest, and it's haunted."

I looked at Poppy first, then back to the man. "Sorry, but...*what*? How can I do anything about that?"

"I thought you were supposed to be smart," the gnome said. "And good with magic and all that crap. Us gnomes are lacking in the spell department. Can't you figure something out to help us?"

"I really think this is a job for the Rangers. I'm not trained to...get rid of haunted houses. I work with potions and charms and..." I thought of the vial in my pocket. "Curses."

"Then un-curse this damn house already, will you? It's driving our population way down. Gnomes are moving out left and right! My grandmother's too old to move and too terrified to stay. What am I supposed to do?"

"Figure it out!" Poppy said, frowning at him. "It's not Lily's job to go traipsing into The Forest to check out a house that *might* be haunted from a gnome who *might* be telling the truth."

"Of course I'm telling the truth!" His face turned a shade of red dangerously close to purple. "I wouldn't be asking for help if I could solve the problem myself. Gnomes hate asking for help."

"That's true," Poppy admitted, turning to me. "Stubborn little creatures. I don't think he's lying. The house might not be haunted, but he thinks it is."

"I'm right here," he said. "And I have a name. Chuck."

"Chuck," I said. "Do you think the house is haunted or cursed?"

"I don't know the difference. I didn't study a whole lot of magic."

"I'll come check it out," I said, sighing. "But no promises. If it looks dangerous, I'm not going inside."

"Darn right, she's not!" Poppy stuck a hand on her hip, leaned forward, and poked her finger right under the gnome's nose. "I swear on your grandmother's life, Chuck, if you harm a hair on Lily's head I will sic her boyfriend on you."

"Ooh, scary," Chuck said. "Who's her boyfriend, the old coot who runs this place with her?"

"Gnomes have no sense of age. That's disgusting." Poppy wrinkled her nose. "Her boyfriend is Ranger X."

At the last initial in his name, Chuck stilled completely. His red nose turned a lighter shade of pink, and the purple coloring in his forehead resumed its ruddy skin tone. "Er, right. Never mind then. Forget I asked. We'll figure it out."

"No, wait, Chuck—I'll come with you." I stepped forward, looking to Poppy. "He's right; it's my job to help protect The Isle, and if there's a curse instead of a haunting, maybe I can help."

"It's not haunted," Poppy argued. "But if it makes you feel better to check it out, at least wear a Comm device, and if anything—and I mean anything—looks wrong, don't step foot near it. Hear me? I'll be at work. Call me if you want backup."

"Don't worry. I'm sure it's nothing."

"That's what my sister said," Chuck muttered.

"What happened to your sister?" Poppy asked.

"Let's just say she doesn't live in our colony anymore. The hauntings pushed her away. You ready, Mixologist? Grab your gun."

"I don't carry a gun."

"What good are you then?!" he snapped. "I thought you used to be a human."

"On that note, I'm heading out," Poppy said, blowing a kiss in my direction as she made her way out the front door. "Stay out of trouble, Lily."

"Wait here," I said to Chuck once Poppy had gone. "I need to grab something."

"What sort of nut you got in there today?" Gus asked from his seat at the bar as I slunk into Magic & Mixology. "He sounds like an odd case even for you."

I leaned against the counter, surveying the sandy ground, the gleaming wood bar, and the tables beyond. The sound of waves always seemed amplified here, driving home the beachy atmosphere.

Gus stared at the chalkboard behind the counter where the Mixologist's list of cocktails was displayed. I watched him for a moment, then frowned.

"I don't *only* get nuts coming in here," I said. "I get people looking for help."

"And what does this guy need—a hole in the head?"

"He's worried about a house near The Forest." Even as I said it aloud, I cringed a bit. "He thinks it might be haunted."

Gus snorted into his cup of coffee. "Right, sure. Have fun with that one."

"I'm glad you're concerned about my safety."

"The gnome colony is *barely* in The Forest. It only qualified on that as a technicality. That boyfriend's cabin of yours is in a more dangerous location. You're hardly going past The Twist."

That made me feel a little better about the whole adventure, but I'd never admit it to Gus. Instead, I pulled the vial from my travel belt and handed it over. "Have you ever seen this before?"

Gus watched the curling black smoke for a long moment. So long that my hand tired of holding it, and I set it onto the counter in front of him. He stared for so long that eventually I poured myself a cup of coffee while I waited.

Finally, he moved. One finger—the littlest one—pressed against the outside of the glass. At the first sign of contact, he flinched. "What *is* that?"

"I don't know. That's why I asked you."

"I've never seen this magic before."

"Nobody has. Hence the reason I'm looking for some help. I need to reverse this curse, or whatever it is."

"It ain't a curse," Gus said. "I can feel when something's cursed. This is... this is something else entirely."

"Any ideas?"

"I've seen things similar to it before..." He frowned and picked up the bottle between two fingers. "But that sort of magic ain't a spell. It's not a charm, an enchantment, or even a curse. This is elemental. Basic. Some sort of primal magic, and I don't like it. Where you find this?"

"I didn't find it, I was taken to it."

"They Zapped you, didn't they?"

"How could you tell?"

"Lily, you were gone for five minutes before Poppy arrived. Even I can't ignore that much," Gus said with a slight smile. "Yes, if you're wondering, time is compressed between Zappings. It might've felt like hours, but it was only minutes. Were you on official agency business?"

"Yes, and sworn to secrecy. I can't explain everything, but I do need to break this. Or reverse it. Or something."

"Does it feel familiar to you?" Gus looked at me with curiosity. "Any sort of magic you've seen used in the past?"

I swallowed, alarmed he'd seemed to read my mind.

"Feels a bit like mind bending, doesn't it?" he asked. "I thought so, too."

"It can't be, though. That doesn't make sense."

"This ain't blood magic," Gus said, twisting the bottle closer to him. The vial sat an inch from his nose, black as coal, beaded like mercury. "Blood magic doesn't work like this. But it's that primal, evil sort of magic. The sort of magic that latches onto anything good and turns it dark."

The way he spoke sent whispers of fear across my skin. "How do you know?"

"I've lived many years, Lily Locke, and I've seen things you haven't even dreamed of. This isn't the first time the dark has tried to taint the light, and it won't be the last."

"What am I supposed to do about it?"

"Exactly what you're doing." Gus snapped the vial into the palm of his hand. "Go check out that haunted house."

My jaw fell open further. "But—"

"Give me some time with this. There's something niggling at the back of my brain, and I need some peace and quiet to think. When you come back, we'll talk."

"And this haunted house? What do you think about it?"

"I think it's a bunny rabbit," Gus said. "The gnomes are stubborn people, sure, but they're also cautious. I've been past that house a million times. Ain't nothing in there except maybe a wild animal. It's been abandoned for years, and there are no such things as ghosts."

"I don't think your pep talk made me feel any better."

"Here." Gus stood, slipped the vial into his coat pocket, and marched his way into the storeroom. "Follow me."

I deposited both of our coffee mugs into the sink before following him into the room with the waiting gnome.

"Take this." Gus pulled down a jar from the top shelf. "Use this. Rids a space of ghosts."

I frowned as he scooped a generous amount of white powder into a bag. I lowered my voice so only Gus could here. "This is nothing but baking flour."

"Maybe if you add the right chant it'll work." Gus's shoulders were practically heaving with a mixture of glee and mischief as he handed over the sack of flour. It had no more magic than a blade of ordinary grass. "Put it in your travel belt, so you can keep your hands free—you know, to fight off the ghosts."

"And how does this chant go? Anything specific?"

"You'll figure it out yourself," he growled. "Get out of here now, before the ghost gets into trouble."

"That's what I've been saying!" Chuck piped up from near the door. "We need to get moving. No time to waste."

With a wave to Gus, a sack of flour, and a disgruntled gnome as my guide, we set off toward The Forest. Though the day hadn't been all bad, thanks to the personalized key from Ranger X, I'd been Zapped, introduced to Wishery, and recruited for a de-haunting mission all in one day. Still, what worried me most was the calla lily in the corner. Blooming and dying, blooming and dying.

He was coming.

Chapter 6

"THIS IS IT." CHUCK stopped abruptly before a little hut buried amid a palm tree grove. "The haunted house."

I surveyed the scene first, taking in the rectangular door built into the rocky stone face of a small hill. Bright palm trees created a miniature forest around the hut, shielding it from view of passersby. The oasis looked more like a vacation home than a dark and scary place.

"I thought you said it was in The Forest." I stepped closer, peeking through the palms for a closer look. The house itself was half built into the rocky hillside, made from old lumber that looked somewhat like driftwood. A cross between a beaver dam and a log cabin.

"The Forest is right there." Chuck pointed beyond the house where, in the distance, the blackness of the shadows stood.

In recent months, I'd had to venture in more and more often. It was home to specialized ingredients for many of my potions, and I refused to ask Ranger X for an escort every time I needed to refresh my Dust of the Devil supply. No matter how many times I'd been through The Forest, it never got easier.

Luckily, this house was *not* in The Forest.

Gus's words rang though my head, and I wondered if it wasn't an animal who'd gotten locked inside. I waved for Chuck to follow me as I crossed a tiny stream that wound in a loose triangle around the house before pouring into a glittering little waterfall no taller than my waist.

"It's charming," I told Chuck. "I'm sure it's nothing. Probably just a raccoon."

"What's a raccoon?"

I stiffened, having to remind myself that this was a magical island, not downtown St. Paul. "Or, you know, a fairy."

"Maybe it's one of Glinda's rug rats gone rogue."

"Maybe."

"Or one of them new...what are they called? The things that live near the volcano."

"Fire Fox?"

"Yes." Chuck now seemed enthused. "Let's go. I've heard they're cute. I bet one got lost and decided to rest here."

We crept toward the front door of the makeshift residence, and the faint scent of charred logs became stronger. "Do you smell burning?" I asked. "Where is that coming from?"

Chuck sniffed, then shook his head. "Gnomes don't sniff too good. I can't smell a thing."

Another few steps closer, and we were near enough to reach out and touch the door.

"Go on," he said. "I'm the one who called you for help."

I reached out, heart pounding, toward the rugged knob. A part of me hoped it would be locked and shut tight with no reason for us to go inside. As my fingers closed around the handle, a hand reached out and grasped my wrist.

"Don't be stupid!" Chuck said. "Get the potion ready. Who knows what's in there? What if the Fire Fox is rabid?"

I struggled to catch my breath and fight off an eyeroll all at once. From my belt, I withdrew the bag of flour and wiggled it in front of Chuck's face until he gave a pleased nod.

"Better," he said. "You can never be too careful."

I untied the baggie just to make him happy, then resumed my position with my hand against the door. Before I could open it, there was a shuffle of movement from inside.

"Did you hear that?" I whispered. "There's something in there."

"Or someone." Chuck's eyes were wide. "I told you that it's *haunted.*"

I cleared my throat and knocked on the door. My desire to get this over with was stronger than my desire to run away. If we didn't solve this today, Chuck would be back.

"Hello?" I called. "Is someone in there? This is Lily."

"The Mixologist," Chuck piped up. "And she's got some dangerous potions ready to fire if you don't come out with your hands up."

"I'm not firing any potions. We just want to ask you some questions."

A quiet thud came from inside, and then the shattering of glass. Chuck jumped, stumbled backward off a rock, and landed with one foot in the stream. Swearing, he yanked his foot out and scowled as I knocked once more.

"Everything okay in there?" I asked. My adrenaline was in overdrive. My fingers clutched the bag of flour as if it had the power to save my life. My ears thudded with the sound of my heartbeat. "We're just here to say hi."

Chuck returned to his position on the rock. "Well, go in there! Something is happening."

"I can't just waltz in. It's not my home!"

"It's been abandoned for years; that's the problem. It used to belong to the Witch of the Woods—like, a hundred years ago. Then she got frustrated with all the visitors stumbling by and moved into The Forest. Nobody has been allowed to live here since. The Forest protects it, you see."

I'd seen firsthand the way The Forest, nature, and all living things on The Isle protected its grandmother—the Witch of the Woods. I understood that piece. What I *didn't* understand was the racket coming from inside the abandoned building.

"Hello?" I called again. "I'm going to try the doorknob in case you need help. Tell me to stop if you don't want company."

Another piece of glass shattered. Chuck's eyes grew wide. Our gazes met, and I twisted the handle and threw the door open.

A cloud of screeching, vibrant orange in a flash of white came flying at us. I reacted on impulse, throwing my hands in the air, which sent flour sailing everywhere. The screeching grew worse, morphing into a pained shriek as Chuck yanked my arm and together we tumbled down the slope and landed in a heap at the bottom.

"What was that?" Chuck leapt to his feet prepared for a fight. "I told you there were evil spirits in there! Where's your potion? When's it going to start working? Did you say your chant? I didn't hear any chant."

"Chuck!" I gasped, holding onto my stomach as I recovered my breath. I'd landed on the stump of a tree and it'd taken all the wind out of me. "That's not...an evil...*spirit*."

"You're nuts. Did you hear that thing? Ain't no human ever made a sound like that."

"Because it's not a human!" Voice still raspy, I made my way to my feet and pointed toward the entrance to the house. There, covered completely by flour, stood Tiger. "It's a cat."

"A...cat."

"Come here, cutie," I said, making my way toward Hettie's kitten. Thanks to the flour, his coat no longer shone vibrant orange, but a powdery white. "Sorry, buddy. It'll wash right off."

"What do you mean it'll wash right off?" Chuck lifted an arm to his nose, took a sniff, and inhaled a nose full of flour. A coughing fit took hold, and when he finished, he faced me looking extra disgruntled. "What is this?!"

The cat wasn't the only one covered in flour—Chuck looked like a very short, very wide ghost with a tomato for a nose.

"Is this a joke to you?" Chuck shook himself, causing a cloud of dusty white to settle at his feet. "This isn't magic, is it? This is just you and that assistant of yours having a good chuckle at the stupid gnome."

"No, Chuck—that's not it at all. Gus just doesn't believe in ghosts."

"Then he should've just said that. You went along with it, too. You're not any better."

"I'm really sorry." I stepped toward him, still clutching Tiger to my chest. "None of this was intended to make fun of you."

"Well, now y'all can share a laugh." Chuck dipped a hand in the water in an attempt to free himself of the flour, but it only made him a pasty, sticky mess. He shook his hand off, spattering bits of doughy goo everywhere. "Hope I brightened your day."

"Chuck—wait! Please. This wasn't a joke. You're right, something was living in the house. We can say it was haunted if you prefer."

The idea seemed appealing to the gnome, but after considering it for a long minute, he shook his head. "Forget it. Thanks for your help, Miss Locke."

"Chuck..."

He'd already turned away, his feet leaving trails of powder behind him. I started to follow him, but he didn't seem interested in talking. I had to find a way to make it up to him somehow, a way to apologize.

"Did Hettie send you?" I squeezed Tiger a little closer and nestled my cheek against his fur. "Is she trying to cause trouble?"

The cat looked at me, hissed, and then jumped from my arms.

When I reached to pick him up, I caught a glimpse of my face in the water's reflection. The gnome and the cat weren't the only ones covered completely in white. My face, my clothes, every inch of me was a complete and utter mess. No wonder he didn't recognize me.

I debated heading to Ranger X's cabin. I did have a key now, and we were close enough, but I looked like a mummy and probably smelled like an old cake without any of the sweet. However, it would be far more practical to meet my grandmother and return her cat. The least she could do was feed me.

"Come on," I said to the cat. "It's getting late, and you've haunted this house for long enough."

Tiger fell in line as I tightly shut the door of the hut. I still couldn't shake the scent of burning. I pulled open the door once more, poked my head inside, and peeked around.

Nothing struck me as unusual. Old utensils, plates and bowls lay scattered around a small corner kitchen. Two broken glasses lay on the floor, courtesy of the cat.

The rest of the cabin looked livable, though old and untouched. A small bed sat in one corner with a lamp next to it. Everything had a layer of dust on it from what I could tell in the dim lighting.

I closed the door once more and backed away.

Even as we marched toward The Twist, the smell of burning lingered behind.

Chapter 7

"WELL, LET ME GET THE eggs and sugar," Hettie said, flinging her door open. "And we'll make a cake with you!"

"Ha-ha," I said, stepping through the front door. A layer of flour flooded to my feet, and I guiltily looked down at the now-white rug. "*Oops*, sorry. Do you have a change of clothes?"

"No worries, we're actually sitting outside. We'd love to have you join us! To what do we owe this honor?"

"Which part?" I looked down at the cat as he slunk between my legs. "The visit, the flour, or the return of Tiger?"

"All of it!" My grandmother threw her hands in the air, her nails glittering against the waning light. Shards of purple polish decorated her fingernails and matched the puffballs swinging around her violently pink sneakers. "You haven't been stopping by nearly enough, Your Perkiness."

"Nope," I said. "We're not doing this nickname thing again."

"Fine. Well, come and join us out back. I'm sure Peter would love to hear the story of how you got covered in flour. I know I would."

"Peter?" I followed my grandmother as she wound her way through her front yard to a small clearing at the edge of The Twist.

Only those of us with West Isle Witch blood could make it through without a guide—apparently, my grandmother and her daughters had been the only women foolish enough to settle down on the same half of the island as the The Forest. In response, Hettie had made it exceedingly difficult for anyone else to visit her house.

"Yes, Peter."

"I didn't know you had company; I don't mean to interrupt."

"Well, I didn't plan for him *or* you, but I do love surprises." Hettie smiled and gestured toward a small brick patio surrounded by fairy lights and flowers of all shapes and sizes. "Peter, this is my granddaughter, Lily. Lily, please meet Peter."

"You're...y-y-you're the Mixologist," Peter stuttered, standing up so quickly the wicker chair beneath him toppled to the bricks. He bent, righted the chair, and grimaced.

"You can just call me Lily. Please. Pleasure to meet you."

"Excellent, excellent," he said. "I never fancied I'd meet you outside of the bungalow. It's absolutely *my* pleasure."

Peter reached for my hand. I made my best attempt to dodge the shake, but I wasn't fast enough. He clasped my hand in his, gave it a few pumps, and then leaned in to give the top of my hand a quick kiss.

And inhaled a breath of pure flour.

"I'm sorry," I apologized, backing away as he launched into a sneezing fit. "It's been quite a day. I really should be getting home; I just had to return my grandmother's cat."

"Sit down," Hettie instructed. "We don't mind a bit of powder. Do we, Peter? You must be hungry, Lily."

Peter shook his head, his eyes watering. "I don't mind at all."

I took one glance at the platter of meats and cheeses on the table and agreed, just as my stomach growled. While I fixed myself a plate, Hettie poured me a glass of wine, and then turned her attention to Peter.

"Catch Lily up, will you?" she asked. "She's obviously been having some fun without us and probably hasn't heard the news."

Peter nodded. "As you know, I'm a reporter for The Wicked Weekly—"

"The best newspaper for magical folks," Hettie interrupted. "You should have copies delivered to your door every morning."

"I'm familiar," I mumbled around a mouthful of prosciutto. "Familiar with the paper."

"Maybe you'd recognize my name if you read one of my articles." Peter proudly puffed his chest outward. "I write an unsolved crimes column. Personal interest sort of thing."

"Ah, of course," I said, though I wouldn't recognize his name if it were printed on a billboard. "I'm sure I've seen it before. I'm horrible with remembering names and titles, sorry."

Peter de-puffed a little and sighed. "Newspapers are going out of fashion these days. It really is a travesty. Have I told you—"

"Peter," Hettie prompted. "Stick to business. Tell Lily why you're here!"

"Oh, of course. I'm here to interview Hettie for a piece I'm working on."

"An unsolved crime article?" I looked between the two, then focused on my grandmother. "Is that why you're wearing...*that*?"

"Oh, this old thing?" she tittered. Then she straightened, looked down, and preened before us both. "Yes. Actually, I thought I was going to have my picture taken, but Peter here says there's no space. Can you imagine—no space for *this*?"

On top of those pink sneakers and violet pompoms, she wore a bubblegum colored pantsuit with bell bottoms wide enough to fit at least ten of her legs. Sequins adorned the bottom and fur lined the wrists of her jacket. The only non-pink flash was the purple glitter of her nails and the bright shine of her blue-tinted eyelashes.

"I think we could probably get a picture of this. Don't you, Peter?" I asked him.

"But the column...there's hardly space for my words, let alone..." He melted under my gaze. "Sure, sure. Certainly. Must commemorate this night."

He fumbled for the camera around his neck, lifted it, aimed, and then snapped a few photos. When he finally returned the camera to the table, Hettie let out a sigh.

"How wonderful," she said. "I always wanted to be in the paper."

"Why is Peter interviewing you?"

"Because I'm *interesting*," Hettie said. "And maybe because I have insider information into the disappearances."

"What disappearances?" I asked. "I haven't heard of any disappearances."

"Drew and Jonathon," Peter said with exasperation. "You'd know if you read my column."

"Drew and Jonathon..." I turned the names over in my mind as they slowly rang a bell. Then, it clicked. "*Oh*! You write that column. The *conspiracy* column."

I slapped a hand over my mouth as soon as I said it. Peter's eyes darkened, and a flash of anger flittered across his gaze.

"It's not a *conspiracy* column; it's a detailed investigation of crimes that don't receive broad enough attention. Every case deserves attention."

"Right," Hettie said. "And I'm going to give this one my attention."

"Drew and Jonathon have both been missing for weeks now. Mark my words, there will be more disappearances. These were just the first."

I kept my mouth shut this time because I had finally placed where I'd heard Peter's name before. *Gus.* Gus read Peter's column every morning, and it was one of the only things that made him smile. He read it like a comic strip, taking every word as fiction.

I'd heard him say on more than one occasion that this Peter fellow was a kook, a nut, someone who needed to find a real job. In Gus's defense, many of Peter's last stories had ended up with very logical explanations.

He once claimed a UFO had landed in The Forest. In reality, it'd been a training maneuver by Glinda's Forest Faeries. He'd also tried to prove—and failed—that the Rangers were cyborgs. Having dated Ranger X for a while now, I could say with certainty that statement was completely false.

"I thought Drew and Jonathon both voluntarily left The Isle," I said. "I read a story on their supposed disappearances."

"You can't trust those articles."

"I don't know... from what I read, it said that Jonathon had a horrible relationship with his parents. Drew had packed his bag weeks before. Maybe they just took off."

"Sure. But when the next disappearance strikes, don't come crying to me with an apology," Peter said, his eyes wide. "As the Mixologist, you should be ashamed of yourself for listening to that rubbish."

"Nobody speaks to my granddaughter like that," Hettie said, rising to her feet. "She didn't ask to be the Mixologist, and she's doing a darn fine job of filling some big shoes. If you truly think there's a problem here, you need to be talking to the Rangers."

"I thought you believed my articles, Hettie. I'm disappointed in you, too."

"Thanks for coming by," Hettie snapped. "You can see yourself out."

"Actually," I said, clearing my throat. "He can't."

"Oh, right," Hettie said, cracking her knuckles. "The stupid Twist."

"I should get going, anyway." I quickly finished my last bite of cheese and cracker. "I can walk him out."

"Thanks for the information, Hettie," Peter added tersely. "I hope we can do this again."

As Peter followed me out of The Twist, a magical labyrinth Hettie had created to keep unwanted guests away from her home, I glanced at him out of the corner of my eye. "What sort of information did you need from Hettie, anyway?"

"She knew Drew. Or, at least, she said she did. Turns out, she ran into him at the grocery store and asked him for a sample."

"That's Hettie for you."

We walked in silence through The Twist. I kept just a few feet ahead to guide the way, finally parting the branches before the front gate.

"Goodnight," I said with a wave, pointing my feet toward the bungalow.

"Wait, Lily."

As I turned back, he hesitated a second longer.

"I know you don't believe me," he said. "But I *really* think there's something different about this. I might've made mistakes in the past, but not this time."

"Like Hettie said, this is probably a job for the Rangers. If you'd like, I can talk to Ranger X about it. I'm not sure what else you'd like me to do."

"I've *tried*. The Rangers have determined it was nothing. All signs pointed to Drew and Jonathon running away."

"Is there a reason you don't believe them?"

"It's just a feeling. Things aren't adding up."

"Look, I'm really sorry, Peter. I'm not saying you're wrong—I just don't have any control over the matter. Drew and Jonathon are both adults. If they left The Isle, they left. I don't know what I can do that the Rangers couldn't."

"Next time." Peter nodded at me, a sardonic grin on his face. "Next time it happens you'll come talk to me, and I'll forgive you for not believing me."

"I didn't say I didn't believe you."

"Whatever you say. Have a good night, Lily."

I made my way toward the bungalow, my head full and my heart feeling heavy. I'd been on a rollercoaster of a day—starting with a key to Ranger X's home, MAGIC, Inc. Zapping me off to Wishery, to the gnome issues, and now after all of that, Peter.

I felt bad. I felt bad for hurting Chuck's feelings, and I felt bad I couldn't be of more help to Peter. But the issues were piling up on my plate, and as much as I wanted to solve everyone's problems...I was only human.

Well, technically I'm a witch.

But magic can't solve everything.

Chapter 8

A SOLID NIGHT'S SLEEP was just what I needed. A fresh start, a clear head, and a burst of energy to deal with the contents of the vial, the everblooming lily, and whatever obstacle the world threw at me next.

Unfortunately, a solid night of sleep was not in the cards for me. Warnings from Peter, Chuck, Lizzie and Ainsley, and even Gus swam through my dreams and caused fitful rest, drawing me out of bed barely past sunrise.

I slunk downstairs, surprised to find the storeroom empty. Gus had been puttering around here until the wee hours of the morning, and I half suspected he'd planned to stay all night examining the vial. He seemed to be stuck, something hovering at the tip of his consciousness, even after we'd slaved over its contents for hours last night.

We'd come up empty-handed. Whatever spell sat inside that vial, it was a form of magic we'd never seen before. Hints of some elemental magic appeared to exist within it, but somehow, someone had morphed and twisted its pure form into a new strain of magic.

We'd crack it, sooner or later. With Gus by my side, I had faith we could figure out an antidote. The main issue was time. Our clock was running out. The longer Wishery remained under the influence of The Faction, the more dangerous it would be.

I moved to the bar, made a quick Caffeine Cup, the magical world's coffee equivalent, and returned to the table in the storeroom.

As I sipped, I watched the twisting black smoke. Eventually, I stood and paced my way around the room, carrying the vial with me.

The calla lily in the corner bloomed faster than ever before. I paused, leaned near the flower, and it bloomed again. Twice in five minutes. Unheard of.

Clutching the vial, I moved back to the table, my heart racing. Surely it meant something; there was no other explanation. It had to be an enchantment of some sort—a note, a warning.

As soon as I sat down at the table, it calmed.

I waited, watched. For ten minutes, it held its bloom before crumbling to ashes.

When it didn't start to bloom immediately, I stood up again and crept closer.

As I inched toward it, the stem began to grow, to preen itself before me.

When I stopped, it stopped.

With a jolt of understanding, I glanced down to find the vial still tucked in my hand. On a hunch, I left the vial back on the storeroom table, and then paced around the room once, twice, three times more.

On my next round, I lifted the vial and cupped it in my palm. I took a few steps closer, and the very tips of green, the first shoots of a new flower poked through the dirt. Another two steps, and the lily had leaves—big, healthy green leaves. It grew before my eyes.

I extended the vial toward the flower.

The lily grew and bloomed into a flower bigger than ever before.

I jerked back in surprise, releasing the vial on accident as I lost my balance and stumbled toward the table. The vial landed in the pot and the shoot lost all sense of reality.

It burst toward the sky, developed a flower, bloomed big and bright and relentless, and then shattered to dust. Then again and again, like fireworks, until I scrambled for the vial and pulled it back to my chest.

At once, the flower's progression stopped.

"Well," I said, looking down at the vial. "If I had any doubts as to who's responsible for the cloud around Wishery, they're gone now."

The next second, a *thunk* sounded against the door. I quickly tucked the vial into a safe spot on the shelves, then made my way to the front of the room and rested my hand against the knob.

The discovery of a relationship between the flower and the vial had me on edge. I couldn't put my finger on which part had me spooked—all of it, I supposed—but I halfway expected the person who gave it to me, a man most likely my father, to be standing on the other side of that door. He was someone I desperately wasn't ready to face.

With a deep breath, I peeked through the peephole. Nobody there.

I briefly considered Chuck's complaint while thinking I should probably get a lower peephole, too. After a few more minutes and no sounds coming from outside, I scrounged up the courage to open the door.

I held my breath as I peered out and waited for the other shoe to drop. The mystery man, the surprise visitor.

Nobody.

It wasn't until I looked down at the ground that I realized the source of the *thunk* against my door hadn't been human at all. It'd been a newspaper slapping against the porch.

With a laugh of relief, I bent over and retrieved the paper, giving one last scan around the area just in case. Quiet, calm—just the waves on the sand rolling across miles of shoreline...and me.

I brought the newspaper with me to the table as I recouped my cup of coffee. I nearly spit it right back out as I caught sight of the front page headline: **THIRD DISAPPEARANCE IN THREE MONTHS.**

Underneath it was a name I recognized. Peter Knope—the very same Peter from my visit with Hettie yesterday.

"You really are growing up," Gus said, startling me with an unexpected appearance in the doorway. "Look at you up early enough to get the newspaper this morning. Did you even know we *got* a newspaper?"

I cupped my mug and narrowed my eyes at him. Normally, he woke hours before me and brought the newspaper inside, read it, and discarded it before I rolled out of bed.

"I couldn't sleep."

Gus nodded. "Me neither. That vial—"

"Have you seen this?" I held up the paper.

"Since you have it in your hands, no, I haven't seen it."

"You don't get them at your house?" When there was no answer, I glanced up to find Gus watching me with a look of discomfort on his face. I realized the source of his unease and held in a muted chuckle. "You spent the night at Mimsey's."

Gus busied himself by leaning in and taking a look at the article. It lasted only a second, however, until he saw the byline beneath the headline. "Whatever you're worried about, you can rest easy. That Peter fellow is a quack."

"I met him yesterday. He thinks something nefarious is happening with these disappearances."

He snorted. "Right."

"What if he *is* right?"

Gus stomped over to the shelves and pulled out the vial. "So what? There's nothing we can do about it. What we have to do is get started on *this*."

"I'm going for a walk first. I need to clear my head and talk to Ranger X about these disappearances. Maybe Ranger HQ does need to be involved."

"Good—I could use some quiet time."

"We'll meet at lunch?" I folded the paper and tucked it under my arm. "Call me on my Comm if you discover something."

Gus nodded, already bent over the bottled storm cloud. "Don't get sucked into that Peter nonsense."

"What?" I turned, already at the doorway. "I'm not *sucked in*. I'm just investigating what might be a genuine concern."

"I heard that gnome talking to you yesterday. *Now* it's this Peter character. I'm afraid people aren't understanding that your job is to be the Mixologist, Miss Lily. It's not your duty to solve every little issue on this island."

"My job is to help. To *Do Good*."

"Your job is *here*. In this very room. You understand magic in a way nobody else does. Rangers can run down missing persons and check out haunted houses." In a moment of surprising clarity, Gus met my eyes. "Don't get yourself mixed up in dangerous situations that can be avoided. I know you want to save the world, Lily, but the sad truth is that you can't save everyone."

I swallowed, the nugget of truth difficult to digest.

"You and me working together, cracking the code to this...this *black magic*," Gus said, tapping the vial with a finger. "Now that is how you can save a city. When you can save a city, you don't have time to be saving a gnome."

"No, that's not—"

"Just think about what I said. It's your choice, but when you asked me to be your assistant, I earned the right to give you my opinion."

Forcing a nod, I pulled the door closed behind me. The walk to Ranger X's cabin was more somber than usual. My heart felt heavy this morning, though I couldn't put my finger on exactly what bothered me the most.

Clearly, Gus had meant what he'd said in a rare moment of concern, his protective instincts floating near the surface. Even so, a part of me couldn't help but wonder if he was wrong. My job was to help people.

But how could I possibly know who needed helping the most?

Chapter 9

RANGER X'S DOOR WAS locked when I arrived. With a cheeky smile, I withdrew the new key from my pocket and fitted it into the keyhole. I hesitated for a moment, debating knocking first, and then decided against it.

After all, he'd told me surprises were welcome.

He should be home, and I could use a fun surprise. Unless he was on a case, X didn't often get to work this early. The sun had just begun to shed its warmth on the world, the pink hues slowly fading to orange and yellow above a bright blue sky.

As the door slid open, I peered toward the bed, hoping to find him there—to surprise him with a kiss and slide in next to him. A bit of body warmth would go a long way this morning.

One step into his home, however, told me that wouldn't be happening.

The shower sounded from the bathroom, and I blew out a sigh of frustration. I should've guessed he'd already be awake. The smell of freshly ground coffee pulled me in further, and I closed the door behind me and took a seat at the table.

X's paper lay open, already rifled through. I poured myself another cup of coffee, returned to my seat, and perused the story once more. The title above Peter's name rang through the space as the threat of another missing person weighed on my mind.

I sipped my coffee and read about Manuel Artina, a young wizard who'd recently become engaged to a fellow island witch named Sophie. According to the article, the two had been dating for over a year and were madly in love. Their wedding date was in three months, and both were reported by family and friends to have been thrilled.

My heart broke at the picture of Sophie and Manuel. The two were wrapped in a loving embrace, Sophie watching her fiancé through big, wide eyes as her arms wrapped around his neck. They looked like two young adults without a care in the world.

The photo had been taken two days ago.

One day before Manuel disappeared.

The official story was that he'd run away, gotten cold feet before the wedding, which could possibly be true. A theory I might've believed had it not been for the image attached to the article. The pair was without a doubt in love.

Or, they were very good actors, I thought, standing to top off my mug of coffee. The love in Manuel's eyes, and Sophie's mirrored feelings, seemed impossible to fake. If anything, it reminded me of the way X looked at me when we were alone.

I was so wrapped up in my thoughts I hadn't heard the shower turn off, nor had I heard the door open, nor had I heard Ranger X leap toward me.

The next thing I knew, I was flying through the air with a set of large muscled arms wrapped around my body. As I squealed in shock, X stumbled in recognition. We hit the bed with an *oomph*, the wind knocked out of me as Ranger X fell on top, pinning me to the mattress.

I wheezed for breath as X regained his composure.

"Lily! What the hell were you thinking?" He moved quickly, releasing my hands and pulling me into a sitting position. The fear left his eyes, replaced immediately by remorse. "I'm so sorry, I heard a noise in the kitchen and thought it was an intruder. I didn't have time to look before I pounced, and..."

I raised a finger, still sucking in air in a very unladylike manner.

"I'm so sorry," he repeated, running his hand over my head. "How did you get inside?" He closed his eyes as the realization of my key-holding status returned to him. "I'm so sorry—I wasn't thinking. I just reacted. Did I hurt you? I'll call—"

"I know," I said, interrupting as I let my hands fall on his shoulders. I gave a few squeezes until he leaned against me. "Relax, I'm fine. I'm just not used to being tackled into bed from across the room."

A painful grimace spread on X's face. "I'm so sorry—"

"Give me a kiss, please."

"Lily, I'm not in the mood. I almost took the wind out of you. I tackled my own girlfriend, and—"

"—and you're not very good at making up for it. It's my fault, too. I probably shouldn't have surprised you for the first time so early in the morning. Forget it."

Ranger X turned to me, his eyes filled with remorse as he took my face between his palms. "I would never hurt you. I'm sorry. You're always welcome here. I'll be better."

"You've been alone in here for a long time. It's natural for you to be on guard. I'd be worried if you *weren't.* But there is a bright side to all this!"

"What's that?"

"I hoped I'd find you in bed." I winked at him, then inched closer so my lips hovered just over his. My arms snaked around his neck as I dragged him next to me on the bed, his body warm against mine as he finally began to relax. His hands traced up my sides, trickled over my back, and held me to him as he gently returned my kiss.

"There," I said, finally breaking the kiss after a few minutes. "Are you convinced I'm *fine*?"

A pained look crossed his face, this time for an entirely different reason. "I wish I didn't have to get to work."

"You're too honorable to forego your duties," I teased. "But today, I'll let your honor slide because I have work, too, believe it or not. And I came here to ask you a question."

"What is it?"

I sighed, remembering Manuel's face in the image. "The newspaper—did you read it?"

"You're worried about the disappearances."

"I talked to Peter yesterday."

"Peter?"

"The reporter who wrote the article."

Ranger X frowned. "Any particular reason why you spoke with him?"

I dove into the particularly long and somewhat cringe-worthy story of my day after we parted ways yesterday morning. I left out the confidential information from MAGIC, Inc., and some of the embarrassing bits about baking flour, but I left the rest of the details intact.

I had also, thus far, avoided the fact that my father might be the head of The Faction and somehow connected to everything happening on The Isle. I dreaded telling X, but knew it was becoming more urgent that I filled him in on it.

"The public seems convinced Peter is crazy, but I don't know," I said. "When we walked through The Twist, he was talking to me, and it felt like he meant what he was saying—that it wasn't just some publicity grab. He's genuinely convinced something's happening with the disappearances, and I—"

"So am I."

"—think it might be worth looking into...wait, *what*?"

X gave a gentle laugh, then reached for my hand and gathered it in his. He traced soft lines along the outer edges of my fingers, the movements so hypnotic I lost my train of thought.

"We've been looking into it."

"Who is *we*?" I asked. "And *what* have we been looking into?"

"The Rangers. We've been following the disappearances closely and keeping an eye on them."

"And?"

"And I have a theory."

"Wait a minute." I held up a finger from my free hand and rested it against my forehead. Blinking for a long minute, I let the pieces settle into place before speaking. "You're saying that Peter might be right this time? These aren't coincidences?"

"It's always a possibility."

"Right. But his last two predictions have been completely off-base. Gus seems to think he's looney tunes."

"Well, his last two stories were wrong. Although, we did ask that Glinda's fairies run their drills by us first in the future, so as not to upset anyone."

"How do you know this time around is different?"

"Because of the evidence we've found. We take every complaint seriously—yes, even Peter's. We look at the facts, assess, and go from there. This time, we have reason to believe the disappearances might be linked."

My eyes felt like saucers. "But he said you guys weren't looking into it."

"He *assumed* we ignored him." He hesitated. "Peter's a reporter. He gossips—that's his job."

"I think his job is to *report*—"

"If I gave wind to Peter that we thought he was right," Ranger X said, straining for patience, "he'd have a field day with it. He'd be begging for quotes, photos, confirmation. We're keeping our investigation private."

"The newest story—Manuel and Sophie." I nodded toward the paper still spread on the table. "What do you think?"

"Word came in during the night about Manuel being gone, and—"

"Wait a second..." I ran a hand over the bed, the covers still unrumpled, as everything clicked into place. "You haven't slept yet."

"No. I came home to shower and return to the office."

"Why is this happening?" I shook my head. "Three people going missing from The Isle is somewhat alarming. People don't *leave* here."

"Have you ever heard of the SINGLES program?"

I pursed my lips and shook my head. "Sounds like some sort of dating thing."

He barked a laugh. "No. Then again, I suppose there's a form of matchmaking happening. It involves The Faction. A program that has been around for many years—longer than I've been alive."

"I don't understand. How haven't I heard about it?"

"It only resurfaces during specific times. We haven't been concerned about it for a while, though Ranger HQ always keeps an ear to the ground for word of it happening."

"What specific times?"

"The SINGLES program is for those who have no attachments. Orphans, children or young adults who have little or no family support at home. Those with bad luck, tough lives, the works. Some might call them *high risk*. Besides the children, there are the adults who are struggling, looking for a place to belong."

"Do they...apply to this program?"

"No. The Faction calls it *recruiting*. We call it *kidnapping*."

"They take kids from their homes?"

"The Faction targets those who they believe nobody will miss." Ranger X's eyes shifted to stare through the window, his voice quieting. "I don't know for sure what happens once they *recruit* them. All I know is that most of them never come back."

"Why would they do this?"

"They're building their ranks. An army, if you will."

"With children?!"

"And adults—and you must remember, this program has been around for a long time. Those children will *become* adults."

"They don't try to escape?"

"I'm sure they do...at first. But I imagine the leaders of this program are very smart and skilled at what they do. Perhaps there's magic involved, or perhaps the leaders manage to convince their recruits that their new family is The Faction."

"But—"

"The Faction promises to care for them, to feed them, to include them as one of their own. You must understand, Lily, that for someone who has no place to go, those are magic words."

"And you think The Faction is behind it? You're *positive* these disappearances are related to the SINGLES program?"

"Almost without question." He waited a beat, watching my face. "Yes, that would mean they're building an army, which doesn't surprise me. We've seen the signs arriving."

"I have to tell you something." My fingers twisted, rolled over one another in my lap. "It's about my family. And The Faction."

"What are you talking about?"

"The night of Zin's Ranger ceremony, I learned some new information about my past."

"Who came to you?"

I debated keeping Trinket's name to myself, but eventually decided against it. "Zin's mother. She had enough evidence that it convinced me to listen."

"Evidence about what?"

The words began to pour out, my voice shaking as I recounted Trinket's story. I told him about how my mother and father had met on The Isle, but my father had left for school. Once my mother had found out she was pregnant with me, she'd followed him to share the good news.

Except when she'd arrived at his dorm room, she'd found it gone. Burned to the ground. My father was dead...or so everyone suspected.

Sometime later, my mother had figured out that all was not as it seemed—instead of perishing in the fire, my father had lived. He had been *recruited* to The Faction and groomed to be their leader. A ghost—that's what they called him. It was one of the reasons The Faction was so difficult to pin down. Their leader had been dead, supposedly, for years.

"The calla lily," I said, finishing up. "The one that blooms in the storeroom—I think it's linked to him. A warning of some sort. It's been going off like mad."

"Why do you suspect this man has business with you?"

I digested the question for a second. "Because he's my *father*."

"Lily—stop, don't cry." Ranger X's face twisted in dismay as a tear slid down my cheek. He leaned in, wiping it from my face. "I'm sorry. What did I say?"

"Nothing. You didn't say anything wrong." I sat stiffly, unable to let my head collapse against his chest though I desperately needed the support. "It's just a stupid tear."

"You know that your father being involved in The Faction—allegedly—doesn't change anything. The way I feel about you, the way anyone feels about you. A man you've never met can't hardly call himself your father."

"His blood runs through me." I flipped my arm, exposing the blue veins. "If he can be recruited, how do we know that I'm not next?"

"No, absolutely do not think that. He made a choice."

"And maybe—"

"Lily." X's voice was firm, solid. Demanding attention. Pressing my head to his chest, he waited until I relaxed against him. "We are all responsible for our own choices. We are all capable of bad choices.

But we are also capable of greatness. *You* are capable of greatness, and you've already proven it."

I swallowed hard, wanting to believe him with every beat of my heart.

"Whoever your father may or may not be is irrelevant to the good you've done."

"The vial," I said, changing the subject. "I think it's linked to the calla lily, which might link to The Faction. I need to find a way to reverse that spell."

"But you can't tell me why?"

My eyes flashed up at him. "I'm sorry, but the details are confidential."

"Who knows about all of this?"

"Gus knows pretty much everything. Trinket knows about my father. I figured the rest of The Core should know, but I was waiting for the right time to share. I wanted to tell you first."

He kissed the top of my head. "I think you're right. We'll all need to be as educated as possible if we stand a chance against The Faction."

I sighed, not looking forward to calling a meeting with Harpin. "I should gather them today. With Jonathon, Drew, and Manuel gone, we don't have time to waste."

Ranger X stood first, silently agreeing. "Do you want me to be there when you tell them?"

X had recently been invited to join The Core, but he'd turned it down due to his position at Ranger HQ. Instead, he'd offered to help when needed as a consultant.

"I would appreciate it," I admitted. "Let's meet outside The Twist at ten this morning. I'll notify the others."

"Lily, there's one more thing."

"Yes?"

As we prepared to leave his home for the day, Ranger X strode up behind me. "Remember what I said. No matter what anyone tells you. Me, Harpin, Trinket—you are a wonderful Mixologist. A brilliant person. And, more important than anything else, you make me the happiest man alive."

Chapter 10

"WHO ARE WE WAITING on?" Hettie asked, puttering around in her treehouse. She had a teapot bubbling over a small flame and a tray of crackers set out on a sawed-off stump. "I thought I heard Gus—"

"I'm right here," Gus said, pulling himself up the ladder to the treehouse. "I'm getting too old for this monkey business."

"Well, that's sad." Hettie put a hand on her hip. "You're dating my daughter, which makes me feel *really* old. You know, since I'm her *mother*."

I looked between the two faces as Ranger X ignored everyone, standing on a platform supported by a particularly thick branch in the corner. He hadn't been amused when I'd explained that we held meetings for The Core in a tree.

"Maybe you should lift some weights," Hettie suggested. "Might help you climb that rope ladder a little faster."

"Hettie," I warned.

My grandmother tilted her nose to the ceiling, which was as close as she came to a truce. "I'm assuming Ainsley can't make it on short notice?"

"Of course not," an oily voice said as Harpin appeared in the space Gus had been standing in moments before. "No loss. I didn't agree with inviting that agency witch in the first place."

"Funny. I feel the same way about you," Gus said. "Unfortunately, you're still here."

Harpin, dressed in his long black robe despite the summer heat, sneered back.

"Children!" Hettie clapped her hands. "I have a pie in the oven, so let's make this quick. Lily, you called the meeting, so what is it you wanted to discuss?"

"Well..." I sucked in a breath, thrown off at the sudden turn of attention. "I called this meeting, um, because I wanted to explain—"

"Let's keep things moving," Harpin interrupted. "I had to close my shop for this. What's so important?"

Ranger X made a terrifying sound in his throat, but Harpin didn't seem to notice. Nobody liked Harpin, and I still found myself wondering why Hettie had seen it necessary to invite him into the group in the first place.

"I recently learned some information about The Faction's leader," I continued. "Before my mother disappeared, she entrusted Trinket with a secret."

"Do you have a name?" Harpin pressed.

"My mother gave Trinket the name of my father. Not only that, but she told Trinket she had every reason to believe that my father was being groomed to be the next leader of The Faction."

Unsurprisingly, the reaction came as stunned silence. There was a rustle of leaves as the breeze changed, the crack of a board as X shifted his weight, but from the rest of the group came nothing.

Until everything came at once.

"*What*?!"

"No. It can't be."

"Names? *Who*? How?"

"I can't believe my daughter kept a secret like that from me!" Hettie screeched. "Years. *Years*! She's been hiding this!"

"How long have you known?" Gus asked, his face turning red. "And not bothered to *tell* me?"

"I'd like to point out that there's only one person who doesn't look surprised," Harpin drawled, glancing pointedly at X. "Lily must've shared the secret in pillow talk *first.* Before all of us—the team she's supposed to trust the most—were told."

Another silence, this one precarious, followed Harpin's observation. My hands shook. I hadn't asked for this—any of it. I didn't *know* the man claiming to be my father. I hadn't *asked* to join The Core. My blood boiled, frustrated that somehow it was all my fault.

Before I could defend myself, Ranger X surprised everyone as he threw his head back and laughed. This silenced the room faster than my news. X laughing in public was a rare and quite noteworthy event.

"What's so funny?" Harpin dared speak first. "Why is *he* here, anyway? He declined membership."

"Lucky thing I declined," X agreed. "If the Ranger business operated like this, we'd never get anything accomplished."

Harpin stepped closer to X, his hands balled into fists. "We were doing just fine before you arrived."

X held up his hands in submission. "I'm just here as a consultant. I was asked to be involved in The Core, and I only showed up this morning because Lily asked me to be here."

"Why am I not surprised?" Harpin turned his beady eyes on me, flicking his gaze from head to toe before snorting in derision. "I should've guessed she couldn't stand to break the news to us alone. Without her boyfriend holding her hand, taking the flak for her. In fact, why is Lily here? She's been a witch for all of five minutes while the rest of us—"

A crack sounded as the branch holding the small platform beneath Harpin's feet shuddered. As we watched, Harpin rose into the air, his words turning into a garbled, strained grunt of noise. Suspended above us, his face morphed to a deadly shade of purple as his breath vanished. Choking, held up by nothing except air... and magic.

X stood with his hand outstretched before him, his fingers pinching the air together as if squeezing the life from Harpin's throat. He remained at the far corner of the treehouse, his face a passive wall against all emotion.

"X, stop!" I cried. "Leave him alone!"

"His Uniqueness," Gus breathed, staring in awe at X. "He has telekinetic abilities."

When Ranger X spoke, it was low, and calm, and matter of fact. "You're wrong, Harpin. I'm not doing this because of Lily. I'm doing this as a favor to you. If you talk to people like you just talked to Lily, you'll wind up in trouble. *Others* may not be so kind as Lily."

Harpin barely managed to squeak a response. His face erred on the side of purple.

"I don't particularly care what sort of trouble *you* find yourself in," Ranger X continued. "But if you're a true member of The Core, you better start acting like it. Otherwise, you'll get everyone in trouble. Everyone here, and everyone on this island that you've sworn to protect."

"Let him *go*," I pleaded. "You're going to kill him."

Ranger X blinked at the sound of my voice, and then he did as I said. His fingers widened as he allowed Harpin some air. Harpin sucked in a few raspy breaths.

"You shouldn't even be here. You don't belong." Harpin dared argue while still locked under the spell of X's powers. Even Gus flinched. "Go back to where you came from."

"No, I don't belong here, but we—the Rangers and The Core—are in a partnership. If we can't get along, we won't stand a chance against whatever the future brings."

To punctuate his warning, Ranger X let Harpin collapse onto the floor. Harpin scrambled desperately to stand, but was unsuccessful. He slumped back down, wheezing in a breath, and it was a long minute before he could pull himself to his feet.

"You're a monster," he spat at X. "Some Ranger you are."

"Watch it," Gus said, stepping between Harpin and X. "He's the most respected Ranger The Isle has ever seen, and if word gets out you've disrespected him—"

"It won't," Ranger X said. "Everything we've discussed here today is completely private."

"Or else...*what*?" From somewhere, Harpin found the oxygen to speak, to smirk, to press buttons. "You'll use your *secret magic* on me again?"

Ranger X's fingers twitched, but he resisted as I laid a hand on his arm.

"Stop it!" I hissed at them all. "This isn't about X or The Core. And you can't be mad at me, Hettie, or at Trinket, for protecting a secret she was sworn to keep. Gus, I trust you with my life. You know I tell you everything as soon as I'm ready."

Gus stared into space while Hettie bowed her head and looked away.

"Harpin, just stop being so horrible. If you're not interested in making friends, fine. But we have to work together, and there's no way around it."

Next up, I turned to Ranger X. He'd crossed his arms and was glowering at Harpin.

"And you," I said, more gently. "I invited you here because we *all* need to work together. Just like you said. I love you," I said, ignoring Harpin and speaking only to X. "But I can defend myself."

"Sure," Harpin said. "But when push comes to shove, he'll be here to save the day. It's no wonder with his Uniqueness."

Ranger X's breath hitched. I could feel a flood of tension as I leaned into him, a wave of understanding as he realized what he'd done. He'd exposed himself, his Uniqueness, to everyone here. Something so sacred to him that he'd taken every precaution to protect it all this time.

And we all knew.

By the time I looked back to him, he was gone.

"X!" I yelled after him, but I couldn't move as swiftly or as smoothly as he could. So, I turned my rage on Harpin as I headed for the ladder. "Look what you've done. You've divided The Core, The Rangers, and next up, it'll be an island divided."

"Lily, wait—" Hettie called.

"I'm through with this. The Core. X was right," I said, my feet searching for the ladder. "I'm done here. We're done."

Grasping onto the thin ladder, I slid more than climbed down, sprinting toward The Twist. Ranger X might be able to make it out himself—after all, Hettie had been required to provide a key potion to her labyrinth for Ranger use.

"X, wait!" I huffed as I ran, but there was no answer.

I threw myself into the rush of flowers, bushes, and weeds. Blooms the size of chairs drifted into the path, and vines as thick as my leg wound underfoot. Water fixtures spurted and danced beyond, birds chirped and wildlife rustled.

I called again, and still nothing.

"*Please*, wait—" As I sprinted around a heavily foliaged curve in the road, I ran smack dab into a figure and lost my breath.

"Lily—it's you." Mimsey reached out, her nails gripping my shoulders. "I need to talk to you."

"I'm sorry, can this wait? I was looking for X, and—"

"I helped Ranger X out of The Twist. He was moving quickly and asked for my help. I'm sorry, I didn't know."

"I need to find him."

"This is important." Mimsey's wide eyes found mine, her short, plump frame trembling as she gripped me tighter still. "I need to talk to you about Poppy."

I hesitated, listened, but The Twist had swallowed any last traces of Ranger X's movements. He obviously didn't want company right now, and if he wanted to be alone, well, I'd never be able to track him.

"Okay," I sighed, letting the thoughts of Ranger X ease to the background. "What is it?"

"I'm worried about the disappearances. I think Poppy might be next."

A chill ran through my blood. "Excuse me?"

"Poppy is a vampire," Mimsey said, her eyes filling with tears. "I'm a witch."

"Right," I said. "What does that have to do with the disappearances?"

"A witch..." Mimsey fumbled. "Can never have a vampire baby."

My blood ran cold. "What are you saying?"

"I'm saying that Poppy is adopted," Mimsey said, her eyes orbs of fear. "And I believe The Faction is after her."

Chapter 11

WE WALKED ALONG THE shore outside the bungalow, the sound of the waves masking our conversation. We were alone, the sun warm on our backs, our feet shuffling through the water.

I spoke first. "Does Poppy know?"

"No." Mimsey's face pinched in pain. "At least, she never said anything. Never asked questions."

"Why didn't you tell her earlier?"

"I always meant to! It wasn't a plan to keep this a secret from her, but I guess... I just always assumed it would be obvious. I'm a witch. She's a vampire."

"Then time slipped away, and it became harder and harder to tell her?"

Mimsey nodded. "I tried, several times. But I couldn't...or, at least, I didn't want to. I didn't want to break *us.* We'd always been mother and daughter, just the two of us. I didn't want anything to change."

"Nothing would've changed, Mimsey. Family is what you make of it. It's who you love. You and Poppy love each other so much—nothing will change that."

"Maybe if I'd told her as a child, but now?" Mimsey raised a pudgy finger and swiped a tear from her eye. "It's too late."

I started to respond, then changed tactics. "One thing, Mimsey. If witches can't have vampire offspring...what about Zin? She's a Shiftling. Her mother is a witch, so does that mean—"

Mimsey shook her head. "Zin's father was a shifter. When shifters and witches mate, their children can be either. As for her Shiftling characteristics—that's something else entirely, something special. A mutation like having two different colored eyes or... I don't know, red hair. Something unpredictable."

"How did it happen? You finding Poppy, I mean."

"Poppy." Mimsey paused for a smile. "I suppose she found me."

I waited, resting in Mimsey's smile as she searched for the words to continue.

"You know, your grandfather brought her to me."

"Harvey? The last Mixologist?"

"The one and only. My father was a good man."

"Where, er—how did he come across Poppy?"

"I'll have to start at the beginning for that." Mimsey's eyes darkened. "As you probably know by now, The Faction has been active in one form or another for a very long time. Many years ago, when Poppy was a baby, they'd implemented a recruitment type of program."

"Are you talking about the SINGLES program?"

"So, you *have* heard of it?"

"Ranger X told me this morning," I said, watching Mimsey's surprised expression. "He believes the program might be active once more."

At this, Mimsey crumbled to the sand, sitting with a hard *thump* before resting her head in her hands. "I knew it, I knew it," she sobbed. "They're back."

"But why would they be after Poppy?"

"She was one of the first vampires recruited to the program," Mimsey said, jagged breaths halting her words. "Her real mother passed away during her birth—or so we believe. Nobody knows whether or not her father was ever in the picture, but he wasn't around when they found her. We tried to look for him, but nothing."

"And the SINGLES program takes in orphans."

"The younger the better. They groom them. Can you imagine?! My poor, sweet Poppy being groomed to be one of *them*."

"How did my grandfather wind up with a baby vampire?"

"As soon as the people of The Isle learned what was happening, they sent a task force to disband the program. A combination of Rangers and volunteers. Your grandfather offered to help."

"Was their mission successful?"

"They disbanded the program and freed most of the children and young adults who'd been kidnapped. There were few adults, but they, too, were freed."

"So, it was successful?"

"That's a complicated question." Mimsey gave a tight smile. "If they're back, that means the program wasn't obliterated for good."

"You said there were others rescued along with Poppy. Where did they go?"

"They were placed with families around the country. A few came to this very island. Among the few who were brought here, one of them was my daughter." Mimsey's wrapped her arms around herself and hugged tight. "The day they disembarked from the boat, I saw her in his arms. Poppy wouldn't let go of your grandfather—not until I reached for her, and then she came to me."

A hard lump arose in my throat. The love Mimsey had for her daughter—blood related or not—radiated from her. There was nothing I could say to make this easier.

"I guess I never felt the need to tell Poppy she was adopted. She's mine, she's always been mine, and I've never seen her as anything other than my daughter. I've never had a single doubt we were meant to be a family."

I ran my fingers through the sand, staring into the water. "Why'd you come to me? Are you ready to tell Poppy?"

"I need to warn her. I'm worried, Lily. What if she doesn't take the news well?"

"If you tell her the same story you told me, I'm sure she'll understand. Poppy loves you more than anything."

"Do you think?"

"I'm positive."

Mimsey nodded. "Is there something...*anything* we can do to protect her?"

"Are you sure she's even a target for the SINGLES program this time around? She's not alone, not an orphan anymore. I'd argue she's quite the opposite of what they're looking for in a recruit."

"I thought so, too," Mimsey said. "Until this morning. Did you see the paper?"

"Yes, but Manuel—"

"—was one of the children brought to The Isle on the same day as Poppy. He was an orphan just like my Poppy."

"You think they're bringing back former recruits?"

Mimsey shrugged, helpless. "All I know is that now he's gone."

At the word gone, Mimsey burst into tears, sobbing so wantonly that I couldn't get in a word of comfort. She sobbed and sobbed until finally, she quieted of her own accord and began dabbing her cheeks with my shirt.

"It's going to be okay," I told her once her head rested on my shoulder in the wake of her tears. "Ranger X is already investigating. If there's anyone who can put an end to this, it's his team. And Zin—she's a Ranger-in-training now, too. She won't let anything happen to her cousin."

Mimsey sniffled. "I suppose you're right. And nothing's happened to her yet. I just couldn't bear it if anything did."

"I know, Mimsey. You're her mother. It's natural to be worried."

"If only I'd told her ages ago." Mimsey's shoulders shook with a delayed sigh. "I suppose I should tell her soon. After her birthday. I can't ruin her birthday."

"I'm sure she'll understand," I said. "It's Poppy. Remember that—she's your daughter. Nothing can change that."

Mimsey nodded, then lapsed into silence. We watched the waves ebb and flow, the colors on the horizon change and morph as time quietly ticked by. Eventually, Mimsey rose to her feet and announced it was time to leave.

I followed, watching her trundle away, her big skirts blowing in the wind as she clutched them tight. The water lapped at my ankles as I stood there until she disappeared into the distance.

While I waited, I realized that I should've pointed out the similarity between my story and Poppy's. After twenty-six years of operating business-as-usual in the human world, I'd learned of my true calling, of my true nature, of the place that would become my home. My path as the Mixologist had come clear as I'd settled into a whole new world.

"Lily!" Gus yelled from the front door of the bungalow. "Come inside!"

His voice rang urgently over the shore, and my musing vanished like sand into the waves. He waved at me, gesturing for me to hurry. I moved along the beach and up the stairs to the bungalow, wondering if he'd already forgotten my outburst at Hettie's.

"I need to show you something," he declared, the second I reached the front door.

Confused, I scurried inside as Gus peered out after me, making sure nobody had seen us.

The shoreline remained empty.

"If this is about what I said at The Core meeting, well I don't know that I feel like apologi—"

"No, no, you were right," Gus said, waving a hand. "We were out of line."

I gawked. It might have been the first time Gus had ever thought I was *right* about something. Obviously, whatever he had to show me was more important than our little feud.

He didn't notice my expression, instead gesturing to the vial and leaning over to examine it with full concentration. "Does this look familiar?"

I leaned in to study the swirling black. "Is that—"

"Yes."

"I think I have an idea."

Gus grinned. "I thought you might."

Chapter 12

"I CAN'T BELIEVE THAT didn't work!" I sat back on the workbench while Gus mournfully placed the vial back in a safe place on its shelf. "I was so sure of it."

Gus paced back and forth, the *thunk* of his cane punctuating each step. "I've read the book backward and forward and can't think of what else might work."

Earlier this morning, Gus had pulled out *The Magic of Mixology*, the ancient manuscript that I had inherited by accepting the role of Mixologist. The book itself was big, hefty, and nearly impossible to memorize. I should know; Gus had made me try.

Gus, however, had it as close to memorized as anyone. Leaning over the table, he licked the tip of his finger and thumbed through a few pages. Then he shook his head and thumbed through a few more. "That was the best Dissolver I've ever discovered—I'm sure of it."

Misery had set into his tone. Gus had discovered an ancient, almost forgotten spell in *The Magic of Mixology* while I'd been out with Mimsey. Supposedly, this enchantment could make magic vanish without a trace, dissolving spells completely. It was a quick spell, and a dangerous one, but we'd had to take the risk.

The spell had gone off without a hitch... except for one thing.

It hadn't made a dent in the storm cloud swirling within the vial.

A knock sounded at the front door, prompting a frown from Gus. "Are you expecting company?"

I shook my head. "No, although that's never stopped guests from coming before."

Gus hobbled to the door, opened it, and greeted the visitor with a blank stare. "What do *you* want?"

"Can I speak to Lily?" The voice was higher pitched than expected, and decidedly female. And familiar. "I have some urgent news to deliver."

"Ainsley!" I scurried around Gus and gave her a hug. Behind her stood Lizzie, who I greeted as well. "What brings you guys here?"

"I heard about the meeting with The..." Ainsley trailed off, and I realized she'd been about to say The Core. But, since Lizzie wasn't involved, Ainsley stopped. "How did it go?"

I shrugged. "Could've gone better."

Gus scowled in the background. "I'll say."

"I'll get the details later," Ainsley said hurriedly. "The other reason I came was because I think Lizzie might be able to help."

Lizzie nodded, smiling as she extended a small pamphlet to me. "I thought you could use this."

"What is this?" I asked, accepting it. When she didn't respond, I took a few moments to glance through it, eventually looking up in surprise. "This is the handbook for Wishery magic?"

"Hold on." Suddenly Gus perked back up and lost his scowl. "Wishery is real?"

Lizzie's eyes flitted between Ainsley and Gus. "I thought you said it'd be just us, *Ainsley*. I didn't bring my NDAs."

"Gus is the Mixologist's assistant," Ainsley explained. "Gus, you can keep a secret, right? Lily, would you agree?"

"Of course. I trust him completely," I agreed, pretending not to notice as Gus's face turned a little red before he looked away. "Gus understands magic better than I do. He should hear this, too, if we have any chance of stopping The Faction."

"That's impossible," Gus argued. "Lily understands potions the best—she's the Mixologist. But I'm second best, without a doubt."

Lizzie smiled, nodded, and told Gus she was pleased to meet him. Then she tapped the booklet and spoke to me. "This is what we give to all new hires. Keep in mind, our new hire process is incredibly thorough, detailed, and confidential. This booklet doesn't go to just anyone."

"I'd say not." Gus peered over my shoulder, showing more interest than usual in the conversation. "I've been in this business all my long life, and I've never heard anyone confirm wish magic exists."

"It's obviously confidential," Lizzie said, miffed. "That goes without saying."

"*Obviously*," Gus said. "Speaking of wish magic, I'd just like to apologize for one particular wish I made last week."

"Yes, I remember." Lizzie shifted uncomfortably. "You speak of a certain wish involving the painful death of—"

"Yeah, that one." Gus cut her off. "Didn't mean it. I was upset."

Lizzie offered a polite smile. "We looked past that one. Anyway, Lily, take a peek in there and let me know if you have any questions."

I thumbed through, but the manual was self-explanatory. I closed it before meeting Lizzie's gaze. "How does one acquire wish magic? Are the new hires born with it? Do they learn it? Is it gifted to them?"

Lizzie smiles. "They wish for it. Before they even know it exists."

"And according to wish magic rules, if their wish is unharmful, unselfish, and filled with wonder... it might be granted."

"Exactly. It's the *only* way true wish magic can ever be gifted."

"How old were you when you wished for it?"

"Eleven," she said. "Of course, I didn't know *wish magic* existed. Instead, I had wished for a career that would allow me to make others happy. A few years later, I got called for a job interview at Wishery, and I've never looked back in my three hundred years of service."

Gus flinched outwardly at this. "Three hundred?"

"I age well," she said with a flicker of a smile. "Anyway, I hope the handbook helps. I don't know how, but it appears wish magic is essential to The Faction's plot; otherwise, black magic wouldn't be haunting our city. Have you any thoughts on how to rid us of it?"

"We thought we were close, just before you arrived," I said. "The Dissolver didn't pan out."

"Lily will pull through," Gus said sounding more confident than I liked. "She always does."

"I know," Lizzie agreed. "Ainsley said the same thing."

Ainsley winked. "That's right boss. We have faith in you."

"I'm *not* your boss—" I started, but was interrupted by a crackling noise.

"We're about to get Zapped," Ainsley said, giving me a kiss on the cheek. "Duty calls, boss. We'll see you soon. Get in touch if you need anything."

Seconds later, they were gone.

"Wish magic," Gus said. "Who would've thought?"

"What I *can't* think of is how this handbook is going to help us."

"Read it. Absorb it. Let the words simmer back here." Gus tapped my skull. "I'll keep going through *The Magic of Mixology*. Something is bound to turn up."

He hadn't quite convinced me, but I couldn't think of anything else to do except get started. We hadn't worked five minutes before another knock sounded from outside.

"Your turn to answer," Gus said.

I pulled myself up, but before I could reach the door, it burst open on its own.

"Sorry." Hettie stood framed in the doorway with her arms crossed and a frown on her face. She caught sight of Gus. "Oh, good. You're here, too. That means I only have to apologize once. Are we all good?"

"Apology accepted," I said. "I'm sorry, too. I shouldn't have walked off like that."

"Have you come up with a theme for Poppy's party?" Hettie stepped the rest of the way into the storeroom, closing the discussion.

I quickly slid the Wishery handbook under *The Magic of Mixology* before nodding in agreement. "I have, but I'm still working on the potion to go along with it."

"What's the Mix called this time?"

"Long Isle Iced Tea."

Hettie clapped. "That is fabulous! Can I try it?"

"Not quite," I said, flinching. I'd tested the potion on myself and Gus, and while it had worked fine on me, Gus had developed a slight reaction to it. An hour's worth of painful hiccups. "I'm still working on the final touches."

"What does it do?"

"When it's drank, the potion will change its user into the costume most desired."

"The theme is *costume party?!*" Hettie's smile couldn't grow any brighter. "You're telling me that if I want to be a princess or a ninja, it'd turn me into a princess or a ninja for the evening? Or better yet... *a princess ninja*?"

"That's the goal."

"What would he turn into?" Hettie asked, nodding toward Gus. "I don't see him as having much imagination."

I shrugged in Gus's direction. "That's the mystery! We'll have to wait and see."

"Oh, Lily, if you weren't the Mixologist, I'd suggest a career in party planning. This is sure to be the party of the year. At least, until my birthday rolls around." Hettie shot me a coy glance. "*Right*?"

"Don't give up your day job," Gus murmured to me. "Party planning is overrated. *Parties* are overrated. Who needs to plan a party? Just show up and eat food."

"What did you say to X?" Zin asked, flying through the door without warning. She had a finger outstretched and accused each one of us in turn. "Who's the genius who pissed off my boss?"

Hettie, Gus and I all shared a guilty look.

"Uh," I started. "What do you mean?"

"Don't play *stupid* with me. I know someone in this room said something to set him off, and I've got a bone to pick with whoever it is." Zin narrowed her eyes at me. "Was it you?!"

"What are you talking about?"

"He just extended our training an extra *two hours* per day. I'm already working so much I barely have time to eat or sleep!"

"I'm sorry, Zin," I said. "We—"

"I love my job," she interrupted. "But I need a break. Whoever is responsible for X's rage—fix it."

"Did he mention what he was mad about?" Hettie asked, too sweetly. "Any hints or names or threats?"

"Does he ever *talk* to us, except to give us instructions?"

"Fair," Hettie agreed. "He is that strong and silent type."

"Maybe so, but I'm not the only Ranger annoyed right now, and that's saying something. Most of the team thinks X walks on water."

"Well, I'm not surprised," Hettie said, admiration on her face. "He is a perfect specimen of man."

Zin scowled at her until I stepped between them and shook my head at my grandmother.

"Fine, truce," she agreed, looking past me to Zin. "Let's put this behind us. Now Lily, where's the potion for Poppy's party?"

"It's not quite ready. I don't want to risk it—"

"Risk what?" Hettie interrupted.

"A bad reaction. I'm just working out the kinks."

"What sort of kinks?"

"Minor side effects," I said, hedging around those painful hiccups Gus had experienced. "I've made some adjustments since the last time."

"What does it do?"

"It's top secret," Hettie blurted, before I could explain. "She hasn't even let me try it." Picking up the jar of Long Isle Iced Tea, she examined the contents. "I'm dying to taste it."

"Lily, let me help." Zin moved another step closer. "I train for things like this; if there's a side effect, I'll be able to handle it better than anyone else."

I took the small glass jar from Hettie and swirled the potion. "I don't know..."

"Can you reverse it?"

"Of course—I have the antidote ready."

"Well, what's the worry then?" Zin pressed. "I have to be at work in an hour. Let me take it quick, you can spot any lingering problem areas, and then reverse it."

I hesitated still, so Zin reached around me and began pouring the mixture into a chalice embellished with bright amethyst gems. She did have a point; I'd eventually have to test it again before using it on partygoers, and Zin was more durable than most.

"Here's the antidote." I held up an even smaller jar filled with a powdery pink substitute, giving her the go ahead. "A pinch of this, and you'll be right as rain."

Zin picked up the chalice and took a sniff of the ingredients. "Fruity." Then, she tipped the potion back and swallowed it in a gulp. "Okay, now what?"

"It shouldn't take long." I took the cup from her hands, then waited for the magic to kick in.

Hettie folded her hands and waited patiently, and even Gus looked up from his ancient book of spells.

"I can feel it," Zin said. "It's tingly, and it's making me warm, and...*oomph*."

Zin bent in half like she'd been hit by a sack of bricks. Her dark bob flew forward and spread over her face, and her all-black attire began to lighten in color and shift in size.

Her clothing then morphed completely, her hair lengthening and knotting above her head. Her pants reached a shade of snow-white before continuing toward pink, eventually shriveling at the ankles, the calves, the thighs, until the material dissolved into a pair of tights complete with a puffy little skirt.

When she looked up, all her dark eyeliner was gone, her thick black lashes slimmed into dainty little things. Blush lightened her face, and a pinch of glitter had worked its way into the bun on her head.

Zin had become the perfect little ballerina, ballet shoes and all.

"Oh, how cute," Hettie said. "She's *adorable*!"

"What is this?!" Zin screeched indignantly, scanning her tight-covered legs and the slippers on her feet. Her leotard had tiny little straps and a curvy neckline entirely unlike Zin's style. "Why am I dressed like a ballerina?"

"You look gorgeous!" Hettie declared. "I always told your mother she should put you in dance. I knew you would've been a star."

"Surprise!" I waved my fingers. "Costume party."

"So, the theme to the party is costumes," Zin figured. "Are they random?"

"Even better," Hettie said with a wink. "It changes the user into the costume they most desire!"

"But I don't *desire* to be a ballerina." Zin stuttered, her hands too busy playing with the tulle around her waist to sound convincing. "I want to be—"

"We know, we know," Hettie said. "You want to be all badass and dark and mysterious. I sort of thought you'd turn into Ranger X."

Gus grunted in agreement.

"On the positive," Hettie continued, "it doesn't look like there are any side effects this time around. Except for Zin's embarrassment."

"Good call on the stabilizer, Lily," Gus said. "Worked like a charm."

"Right. Well, this has been a good laugh for you all, but I have to get ready for work," Zin said. "I have to report for duty in thirty minutes, and I have errands to run first."

I extended the vial of pink powder toward Zin. "One pinch and you'll be good as new."

Hettie sighed as Zin ingested the antidote. "This is going to be a great party. I can't wait to see my costume. And Gus's. And Ranger X."

"Why am I not changing?" Zin looked down, her tutu still completely pink. "I don't feel anything."

"Give it a few minutes," I said. "It's a pretty big reversal."

However, five minutes later when there were still no signs of Zin changing back to her former attire, I began to worry. And work—double-checking my formulas and math and Mixology.

Ten minutes more, and Gus dived in, too. Together, we analyzed every inch of the antidote while Zin tapped her foot in annoyance.

"I knew I shouldn't have let you bait me into trying the potion." Zin looked between Gus and myself. "Well? Gus doesn't look happy. Why doesn't he look happy?"

"The stabilizer you added?" Gus mumbled to me, a hint of sheepishness on his face, "I think it had a reaction with the sweetener."

I grabbed *The Magic of Mixology* and pulled the ancient text toward me. Thumbing through the pages, I flicked over the spell in my head until it hit me. "Oh, no. It cancels the effect of the silver."

Gus held up his finger like a lightbulb. "Correct."

"I should've caught that. It makes the antidote useless."

"*Should've caught that*? Yes! Yes, you should have." Zin threw a hand in the air. "Now what am I supposed to do? I have no extra clothes with me. My old ones are... where are they, Lily? Incinerated? I have to be at work in under ten minutes."

"Sorry," I said, flinching. "Really sorry, Zin."

"This is a mess. You're all a mess." Zin glared at her grandmother. "I came here to yell at you, and I should've done that and left."

"Shoulda, woulda, coulda," Hettie chirped. "There's no need to be so upset with Lily when you volunteered for the job. Nobody's saying you can't go to work dressed like a ballerina."

"I'm in Ranger training. I will be laughed out of HQ."

"I doubt it. Most Rangers are men. You are a beautiful woman," Hettie said. "Maybe they'll enjoy the show. You can kick butt in a tutu."

Even Gus looked impressed with Hettie's assessment, and I had to admit the point was valid. Zin, however, looked underwhelmed with Hettie's solution and huffed out of the room.

"I think she looks adorable," Hettie said as she left. "If I had legs like hers, I'd walk around in a tutu all day, too."

"I feel bad," I said, turning to Gus. "I have to come up with a way to reverse the effects. Do you think adding thyme to the antidote will wipe out the sweetener and let the silver work its reversal?"

Gus grinned. "Of course it will."

"Why didn't you tell me that ten minutes ago?! Now Zin has to walk around looking like a ballerina."

"You've got to learn to think under pressure," Gus said. "I won't always be around to save the day."

I shook my head, setting to work re-mixing the antidote. "I have to get this to Zin. While I'm at Ranger HQ, I'll find X and set things right so he'll stop taking out his frustration on his employees."

"Great. I'll let you handle this," Hettie said. "Now's my time to leave."

"She always comes to make a mess," Gus said, watching my grandmother leave. "And then leaves us to clean it up."

I sighed. This afternoon was shaping up to be one pile of joy after the next: fix a faulty potion, make amends with my cousin, settle my seething boyfriend, and prevent Wishery from being destroyed.

No big deal for the Mixologist, I thought wryly.

The fact was—I had no idea where to start on the contents of the vial. My pulse quickened as I sealed the antidote into a container for Zin, watching out of the corner of my eye as the calla lily slowly bloomed into another perfect flower.

Time was running out.

Chapter 13

THE ANTIDOTE EXCHANGE with Zin went quickly.

I found her lurking in the bathroom at Ranger HQ. Elle, the gorgeous, over three-hundred-year-old receptionist, pointed me in her direction as I signed into the building.

Grudgingly, Zin swallowed the antidote and reverted back to her normal self. It was only after she'd inspected her newly regenerated attire and found it perfectly intact that she reluctantly admitted she liked the idea of a costume party.

With one relationship repaired, I set out in search of my next target.

"Hey, Elle—do you have any idea where X might be this afternoon?"

The silver-haired beauty raised exquisitely manicured fingers to her lips and grimaced. "He's in a mood today."

"So I hear," I said with a sigh. "And I'm afraid it's partially my fault."

"He stomped into The Forest an hour ago after clocking out. Usually that means he needs some time to cool down. Let him wrestle were-bears, or whatever he does in there. I'm sure he'll calm down by the evening."

"I wish I could, but I really need to fix this."

"Honey, if you want my advice, there's nothing to fix." She offered a flickering smile. "Whenever he gets this angry, it's usually something he did himself. A mistake he made, a decision he's worried about."

"I know, but I pushed him to *make* a mistake. So, we're back to it being my fault."

"I *guarantee* he won't see it that way. Ranger X takes pride in making all of his own decisions. If he made a mistake, even on your account, he'd still blame himself."

"Any idea where he goes in The Forest?"

"No, I'm sorry. He wouldn't even be happy that I told you he went there at all."

"I know, but—"

"Just wait it out, Lily. It'll only make things worse if you go chasing him down. He loves you, and you love him. He'll come back soon."

I groaned as I stepped back from the desk and headed toward the elevators to the outside world. "Thanks anyway."

"See you soon," she hummed. "And be careful out there."

The second I appeared above ground, I turned my feet away from the Ranger HQ entrance and started to make my way deeper into The Forest.

The familiar dampness, the heavy weight of the air, settled on my shoulders. The world here was a bit too quiet, a bit too still. So stuffy it was nearly impossible to find a full breath of oxygen as my feet pulled me underneath the giant trees.

I closed my eyes and inhaled, and exhaled, practicing the almost meditative-like state that Liam had taught me to get through The Forest. Directions here didn't work in any normal capacity. The trees, the shrubs, the wildlife—all were alive and moving, bending their limbs to the songs of the universe and changing the course of The Forest with each passing breeze.

I'd improved at my ability to listen, to feel, to guide my way through. I still avoided the need to venture in alone as much as possible, but often it was a necessity. Dust of the Devil—the dangerously blooming plant required for Poppy's Vamp Vites—bloomed in only one location. That location was deep within The Forest.

As my feet wound their way through the undergrowth, I focused on that very thought—I was overdue for a harvest from the plant, and it would give me a good excuse as to why I'd come to The Forest in the first place.

My footsteps sprung light and easy, and I made my way toward the flower-laden tree in record time. I'd only paused once or twice to listen, but it hadn't helped. Something was amiss within The Forest. It was as if every branch and leaf had been stunned into complete silence. Not a single creature or critter had brushed past my legs as I picked my way through the undergrowth.

When I approached the clearing where the Dust of the Devil plant lived, my suspicions crept up higher than ever. The faerie who lived on the mushroom here, Ferrah, a Tinkerbell with sex appeal, had vacated her post. She never vacated her post. Ferrah loved to sit and smoke her fake cigarettes and tell stories to anyone who stumbled deep enough into the wilderness.

Suddenly uneasy, I focused on the task at hand. Gather the flowers. Do not linger, do not inhale their scent, do not get sucked under their enchantment like a sailor to a siren.

I gathered three flowers and reached for a fourth. The second I plucked it, I heard a noise. *The* noise. A popping, almost as if a log were on the verge of collapse. I whirled around, expecting to come face to face with a wild animal, but...*nothing*.

"Hello?" I called. "Anybody there? Ferrah?"

No answer.

The fumes from the Dust of the Devil flower grew stronger. I hadn't capped the vial quickly enough, and the scent began to pull me under, to gather me in a loving embrace and carry me away on a light melody.

I let it happen for a moment, blithely drifting away, letting my eyes close until—

Another noise.

This one louder, too loud to ignore.

Snapping to attention, I shoved the flower in the vial, sealed it shut, and quickly stowed it away in my travel belt. Still shaken by the Dust of the Devil's spell, I glanced up. Again, I saw nothing.

"Hello?" I called. "I'm not here to hurt anyone. I'm Lily Locke, the Mixologist. Is anyone there?"

Only silence spoke back.

The eeriness of being watched, however, only intensified. I moved quicker, faster. Somehow, despite the spine-tingling sensation increasing, I didn't feel afraid.

I forced myself to trust in my gut reaction. The Forest and its natural magic had a way of protecting those who respected it. I'd been in danger in The Forest before, and I'd always known. Always sensed it.

I couldn't piece together why this sense of calmness had settled over me. I didn't dwell in The Forest regularly, and I never wandered about aimlessly. It wasn't as if I knew its paths inside and out. As I began my journey out of The Forest, deciding to wait for X at his house, I found myself pulled in a new direction.

A short while later I stumbled from the grip of The Forest into brilliant rays of sunshine. Glancing around, I realized I'd emerged at a different location than the one I'd entered. I'd popped out in a sunny little oasis bordered by palm trees that looked unfamiliar to me.

Confused, I stepped further from The Forest, giving my brain time to process. *Why had The Forest spit me out* here? The Forest had never before pulled me in a new direction. It usually sent me exactly where I'd wanted to go.

That's when it clicked. This place wasn't new to me at all.

I'd been here before, and recently. Through the palm trees, I spotted the little house that Chuck had claimed was haunted. I'd popped out on the opposite side of the oasis, hence the reason it had looked unfamiliar.

With a giddy sigh of relief, I realized it was only a short walk home. Whoever had been following me in The Forest would have to wait another day for whatever business they had with me.

Still, I hadn't resolved things with Ranger X. I shouldn't have been surprised that I couldn't find him in The Forest, but the disappointment hit nonetheless. I'd almost hoped The Forest would bring us together.

Elle was right, I supposed. Time would calm him down.

Resigned to letting X stew alone, I glanced around, locating the worn footpath that would take me back to the bungalow. I took one step and stopped. Silent, listening.

Something had moved.

Something was different.

Something was alive.

My chest felt like it'd been hit by a brick, my lungs constricting until I could hardly breathe. I ducked behind the nearest cluster of bushes, watching a small spiral of smoke curl up from the chimney of the old shack, long ago abandoned by the Witch of the Woods.

Cats couldn't start fires. Neither could most wild animals. This time, it wasn't Tiger hiding out innocently in the cottage. Which meant that something else—or someone else—was inhabiting this home.

I remained crouched in hiding as my eyes stayed glued to the front door. The windows were grimy, and I strained to see through them, to locate movement through the windows. Aside from the curling smoke, which now made sense with the burned smell I'd detected, the house rested quietly.

A squirrel skittered over the front lawn, and a small family of birds made their way to the stream before the cottage. They landed, drinking from the water while the smoke continued to rise.

I watched everything—every movement, every wisp of a breeze, and yet I could find nothing save for the smoke.

Inching forward, I craned my neck for a better glimpse through the window, almost disbelieving my eyes as a shadow flickered behind it. A whisper of darkness behind the grime.

I held a brief debate with myself, muttering the pros and cons list for pushing forward and demanding the inhabitant show themselves. On the cons list, however, was the fact that *nobody* knew my whereabouts. I hadn't intended to come here, so if things went south, not a soul on this island would have the first idea of where to look.

My decision made, I began to back away. I eased under the cover of The Forest, keeping just along the edge as I traced a roundabout way toward home. The canopy kept a layer of shade over me, and I made good time traveling along the ridges until a large tree diverted my path.

Keeping close to it, I eased deeper into The Forest for just a second.

Just a moment to inch around the fallen tree.

A hand circled my wrist, pulling me into the darkness. A firm, strong grip that had no intention of letting me go.

My heart nearly burst, my pulse racing as adrenaline flooded my body. My instincts kicked in, sending my legs and body bucking as my fingers scratched like a wildcat.

"Lily, it's me!" Ranger X called, exasperation clouding his words. "It's just me, sweetheart. It's *me*."

"Why?!" I breathed, sheathing my claws as he gently set me on my feet. "Why would you ever startle me like that? What happened to calling out a *hello*?"

"Why were you running through The Forest?"

"I was walking, not running. And I hardly stepped foot inside of it."

"You stepped far enough inside for me to find you."

"How *did* you find me?"

Ranger X eyed me carefully. "The Forest has a way of bringing me just where I need to be."

"What are you doing here?"

"What are *you* doing here? Did you come here to look for me?"

"No, I was harvesting Dust of the Devil. Poppy's Vamp Vites are due for a refill, and..." I trailed off as his gaze landed on me.

"Why didn't you take the Upper Bridge?"

"Maybe The Forest led me straight to *you.*"

"You were looking for me."

"Of course I was looking for you! You stormed out after our meeting. I had to come find you."

His face clouded with something I initially pegged for anger, but underneath, I wondered if it wasn't more. A hint of shame maybe, or embarrassment.

"I was looking for you," he admitted finally. "To apologize. Sometimes when I'm frustrated, I escape to The Forest to blow off steam. I wander around and let my mind work. The Forest takes care of me, gets me to wherever I need to be. By the time I'm spit back into the sunlight, I usually have a new perspective."

"And this time?"

"It brought me to you. I owe you an apology," he said, taking my hand in his and cupping it between his fingers. "I'm sorry about how I acted at Hettie's. It was your meeting, your team, your place to speak."

"Thank you, but—"

"I hope you can understand I never meant to undermine you." He brought one hand up, ran it through his hair in frustration before meeting my gaze dead on. "I'm beginning to realize that I don't always act logically when matters concern you."

"It's okay, really."

His eyes darkened as he brought his hand down, leaving behind hair standing messily on end. He slipped his arm around my waist and pulled me close. "Walk with me for a bit."

I hesitated, our lips inches apart as my hands braced against his chest. I waited for him to close the gap, to kiss me and make the world crumble away, but he didn't.

My heart pounded against my chest, and his echoed in response. The sizzle between us grew palpable until my entire body shook from hunger to close the space between us, but X seemed to have other things in mind.

"Sure," I eventually managed. "Let's walk."

After a long silence of nothing but the crackle of branches, he spoke. "I don't know what to make of this."

"Of what?"

"I've spent a lifetime straining to keep myself in control. Always in control. Not once since I was a child have I used my Uniqueness without intention."

"Until earlier today?" I guessed, sliding my hand into his as we fell easily in stride.

"That... it just happened. Lifting Harpin, restricting his airway—no, I didn't intend for any of that to happen."

"It looked purposeful."

"Maybe in my subconscious, but it wasn't logical. I just acted, and before I realized what had happened, it was too late."

Uneasily, I shifted next to him. "Was it because of me?"

His eyes flashed to me. "This isn't your fault, Lily."

"It is a little bit."

"I'm just trying to absorb what it all means. I *can't* be out of control. Ever."

"You're a person just like everyone else. We all lose control sometimes. It happens."

"*Everyone* might make mistakes, but *everyone* cannot be head of the Ranger program. I've been granted that honor, and my path is incredibly clear. It is *why* I have my position—I am not everyone. I *can* block off my emotions."

"Maybe you can't."

"Whenever a Ranger makes a decision with their emotions instead of their brains, we play a dangerous game."

"You didn't really hurt Harpin, and he was being quite rude—"

"That's no excuse. I deal with people and creatures who've done bad things. Most of them aren't polite when we arrest them."

I pulled him to a stop as we reached a small clearing. A lump had grown in my throat, and I didn't know what else to say. I had nothing to add, no insights or advice. I just knew that X was spiraling lost, and I was starting to go with him.

Jasmine circled us, small white flowers blooming amidst the darkness, thousands of little stars amongst the greenery. The moment was filled with sweet intensity as I brought my gaze to land on his glittering eyes.

"What you're not saying," I began, "is that the problem with all of this is me."

"No, that's *not* what I'm saying at all—"

"If it weren't for me, Cannon, would you have lashed out at Harpin or would you have walked away?"

He took a breath before responding and let it out slowly. "I don't know."

"We both do," I said, feeling a little cross. "The answer is no."

"It doesn't matter."

"Of course it does! Obviously you're worried because you've used powers you haven't used freely in years. And you didn't *try* to do it. That's dangerous, X. You know it, and I know it. What I *don't* know is where we go from here."

"It doesn't matter. The Core—you're all bound to secrecy, yes?"

I nodded.

"Then they will not share what happened. The secret is safe."

I flinched. "Unless the group is dissolved."

His gaze faltered as he shot me a questioning glance. "What did you do?"

"You were *right*! We weren't working together. The only thing the group of us have in common is my grandmother. Half of us don't like one another. Maybe it's a bad idea to force something."

"Your grandmother brought the group together because you are all talented. And you're needed now more than ever—all of you."

"*Help* is needed, yes. Not a bunch of misfits who can't get along for ten minutes."

"You wouldn't have left the meeting if it weren't for me."

"You wouldn't have used telekinesis if it weren't for *me*." I stepped back, the space where his fingers had been now blindingly cold. "You wouldn't be having any of these issues, or thoughts, if it weren't for me."

"You're the Mixologist, Lily. You are worth it. As a Ranger, if someone threatens you, it's my duty to protect you above all else."

"Is that all this is?" My eyes smarted with tears as a pit gathered in my stomach. "It's all about me being the Mixologist. *That's* why you care so much?"

"If you think that's what this is all about," Ranger X growled. "Then you don't know me as well as I thought."

"Then tell me what you want me to say! You bring me here and tell me you're confused, that you're dangerous, all because of me. Well—the only solution I can think of to solve that problem is to keep me away from you."

His hands came to rest on my shoulders, his grasp so hard and so firm it might've bruised. A tangle of furious heat followed, his lips meeting mine in a vicious war, a kiss that spilled over frustration, hurt, and underneath it all, the ache that simmered between us.

My body vibrated under his touch. He pushed and pulled, teased the heat from me as his grip grew softer. My stomach tightened as we connected on a visceral level that had my veins turning to molten lava.

And then suddenly, my feet no longer touched the ground. We were circling, rising above the clearing as the sweetness of jasmine wrapped around us.

His arms held my waist, tight and sure. My mind was far too hazy to process the fact that we were floating, drifting toward the treetops. My hands fell to my sides, my body melding against X's as he gripped me against his chest.

He feasted, his tongue pressing into my mouth as we ascended still higher—five, then ten feet from The Forest floor. Spiraling in a wash of heated sparks and chilled air, his scorching touch against my bare skin.

This must be magic. *His* magic.

Some sort of latent power taking over in the rush of emotion. The desire, the anger, the frustration—he'd lost control, and the dam had opened and spilled out.

Light glowed from X, radiated from every line of his body. An aura of power surrounded us second to none I'd ever seen before. He must have held this much inside, this strength, for years and years, until he overflowed with it.

"Cannon," I whispered, still not digesting the fact that we hovered in a golden cloud of dust just under the treetop canopy. A tear finally slid down my cheek, and I tasted salt. "What does this mean for us?"

He caught sight of my face, the sparkle of wet against my cheek. Took the moment to kiss each glimmer away before gently easing us back down to the ground.

We stood in an embrace, my gaze focused on the grass beneath our feet.

The longer he went without speaking, the tighter my fingers wound into his shirt. "What was that?"

When he didn't respond, I looked up to catch a faraway expression in his eyes.

"What *was* that?!" I yanked his shirt closer to me. "Cannon, talk to me!"

X leaned his head back in response. It lolled back, his chin tilting upward as his hands rose of their own accord. He stood broad, like a perfect image of the Vitruvian man, strong and sturdy and distant.

His hands rotated until his palms faced the skies above, and then, as if from nowhere, two columns of golden light radiated from his palms and burst upward, parting the treetops with a ripple of bright light.

A metallic cloud of dust drifted around us, the silence new and all-consuming. I backed away from him slowly, watching as my heart raced. He didn't seem to hear me, see me, or even notice my presence.

I called his name, but he didn't respond. I called again, and still nothing.

The beams of light grew stronger, more intense. They pulsed with a brightness made from lightning bolts and stardust, and grew wider, taller, brighter until everything came to an end with resounding quiet.

Slowly, his head sank back into a normal position as his gaze met mine, finally, as the columns from his palms evaporated to nothing. I stepped toward him, but he shook his head and murmured only two words. "I'm sorry."

Then he collapsed, lifeless to the ground.

Chapter 14

"GUS!" I YELLED, HAIR flying behind me as I raced across the beach. The waters whipped in angry currents behind me as I burst through the door of the bungalow. "Gus, I need you to come with me, *now*."

He took one look at me, rose to his feet, and moved. He didn't bother to ask any questions, and for that, I was grateful. Together we raced back toward The Forest, the place where X had fallen seared into my mind.

"What happened?" Gus bent on a knee and ran his hand over X's face. "He's out cold."

"I know. We were...walking together, and—"

"Tell me the truth," he demanded. "Don't censor a word. We have the head Ranger knocked unconscious, and there's no time for privacy."

"We argued," I said, fear clutching at my chest. "About the meeting this morning. I stopped us here to talk, and things got heated. We were almost yelling at one another when all of a sudden, he kissed me."

Gus maintained eye contact, no judgment in his gaze. "And?"

A new wave of respect for my assistant washed over me. "We kissed, and then...um, we sort of floated."

"You floated?"

"Floated *up*. There." I pointed toward the canopy. "It wasn't like we *tried* to do that, but there must be some magic at work or...or something. Maybe his power?"

"He's breathing. Vitals seem to be fine. What makes you say it was his power?"

"Well, we've kissed before, you know, and we've never floated up anywhere. I've never flown anywhere without a broomstick."

"How'd you get back down?"

"We just sort of...descended. I asked him a question and maybe that broke the spell."

"And when you landed?"

"His expression got distant, as if he couldn't see me or hear me. Like he didn't even know I was around. Then a light shot out of his palms toward the sky."

"What color was the light?"

"A golden, sunlight sort of shade, I suppose."

"We need Trinket."

"What does Trinket have to do with this?"

"I'll explain when you return. Get to her house and back as soon as possible. I'll wait with him."

I took off without question. Rushing toward Trinket, I hurtled through her neat front yard and pounded on the front door, unable to keep from wondering what Zin's mother had to do with any of it.

"Lily?" Trinket opened the door, not bothering to hide her look of dismay at my disheveled appearance. "What is it?"

"We need your help. Gus requested you."

"Where?"

"Just inside The Forest—not far from here."

Trinket narrowed her eyes. "Why did Gus ask for me?"

"I don't know. He came to help me revive X—"

"Revive Ranger X?!" Her look of concern turned to alarm as she briskly began to slip into her shoes. "What happened?"

"Golden rays of light sort of...*um*, shot out of his hands, and then he fell unconscious."

"Oh, dear." Trinket exhaled a breath, looking decidedly less worried all of a sudden. "This certainly won't be pleasant for him."

"What is it? What's happening?"

"He'll be fine. Let me grab my things, and we'll get this cleaned up quickly."

No less than a minute later, we were both striding quickly across the lawn.

"He'll be fine," Trinket said, a pace behind me. "No need to run."

"You haven't even seen him, yet! How can you possibly know that?"

"Because I know *exactly* why Gus called me." Trinket fished for a tool that looked like a compact mirror and extended it in her palm. "This will fix him right up."

"Then what is wrong with him?"

"Lumiette, of course."

"Lumiette?"

"You've never heard of it?" Trinket raised an eyebrow. "I'm surprised you didn't suffer from it yourself when we first brought you to The Isle. Ranger X, however, should have known better."

"Better than to do what? Was it the kiss?"

Trinket's other eyebrow joined her first, a little too high on her forehead. "This has nothing to do with kissing, I assure you."

"Then what is it?"

"Lumiette is a sort of affliction that mostly affects children."

"Then why would X or I have it?"

"Because the reason Lumiette forms in the first place is from an excess of power in the body with no outlet. If the power has no place to go, it will build and build until it breaks free."

"Is that what it was? The light?"

"I imagine," Trinket said. "Although I've never seen anything so drastic. Usually it manifests in a small halo around a child's head. In this case, the reaction was intensely more profound. You see, Ranger X has more power than most paranormal beings, and I'd guess he's been repressing it for too long. Like anything, the longer—the more intense—the compression, the more dangerous when the energy is released."

We reached the edge of The Forest, and Trinket waited for me to enter first.

"Gus called *me*," she explained as the leaves swished around us, "because I have seven children. Since children are so raw, so pure in their power, and they have no real way to control it, magic leaks from them when they're emotionally distraught, incredibly tired, or otherwise fragile. I've been dealing with Lumiette for the last thirty years of my life."

We wound through the tree roots bubbling under the ground and Trinket paused to find her footing. "It's likely Ranger X showed some fissures of it earlier today, or this week—a few small bursts, possibly, and that weakened his armor. Think of it like a window—a few tiny cracks, and the pane becomes incredibly vulnerable. Now, if he's had an emotionally difficult situation, and that glass shatters, you have a classic case of—"

"Lumiette?" Gus looked up from his post over Ranger X. "Was I correct?"

Trinket kneeled, sweeping her ankle-length skirt to the side. She brought her hand up, felt over the top of X's head, and then brushed a thumb over his lips.

"Yes," she said finally. "Ice cold lips, the rest of him boiling up."

"Will he be okay?!"

"I already told you he'll be fine," Trinket snapped. "And I meant it."

"I'm allowed to be worried," I said. "Not only do I care about him, but he's the head Ranger on this island. One of the most powerful men here. If he's unconscious, it's a bit alarming."

"I'd give you that argument," Trinket said coolly. "If someone else had made him unconscious."

"What she's saying," Gus added, "is that Ranger X knocked himself out. If ever there was a person who could take down X, it's himself."

Trinket pulled out the compact she'd put into her pocket earlier and flipped it open to reveal a honey-colored gel inside. Sticking one finger into it, she dabbed some over X's lips until they were covered in a glossy sheen.

Then she snapped the compact closed, handed it to Gus, and wiped her hand on her dress. Carefully, she brought her fingers to his chin and pressed it upward, forcing his mouth fully closed.

"There he goes," she said, after a long minute of holding there. "He needs to ingest enough of it for the process to work."

"What's in it?"

Gus simply handed me the salve. "You tell me."

"Do not use this as a teaching moment. My boyfriend is unconscious."

"Every moment is a teaching moment," Gus said, undeterred. "What's in it?"

I hesitated, then surveyed the compact and began my normal assessment of a foreign substance. Eventually, I reached the taste test, and I dipped my finger in and dabbed a bit on my tongue. The taste was sweet, a lemony honey mixture pleasant to the senses.

"Calming—there's chamomile and lavender..." I watched as X, even in his unconsciousness, ran his tongue along his bottom lip. "Honey for taste."

He stirred shortly after, rustling against the ground, fighting back weakly as Trinket held his mouth shut.

"Guarana," I said, tasting the buzz of caffeine. "For energy."

"Very good," Gus said. "And?"

I tasted again, considering. "Well, we have chamomile and lavender for the calm, guarana to revive him...I'm assuming we have one more ingredient that will soak up any extraneous energy running through his body."

Gus nodded, looking somewhat impressed.

"It's not..." I scrunched up my face and tasted again. "No. Please tell me I'm wrong."

Gus grinned. "Why do you think we need to add so much honey?"

I quickly closed the compact and handed it over to Gus. "You are *so* rude."

Trinket looked mystified as she glanced between us.

With glee, Gus clarified. "Liver. Absorbs the energy, just like it's made to do when it's inside our bodies. Works the same with excess power."

"Your grandfather created Obscurita," Trinket said as she took the compact and slid it back into her pocket. "As a matter of fact, he made it for your mother."

"My *mother*?"

"She had power coming out of her ears from the day she was born," Trinket said, a faint smile playing at her lips. "I think she's the only person—well, besides X, now—that's ever gone unconscious from Lumiette."

Gus nodded in agreement. "The Isle thought she might be the next Mixologist for a moment. She wasn't, but she had the strength for it. Must've passed it along to you."

"Your grandfather developed Obscurita when your mother knocked herself out," Trinket said. "Before that, we gave children an ice pack, a lollipop, and set them in bed until they calmed."

I inched closer and kneeled, too, my hands landing on X's shoulders. "He really will be okay?"

"I *told* you that," Trinket snapped. "He should regain consciousness in another minute or two. We'll have to walk him home, as his legs will still be wobbly. I imagine he'll feel somewhat like he's been electrocuted."

"Is that all?"

"I'll leave this with you." Trinket slipped the compact out once more and handed it over. "Apply Obscurita every four hours or so—it should be easier once he wakes. Don't let him convince you he doesn't need it. He does, otherwise the extra energy will spark in his blood until he has another episode. He can resume work tomorrow."

"He won't want to wait until tomorrow."

"Well, he should if he's smart, or he's risking his own health and the safety of those around him," Trinket said, rising to her feet as X stirred again, his eyes flickering open and snapping shut in rapid succession. "Tell him that, and maybe he'll rest."

I ran my hand through his dark locks, my fingers toying with the strands. "Is there a way to prevent this from happening again? What if we hadn't been around to revive him?"

Trinket brushed her skirt against her legs. "I imagine if you weren't around when this happened, he wouldn't have let his emotions get the best of him."

"What's that supposed to mean?" I moved X's head so it rested in my lap. "Are you telling me to stay away from him?"

"You asked how to prevent another episode, and I'm giving you my advice. There are two main options, one is better than the other."

"And they are?"

Trinket watched X's face as she spoke. "The first is the best, but it will be the most difficult. He'll need to step back and begin training his energy, his power. If, and this is a big if, he can learn to corral his raw powers after all this time, it could keep these episodes at bay."

"You make that sound difficult."

"It is. He's stubborn, and he's a man. He'll argue that he can control his emotions, but as history has already shown—he can't. Nobody can, not completely."

"I can," Gus growled. "I have no emotions."

"And Mimsey is fat," Trinket said.

Gus stood, his hands clenched into fists as his eyes blazed. "What did you say?"

"No need to get your feathers ruffled," Trinket said in a lofty voice. "I know very well that my sister isn't fat, but I needed to prove that you, yes, even you, Gus, can have what's called *an emotional reaction.*"

Gus eased his fingers open and sullenly stepped back.

"What's the second option?" My fingers gripped X's hair tightly, winding their way through as if that could keep him safe.

"The one he's chosen for the last number of years. Maintaining little to no serious emotional ties," Trinket said. "He obviously managed to keep himself contained for longer than most, and I imagine he succeeded because he prevented all connections from beginning in the first place."

Everything in me shrank away as Trinket's implication hit me, biting and painful to realize what she meant.

"It might be best for the short term to keep your distance," Trinket said gently. "I'm sure he'll make the right decision, Lily."

"But—"

"He'll have to make that decision one way or another. If he chooses a life with you, he won't have the option. Should he have children..." She paused, her voice easing into a softer tone, one she rarely used. "Children are pieces of your heart that you can't control from the day they're born. I have seven pieces of me, my heart, running around, and no matter how hard I try, I can't keep them from harm."

I was still reeling as she wheeled around and began a fast trek toward the clearing out of The Forest. I called after her, but she didn't stop, and I couldn't leave Ranger X's side. Even as I watched Trinket leave, one of Ranger X's hands reached up and grasped at my arm.

"Let her go," Gus murmured. "I don't think that last bit was about you."

"No, *really*?" I turned to him. "It doesn't mean she couldn't use someone to talk to. *Seriously*. Men, sometimes."

"Zin has been training her whole life to be a Ranger. Shouldn't Trinket be used to that by now?"

"I'm sure that doesn't make things any easier."

"Lily." Ranger X finally spoke. "Where are we?"

"X, you're awake!" I let my hand rest against his cheek, skim across his face, and come to rest with my thumb against his lips. "We're just inside The Forest. You had a spell of...wooziness. Take your time, and when you can stand, we'll take you home."

Ranger X frowned, brought a hand to his forehead and massaged it, as if trying to bring back his memories. "But what happened?"

"We'll talk about it later," I said. "Right now, just focus on..."

I trailed off as he ran his tongue over his lower lip once more, his eyes flickering with understanding at the taste. "Obscurita? The antidote for Lumiette? But that's impossible."

"Ain't impossible if you never use your magic," Gus said with a chastising frown. "You should know better, X."

"But I always—"

"Closed yourself off, yep." Gus nodded along. "We all know how this works. Looks like you've got some stuff to figure out, don't you?"

"Gus! Let him rest," I snapped. "We'll talk about it later. How do you feel, X?"

"I'm fine." He struggled to his feet, pulling himself upward with painstaking care. He reached for a nearby tree branch for support. "I'm fine. I can see myself home."

"Stop being so stubborn!"

"Stubborn?"

"Yes!" I stood, too, frustration bubbling behind my words. "Maybe if you hadn't been so stubborn in the first place, we wouldn't have gotten ourselves into this mess."

"*We* didn't do anything. This is all *my* fault."

"And now it's *my* problem. I love you, so if you go unconscious on me, of course I'm going to worry."

"Lily—"

"Stop arguing and listen to me." I linked my arm through his. "We're going home, and you're not moving until tomorrow. Understood?"

A quiet laugh from Gus caused my hackles to rise once more.

I turned to him. "Something funny to you, Gus?"

"Nope. No."

"Can you *please* go back to the bungalow and work on the vial after you help me get him to bed? See if you can tease the potion ingredients out, separated individually, so when I return from taking care of this stubborn man, we can move forward."

Thankfully, Gus recognized my mood as one not to be prodded. He looped one arm around X while I took the other side, and together, the three of us limped toward X's cabin.

By the time we arrived and laid him in bed, X had thoroughly exhausted himself. I re-applied the salve to his lips as he drifted to sleep, then accompanied Gus outside.

"I'll be back tomorrow," I said. "If you have any luck with the vial, let me know, and I'll get Trinket to come watch over X."

Gus nodded. He began to stomp away, but at the last second, he turned back. "Lily, do you need anything?"

"Like what?"

"You seem...upset."

"I am upset."

Gus still looked confused, so I went ahead and unloaded.

"I'm upset because my boyfriend is getting himself injured. He's injured *because of me*."

"It's not your fault, Lil—"

"That's not it." I held up a finger. "I'm upset because there's a vial I can't dissect. I can't figure it out, and that is my *job*. It's my career, my life, my...everything to understand this level of magic."

"No, Lily—"

"I'm also upset because Trinket's upset. Something's going on with Zin, and I hate that nobody is figuring out why. I'm upset because the gnome was right, and there's something funny going on at that house—haunting or otherwise. I'm frustrated because we've had three disappearances from The Isle in so many months. On top of that, I haven't eaten a good meal or slept through the night without horrible dreams for a week. Is that enough?"

Gus started to reply, but I raised a second finger.

"Oh! And all of The Isle, as well as MAGIC, Inc. and the mainland are watching and waiting for me to save the day. Is *that* good enough?"

Gus stared back at me, flabbergasted. "How do you have room in your head for that much worry?"

"Goodbye, Gus."

"Take a breath. It will be okay."

"How can you say that?!" My voice exploded from me. "Did you not just hear a word I said? Everything, everything is resting on my shoulders right now!"

"And that," Gus said with a smile, "is why everything will be okay. Take care of X. I'll let Ranger HQ know he will be indisposed for a while."

He left, striding toward home, leaving me to digest what he'd meant. It had sounded almost like a compliment, but at the moment, it wasn't feeling like one. It was feeling like a gigantic burden.

I stepped back inside X's home, locked the door, and eased onto the bed next to him. For many minutes, I watched him sleep. As I monitored his temperature, I wondered what choice he'd make.

Would he choose the unpredictable road, the one to make him vulnerable from all sides...or would he play it safe?

The question played over and over in my mind until eventually, my eyelids began to droop, and I eased my legs under the covers, too.

Then, I slept.

I slept for several hours, finally rising when the sun had started to sink. I made a quick dinner for myself and tried to share it with X, but he floated in and out of delirium all evening.

I reapplied the balm several times, and each time it disappeared faster and faster, absorbing the energy just like Trinket had predicted.

Finally, night came, the moon rose, and I moved back to bed and attempted to sleep. However, I'd slept well earlier, curled against X's feverish body, and my mind was restless. I couldn't drift off, so eventually I gave up trying and climbed from bed.

I opened the front door and sat on the front steps, watching as a shooting star traipsed across the sky. The moon hovered, a silver path of light leading from it to the edges of the lake around us, further than the eye could see. For a moment, I debated wishing on a star.

Wishery, I thought. I wondered if they would hear my wishes through the fog.

Then I pondered, yet again, how there could possibly be a form of magic in that vial nobody had ever seen before. Wish magic existed, Lizzie had confirmed it. Used for good only, which meant it couldn't possibly be wish magic that swirled in the vial.

Unless...I stood and paced back and forth in front of X's home. My mind worked through a series of scenarios as I formulated a plan, hoping, praying, needing to believe that it might work.

It wasn't until the new hours of the morning that I climbed back into bed, exhausted, and slept again.

Chapter 15

I WOKE THE NEXT MORNING to the scent of coffee and the sound of water running.

My eyes eased open carefully as I stretched luxuriously in bed.

For one moment, everything was as it should be: I'd slept, mercifully without dreams, and felt rested. My body sunk into the soft embrace of X's bed as the fresh brewed caffeine gently teased me to consciousness.

The sound of the shower running brought me back into the normal routine so quickly and thoroughly that it nearly washed away the memories of how I'd ended up here yesterday.

Then, a *thunk* sounded from outside—the newspaper hitting the door, I imagined—and everything jolted back.

Lumiette, the vial, wish magic.

I bolted out of bed and rushed to the door to retrieve the paper.

Returning to the kitchen, I poured myself a cup of coffee and skimmed the front-page headline, setting the carafe down with a heavy thud as the first one caught my attention.

FOURTH DISAPPEARANCE—WHO WILL BE NEXT?

Peter's name appeared under the headline again. I settled at the table, forgetting all about the coffee I'd poured as I inhaled the article. Another missing person, the second this week. Either there was a wild explanation for all of this...or things were escalating, and fast.

This missing person was a woman, reported to have been a loner most of her life. Consistent with the first two missing persons. So far,

Manuel was still the outlier in that he'd been the only one with a serious relationship and no desire—allegedly—for a way out.

The woman newly missing was named Magdalena Sprite. According to the article, she had a human father and a witch mother, both of them long since deceased. She'd raised herself since her fifteenth birthday.

However, she'd done well with her life and now had a career making custom school robes for Cretan. According to Peter's article, she'd loved her job, had purchased a quiet little hut on the northeastern shore of The Isle, settling there for the long haul.

She hadn't, however, had many friends or acquaintances, so most of the quotes about her came from neighbors who'd seen her in passing, or the owners of local shops.

"Good morning," X said, startling me into dropping the paper. "Sorry, I figured you'd heard the water shut off."

"No, it's...another disappearance." When he didn't look surprised, I continued. "Had you already heard?"

"He gave a slight nod. "Message came through this morning—it's what woke me up."

"Right." I blinked, shaking my thoughts back to the present. "How did you sleep? How are you feeling?"

"I feel fine," he said, running a hand behind his neck and hooking it there. "I felt fine yesterday, but that salve you kept putting on knocked me out."

"Sure, that's what knocked you out," I said, forcing my eyes not to linger too long on the arm crooked behind his head. His gorgeous bicep was a prime candidate for admiration, and I couldn't let it distract me from the conversation we needed to have. "It was the *salve* that knocked you out, and not the fact that you'd stored up nearly thirty years of power without giving it anywhere to go."

"They're saying it was Lumiette?"

I nodded. "Trinket and Gus agreed. They were correct, I'd imagine, seeing as you're looking much better today after the antidote."

"It was nothing." X moved to the counter and poured himself a mug of coffee. "A mistake."

"A mistake that knocked you unconscious."

"Well, it shouldn't happen again soon, eh?" He continued with the lighthearted tone, his eyebrow raised as he faced me. "I think we can call it good for the next thirty years."

"That's not what Gus and Trinket seem to think."

"Is it any of their business?" The lightness faded fast from his tone.

"I think it is, seeing as you are the head Ranger on this island. You protect all of us." I swallowed, hating to say the next part. "Including me."

"They're worried I'll hurt you?" X growled, whatever light that'd been on in his eyes now sucked away, a vacuum of dark filling them instead. "I would never hurt you."

"Who cares whether or not you hurt me? What about yourself?" I stood, leaving the paper to flutter to the floor. "What if I hadn't been around, or Gus, or Trinket? Would you've lain unconscious in The Forest until the creatures ate you alive?"

"They wouldn't. They know better than to eat *me*."

His lips turned up in amusement, but I ignored it. "Fine. Until The Faction found you? Until...your body shut down? I don't know, X, but it didn't seem like you had any choice in the matter at all."

"They're not worried about me. They're worried about me being out of control around *you*." His jawline set firmly. "They think it'd be an accident. That I'd have another episode and you would be collateral damage."

"Forget about me! This is about you. It's unhealthy, whatever you're doing. You can't keep this locked inside of you. If I'd known, I would've asked you to address it long ago."

"Well, I can't just *let it out*, what do you suggest I do?"

"What?" I stepped back, somehow hit by surprise to hear he had already rejected the first option. "Why not?"

"I told you—using my Uniqueness puts me in a vulnerable position. When I use my magic, I'm at my weakest. It takes time to recover from that, and I can't afford to be weak."

"Then what do you suggest?"

"I suggest I keep doing what I've been doing all this time." Ranger X sat at the table and reached for my hand. "I'm good at keeping things locked inside."

I backed further away. "You are," I said slowly. "Until you aren't."

"What is that supposed to mean?"

"What does the future look like for us, X?! Admittedly we haven't talked about it much, but Trinket brought up a few interesting points yesterday."

Ranger X's hand remained extended, waiting for me to take it. "Lily, please. Let's figure this out together."

My hand reached for his of its own accord. "You have to take care of yourself."

"What did Trinket say?"

"She said..." I couldn't bring myself to make the leap to *family*. "Just trust me. I think it would be best if you considered all your options."

"I don't think I have an option." X's jawline was firm. "Lumiette rarely—if ever—renders a person unconscious. I believe the reason it took such a toll on me is because I was already in a weakened state in the first place because I'd used my magic on Harpin. I can't afford to be *weak* in my career."

"That's not why it knocked you out! It knocked you out because *your* power was too great inside of you!" I gripped his hand tighter. "You're the most powerful person on this island. You have to find a way to control it."

"I can't risk it. As of today, I will return to my old pact to never use it. Not for anything."

"That can't be the solution. Nobody else has that option," I said. "I can't just turn off my Mixology magic—the island would suffer."

"Trust me, everyone's better off if I keep the telekinesis hidden."

"Then you will have some thinking to do," I said, reluctantly pulling my hand from his. "Because I won't put you at risk."

"How are you putting me at risk?"

"Don't you understand? This is about you being unstable. *Emotionally.* Don't roll your eyes; you have emotions no matter how much you hide them. You're frustrated right now. Probably angry, and—"

"—in love," he completed softly. "I know."

I swallowed, waiting for him to continue, but he didn't.

"It will be okay, Lily."

"Not if something doesn't change." I shook my head. "There are fissures in your coat of armor, and if you decide to close yourself off and keep all that locked away, you can't afford to have a single weak link."

Another silence followed in which X looked away.

"I am a weak link for you, Cannon."

"That's not true." He rose, closed the distance between us and wrapped me to his chest. "You make me stronger than I've ever been."

"Then maybe," I whispered into his bare skin, "you need to become weaker before you can get stronger."

He smelled of forest and mint, fresh from the shower, his skin smooth against my cheek. I let my hands ease around his waist for a moment, just a moment, before I pulled back.

"I really have to go," I said. "Gus is expecting me at the bungalow."

"What am I supposed to do?"

"I can't tell you that. I'm just asking you to think about it." I opened the front door and let my feet carry me away. I looked back when I reached the front path. "Let me know what you decide."

"Lily—"

"I have to go. I'm sorry."

Chapter 16

"THIS WILL DO," I SAID, after making my way back to the bungalow. "Thank you."

Gus stepped back from the table in the center of the storeroom. He had the vial prepared as I'd asked, separating the elements to the most basic level possible.

Swirling in the glass jar, the cloud of black smoke seemed darker, deeper. The rest of the ingredients had been teased out to the bottom of the vial and lay in shimmering layers of pearly white, startling silver, and intense platinum.

Gus cleared his throat. "Are you sure you don't want to talk?"

"Thank you for your help yesterday."

"You know that's not what I mean."

"There's nothing to talk about. Ranger X and I had a conversation about his condition..." I paused, shaking the vial to see the contents separate. "He has some thinking to do."

"What did he say to you?"

"Look, you don't want to talk to me about this," I said, straightening. "You hate talking about anything that requires emotion."

"Lily, I—"

"I know you care about me, Gus." I set the vial on the table and straightened to face him. "You don't have to say anything more. When I asked for help in The Forest, you came without question."

"Very good," Gus said, a look of relief flooding his face. "Have you decided what to try next on the cloud?"

"Yes." I eased into my seat and pulled the contents closer. "I believe I know exactly what's happened."

Gus's wiry gray eyebrows shifted with curiosity. "Are you certain?"

"You know better than that, Gus." I pulled up my sleeves and circled one hand around the bottle. "I can't be certain until I have a correctly functioning antidote."

"Well?"

"I'll need more silver," I said. "The purest this island has ever seen. Do Mimsey and Trinket carry that at their supply store?"

"Yes. Mimsey mentioned something about a new shipment coming in yesterday. What else can I get for you?"

"Stardust," I said. "Is there a market for that?"

"I wouldn't call it a market." Gus gave me a meaningful stare. "There is one man who could help you find it."

"Liam," I murmured. "Any chance you're able to get in contact with him?"

"I can put the feelers out."

"Thank you. I'm going to go to the supply store, and we'll meet back here this afternoon."

"Lily."

"Hmm?"

"You knew the Mix for the antidote when you walked in here this morning." Gus reverently reached over my shoulder and clasped the vial in his hand. "It had nothing to do with my filtering the ingredients out. What happened?"

"I don't know that I've figured anything out."

"You have a strong theory."

I debated telling Gus how I'd reached my solution. I hesitated, uncomfortable with the idea of sharing my work before I deemed it complete. Poppy called me a perfectionist. I preferred the term prepared.

"Forget it," Gus said. "I'm just the assistant. I shouldn't have pressed—"

"Wish magic," I said, deciding in that instant that Gus didn't deserve me keeping secrets from him. He'd shown nothing but loyalty to me, and I owed him that in return. "You heard Lizzie explain it the other day."

"Some."

"Well, in its inherent form, wish magic is only ever used for good."

"It's impossible to use it in any other way."

I raised my finger. "So everyone thought."

"But..."

"Wish magic is believed to only be used for positive, ever. Many people made many selfish wishes, and they never came true. Of course everyone believed the legends."

"But?"

"But a smart man, or woman, might've figured out how to flip it. How to use the power against itself."

"Just like with X yesterday," Gus said, eyes brightening. "It was only by his own power that he managed to be defeated. Is that what triggered your solution?"

"Partially. It also helped that I saw an excellent shooting star, and I debated wishing on it. Then I found myself wondering how anyone could've come up with a sort of magic *you'd* never heard about. I'm still new here, but you—you're the most knowledgeable person on The Isle."

"I admit it's peculiar."

"Then I realized it had to be magic that had always existed, just in a different form."

"Twisted or morphed or—"

"*Flipped*," I finished. "That's why I need the silver. To reverse its power, just like I used it to do with my Jinx and Tonic solution."

"Pieces of this magic are similar to blood magic."

"Yes, and we know that blood magic takes an unwilling, often a *good* person, and turns them. It's like blood magic on a massive scale."

"The Faction took Wishery," Gus said, frowning in thought. "And used their own wish magic against the citizens."

"They turned the protection inside out and pushed the rightful residents of Wishery away."

"And there's a way to reverse it?"

"I'm first going to add pure silver, then compliment it with stardust granules to stabilize it in its original form."

Gus sat heavily on the bench at the table, folding his hands in front of him. "That's not half bad, Miss Locke."

If the situation hadn't been so dire already, I'd bask in the compliment for a while longer. Instead, I brushed my hands on my legs and stood, gathering a small vial for the road, along with my keys. "I'll be back soon. Tonight, we'll prep the potion. It should be ready in three days."

"Are you headed to the supply store? While you're there, will you pick up some extra beet sugar?" Gus asked. "What do you think about using it to sweeten the Long Isle Iced Teas? Would turn the beverages pink."

At this suggestion, his ears turned the color of said beets, and even I couldn't refrain from a grin. "That's a brilliant idea. Poppy will love it."

Gus bowed his head. "I'll prepare your workstation."

I nodded another thank you, then turned to leave. However, I hesitated and turned back to Gus. "You asked if I wanted to talk. Did you mean it?"

Gus's hands shook, and he pressed his fingers into the table to hide the tremors. "You seemed like you needed an outlet. Didn't want you to lose it, too."

"What do you think?"

"It's not my place to—"

"You're my assistant, and I'm asking your advice," I said, soft but firm. "Should I cut ties with X? At least emotionally until he figures himself out?"

"It might be the easiest solution." Gus met my gaze head on, unflinching. "As Trinket said, that is your first and most direct option."

My arms felt like Jell-O as I processed. I bit my lip so hard it burned, and still, I couldn't force my head to nod in agreement. My hand turned the doorknob, the front door opening to reveal sunlight and...a gnome.

"What did I tell you about getting a stool or something for us height challenged folks?" Chuck stomped through the doorway, not bothering to notice my shell-shocked expression.

"What in tarnation are you doing here?" Gus growled at the gnome. "Lily's got more to worry about than your culture's superstitions. You got a problem? Solve it yourself. She's not your policeman."

"Gus," I said. "It's okay, I—"

"Listen here, both of you." Chuck stuck his finger out, spinning between us with an accusatory point. "You made fun of me last time. Mocked me. I was upset, but I got over it because I'm concerned."

"We really are sorry—" I started, but Chuck hushed me mid-sentence.

"I'm not looking for an apology," he snapped. "What's done is in the past. I came here knowing that you probably think I'm delusional. Well, that's your problem. Here's the deal; there's someone, or some*thing*, making a home out of that abandoned shack, and I bet the Witch of the Woods wouldn't be happy to find out about it."

Gus spoke first. "I don't think the Witch of the Woods cares about a cat wandering through her territory."

"It's not a cat!" Chuck's fingers balled into fists. "There's been more movement than ever—smoke coming out of the chimney and shadows lurking behind the windows. Someone saw a huge animal around there the other day, and we think it belongs to the owner of the house."

"What sort of animal?" Gus asked. "A cat? I already told you—"

I held up a hand for Gus to quiet. Surprisingly, he obeyed.

"I'm asking for a favor." Chuck turned to me, throwing his hands wide open. "Nobody else will listen. You might've been mocking me, but at least you came with me last time. The Rangers threw me out before I got past the front desk."

"Wonder why," Gus muttered. "They don't have time for hallucinations."

"It's not a hallucination!" Chuck growled. "My entire family saw the smoke. There's spirits at work there, or something else. Lily, you've got to believe me."

"I do," I said.

"You have to trust me this time..." Chuck continued for a while before processing what I'd said. "Sorry, what? I *thought* you said you believed me."

"I do," I said, giving Gus a tight smile over Chuck's shoulder. "The other day when I was harvesting Dust of the Devil from The Forest, I saw smoke myself."

"I told you!" Chuck triumphantly fisted the air. "I'm not going nuts!"

"You shouldn't be excited to realize that," Gus mumbled.

Chuck scowled, then decided to ignore Gus and faced me instead. "What do you think, Miss Lily?"

"Lily," I corrected. "I think I should get the Rangers involved. Something's going on there, but I don't think I'm the right person to handle it."

"They won't listen."

"They'll listen," I said. "I am positive."

Chuck considered this for a long moment. "I suppose you are the Mixologist. Probably have more pull than I do."

Gus chuckled darkly. "That, and she's dating Ranger X."

Chuck paled. "Oh, er—right."

"Gus," I said sharply. "That has nothing to do with this. I'll talk to Poppy—my cousin works dispatch at Ranger HQ."

"That would be most appreciated," Chuck said. "The Rangers, they'll send a team out there?"

"We'll get it taken care of," I assured him. "I promise. I'm on my way to the supply store now, and I'll talk to Mimsey and Poppy if they're around."

Chuck seemed mystified that he hadn't had to argue more before getting through to me. He bumbled around some, knocking into the doorway as he stumbled toward the exit. At the last moment, he raised a hand and saluted me. "Thank you, Miss Lily. It was a pleasure to uh, meet you. Er—do business with you. Thank you."

Gus shook his head as the gnome disappeared. "He says he's not hallucinating, but—"

"Gus," I said sharply, and left it at that. "I'm going to find Mimsey and Poppy. I'll be back after I speak with them. Can you get that stardust for me?"

"Lily, wait," he called when I had a foot on the front step.

I waited until he'd click-clacked with his cane to the front door and rested a shoulder against one edge. "Yes?"

"Earlier, I told you that cutting ties with X would be the easiest solution."

"Yes."

"I said it would be *easiest.*" A grim expression settled on his face. "I didn't say it'd be for the best."

"What's that supposed to mean?"

"I don't know, but I'm sure you'll figure it out."

Striding toward the supply store, I contemplated this as my feet crunched first over sand, then over the well-worn gravel path. The supply store sat near The Twist, a short jaunt from the bungalow. I made it quickly, despite my mind being somewhere far away.

"Mimsey?" I called after the bell on the front door tinkled to announce my arrival. Winding my way through stacks upon stacks of antique looking supplies, I searched my aunt's usual hiding place. "It's me! Do you have beet sugar? Oh, and silver. I'm looking for the extra pure stuff—"

I halted immediately after rounding a table piled so high with dusty books it begged to rival the Eiffel Tower.

"Mimsey?!"

She sat behind the register, a big floppy hat wilting around her face. Her rose-pink sundress hung limp around her squashy figure, fluttering lifelessly around her ankles, and her face—streaked with tears—matched the color of her dress.

"What's wrong?" I went to her, scrambling to perch next to her on the desk. "Talk to me. What happened?"

She sniffed so loudly and so powerfully she shuddered. "It's Poppy."

"What about her?"

"Did you see the paper this morning?"

"Are you talking about Magdalena Sprite?"

"Yes. It's the second disappearance this week."

"I know, it's horrible. But the Rangers are looking into it. They'll catch whoever's responsible. *If* someone's responsible."

"Someone is behind this." Mimsey spoke with a deep voice, calm, yet angry. "That's why I told Poppy."

"Told her what?"

"The truth!"

My heart sank as Mimsey's shoulders shuddered. "About what?"

"Everything. Her adoption, the SINGLES program, my fear that she was a high-risk target if it truly is The Faction is recruiting."

My heart thumped, palms sweating. "And?"

"And she's gone."

"What do you mean *gone*?"

Mimsey took far too long to respond, her floppy hat slipping lower over her eyes. Her stare fell vacantly on me. "She's *gone*."

Chapter 17

IT TOOK SOME TIME TO convince Mimsey that everything would be fine. Even when I pulled myself to my feet and Mimsey's shoulders had stopped shaking, neither of us were convinced I was right.

"I have to get going," I said, squeezing her hand. "I wish I could stay longer. Are you sure you don't want to come back to the bungalow with me? Or I could send Trinket over?"

"She's home with the kids today," Mimsey said, waving a hand and standing next to me. "I'll be fine, really. Let me gather those things you need. You said something about beets...silver beets? No, I'm not thinking straight. What can I get you, dear?"

"We can do this later."

"No, please, it'll help me to have something to focus on."

"Beet sugar and silver. The purest silver you have."

"Of course." She bustled behind the counter and fretted for the supplies, returning with her hands full. "Is this plenty?"

"More than enough," I said, accepting the goods. "I have to get back to the bungalow, but I'll swing by Trinket's first and see if any of them have heard from Poppy. Poppy isn't *gone* anywhere. She probably just went for a walk or something to calm down. It's a lot to process."

"Maybe," Mimsey said, but her face furrowed in a frown.

"Are you sure Poppy didn't give any indication of where she was going?"

"We talked over breakfast, and then she took off. I couldn't even tell if she was feeling sad or angry or confused or...all of it, I suppose."

"We all process things in different ways."

"She should be back by now. It's been hours."

"This is big news for her." I gathered the supplies into a bag, then returned my gaze to Mimsey. "She might be a little upset, but she'll come around—I promise. She won't stay angry with you for long...*if* she's even angry at all. I'm sure she's swimming in confusion, and nothing more."

"Why won't she let me help her with it?! I'll answer any of her questions, hold her if she wants to cry, let her scream at me if that'll make her feel better."

Flickers of my leaving X with a decision to make alone returned in waves. "Maybe that's not what she needs. Maybe she just needs to think."

"Maybe," Mimsey said. "But I'm her *mother*. No matter what."

"She will be back in no time. I'm going to look around for her, I'll ask Trinket, I'll mention it to Ranger X. In fact—" I held up the bottle of beet sugar— "this is for her birthday party. It'll turn the Long Isle Iced Teas into a brilliant pink color."

"Oh, she'll love that." Mimsey's face crumpled into a smile, and a few tears leaked out. "She'll adore that. Thank you, Lily."

We shared another hug, and then Mimsey walked me to the front door. I made her promise to let me know the second she heard from Poppy. I promised to do the same.

Tucking the bag of supplies under my arm, I altered my course to swing by Trinket's house instead of returning to the bungalow. The neat front yard appeared before me quicker than expected; I'd sunk deep into my thoughts, into the swirl of concern around X, Wishery, and now Poppy.

Surely, she hadn't gone far. When I'd found out that most of my life had been a lie—the day Mimsey and Trinket had waltzed into my life—I'd needed time to process, too.

It'd taken awhile for me to wrap my brain around a whole new *world*, and Poppy was likely doing the same thing now. If only I could find out where she'd gone to process, it'd save the rest of her family a lot of heartache.

I mentally crossed my fingers as I raised my hand to the front door and knocked. I'd made my way through the perfect white picket fence, over the closely cropped grass, and through the quaintly landscaped gardens without noticing an inch of it.

Only now, as I waited for someone to answer my knock, did I scan the surroundings with a new curiosity. Roses bloomed along a trellis next to the stairs, the scent too potent for the moment. Too sweet, too bright.

I exhaled a sigh of relief when Trinket herself opened the door with an unamused expression on her face.

"Hi, sorry to bother you," I said, my shoulders tense. "Is Zin around?"

"Why would she be around?"

"Um," I hesitated. "She's your daughter?"

"And?"

"And...she lives here?"

Trinket gave me a startled look, which for her was quite rare. Few things in this world shocked Trinket. "Zin hasn't lived here for two weeks," she said, struggling to appear indifferent.

It felt like my chest had caught a sack of bricks. The air snapped from my lungs, and I was left gasping for a breath. "What?"

"She moved out after our last..." Trinket blew air out in a small spiral. "Disagreement."

"Where did she go? What is she doing? Why didn't she tell anyone?"

"Perhaps she's embarrassed. She threw quite a tantrum, and then stomped out of here like a petulant child."

"Where did she go? How?"

"*How*? I imagine she walked, just like everyone else." Trinket crossed her arms over her chest. "Where? I have no idea."

"How can you have no idea?!"

"Because she didn't tell me."

"She's your daughter! Haven't you tried to look? Didn't you ask her? Or ask around, or look for her?"

"Until you have children of your own, do not criticize my parenting, Lily." Trinket stepped through the front door and closed it behind her, lowering her voice to a hiss. "Zinnia is a thoroughly capable adult working for the most prestigious security group on this island. I think she can handle herself."

"But you are her mother! Don't you care where she went?"

"She has chosen not to speak to me." The first flicker of uncertainty crossed Trinket's face, but she banished it instantly. "I will not beg her to change her mind. I will not go crawling to apologize to her. She can come to me when she's ready."

"But..." My heart ached for her, for Mimsey, for Zin and for Poppy. For my own mother, who might have had advice for a moment like this.

"But *nothing*," Trinket said, ending the conversation. "Is there anything else I can help you with?"

"Have you seen Poppy?"

"Poppy? No, not for a few days. Why?"

"She's gone missing."

"Missing?" Trinket straightened. "Where? When?"

"Apparently, she had a difficult conversation with her mother," I said wryly. "And she wandered off afterward."

"I don't like your tone."

"Well, I'm worried about your daughter. And Poppy. They're my family, too."

"Zinnia is fine, as is Poppy. If anything, maybe the cousins are together, gossiping about what horrible mothers they both have."

"I hope so."

The sheer idea of it sliced me some, a jolt to my already fragile nerves. Why hadn't they included me? Without realizing it, I backed down the front steps, retreating in a daze.

"Lily, where are you going?" Trinket called after me. "Is Mimsey at the store?"

I managed a nod. "If you hear from either of them, let me know. Please."

Trinket tilted her chin upward. At the last second, she forced a tilt of her head in acknowledgement.

In one last ditch effort, I tried once more. "Are you sure you have no idea where she's living?"

Trinket began to close the door, but she paused and met my gaze. "I can't imagine it's anywhere decent. Rangers in training don't earn a luxurious wage."

"Why wouldn't she stay with me?" I asked, more to myself than anyone else. "I have plenty of space."

"If she were *speaking* to me, I would ask her." Trinket slammed the door shut, leaving her yard neat, immaculate, and untouched once more.

Grumbling, a mixture of fury and frustration bubbling inside, I headed toward home. I had to relay all of this to Gus, drop off my supplies, and get started on the vial. Then I had to loop in the Rangers to take care of the haunted house and hunt down both of my cousins.

And not forget to plan a birthday party.

I wished my sour mood would vanish. I was healthy, I had an incredible career and family, and I loved my work. There were some problems, but that was a hazard of the job.

Even so, stress knotted my shoulders, a headache easing its way into my skull. I'd offered both Poppy and Zin a place to stay. *Why had neither of them taken me up on the offer*? Why go out on their own?

They hadn't even come to me for help or advice. *Two weeks* Zin had been gone, living somehow on the meager edges of a salary. The more I walked, the more I thought. The more I thought, the more hurt I felt that she hadn't confided in me.

I'd thought we were family. Family counted on one another, and...

I stopped at the sight of smoke curling in thin wisps toward the sky.

The haunted house.

A large dark animal.

Shadows in the window.

My back snapped rigid, my temper boiling as I changed course.

I no longer feared the thing hiding in the abandoned house.

In fact, the two of us needed to talk.

Chapter 18

THE HOUSE HAD SAT FORLORN, silent and unused, for so long that even its most recent inhabitant had yet to wipe the loneliness from the air.

If anything, the most recent tenant had taken drastic measure to ensure the house looked as if it remained *empty.*

Unfortunately for her, I knew better.

The bed was roughly made, same as the last time I'd peeked inside. No dishes sat out of cupboards and the trash was empty.

It was easy enough to see how the gnomes believed that only spirits dwelled here. I also had a feeling the person *haunting* this space had used their wit and skills to prey on the superstitious culture of the gnomes living next door, encouraging their theories of ghosts and hauntings.

I sat at the table inside the small kitchen, my hands folded carefully as I waited. I must've waited thirty minutes already, but I wasn't going anywhere.

As I sat waiting, I surveyed the space. It wasn't so bad, I thought. Livable, especially for an animal.

I didn't bother to peek in the cupboards or scrounge for food—I knew there wouldn't be any. Surely Zin would've taken pains to eat outside the house, only spending time here to sleep. And, since she'd likely worked the night shift, she should be home any minute. Zin wouldn't have gone far judging by the smoke.

I waited, and waited some more, until the soft rustle of grass and crunch of gravel underfoot signaled the arrival of someone outside.

I tensed—a moment of panic settling in as I prayed my suspicions were true. If not, I could've walked into a trap. A thought I'd been too angry to consider until now—and now was too late for me to be wrong.

The doorknob turned, sending my pulse skyrocketing. The door pressed open slowly, and as it did, the glint of sunlight off black fur caught my eye.

Zin had partially transformed back to her human self, yet a lingering sheen to her dark hair and laziness to her gait gave away the jaguar form that had allowed her to escape unnoticed.

She stretched, rolled her neck and cracked her knuckles, and then turned around and froze. "Lily?!"

"Nice digs you have here."

"What are you doing here? How—"

"How did I find you? I'm psychic."

"But—"

"It wasn't all that hard once things started coming together," I explained, waving a hand across the room. "A house in use, dark shadows, reports of a large animal coming and going, a Ranger in training who has the skills to live out here alone."

"How did you know—"

"That you moved out? Trinket told me this morning."

"It's none of her business!"

I cocked my head to the side. "She didn't come to *me.* I went to your mother's house to find *you.* She told me she didn't know where I could find you. Did you honestly think nobody would notice?"

Zin crossed her arms and scowled. "It's not that unreasonable. It took you *two weeks.*"

"Because you have been hiding it from everyone!" I stood up, my chair scratching away from the table. "You're a Ranger, Zin. You're excellent at your job. If you want to hide things from people, you shouldn't be surprised when it takes us awhile to catch on. How have you been surviving here?"

"Shifting in and out of my jaguar form." Zin hung her head, sullen. "I come in when nobody's around. Usually. I can feed easier in that state, too—you know, if I run low on supplies."

"Your mother said you'd have had to find a cheap place to live on your salary."

"And I found one for free."

"You're living somewhere that doesn't belong to you. What if the Witch of the Woods found out?"

"I'm assuming she knows. I am a Shiftling, Lily. I spend plenty of time in The Forest in animal form. There's not one of us—the creatures—who don't know of her, respect her. She's the grandmother to this island and all of the wildlife on it."

"Why go through the trouble?" My words came out blazing with heat. "Why not just stay with me? I have asked you to move into the bungalow. Multiple times."

Zin didn't have a response, so I moved around the table and stood directly before her.

"I offered you a place to stay, and yet you hid from me. From us, from your family. What is family for if not to help?"

"I don't need help!" Zin roared, her eyes turning more golden by the second. Even her hair grew a shade longer in her fury. "I'm soon to be a full-fledged Ranger. I'm a Shiftling. I should be able to take care of myself, and that's exactly what I'm doing."

"You *can* take care of yourself! Nobody's arguing with you on that. But you can't do everything! Why sneak around here when you could live, openly and easily, at my place? There's no shame in it."

"Ranger X would never lean on another person for help."

"You can't know that."

"He's self-sufficient, and he's strong and powerful and capable."

"And he's the golden standard of Rangers, is that what this is about? You're trying to be *like* him?"

"He made Head Ranger for a reason. Everyone on The Isle respects him. And if they don't respect him, they fear him."

"I don't disagree, but that doesn't mean he's free from problems."

Zin had a retort ready, but pulled it at the last second. "What's that supposed to mean?"

"Nothing. I don't understand why you—all of you Rangers—seem to think it's a sign of strength to be completely independent of anyone you love."

"That's what it *means* to be a Ranger."

"But is that what it means to be a *person*?" I shook my head, letting my shoulders sag and my hands drop to my sides. "It's pointless to argue with you. With X. You both have your beliefs, and I'm clearly not going to change them."

"This isn't even about me, is it?"

"You know what? I don't know." I rested a hand on the doorknob, my fingers clenching around it. "I thought this was about family, and love, and trust, but I suppose it's not. Love and trust aren't one-way streets."

"Lily—"

"Wise up, Zin," I said, casting one last glance over my shoulder. "I love you. You're the closest thing to a sister I've ever had. But you didn't even *think* to ask why I came looking for you in the first place."

Zin's eyebrows crinkle in confusion. "I assumed—"

"That I wanted to give you a lecture," I said. "Well, that wasn't my intention."

"Then what was?"

"Poppy's gone missing." I pulled the door open and stepped outside. "I know you care about her. Why don't you use your Ranger skills to find her instead of hiding from your family? While you're at it, maybe you can let your head Ranger know, too."

"Poppy's missing? Where? How?"

"That's the million-dollar question, isn't it?"

"But—"

"I'm going home," I said, raising my hands as I stepped away from the cabin. "My door is open. It's always been open for you, and it will remain that way forever. Asking for help, or accepting it when it's offered, is not a sign of weakness, whatever X might say. I'm your family, Zin. Don't forget that."

I closed the door behind me, and turned toward home. I made it halfway there before I heard the shuffle of footsteps trailing behind me. My heart soared as I turned, a smile on my face, to greet Zin.

My spirits fell when instead of my cousin, I found a small gnome jogging to keep pace.

"Miss Lily!" Chuck called, still a few paces behind. "Wait a second!"

I stopped, willing my heart to slow and my well of patience to refill. "Hey, Chuck."

"I heard you giving the spirit a piece of your mind back there," he said. "That's what it was, right? A spirit?"

I shook my head. "No, I'm sorry. Just one of us."

"One of...us?"

"An Islander camping out there. Nothing more than a misunderstanding."

"Does that mean you took care of it?"

"I don't know, Chuck." I pursed my lips and gave a tense shake of my head. "I sure hope so. Either way, you're safe. I promise."

Chapter 19

"LILY," GUS SAID, TAPPING the table repeatedly. "I said it's time for a break."

I looked up, surprised to find darkness outside the bungalow windows. "What time is it?"

"Nearly ten o'clock. You've been at this for almost ten hours straight."

"You never tell me to take breaks."

"I've never seen you work so intensely." Gus adjusted a few vials on the shelf, cleaning up the mess I hadn't realized I'd been making. "Throwing yourself into your work to forget about something?"

"Not one thing," I said on a sigh. "Everything."

"Well, maybe you should get stressed more often. Look at all you've accomplished."

I followed Gus's sweeping arm across the room. A hint of satisfaction burned at the realization of all we'd accomplished. It wasn't enough to wash away the stress entirely, but it helped fight back fatigue for the time being.

"Helps the time pass," I agreed. "Thank you for all your work today."

"I can't believe I'm telling you this, but sinking into your work will not solve everything else."

I raised an eyebrow at Gus. "I can't believe you're telling me that, either."

He grunted, and then turned back to sorting the vials as I paced along the north window, surveying my handiwork.

From left to right, there were multiple canisters filled with bits and bobbles of potions, ingredients, and more. Silver, soaking up the sunlight, sat in the largest one. The silver dust would need to be as strong as possible, and absorbing the rays of sun would help it reflect when the time came to activate the antidote.

The vial, ingredients teased apart, sat on a shelf below it, hidden in the shadows. The blackness whirled faster, more violent by the day. When Gus had teased the smoke out of the curse, it turned more dangerous, more volatile. Just standing near it had me on edge, antsy to dispel its effect once and for all.

Next, there were small packets of ingredients needed for the rest of the antidote, and I'd kept those sealed inside tiny, airtight jars. Beside those sat the fresh mixture for Vamp Vites, which still needed to simmer before I added the Dust of the Devil. It'd be ready for Poppy tomorrow, and with its readiness, I hoped Poppy would return, too.

Lastly, a vase of neon pink liquid bubbled over a tealight. Long Isle Iced Tea, now perfected and beautifully safe. Earlier this evening, I'd turned into a bird while Gus transformed into a pirate. We'd both made it back in one piece. No lingering side effects, no painful hiccups. I only had to create it in bulk to be ready for Poppy's party.

A party that wouldn't happen if Poppy didn't return soon.

"You shouldn't let things with X bother you so much." The clink of glassware accompanied Gus's voice. He had a way of speaking with his back to me, as he organized shelves, that was more honest. "I harp on him a lot, but the kid loves you."

I smiled at Gus's calling Ranger X a kid, but the glimmer of amusement didn't linger. "It's not just about that."

"What else is bothering you?"

"I went back to the haunted house today, and—"

"Lily, how many times do I have to tell you that's not your job? I thought you were going to involve X. Is this because you two aren't speaking? You can't let personal spats get in the way of making solid decisions. Your safety comes first."

"It's not a spat. I'm not upset, I'm just waiting for him to come to a decision."

"And in the meantime, you're putting yourself at risk."

"I didn't put myself at risk! I made a calculated guess, and it paid off."

"Of course you did, but what if it wasn't Zin living there? What if it was something else, someone worse. What if it had to do with that lily blooming in the corner?"

I watched Gus's nod toward the flower, easing into another white bloom. "Well, I'm just fine, so that means my calculated guess...*hold on a minute*. How'd you know it was Zin? And *why* didn't you say something sooner?"

"I know the island well."

"What's that supposed to mean?"

"It means I keep tabs on things, and I keep an ear to the ground."

"That's why you dismissed Chuck's worry so thoroughly."

"I take concerns seriously, but only when it's a legitimate fear."

"To the gnomes, it was serious."

"Then they didn't do their homework because I discovered Zin had moved in within hours."

"And you didn't tell me?"

"It's not my place. I don't gossip, and I don't share news that's not mine to share. She's not my family; I don't give a rat's arse what she does so long as it doesn't interfere with you."

"With me?"

"I'm *your* assistant." Gus finally set the vials down, turned to the table, and gripped the edge until his knuckles glowed white. "Above everything else, above *everyone* else, my job is to protect and assist the

Mixologist. Above my own safety, I need to protect you. You granted me the honor when you asked me to be your assistant, and I will never willingly let you down."

I'd meant to argue further, to chastise Gus for keeping a secret from me, but his words set me back. Tears had swum in the back of my eyes all day, a lump increasing in my throat as time had progressed. It was everything I could do not to cry, to let it all out now.

"Well, then you needn't have worried about me going there alone." I swallowed and offered him a smile. "I understand now."

"It's why I didn't tell X to follow you. I figured this was between you and Zin."

I nodded a silent thank you.

Gus's eyes slid toward the potions. "You really did incredible work today, Lily. You're learning far more quickly than I'd thought possible."

"Probably just a good teacher," I grunted, before those tears came back and stabbed tiny pitchforks at my eyes. "Thank you."

"I've got the stardust ordered. Liam will have it here shortly." Gus thumped over to the windowsill. He stood by my side and peered at the silver. "What do you think? Three days until it's ready?"

"If we can wait that long. It should *function* at a basic level by tomorrow, but I think we'll need the extra time to strengthen it. If we *have* the time."

"Agreed. As for Poppy's party, are you all set?"

"All set except for the main ingredient."

"I thought you added the beet sugar," Gus said. "Isn't that the last bit?"

"Poppy! I'm talking about Poppy."

"Well, obviously she can't be here, yet. It's a surprise party. Isn't much of a surprise if she finds out about the potion now."

"Hold on." I blinked, slowly facing Gus. "You don't know?"

"I hate games. What don't I know?"

"Mimsey..." I cleared my throat. "She's worried that Poppy has run away."

For maybe the first time ever, Gus looked truly shocked. "Since when? I saw Mimsey last night, and she didn't say a thing."

"They had a, um...chat this morning, and it didn't go so well. I'm sorry," I added at Gus's stricken face. "I'm sure she was just waiting until she saw you to tell you."

"Here I am," he said, in a gravelly, frustrated tone, "thinking I know everything there is to know about this island. I knew about Zin, I knew about X. I recognized Lumiette and knew to call Trinket. I can recite *The Magic of Mixology* backward and forward, and yet, I didn't know that Poppy went missing."

"We don't know that she's actually *missing*. She might have gone somewhere alone, privately, to process. I'm sure that's what it is."

"Process?"

My lips tightened into a line, and I gave an apologetic shake of my head. "I'm sorry, Gus. It's not my place—"

"—not your place to share their secrets, I understand."

"Go to Mimsey."

"I don't need to ask her. Between the disappearances and what I know from assisting Harvey for more years than you've been alive, I have a good idea of what's going on. I know what Poppy is."

"Mimsey still needs you," I said, swallowing my surprise. "But why didn't you—"

"It wasn't my place to get involved in family matters then, and it's not now, either. She obviously doesn't want me there, or she would've asked."

"Gus." I rested my hands onto the table and leaned forward. "Go to her. She *needs* you there. Don't make this harder on her by forcing her to *ask*."

"I'm not supposed to know about it."

"You're not supposed to know a lot of things, yet you somehow find out about them all. Exhibit A: Zin hiding in the cabin."

He moved to stand, but sank back to his chair after only a second. "I can't."

"Fine." I reached for *The Magic of Mixology*, hauling the book away from Gus as I tucked it under my arm. "Stay here and sulk. What do I care? Nobody listens to me, anyway. We can work more. Can you grab me the vanilla bean? I think the potion needs a balancing agent."

"I'm not sulking."

"The vanilla bean, please." I took a seat at the table, humming as I flipped through the pages to find a particular Mix. My finger landed on the potion for Sleep Syrup. I had a feeling I'd need a little help drifting off tonight.

I quickly memorized the list of ingredients, then moved to scanning the shelves for dried chamomile. I found it quickly, then reached for the lavender.

"What are you doing?" Gus's eyes followed me relentlessly.

"Working." I continued, pulling out a stalk of fresh lemon grass and reaching for a knife to slice it.

"What did you mean that nobody is listening to you?"

I began chopping, the violent motion somewhat soothing. "I've been offering Zin a place to stay since I showed up here." *Chop, chop, chop*. "She declined. Now she's living like an animal in an abandoned hut."

"It's her choice."

"Sure is," I agreed. "Which is why I'm not going to say anything more about it. I hope she feels comfortable enough to take me up on my offer to stay here. It's not out of pity; it's not because I think she's helpless. It's just because I love her."

"She wants to be independent. To let everyone know she can take care of herself."

"Great." *Chop, chop, chop-chop.* "She's independent. I didn't know that being independent and leaning on your family were mutually exclusive."

"Lily, your fingers."

Chop, chop, chop. "What about them?"

"Be careful! You're going to cut one off."

I continued chopping to his dismay. *Choppity-chop. Chop. Chop.*

"What would I even say to Mimsey?"

Finally, I stopped and rolled up my sleeves. "Don't say a word. Just give her a hug and let her talk."

He moved slowly, as if his joints creaked with each motion, but he made progress nonetheless. "Will you be fine here by yourself tonight?"

"Yes, go. I promise everything will be fine. Take as long as you need."

"Thank you."

His simple phrase, soft and sincere, made every pain from this day worth it. Every ache, every risk, every word I'd spoken. I leaned in to him, the first tear of the day falling as I brushed a tiny kiss against his cheek. "Thank you, Gus."

From the doorway, I watched as he limped toward Mimsey's place. I couldn't help but wonder if he'd find mother and daughter there, reunited as they should be, or if he would find a mother alone, wishing for her daughter to return.

I glanced up at the sky, debating another wish as the first star blinked brighter and brighter. *No*, I thought, turning inside and closing the door.

The Wishery crew had enough on their plates. Later, once this was all wrapped up, maybe the Wishery team could grant my biggest wish.

Standing over my work for the day, I willed time to go faster. The silver glinted under the moonlight, gaining strength and resilience.

Patience. It would take patience and careful planning, but in three days, we should have a solution.

I moved to tidy up my work station and close up for the night, exhausted from the day's work. I had yet to hear from Ranger X, but I'd left the decision in his hands, and now I owed him the time and space required to think.

Before I reached the light switch, however, the door flew open behind me and crashed into the glow of the storeroom.

A figure stood outlined there, backlit by the stars. The waves were loud tonight, accompanying his appearance with a dramatic flourish and a raging melody.

"Lily," the man said, sounding hoarse. "I need help."

I couldn't find my voice to respond, so I shook my head in shock.

His fingers trembled as he stepped inside. "I'm *next.*"

Chapter 20

"TELL ME EVERYTHING," I said, once I'd shut the front door and set a pot of warm water to boil. "Start from the beginning. Why do you think you're next?"

Peter Knope, columnist of *The Wicked Weekly*, sat huddled on the far bench at the storeroom's center table. His hands curled around one another as they rested on the wooden surface. "I'm sorry for barging in like this, but I didn't know where else to turn."

"I'm here to help if I can, but you're going to have to explain more thoroughly."

He nodded briskly, glancing over his shoulder with a hint of paranoia. The confidence he'd exuded the other night at Hettie's had vanished, worry taking root in its place. "Yes, of course. You read about Magdalena Sprite's disappearance, I imagine."

"Yes, and Manuel, and the others."

"I'm next. I just know it."

"How can you possibly know that? Do you know who's behind the disappearances?"

"The Faction, most definitely."

"We all suspect that, but do you have proof?"

He tapped his head. "I *know*. I know they're up to something, and I can follow the patterns in their recruiting. I'm the perfect candidate."

The kettle began to whistle, pleasing me with a break from this conversation. I hurried into the bar area and began quickly pouring two cups of hot cocoa, dotting marshmallows on top.

Storm clouds hovered far in the distance, and the waves around the island howled in dismay. We rarely saw bad weather on The Isle. Even the air seemed to stand on end.

Then again, everything about these past few days had been alarming. Including the fact that I had a newspaper reporter in my home, claiming he'd be the next victim of a sequence of disappearances. It was an evening ending in firsts.

I carried the two mugs back. Plunking one in front of him, I watched as shaky fingers crept forward and circled the ceramic for heat.

"I have a few questions for you." I took a sip of my hot chocolate, pausing to let the sweet warmth slide into my stomach. "Why'd you come to me, anyway? Isn't this a case for the Rangers?"

"I went to them earlier today. They told me to get in line. Apparently thirty-four complaints came in this afternoon from people saying the same thing as me."

"Yikes."

"I'm different, I swear. I told the Rangers that, too, but they told me everyone said the same thing." He blew out a breath, his shoulders sinking into the sigh. "I don't know how to convince them otherwise."

"Did they say they'd follow up?"

"They follow up on every lead, but they told me the Rangers are stretched thin—even the trainees are working overtime. They set up a time for me to come back tomorrow."

I frowned. "So why don't you go back tomorrow?"

"Because I won't be here tomorrow!"

I glanced outside. "It's almost the middle of the night. Don't you think you can wait a few more hours and return? I guarantee nothing will happen to you at Ranger HQ once you get inside."

"My appointment's not until ten a.m.. If they take me, I'll be long gone before then."

I took another sip, fishing around for one of the marshmallows stuck to the edge before continuing. "Why do you think you're different, Peter?"

"The Faction seems to be behind this, wouldn't you agree?"

"I think it's a fair guess, but it hasn't been confirmed. Assumptions are dangerous."

"Play along with me. The Faction is recruiting for something. They're not kidnapping us for no reason. They're ruthless, but not unintelligent."

"I agree."

"And even if it's not The Faction who's behind this, my logic still stands," he continued. "Whoever's taking us needs us for a purpose—and it's not to kill us. At least, not immediately."

"I'm following you so far."

"Naturally, then, if we discover the correct pattern, we should be able to predict who's next."

"You're telling me you've discovered the pattern?"

"*One* pattern," he hedged. "But I believe it's the correct one."

"I'm listening."

"Magdalena Sprite—kidnapped most recently. She makes cloaks for all of the Cretan folks, and she's considered highly skilled at her job."

"Right."

"Manuel trained as a Healer," he said. "It's a little-known fact because he never pursued it into a full-time position. He owns a small herb business with his soon-to-be-wife, Sophie."

"How did you—"

"I'm a reporter. Digging for information is what I do. The first two disappearances—Jonathon and Drew respectively, had one thing in common. A love for games."

"Games?"

Despite his paranoia, Peter took a moment to preen boldly, his pride shining through as he smirked. "The two were loners to the outside world. But to the underground gaming club on the island, they were big time leaders."

"Games? What sort of *games*?"

"Human games. Card games, board games—anything and everything that doesn't require technology. Behind all of these games is yet another thing binding them together. Strategy. *Battle* strategy."

"You've lost me."

"The prerogative to many of these human games is to take over the world. Of course, it's only a *game.* But the club is extremely competitive, and often the members take their gameplay incredibly seriously. Jonathon and Drew were, without a doubt, the masterminds behind it all."

"Why has nobody come forward with this information yet?"

"Probably because it seems irrelevant. To everyone on the island, they looked like two loners who didn't have much contact with others. But when tied together, and grouped with the rest of the missing persons..."

"You are going to have to be clearer. You're losing me."

"The Faction, or whoever you argue is behind the kidnappings, is building something. Something big, a framework for something more. If they wanted to kill us, they would've. If they were out to prove a point, they would've moved on it already. They haven't, which I take to mean there's a larger plot at work."

"What is it you think they're building?" I asked, already knowing the answer.

Throughout this entire conversation, X's words about the SINGLES program had been in the back of my mind. I had a feeling that if Peter had gotten this far with his deductions, the leap to the next step wouldn't be difficult to make.

"An army," he said in a hushed voice. "I don't know how they're getting Manuel and the others to cooperate, but I don't doubt it's possible."

"How do *you* fit into the pattern?"

Again, a smirk of confidence crept onto his face. "Well, because I figured it out."

"Have you told anyone else?"

"No, but—"

"Then how would they know?"

Peter's face crumpled in dismay at this. "How would they know? Because everyone knows about me. I'm one of the lead reporters for *The Wicked Weekly*."

I remained silent, unwilling to spout the public opinion of his column.

"There's more," Peter said. "My parents and I haven't spoken for years. I'm not married, not dating—I don't have a whole lot of friends."

"I'm sure that's not true—"

"I'm not looking for sympathy. I'm just stating the facts. People think I'm off my rocker, but I don't care. I'm on *their* radar, Lily, I'm sure of it. I haven't been wrong yet."

I again didn't bother to clarify that he had, in fact, been wrong multiple times over his last several articles.

"Wrong about *this* story," he said, reading my mind. "Why do you think I'm pursuing it so relentlessly? I could be next. Most of all, The Faction is looking for people who wouldn't be missed. I'm not sure there's a soul on this island that would *miss* me, Miss Locke."

My stomach twisted, and I shook my head. "That's not true."

"Pretend it is. Can't you see where I'm coming from?"

"Even if I can, I don't know what to do about it."

"Talk to your boyfriend. I know you have a link to Ranger X."

"I won't see him until tomorrow."

"It's urgent; we need to find him, now."

"No, Peter, we don't *need* to do anything. I'm truly sorry, but he's not here right now, and I can't just leave to go chase him down in the middle of the night."

"Surely you know where he is." The winds grew in intensity outside. Peter watched me for a long moment, but even if I'd wanted, I couldn't give him the answers he desired. Finally, he spoke again. "You *don't* know where he is."

The truth was that I had no idea if X was out working or tucked home sleeping. I had no clue if he'd made a decision with regards to us, or not. I just didn't know.

"I'm tired, it's late, and whether or not I'm dating Ranger X, I can't abuse my relationship with him and push your case to the top of the line. It would be unfair to everyone else who has concerns, too."

"Are you denying I have legitimate concerns?" Peter stood, pushing his empty hot cocoa mug forward. "You're smart, Lily. You know I'm making sense."

"Please, listen to me, Peter. It's not about whether you make sense or not, it's about—"

"It's about me being some quack reporter who nobody takes seriously."

"Peter!" I followed him as he stormed to the door and yanked it open. "Wait."

"Are you going to help me, or not?"

"Stay here tonight, if you want," I said. "You can take the couch. I have plenty of space. We can find X together as soon as the sun rises. It's dangerous outside; I haven't seen storms like this since I've been here. My duty is to remain at the bungalow."

"I'm not looking for pity." He scowled, stepping outside as the wind raised his hair. "I'm looking for help."

"I want to help you, Peter," I called as he strode down the porch steps and away from the bungalow. "Peter! Come back. It's not safe to be outside."

My words fell on deaf ears, the angry wisps of breeze inhaling my last arguments. Even after Peter had disappeared into the darkness, I stayed on the porch, easing into the swing and letting it drift back and forth.

Hair whipped over my face, and finally, the tears fell. Angry torrents of them, frustrated rivers of salt staining my cheeks as I watched the waves twist and twirl and spiral onto the shore.

It seemed that everyone wanted my help, yet nobody wanted to listen. As much as I wanted to help them all, to assure every last person that things would work out, I was beginning to crumble.

With Gus away at Mimsey's, and Ranger X lurking who knew where, I no longer had someone to tell me that things would work out. Sitting alone on the porch waiting for the Sleep Syrup to kick in, my emotions, my body, my soul grew battered by the storms. Eventually, I dragged myself up to bed and fell into an exhausted slumber.

I needed sleep. I needed rest. I needed my nightmares—the all-too-real haunts raiding my dreams—to go away.

What I didn't need was the shadow that appeared at my window sometime before dawn or the slither of movement outside my front door.

And when my door blew open downstairs and banged against the wall, the last thing I needed was to be alone.

Chapter 21

"WHO'S THERE?"

I hadn't noticed the shadow outside, nor the slither of movement across the front porch. The clanging of the door, however, had woken me from a fitful sleep.

"I have help on the way—announce yourself." My heart pounded in my chest as I eased down the staircase from my bedroom to the storeroom.

No sound except for the raging wind slicing through the open door and spiraling around the storeroom could be heard. A crash followed, then the tinkle of breaking glass.

I sunk lower to the ground, listening a few moments before finally pushing my head around the corner. A dark shadow was hurtling toward the side door, exiting via the bar.

My lungs constricted, and I couldn't tell if the darkness came in a human form, a creature, or nothing more than smoke itself.

I stared after it, hardly breathing, until another noise pulled my attention to the front door. A new figure stood there, bigger and darker than the last, this one in the form of a man.

Backlit by the moon, covered in shadows, I couldn't make out his features. I pulled my head behind the doorframe. A sob rose in my throat, flashes of everything I had yet to accomplish blinking into my mind: prepare the vial for Wishery, find Poppy, help Zin secure housing, make amends with X—all of it still lingering.

And then he spoke. "Lily?"

I gasped.

"Lily! What happened?!"

Ranger X's voice broke through, releasing the silent sob I'd held back for too long. He moved through the storeroom before I could uncurl myself from the ball I'd crumbled into, and he had me in his arms before I could utter a word.

"Who was here? What did he do?" Ranger X pushed my hair back from my face, almost violently pleading with me. "Talk to me, Lily."

"How did you..." I hiccupped, sobs wracking my body.

"Something felt wrong, so I came to you."

I blinked up at him. "That's it? A feeling?"

He kissed my forehead, relief flooding his face as he saw me unharmed, heard my voice, touched my cheek. "I'm so sorry, Lily. About everything. Leaving you alone—where the hell is Gus? I instructed him not to leave you."

"You instructed him?"

"Do you hear that?" Ranger X pressed his cheek to my forehead, and the wild storm grew outside. "I'd never leave you alone tonight. I would've come sooner, but I had...business. I've been working all day, all night. Things are happening, Lily."

"I know," I whispered. "Look." The calla lily in the corner had grown, bloomed to a flower the size of my head. "We can't stop it."

"Stop what?" Ranger X stiffened. His chest big and strong and firm as he pressed me harder against him. "Was it...you don't think it was him that was here tonight?"

"My father? No," I said. "I just saw...well, a shadow, just before you came through the door. Nothing more than a shadow."

"They say he's a ghost."

"I don't know," I finally murmured. "All I know is that things aren't right. Nothing's right. There's havoc on the island, and it's impossible to ignore any longer. I mean, look at us."

"What about us?"

"You and I are arguing. We rarely argue."

"Lily," he rasped. "Where is this coming from?"

"Our talk, earlier. You have to decide what to do."

"Think about what to do, yes. Not whether or not it means being with you. It wasn't an argument, it was a..."

I rose to my feet, the wind cycling through the door and whistling behind my words. "If you are in a relationship with me, your emotions are involved. There's no way around it. That's what love is—being vulnerable. If that puts you or your Rangers at risk, then you'll need to figure out what to do about it."

"Yes, but—"

"You didn't seem to want to go the second route, which leaves only the first. Cutting emotional ties. I *am* an emotional tie. If I weren't, you wouldn't have come here tonight."

"Come home with me," X demanded. The windows rattled and the door banged against the wall. "I don't want you here alone. We'll discuss this later."

"Screw later! We're talking about this now."

"Now?!" X, framed by dark black clouds, looked positively menacing. His eyes glinted onyx black and his lips curled into battle. "Fine. But there's nothing to decide."

"Have you not been listening to me?"

"Of course I have." He stepped toward me, the black of his pants, his shirt, fitting the frightening image of him. All mass, all muscle—no wonder the islanders respected him so. "But there's no decision to be made."

"What are you talking about?"

X stood inches away from me, our breath intermingling with the heaviness in the air, the humidity stifling. The scent of him, like lumber and fire and outside, lingered around us.

If things were different, I'd ease my arms between his, clasp my hands behind his back, and let the beat of his heart carry me away from this place. The brewing anxiety, the inky unsettledness easing its way into the hearts of our people. But things weren't different, not yet, and we reached a standoff, both of our fists balled at our sides.

"I can't believe you'd even think there was a decision to be made here." X's voice was a whisper, deathly still. Even the storm seemed to halt for a moment. "If I have two options, and one involves losing you—I will always choose the other."

"But—"

"End of story," he snapped. "I will always choose you."

"You can't mean that."

"Where do you think I went tonight?"

I shook my head, unable to speak. In response, X held up his fingers. No moon beamed through the windows, no stars cut through the storm. Utter darkness surrounded us save for the glint in X's eyes, and...the halos around his fingers.

"What is..." I cleared my throat. "What is that?"

He held up his hands, the glow around the edges of his fingers as bright as if he'd dipped his fingers into liquid gold.

"I won't let it happen again," X said with a vengeance. "You belong to me, and I belong to you. Everything else is secondary. What must I do to prove that to you?"

The lump that'd been growing in my throat choked me, and the tears spilled freely as I finally collapsed into his arms. His hands stroked my back, teased through my hair, and held me against him.

"I almost lost you once to my job, and I almost let you go," he said, his voice raspy. "I've learned from my mistakes. You are my strength, Lily, not my weakness, and together we are stronger. I won't ever doubt us again." He paused, pressing me closer to him, refusing to let go. "My responsibility is to The Isle, yes. But first, it is to you."

"I believe you," I said. "I'm sorry. I'm so sorry I doubted you, but I—"

"It's not your fault; I didn't handle the attack well. Lumiette—it was a surprise. A children's disease struck me down. I didn't handle it well, and I needed time to deal with it. I should've been clearer about that."

"No, I should've trusted—"

"Let's go upstairs. We're done down here for tonight, and I'm not leaving you alone."

I scanned the contents of the storeroom one last time before locking up for the night. Nothing appeared to be damaged from the wind that came through, but I'd heard breaking glass. Cleanup, however, could wait until morning.

Instead, I took X's hand, allowing him to lead me upstairs to my bedroom.

He looked wonderful with his black shirt melted to his body, his pants slick from the rain he slogged through on the way over. Even his eyelashes glittered with raindrops, and his hair was tousled and shaggy.

While I surveyed him, he eyed my matching satin pajamas, now all but see-through and useless after having his wet clothes pressed against them. His eyes darkened, glinting, and I gave a shake of my head.

Together, we burst out laughing.

"Come," he said. "Take a shower and get warm."

I moved to the bathroom, turned to face him at the door, and crooked my eyebrow high. "Alone?"

Chapter 22

THE NIGHT PASSED IN a delightful tangle of limbs as we slept wrapped in each other's arms. Mercifully, the storm let up around daybreak, X slipping from bed shortly after. He was in the shower when the thunk of the newspaper—a sound that now brought dread with it—hit the front door of the bungalow.

I eased out of bed, threw on one of X's old shirts, which was long enough to be a dress, and crept outside to get the paper. To my surprise, I wasn't alone.

"*Any comments?*"

"*Lily Locke? What do you know about the disappearances?*"

"*We're told Peter spoke with you late last night—*"

I halted on the front steps in an awkward position, halfway bent over to retrieve the paper, to find no less than six reporters with notepads shoved under my nose, pencils scribbling away.

I didn't have time to think, to shriek, or to yell at them. I merely froze, staring dumbly at them with my hair in the style of a rat's nest, and my clothing fit for nothing but sleep. My feet were bare, as were my legs, and finally the chill of skin against dewy ground jolted me awake.

"We're here to ask you some questions," a reporter in a top hat said. "Is Ranger X with you?"

"What's going on?" X called, stepping into the storeroom. "Lily, are you okay?"

His eyes locked on me, probably saw the fear in my face, and made quick strides across the room. I tried to stop him, to keep him away from the mess, but my intentions backfired. Ranger X and I hadn't kept our relationship a secret, but we also preferred it not be splashed across the newspapers.

He wore no shirt and no shoes, and his black pants clung against his figure. He looked incredible. That wasn't the issue. The issue was that he stepped directly behind me and in front of the open door. A group of hungry reporters turned their eyes from me to the figure standing at my shoulder.

"Ranger X, question—"

"—know anything about Peter—"

"—disappearances are alarming. What are the Rangers doing to fix this?"

"Why are you spending your time with *her* instead of solving the issue?"

That last question froze everything. As if time had stopped completely. I'd heard the way the reporter leaned on the word *her*, and it hadn't been complimentary.

Ranger X stiffened against me, his arm coming down to rest on my shoulder and squeezing, squeezing tighter until I had to shift slightly to relieve the pressure.

The reporters near the back squirmed, everyone looking mighty uncomfortable. Except for the one who'd asked. He continued to stare in blatant obliviousness up at X until another elbowed him in the ribs.

Looking around, the reporter in question must've realized his mistake and slunk back a step, mumbling an apology underneath his breath.

Ranger X took a step toward him. It wasn't meant to intimidate, but it did nonetheless, and the reporter blinked furiously, scanning for a way out of the situation.

"If you had a woman like *her,* maybe you'd understand," he said with a crooked, terrifying sort of smile. "You may apologize to Lily. After all, she is *your* Mixologist,"

"Yes, o-of course." He turned to me. "Sorry, your honor."

"Well, no need to go overboard," I mumbled. "Let it go, X, it's fine."

"I don't ever want to see you on this property without an invitation again—any of you. If you have concerns about how the Ranger program is protecting The Isle, you may inquire at HQ like the rest of the population. We will promptly address your concerns."

"So, you're working on the disappearances?" A timid, yet stupidly brave reporter pressed on. "Just one word for our story?"

Ranger X gave him a pleasant smile, one that brimmed with fury. "You may inquire—"

"Inquire at HQ, understood."

"And, if you feel the Rangers are not up to your standards," X said, resting a hand over my shoulder and against the doorframe. "Please feel free to submit yourself for the next Trials."

At that, the reporters backed away.

Ranger X pulled me inside, then shut the door, latching it with surprisingly gentle movements. "I apologize for that."

"You have nothing to apologize for." I watched over his shoulder out the window. A few of the reporters lingered on the edge of the property, watching us through the glass. "They showed up here and invaded our privacy."

"They won't do it again. I might've come off as harsh, but I'm simply not willing to share our time alone with anyone. For any reason. They can ask questions on work time."

"Speaking of alone time..." I cleared my throat and gestured out the window. "They're still watching us."

He cursed under his breath and stomped toward the window.

"I can't tell if they're more interested in the disappearances," I joked. "Or your love life."

Ranger X had his hand on the window and, instead of pulling the curtains down like he'd been about to do, he threw the window wide open. A thoughtful expression appeared on his face. "Come here."

"What?"

"Here," he demanded. "Now."

"But—" I held up a hand and weakly gestured outside. "They're just waiting for something to happen."

"Are they?" His eyes twinkled with mischief as he reached for me.

I didn't realize what was happening until a second later, he had my back pressed to the wall and his lips on mine, his arms sliding around my sides and melting me against him.

The kiss itself was delicious. His hands teased the band out of my ponytail, letting my hair loose as he ran his fingers through it, not caring who in the world saw.

The world darkened, the reporters vanished, and all that existed was us.

"Cannon," I murmured when he finally allowed me a moment to breathe. "That was...*wow*."

He winked, then glanced out the window and waved. "Yeah, I think they would agree."

Six male jaws sat wide open. Hugely open. The reporters stared with unabashed amazement through the window.

At X's glance upward, they all simultaneously began marching away, several of them attempting to jot down notes as they walked. I leaned against X, sharing a quiet laugh as the bungalow finally recouped its privacy.

"You didn't need to do that," I said, my head against his chest. "I know you prefer to keep private matters under the radar."

"Private matters, yes." He planted a kiss on my head. "I have no desire to keep you private. The whole world can know for all I care. It won't change a thing."

I was a gooey mess as we wandered to the kitchen for some coffee. He poured cups for both of us, just as I realized that I'd never actually gathered the paper. Scurrying to the front steps, I retrieved it and set it down on the table without reading it.

"When the reporters were outside," I asked softly. "Did you hear them mention Peter?"

"Peter? The conspiracy columnist?"

"I suppose."

"What about him?"

"He came to visit me late last night and asked for help."

Ranger X plunked two mugs on the storeroom table and sat down across from me. "With what?"

"He said he'd be the next person to be...disappear."

As usual, X didn't respond immediately, preferring time to work through his thoughts before leaping to conclusions. "And you believed him?"

"I didn't think it was urgent, but I didn't doubt he believed the theory himself."

"He always believes himself," X muttered. "That doesn't mean he's right."

"Fair enough, and that's what I told him, but what if..."

Ranger X unfolded the paper, ushering in silence from both of us. The front page was a photo of Peter with a byline from none other than himself. The title of the article: **I'M NEXT**.

I stood, rounding the table to read the article over X's shoulder. It seemed that Peter had written and prepared the piece, slipping it into this morning's edition, probably late last night. It didn't provide all the details that he'd mentioned, but it explained he would be the next to go.

The last line, in particular, was a cry for help.

Lily Locke, he wrote, *will have the answers.*

"I don't have any answers!" I cried, though the reason the reporters had shown up at my doorstep had now become clear. "What answers?!"

"Calm down. We don't even know if he's missing."

"Can you have your Rangers check?"

"Already on it. We should hear back soon."

Almost to the tee, his Comm buzzed, and Ranger X listened to the message with a blank expression. When the Comm ended, he looked up, and his expression confirmed what I'd already guessed.

"He's gone," I said, frozen in place. "And I sent him away last night. I offered to let him stay, but—"

"Lily. *Lily*," he repeated when I wouldn't stop trembling. "It's not your fault. If he was concerned, he should've come to Ranger HQ."

"He did, but he was sent away. Apparently, there's a long list."

Ranger X pinched his forehead. "It's not up to you to save the world, contrary to everyone's beliefs."

"I didn't do everything I could to save him. I told him to go back to you in the morning, and—"

"And that's what you should have done. You offered him a place to stay? That's more than you needed to do. If he turned you down, that's on him."

"He asked me to get in contact with you. I refused and said I didn't want to abuse my relationship with you and ask for favors. I told him to wait in line with everyone else."

Ranger X pulled me into his chest. "No matter how hard we try at Ranger HQ, we can't save everyone and prevent everything. We do our damndest to make sure we do, but at the end of the day, we have to follow a process. We must be thorough and orderly, or else we'll have chaos."

"But—"

"Thinking about what might've been different will get you nowhere," X said firmly. "What can we do to get him back?"

I tried hard to listen, to digest X's words. Little by little they slipped into my consciousness, and finally, I nodded.

"I must get to HQ."

"X," I said, as he turned away to go upstairs and get dressed. "Thank you. For everything."

"You don't have to thank me for anything."

"Yes, I do. All you've done for me, all you've—"

"Whatever I've done for you, you've done for me tenfold," he said, reaching for my hand and squeezing it. He brushed his lips against mine in the softest kiss. "Be safe today. Keep me posted with anything you find."

"I need to start testing the antidote for the vial," I said. "Then find Poppy, talk to Zin, and hunt for Peter."

"Leave Peter for me to handle."

"Why?"

He shifted uncomfortably. "How do you know he's not doing this for attention?"

"Doing *what*? Kidnapping himself?"

One of his shoulders raised in agreement. "You have to admit, it's getting eyes on his article. People know his name today, and he's finally been right—for *once*."

"He wouldn't do all of this for attention."

"And you know him well enough to swear on it? Look, Lily," Ranger X continued quickly. "You see the good in everyone, and I love that about you. But sometimes it's not the good you need to be looking for."

"Of course it is! I'm skeptical, too, but there was something different this time. Peter was really upset last night."

"Or a great actor."

"He wasn't acting!"

"Just let me and my team investigate, please? Don't put yourself in the middle."

"I can't promise that."

"At least promise me you'll be careful."

I nodded, recognizing this as an olive branch. "I'll do my best. You do the same."

"Agreed. Then, tonight, we'll meet. You'll not stay alone until things are safe."

"That doesn't sound like I have much of a choice."

"I'm hoping it's not hard to convince you," he said, a question hinting around his statement. "I won't comment if you look into Peter's disappearance, but you can't fight me on this."

I extended a hand, waiting for his to join mine. "Deal."

When X was finished getting ready, we headed back downstairs, and he left for HQ. As I took stock of the storeroom in the light of day, it hit me that Gus hadn't yet arrived. Usually, he'd grab the paper, sparing me from the humiliation of being spotted in my pajamas. A tickle in my spine had me wondering if things were worse than I'd thought at Mimsey's.

Before I had the chance to worry more, a sound from the front door had my shoulders at ease. "Gus," I said, turning. "You'll never believe what happened this morn—"

However, it wasn't the grumpy old man I'd expected standing in the doorway. Instead there stood a small, petite woman with eyes full of uncertainty. *Zin*.

"I hope you don't mind," she murmured, holding a duffel bag as she shifted from one foot to the other. "I'd like to take you up on your offer. Do you mind if I stay here for a while?"

Chapter 23

"I REALLY CAN'T HAVE more," I said, waving Zin off as she attempted to pour me another Caffeine Cup. "This would be number six for the day."

"Ah, you were up early with X?"

I nodded, filling Zin in on the morning events—the paparazzi attack, Peter's disappearance, the scare last night.

She frowned. "I'm sorry you had to go through all that yourself. If I'd been here, maybe—"

"It worked out fine. It's unusual to see a storm like that on The Isle, and I suppose it freaked me out. I'm sure last night was nothing more than a strong wind."

"No, Lily, I mean it." Zin's hair framed her face, the dark strands making her pale skin stand out further. "I was being stubborn and stupid, and I'm really sorry."

"Forget about it."

"No! It's not okay. Ever since I found out I was a Shiftling, I've been feeling...I don't know how to describe it. Off."

"In what way?"

"I don't know—just different." Zin looked up from her mug and found me there. "It's a combination of things. Part of me thinks I don't belong. Not here, not anywhere. Another part of me feels this huge pressure. Like I am expected to be something extraordinary because of my Uniqueness, and I'm just not."

"You are."

"That's what I mean! People keep telling me that, but I didn't *do* anything to become a Shiftling! It's like being born with...I don't know, two different colored eyes. Red hair. Long legs. I can't *help* it. I don't feel any different, and I don't act any different. Except maybe stupider."

"You're not acting stupid, Zin, you're readjusting to a huge piece of information. It's a big thing, whether it feels like it or not."

"The pressure, though, to do amazing things—"

"Stop! When I said you're extraordinary, it had nothing to do with being a Shiftling."

Zin's eyelashes fluttered. "But that's the only thing that sets me apart from anyone else."

"That's so entirely false. I thought you were great from the day I first met you."

"You did?"

"Of course!" I smiled at her and waited until she smiled back. "You're amazing because you work harder than anyone I know. The determination you have..." I shook my head. "If I had half of it, I'd be the best Mixologist this island has ever seen."

"Lily—"

I raised a hand. "Zin, you changed a decade old society, the Ranger Program, to include women. Do you know how *big* that is?"

"It wasn't easy, I guess."

"No, and the best part? There was no magic involved. You were worried if you even had a Uniqueness."

"Yes, but—"

"But nothing! Generations of witches and wizards and shifters and all sorts of paranormal folk have come before you, and never once has a woman made it to the ranks of the Rangers. They still wouldn't if you hadn't broken through the barrier."

"Yes, but—"

I halted her with a raised hand. "That's why you're incredible, and that's why people admire you. So what you're a Shiftling? You're still the same Zin we know and love. Sassy and dark and brooding and badass."

"I'm not that sassy."

"You can be," I said with a wink. "But that's not the point. The point is that being a Shiftling shouldn't change anything except to add another tool to your toolbelt. You're already a Ranger, so use it to your advantage to help others."

"You're the Mixologist," Zin said, hesitation in her gaze. "You have even more pressure than me. How do you deal with it?"

"That's the thing." I gave a dark laugh. "I'm not special, either. People seem to think I am, but I've been born into this role—I don't feel as if I've earned it."

"But you are still learning. You're new to this, and—"

"And so are you?" I offered her a small smile. "I don't always deal with the pressure well, Zin. "Sometimes I cry, and sometimes I lean on Ranger X, and sometimes I count on you and Poppy. So, I guess there's your answer: I don't do it alone."

Zin shook her head and pushed her cup away. "I feel so embarrassed. I'm sorry I didn't come to you for help."

"There's nothing to be embarrassed about. It's already forgotten."

"I just... on one hand, I wanted my independence so badly that I forgot—" Zin stopped abruptly. She blinked, then blinked again. She'd never cried before in front of me, and it seemed she wasn't happy about the threat of tears now. "I forgot that I was lucky to have you all. And now, it's too late."

"It's not too late!"

"Poppy's gone! Still missing!"

I bit my lip. "Then, let's find her."

"How do we start?"

"We still don't know that she didn't run away. You know as well as I do that learning something new about yourself can be hard."

"You learned about a whole new life of magic and witches and Mixology—"

"—and you learned of your Shiftling nature. Even X is learning new things," I said. "And Hettie. We all do it, and we all process it differently. Poppy might be sorting through things on her own."

"I think we need to assume something has happened."

"Why?"

"Because if she's off licking her wounds, she'll be back. But if not, we're wasting time."

"You think this might be linked to the other island disappearances?"

Zin tilted her head to the side. "It's hard to say. She doesn't fit the bill, but it's possible."

"Mimsey thought so, too," I said, and filled her in on the full story. By the time I finished, Zin's face was even paler than before. I pushed the newspaper toward her. "We've got five disappearances now including Peter."

"Six if you count Poppy."

"Peter thinks they're all linked," I said. "Which means we should start from the beginning."

"Hello, Jonathon," Zin said, looking at the photo from the first person to go missing. "Let's hear your story."

Chapter 24

JONATHON'S STORY BEGAN at a large house that looked more like a southern plantation on the mainland than it did an island beach home. Tall white columns held up a sturdy roof while a manicured front lawn sloped toward the grandiose front doors.

Zin shot me a look as we approached the outside gates. "We didn't come around this area much as kids."

"Where are we?"

"This is a small colony for politicians, some of the island's business people, islanders like that. I'm guessing our friend's parents have something to do with MAGIC, Inc."

"Really?"

"There aren't that many companies for magical folks that pay real well. And typically, paranormals don't care about money all that much."

We approached the door cautiously, Zin sniffing around for protective spells and alarms while I climbed the stairs and knocked on the door. An older gentleman answered, and I gave him a polite smile.

"Are you Jonathon's father?"

"Oh, no. Mr. Pritchett is not available at the moment."

"Um, is his wife?"

"No."

"Charles, is that my masseuse?" a voice called from behind. "If so, tell him he's late, and I won't stand for—" The woman belonging to the voice stopped talking abruptly as she appeared in the door behind Charles. "Who are you?"

"I'm Lily," I said, "and this is my cousin, Zinnia."

"And what do you want?" The woman had severe gray hair and a long stick between her fingers that looked like an elegant cigarette. A fur thing was draped around her shoulders as she lounged against the doorframe.

"Well, we came to talk to you and your husband—"

"My husband is busy."

"So I've heard," I said. "Maybe you have a second? It's about your son."

"Henry?"

"No, uh... Jonathon," I said, forcing myself not to look surprised. "You have another son?"

She'd looked mildly disinterested the second I mentioned Jonathon's name. "Of course I have another son. My eldest, who runs the Hex department for MAGIC."

"And Jonathon?"

"What about him?" She looked unperturbed at the mention of his name, and I had to wonder if she even knew he was missing. "Is he in some sort of trouble?"

"No, well, I hope not. Have you seen him lately?"

Mrs. Pritchett frowned, her eyebrows bending inward as she calculated. "Oh, yes. Maybe on his birthday? No, that can't be right. We were vacationing in the Caribbean then. Has it been over a year? My, how fast time flies."

"Over a year!" Zin gaped at her. "How has it been a year since you've seen your son when he lives on your property? He does live here, doesn't he?"

"Yes, but unlike Jonathon, I keep very busy, as does my husband."

"And you haven't seen him in a year."

"I don't feel the need to keep tabs on him," Mrs. Pritchett said, a haughty tilt to her chin. "He's an adult and can handle himself. He lives on our property, but it's his own space."

"Of course." I jumped in before Zin's grumbles outweighed everything else. "But surely you've heard the news that he's missing?"

"Missing?" She turned the word over a few times. "I've heard the rumors."

"He's been gone for well over a month," Zin said. "Even the Rangers are looking into it."

"Like I said, he's an adult, and—"

"An adult who is your son and missing," Zin repeated. "You haven't noticed?"

"Who did you say you are again?" Mrs. Pritchett snapped. "Coming here, asking me questions about my personal family business. It's as if you think you're—"

Charles leaned over, repeating the words into his employer's ear. "Zinnia and Lily. *Lily Locke*."

I hadn't given him my last name, which meant he must have recognized me. At first, the names clearly meant nothing to Mrs. Pritchett. Then, with a slow realization, she turned to face me.

"Lily Locke?" she murmured, just barely above a whisper. "The Mixologist?"

"Yep," Zin said. "The Mixologist."

I didn't have time to agree before Mrs. Pritchett turned, gesturing for us to follow her into an extravagant living room. The couches looked like artwork, and the art looked like pieces of ancient history.

Charles poured three sweating glasses of cool water, handing the dainty pieces of glassware to the three of us on a silver platter.

"Sit," Mrs. Pritchett said. "And tell me why you're here."

I sat, but Zin continued to prowl around the edges of the couches. Mrs. Pritchett mostly ignored her as I began to speak.

"We're looking into some of the disappearances happening on The Isle. Have you read anything about them?"

"Of course. I'm a liaison between MAGIC, Inc. and the warlock association of France."

"That's a mouthful of a title," Zin said. "What does that have to do with the kidnappings?"

"I am current on all society events. What I'm not current on is why you believe Jonathon might be involved." She picked up a photo of her son. It wasn't Jonathon. "I can understand why someone might be after my Henry. Look at the dear boy's face. Who can resist it?"

"Did Jonathon play in some sort of underground game community?"

Mrs. Pritchett dismissed the idea with an extended sigh. "Don't be silly. He shied away from any sort of social interaction."

"There are rumors about him being some sort of brilliant game strategist," I said. "You haven't seen anyone coming and going, anyone who might have more information about your son?"

"They're just rumors. Jonathon's only interest was doing the exact opposite of what we asked of him. Lounging around free of rent instead of pursuing a successful career like our Henry."

For the duration of our stay at the Pritchett's, we were bombarded by 'my Henry' this and 'my Henry' that. Mrs. Pritchett had an entire photo album dedicated to Henry, and she showed us every picture in it.

"Do you think she remembered we asked about Jonathon?" Zin mumbled after we'd said our goodbyes and begged a quick departure. "She couldn't stop talking about Henry."

"No wonder Jonathon wasn't on great terms with his mother," I agreed. "She pretends the poor guy doesn't exist."

"Golden boy and ugly duckling."

"It's sad. I can see how he might be a target for the SINGLES program. His mother hasn't even noticed he's been gone."

"I'd call him a prime candidate," Zin said grimly. "If we hadn't had other disappearances on the island, I'm not sure anyone would've noticed him missing."

"Do you think he has friends in this gaming community?"

"I would imagine, but how do we find them?"

I stopped as we turned onto the main path winding its way up the east side of The Isle. "Do we know who reported him missing? Obviously, somebody noticed."

"And it certainly wasn't *her*," Zin said with a nod toward the house. "I bet X would have that information."

"Let's visit the rest of our list, and then swing by HQ and ask him."

We reviewed our list, looking for Drew, the second person to go missing. Unlike Jonathon, however, this man didn't have any family to speak of. If Peter's research was to be believed, Drew might have a tie to Jonathon via their gaming community. Other than that, however, he was a dead end.

"Who reported Drew missing?" Zin looked up. "Someone had to notice these people were gone. Who?"

"Let's finish up here first. We have Manuel's fiancé, Sophie, to visit, and then Magdalena's family. After that it's..."

"Poppy," Zin murmured. "And Peter."

"We don't know Poppy's missing. Does she have any friends or acquaintances, maybe on the mainland, that she might've gone to visit?"

"Poppy's never been to the mainland. Everyone she knows is here."

"The Isle is a big place. People, creatures, have stayed hidden here for years."

"You think Poppy's hiding out in The Forest?" Zin raised her eyebrows. "She calls me to kill spiders."

I cocked my head to the side, trying to think of some other logical explanation. "I don't know," I said finally. "Let's find Sophie."

"She's not far. Her address lists her right near Main Street."

I glanced in the direction we needed to go. "Any chance you want to take the scenic route?"

"Who are you trying to avoid?"

I squinted. "Harpin."

"Any particular reason why?" she repeated.

"Do I need one? He's a jerk."

"Fine." Zin raised her hands. "Scenic route it is."

The scenic route took us on a pretty little path along the river that split the east and west halves of the island. Flowers bloomed along the edges, and sunlight filtered through wispy clouds and bounced off our shoulders. If we weren't on the hunt for missing islanders, it would've been an altogether pleasant stroll.

We found Sophie sitting outside a small house on her makeshift front porch. She lived on the northeast side of the island, halfway between Midge's B&B and Sea Salt eatery.

The young woman sat on her front porch, staring out at a gorgeous view of the lake, rocking back and forth in a creaky old chair.

"Who are you?" she asked tiredly as we climbed the front steps. "And what do you need?"

"Are you Sophie?" I asked. "I'm Lily, and this is Zin."

She didn't bother to nod. She looked too tired to nod, too worn down.

"We're really sorry to be visiting you like this," I continued, "but I was wondering if we could ask you a few questions."

"The Rangers already talked to me about Manuel."

"I'm a Ranger," Zin said, stepping forward. "And I was wondering if I could get a little more information."

Sophie creaked back and forth, back and forth, one hand on her thin stomach and the other clasped around a tall glass of lemonade.

"If you're a Ranger, why don't you look at the report? I answered everything, and I have nothing more to tell you."

"We're really sorry about your fiancé," I said. "I can't imagine what it's like with him being gone."

"Missing, not gone," she corrected. "I'd know if he was dead, and he ain't dead."

"Missing." I took one step onto her front porch, easing my way closer to her. "That's what I meant. Well, I'm—"

"I know who you are. You're the Mixologist."

"Yes. And I'm here because my cousin is missing. Hers, too." I gestured toward Zin. "We're here on personal business."

"Well, if the Rangers can't find Manuel, I don't know *how* the two of you think you'll be able to do any better."

"Maybe so, but at least we're trying. We'll only take a few minutes of your time."

Sophie took another few sips of her lemonade. "Don't tell me you're one of those who thinks Manuel was looking for an escape from me. We were *happy* together. I love him."

"I believe you. That's why we're here in the first place." I leaned against the railing of the porch and studied Sophie's slowly melting mask of frustration. "I don't think Poppy, our cousin, was looking for an escape, either. Maybe the two are related."

"More than two disappearances now," she snapped. "Who would just take people like that? I mean, all these incidences aren't a coincidence—they *must* be related."

"Someone horrible." I hoped to goodness that I wasn't related to the man behind it all. "Tell me about your fiancé."

"He's incredible," she said, her eyes finally showing signs of life. "He says the sweetest things, and he loves me more than anybody's loved me in my life." Her voice grew a little quieter. "He is just the gentlest soul. People from the neighborhood come by every time something goes wrong, and he always knows the right words to say or the right medicine to give them, or...whatever it is they need."

I remembered Peter's warning that Manuel had trained as a Healer. It made sense The Faction might need his skills—skills that would be otherwise difficult to attain. Professional Healers on the island were hard to come by, and their absence would be felt.

"What was his family situation before you came into the picture?" I asked. "Is there anyone else who might have more information?"

She shook her dirty blonde hair, looking barely older than a child. "It's just the two of us. Neither of us had much for families. People think we're stupid for getting married because I'm so young. I don't think it's stupid at all. I know what I want, and he knows what he wants. Why does it matter that he's a few years older than me?"

"What is it that you want?" Zin asked. "You seem so sure."

Sophie turned her gaze to Zin. "Why, a family. And we were gonna have it, too."

"Sophie!" I climbed the rest of the way onto the porch and knelt beside the rocking chair as she began to cry. "What's wrong? Why are you upset?"

The hand holding her lemonade trembled, and I took the glass before it slipped and crashed to the floor. "We were going to be a family," she said again. "Because I'm pregnant."

Zin sucked in a breath while I reached for Sophie's chilled hand. It was slick with perspiration from the lemonade, and I held on tighter and tighter until she sobbed freely.

Finally, she looked up at me through tear-stained lashes. "I never got to tell him," she sniffed. "I found out the day before he left. I had a dinner planned with all his favorites—fresh fish from the market, potatoes, green beans—and I was going to tell him that night."

"Which night?"

"The night he disappeared," she murmured. "But then I waited all night, and he never came home."

"Do you think—" Zin began to ask, but I held up a hand to silence her.

"We'll find him," I said. "I promise. Is there anything else you can think of?"

"That Peter guy, the one whose face is in the paper today?"

I nodded. "Did he come here?"

"Yeah, and he left me something. Said to give it to someone if he disappeared."

"Give it to someone?" I shot Zin a look of surprise. "Who?"

"He said that some people would probably come around asking questions. Then he said to hold onto this until there was a person I thought could really help us."

She heaved herself out of the chair and moved inside, returning quickly.

"Here." She thrust a small, bulky envelope into my hand. "I don't know what it is, and I don't know what to do with it. I hope you do."

We stayed around for a bit longer, making sure Sophie had everything she needed. I told her to come by the bungalow anytime, and Zin promised to take Sophie's story back to the Rangers and find some answers. Eventually, Sophie thanked us, and we found ourselves back on the sidewalk with an envelope in hand.

"Shall we?" Zin asked. "Open it. She gave it to you."

I slid my finger under the edge, sliced it open, and folded it back. There, wrapped in soft paper, was a key.

Zin leaned in to study it. "Where does it lead?"

"I don't know," I said, flipping over the envelope to reveal the faint outline of a map. "But I bet this will point us in the right direction."

Chapter 25

WE FOLLOWED A LOOSE map drawn on the back of the envelope. Though it wasn't exactly polished, it was clearly the layout of The Isle. My finger followed a dotted line as our feet kept pace with the map's directions all the way to the northernmost tip of the island.

"Where is he leading us?" Zin asked. "And why?"

"Do you think this might be his home? He never did say where he lived."

"Your guess is as good as mine. But what do you think we'll find there?"

"Clues? Information? The rest of his studies? I don't know."

"Do you think it could be a trap?"

I stopped dead in my tracks. The Forest loomed to the west—we'd just passed the Upper Bridge, and we were nearing the rocky shores where few residents lived. The houses in this area were often built on the edge of the cliffs; I wondered if a strong storm wouldn't blow them right into the raging sea below.

"Why do you think it'd be a trap?"

"Peter is..." Zin waited for me to fill in the blank, but I never did. Zin huffed out a breath. "Come on, Lily. I know you believe in the good of people, but you have to admit he was a bit of a nut."

"He wasn't *ruthless*."

"He believed in his own *stories*. The keyword there is *story*. What if this particular tale is a dangerous one?"

I continued shaking my head, but her words had registered no matter how hard I fought them off. "No, I don't think so."

"I don't know if we should do this alone. Why don't you hand over the key to X? I'll go with him."

"Sophie gave me the key. Nobody else."

"I know, Lily, but—"

"But what?!"

"X would kill me if I let anything happen to you."

"Well, I don't plan on anything happening to me, so we should be safe." I turned and began down the gravel road, striding toward the cliffs. "I was given the key, and I'm going to use it. You heard Sophie. The Rangers already stopped by. If she'd wanted them to have the key, she would've given it to them."

"Yes, but—"

"But nothing. I'm going because we don't have time to waste. People are missing, including your cousin. Are you coming?"

Zin's eyes flashed with flecks of gold, and she set her jaw firmly. "Fine, but I'm not happy about it."

"You're a Ranger, Zin. You can make your own decisions."

"I'm a Ranger, which means I have to obey the commands of my boss."

"What did he command you to do? He doesn't even know about the key!"

"It's not about the key."

"What's it about then?!" I threw my arms up, spinning to face Zin. Then, I saw it written on her face. "Oh. *Me.* This is about me."

"Come on, Lily, you have to understand. Ranger X protects his own. I'm his employee, and he'll protect me like he would any brother or sister. But he *loves* you. Can you even fathom what that means?"

I had no response good enough, so I remained silent.

"I'm not saying we shouldn't go inside," Zin continued. "I mean, I think it's probably best to wait for X, but I'm sure he's busy with everything else today. I'm just saying we need to be extra careful. It doesn't hurt to consider all of our options."

"I vote the option of a quick peek."

"Any sign of foul plan, and we take off. No questions asked."

"Understood."

We crept toward the spot marked on the map with a black X.

"I'm still not convinced Peter's not a part of this," Zin whispered as we approached the end of our journey. "What if Sophie is involved, and her fiancé isn't really missing? Peter could've paid Sophie off; she needs money, especially since they're having a baby."

"No. Sophie wouldn't do that."

"How are you so sure?"

"Because I saw the photo of her and Manuel in the paper."

"And?"

"People just can't fake that sort of love. Their body language, the way they looked at each other. They were in love. I don't think Sophie's faking her unhappiness with him gone, either."

"But what if—"

"Time is running out, and Poppy hasn't come back."

Zin forced a nod at my pleading tone. "Let's go."

The front door was locked, as expected. I lifted the key to slip it inside, but realized at once that it wouldn't work—the key was much too large for the lock.

"Are we at the right place?"

Zin double-checked the map. "It says so."

I looked over her shoulder. "The X is a little off-center. Do you think this key isn't for the front door?"

Zin glanced beyond me. The 'backyard' of this place was little more than a rocky cliff that dangled its inhabitants far above the crashing waves. "I don't how to get over there. One wrong step and..."

"We have to try."

"No." Zin took the key and slipped it into her mouth. "I'll go. You wait here."

Before I could argue, she began to shift into her simplest form, the jaguar. She seemed a natural at it, easing gently into the state and prowling around the edge of the house before shooting a gleaming, golden glance in my direction.

"Zin, be careful!" The wind, however, swallowed my words as the beautiful cat began to effortlessly pounce from one boulder to the next. At one point she slipped, sending several rocks cascading down to the treacherous coast below.

Zin made it to the side of the house and shifted into human form atop the rocky cliff.

"What are you doing!?" I yelled, my heart flying through my chest. "You have to shift back!"

She balanced in human form on the ledge, her hands held wide for balance. "I can't open this door with my mouth."

"What door?"

"There's a trapdoor built into the stone."

"You're not safe out there. Come back, Zin. We said—"

Before I could tell her what we said, she inserted the key into a lock invisible to my eye and twisted it.

"It's here!" she cried, excited. "The key fits!"

"I can't possibly reach you."

"One second. I'm going to pop inside. If I don't come back out in five minutes, get help."

"Zin, wait!"

She didn't listen, instead dropping into the crevasse without looking back.

I paced back and forth, muttering curses at Zin under my breath. Four minutes passed, and my curses grew louder. Then five minutes.

"Zin!" I yelled. "Time is up. Where are you?!"

No answer.

"*Zin*!"

I gave the wind thirty seconds of howling before I tested a foot on the ledge, inched over it, and hesitated. Pebbles slipped under my shoes, skittering off the side of the cliff.

"Lily!" Zin's cries sounded muffled. "Help! I'm stuck, it's..."

Her voice trailed off, and my heart leapt further into my throat. I moved, calculating each step before I made it. When a rock the size of my head slipped away and pounded into the abyss, I hesitated again, gathering my courage.

"I'm coming!" I yelled. "Can you hear me? What's happening?"

"Stay where you are!" Zin's voice, still muffled, sounded pained. "I'm going to see if I can..."

Again, she trailed away, sounding as if she were speaking from the bottom of a submarine. A thunk sounded, a screech, and then a guttural yell.

My fingers curled around the root of a tree pushing out of the cliff as I raced forward, still far too distant to be of any help. If I moved any faster, I would lose my balance and tumble downward.

The screeching continued, my palms dampening with sweat at the thought of what might be happening to her. I tasted salt as I moved one hand over the next to another root. One foot slipped, dangled, and I let out a yelp myself.

"Zin!"

At once there was a pop, a fluttering sound, and then silence.

I held my breath, watching the mouth of the crevice for a sign of movement. Meanwhile, I hauled myself higher onto the boulders, the roots creaking beneath my weight. I clung to the tree for dear life, wishing I would've listened to Zin in the first place and gone to Ranger X with the key.

That's when I saw it—a small tuft of feathers barreling from the mouth of the cave. A tiny little bird, a fluffy thing that would fit in the palm of my hand, flapping her wings above the waves.

"Zin?" I stared closer at her little body, knocked around by the strong winds. "Is that you?"

As if in answer, she shifted once more, this time into a larger bird. An eagle, flapping strong, powerful wings until she landed on the rock just above my head.

My arms shook, and I focused on mustering every bit of strength to haul myself up and over, landing in a sheltered nook.

Zin moved a few paces back, then shifted into her human form, landing crouched on the rock face. Her hair was matted with sweat, her eyes wild as she shook her head. "I can't do it. It's not for me."

"What's not for you?"

"There's some sort of safe inside, and it's looking for a handprint."

"A handprint?"

Zin nodded. "I figured I had the key, so maybe it just needed to be touched, or pushed. So, I put my palm against it, and—" she shuddered. "It shocked me. It kept shocking me until I heard you yell my name, and it brought me back. That's when I shifted and got away."

"How do we know whose hand is supposed to be there?"

Zin shook her head. "Maybe it has something to do with the person to whom Sophie entrusted the key."

"I suppose we need to try."

"How?!" Zin glanced further out. "Even after shifting I barely made it across this terrain, and I have nice claws."

I watched with a wispy smile as Zin admired her manicure. I exhaled, scanning the distance between me and the safe. "I don't know."

"What if you get there and it's not your hand?"

"You pull me out of there, and we get Ranger X."

"We should get him now."

"There's no time! If we run back, find him, tell him everything, convince him to return with us... just *no*," I said, firm. "We just need to find a way to get me out there and back."

"I *might* have an idea."

Without explaining, Zin shifted back into the little blue-colored bird and sailed away, bouncing against the strong gusts. I sat, watching until she disappeared around the back of Peter's house.

Zin returned shortly after with a thin wire in her beak. A safe distance away from the rocks, she shifted to human form and extended it. "The clothesline in the back," she explained. "I tore it out. If you wrap this around your waist. I'll carry it in my mouth in my jaguar form and that should help with balance."

"Will it hold my weight if I slip?"

"If you don't slip, we don't have to test it out," Zin said with a wry smile. "Shall we?"

I looped the rope around my waist as she suggested, fingers shaking. When we were ready, I made eye contact with Zin and nodded. "If I fall, you need to get—"

"You won't fall. Now, let's move."

Together, we inched our way across the boulders. I lost my footing once, grabbing onto a set of roots as I started my slide toward the edge of the cliff. Zin yanked the rope in her mouth, her feline body tensing as she guided me back to safety.

Heart still racing, we continued. Inching and inching until the rocks became so slippery with sea spray that Zin was holding nearly all my weight. I balanced on thin points of rock barely larger than my pinky until at last I tumbled over the threshold into the opening of the cave.

There wasn't room for two of us here, so Zin stayed atop in jaguar form while I slithered through the opening and studied the view before me.

All was exactly as Zin had described. We'd reached a small cavern built into the wall of the lakeside cliffs, empty save for a sheen of sunlight and a large stone box in the middle of the room.

In the center of the door was a handprint, sized much larger than my palm. I stepped closer, sucking in a breath as I extended my arm and visually measured my fingers against the stone imprint.

Too large. This wasn't right.

But I hadn't come all this way to give up before trying, so I guided my hand into the imprint, hovering millimeters away from the surface, and closed my eyes. If this didn't work, I hoped Zin would be able to pull me away. Otherwise...

Warmth. I pressed my fingers to the rock, and though a slight tingle shot through my hand, rolling up and over my arms, into my shoulders, and down my back, there was no sign of the shock Zin had described.

Something was at work. I could feel it, sense it.

My hand locked in place with a jolt. When I tried to tug my arm away, I couldn't. Something deep within the rock slid, stuttered, adjusted. I could feel movement there, like gears churning and bolts flipping into place.

All at once, my hand freed itself from the rock, repelled as if by a magnet. I backed away and watched as the door began to slide open. With a gravelly crunch, the safe revealed its contents. A scroll lay on top of a stand, and on the scroll someone had printed another map.

This map had been created with every detail listed on it—much more detailed than the back of the envelope drawing that had gotten us here. Furthermore, it contained elements that extended far beyond The Isle.

As I studied the map, my eyes were drawn to a blinking red light. The glowing dot began to move as I watched, beginning its projector here on the island, then dotting its way across Lake Superior, onto the shore of the mainland.

With curiosity, I watched as it pulsed once, then a second time, just outside of the Twin Cities. I squinted closer, realizing it was just outside the headquarters of MAGIC, Inc.

The dot didn't stop there. After pulsing twice, it slid a little further south, and then stopped entirely and blinked green.

"What is this?" I murmured, wishing I'd listened more closely to Peter. "Where are you taking us?"

"What's going on, Lily?" Zin called.

"It opened! It's some sort of map. I don't know what it means," I yelled up. "There's a blinking light, and—"

"What color?" she asked sharply. "Did it move after you started looking?"

"Yes, it didn't start moving until after I got close to it. The light started as red, pulsed twice, then turned green."

"A tracker."

"A what?"

"Get out of there," Zin said. "It's going to burn up in the next few seconds. It'll be smoky in that cave and dangerous."

As soon as she said it, the edges of the map started to curl, then turn brown. I scrambled toward the mouth of the cave, climbing up as a tiny flame lit along the edges.

"Here!" Zin dropped me the wire. "Put this around you. Has it started to burn?"

"Sure has."

While I tied the cord around myself, Zin changed into her jaguar form. I grasped tight, and she yanked, pulling me up as I scrambled over the ledge. By the time I landed face first on the grass of Peter's backyard, she'd already shifted back to human form and was kneeling beside me.

"Do you know where the tracker led us?"

"What's a tracker?"

"A person can enchant themselves onto a map. They entrust someone with the key, and only the person with the key can see their whereabouts. It works once before incinerating. Did you catch the location?"

"It looked like they were near MAGIC, Inc.."

"Does that mean anything to you?"

Suddenly, everything made sense, and I looked up at Zin. I looked up at Zin. "I know where they've taken him. All of them."

"Where?"

I hesitated, the magical contract burning as the words formed at my lips. I was bound not to divulge the truth about Wishery to anyone, not even Zin. I didn't want to discover the consequences for breaking the NDA when I had so many other things to do.

So, I sighed. "I can't tell you."

"After all we just went through together, and now you can't tell me your great epiphany?"

"No," I said emphatically. "I *can't*."

At that, she frowned, then looked down at my fingers. I moved them into fists so she couldn't see them shaking as I fought back the urge to explain everything.

"Is it related to that vial in your storeroom you've been all secretive about?"

I gritted my teeth and nodded. The tingling sensation grew more intense. I was hovering on a dangerous line.

"MAGIC, Inc. swore you to secrecy," she said, then cursed under her breath. "Even X can't know the details."

"Not unless I get explicit permission. I'm going to contact Ainsley once we get back to the bungalow."

"I understand. Then, I suppose we should get going?"

"I'm sorry, Zin. I just—"

"I get it."

We set off on a silent journey toward home. It wasn't until we were nearly at the bungalow that I broke the silence. "Thank you for your help back there."

Zin gave me a smile, the tension dissipating. "Of course."

"Do you want to come inside?"

"Lily, what do you think about Poppy?"

"What about her?" I asked as we approached the front steps. "I've told you everything I know."

"I mean...do you think she might be one of the disappeared? She's still not back." Zin's voice grew in urgency. "Poppy doesn't strike me as the type to stay away so long; even if she was upset at Mimsey, she'd get over it. They're the best of friends."

"I don't know—"

A wail launched from behind me, interrupting my response as I spun around and stumbled up the steps with Zin close on my tail.

Or rather, Zin as a jaguar. The jungle cat slid onto the porch in front of me, blocking me from whoever was waiting for our arrival. She'd entered into attack mode.

It wasn't long before she retreated. "Mimsey?" Zin said, shifting back at once. She brushed her hands against her leather pants and swept a stray cat hair from her shoulder. "What are you doing here?"

Mimsey watched us with huge tears in her eyes. "You think they took my baby?!"

"No, Mimsey." I moved quickly over to her, catching my aunt as she collapsed in my arms. "We're not sure of anything."

Her dress, usually bright and colorful, appeared dim today. Even her cheeks, normally rosy and pink, had faded pale, and her laugh had all but disappeared.

"She—she's my best friend," Mimsey said. "And it's because of me she's gone. I came here to f-finish planning her party," she sniffed. "She d-deserves the best. Oh, what am I saying? She won't even be here."

"She'll be back, I promise," I said, catching Zin's eye. "We'll have her back by her birthday, I guarantee it. This is *not* your fault."

"How can you possibly promise that?"

"Because I know where they've taken the others, and I'm going after them," I said. "If they took Poppy, too, I'll get her back. I'm going to contact Ainsley, the Rangers—anyone and everyone I can think of who is able to help."

"The Rangers," Mimsey said, dreamily. "I suppose I should...I should report Poppy as missing to HQ."

"I'll go with you," Zin volunteered. "And I'll let Glinda know about Poppy. Maybe she can have the Forest Fairies do a quick search around the island. Then, I'll check in with X."

Zin fell silent, watching as her aunt plodded down the bungalow's front path and stopped just before the water's edge. "Do you think she would miss me like *that* if I were the one gone?"

"Who?"

"My mom," she said quietly. "Do you think she'd even notice?"

"Yes." I slipped an arm around Zin's shoulder and tugged her slight frame toward me. "Trinket is different than Mimsey, but she loves you just as much, just as hard."

"I owe her an apology."

I didn't disagree, merely let Zin rest her head on my shoulder for a long moment. The wind picked up again, and I glanced at the sky. "Another storm is coming. You both should get going."

"Will you be okay here?"

"Gus should be back soon," I said. "There was a shipment coming in today with supplies. He'll be back once he's done with the order."

Hours later, I began to wonder what was taking Gus so long. He should've been back by now, or at least sent word if he needed help.

As I puttered around the storeroom, preparing small vials of antidote, I realized he'd probably caught up with Mimsey. Which was where he should be, I thought. There was a storm heading toward The Isle, and it'd be best if Mimsey didn't have to weather it alone.

If Gus wasn't returning tonight, I needed to get started without him. Making my way over toward the window, I gathered the ingredients into my travel belt, placing the silver, the stardust Gus had acquired, and everything else I'd need into their own little pockets.

Lastly, I picked up the storm cloud contained in the vial and carried everything over to the storeroom table.

I Mixed until everything was just right, the familiar *hum* of magic surrounding me as I worked. A contentedness settling over my shoulders, despite my captivity. This is what I was born to do, my small way of infusing a light into the darkness swirling around the city. I might not always like it, but Mixology coursed through my veins; I lived, breathed, worked with it—even *needed* it.

Lost in my own world, I pulled the silver dust from my belt, muttered an incantation, and sprinkled it into the larger potion. The final step.

A cloud of smoke emerged as I returned the silver to my belt, next to a pink tube of Long Isle Iced Tea, a sample of the black cloud, and a few other necessities. The vial of antidote sitting on the table turned a deep, royal purple as it burst out of the glass, enveloping the room. For a moment, it hovered in the air, thick and smoggy, and then crackled into oblivion, leaving the finalized potion in the vial.

My heart leapt. Joy pounded in my throat as I fought back tears of stress, of happiness, of relief. "Finally," I murmured, resting my hands against the counter.

"Well done," a voice said behind me. "Incredibly well done, as a matter of fact."

I couldn't breathe, couldn't turn around. The voice had a gravel quality to it that held me captive. I knew it, but I didn't. Familiar, but a stranger.

"Hello, Lily," the figure said, waiting for me to peel myself around and face him. "You are your mother's daughter, just like they said."

I struggled to swallow, but failed. My breath came in ragged slices through my lungs.

"I'd ask you to come with me nicely," he said, calm and almost tenderly. "But I don't think we have time for formalities."

Footsteps sounded, a hand reached out, and he plucked the lily from the corner. Before I could move, he muttered words from another language under his breath, closed his eyes, and blew.

A dusty powder burst from the flower, surrounded by a sickly sweet floral scent. I had only a second to react, a moment to lunge for the vial of antidote before coughing, fading, drifting into blackness.

My body crumpled to the floor, weak. A fizzling shot through me, like the last breath of a firework. By the time I landed, I was gone.

Chapter 26

SLEEP FELT SO GOOD, so nice.

I sunk into it, dreams carrying me away as sweetness wrapped around me.

Undisturbed, I continued to slumber, only waking when the intensity of the flowery scent began to fade. It was replaced by the smell of freshly laundered sheets and a slight mustiness in the air. Only once the confusion set in did I find the willpower to slowly, one by one, force my eyes to open and study my surroundings.

I had been placed in a bed, and to my surprise, I wasn't bound in any way to prevent me from escaping. I moved slowly, testing each of my limbs in turn, and yet none of them had been tied back.

As I began to stretch, the soreness hit me. How long I'd been out was difficult to say, but my muscles felt weak, almost too relaxed. As if they, too, had gone to sleep and had forgotten how to function.

A quick scan of the space told me this resembled a bedroom, and I was the only occupant. I eased into a seated position, leaning back against the headboard, and pulled the covers higher to my chest. I'd been changed out of my clothes into a gown that felt like satin.

My breathing sped up, my mind flipping through the curious series of events. I'd been kidnapped—*right*? Kidnappers weren't typically known to treat their captives like royalty. I closed my eyes, struggling to piece together my memories, splicing the line between dreams and reality.

The space around me did feel quite royal. My bed had gauzy draping hung from four posters, the comforter even softer than my nightgown. Directly across the room sat an antique-looking desk, a huge thing with a mirror perched on the top and drawers lining the sides.

In the mirror, I studied the reflection of myself. Pale faced, anxious, my mouth had formed a pout and my eyes were bright and alert. It looked so unlike me that I raised a hand to my face to check for a reaction.

The hand in the mirror raised, too, and I exhaled. That was me, the pale-faced, frightened thing. Climbing out of bed, I caught sight of my clothes hanging over the desk chair. I hurried to them, also finding the belt resting, untouched, on the desk, along with a string of empty vials that had also been tucked there at the time of my kidnapping.

I took stock of my supplies: one vial of Long Isle Iced Tea. A second filled with silver, and a third filled with the black smoke. The last contained the ingredients necessary for a pint-sized antidote against the spell surrounding Wishery. I'd grabbed it off the storeroom table just before I collapsed.

Then, with a sinking heart, I realized there must be no chance for an escape if my captors felt confident enough to leave me unbound and ungagged with all of my supplies intact.

"Oh, you're up! Good evening," a pleasant voice chimed from the door. "I should've knocked first, but I didn't want to wake you."

"Who are you?" I spun to face the friendly voice, my vials clinking as I clasped them behind my back. "Where are we? Why am I here?"

A petite, thin, woman with dark hair secured in a neat bun gave me an easy smile. "I figured you might have a few questions, and so did he."

"Who is he?"

"Never mind, Miss Locke. Did you find your sleeping arrangements suitable? He wanted to make sure you were comfortable."

"Is this *he* you speak of the one who kidnapped me?"

"He would prefer to talk to you himself. I'm just here to ensure your needs are met and you're comfortable. Shall I help you dress?"

"Was it you who helped me into my pajamas?"

"Well, yes, of course. Simple spells. I've been a housemaid for many years, and one picks up a few tricks now and again."

I clutched my clothes in the other hand. "No, I'm perfectly fine on my own. Where are we?"

"Let's get you dressed. And no, I'm sorry those clothes will not do."

"But—"

"Here. I've picked a selection for you." The woman moved smoothly across the room, rested her hand on a doorknob I hadn't yet noticed, and flung it open. "Anything from here will do, except for the blue. I really think the blue will be best for the gala."

"Gala? Which gala?"

"He will explain."

"I don't want *him* to explain," I said, fury building as my feet carried me toward this curious woman. "I want you to explain. You seem nice enough. *He* doesn't."

She chortled in a good-natured way. "I love to see humor around here finally. Everyone's been in such a dreary mood lately. You may call me Belinda."

"Okay, Belinda, I'd like some answers before I put on..." I turned, my eyes widening as I looked into the closet and digested its contents. "A ball gown?"

"Oh, don't be silly. This isn't more than a little evening gown. This, however..." she flicked on the light and stepped inside the closet—a closet as large as the bungalow's storeroom. "*This* is a ball gown. For tomorrow evening."

"What is tomorrow evening?"

"Your induction."

"To what?"

"I've already said too much," Belinda said, her cheeks brightening. "Let me take you to him. Get dressed, please, or I'll have to do it for you again."

"No, I'd prefer—"

"Then move along, move along." She shooed me toward the row of dresses. "I'll be waiting in the hall. Do you prefer your hair in braids or in pins? I have been practicing both, and I'd like to try one without magic."

"I'm confused about—" The bedroom door slammed shut, punctuating my question. My shoulders slumped in dismay. "About everything," I finished, trying the handle. *Locked.*

"It'll unlock once you've changed," she said. "Sorry for the force, but I had a feeling you would need some convincing. It's just a dress, Miss Locke."

Just a dress. I glanced around, thinking none of these were 'just dresses'. We had yellows and reds and pinks, one colored like an emerald and another in a deep, royal purple. Dresses all colors of the rainbow, and I had no idea why I needed to wear any of them.

"Where am I?" I yelled through the door. "What is going on? Why the dress?"

"Put one on, and we'll talk face to face. You're running low on time. You overslept by an hour and a half."

"Probably because I was poisoned! Do you know why he kidnapped me?"

"He never intended to hurt you; he simply wants to get to know you."

I stood before the mirror, retrieving a shiny, silver dress. Shimmering fabric slid down my shoulders and over my back, dusting the floor near my feet as it shifted into place. A perfect fit.

"How...?" I murmured aloud, wondering about the perfect measurements, then chalked it up to magic. It was the only solution that didn't make me cringe.

I finally pulled my chin up to look in the mirror, surveying the silver fabric that glimmered and danced in the light. The gown itself was long and flowing, with lacy sleeves that covered my arms. Elegant, certainly, and very gorgeous. Why I needed it at all was still a mystery.

"How are you doing?" Belinda called. "Did I get the sizing right?"

"It's pretty good," I said, unwilling to admit its perfection. "One second, please. Almost done."

I'd dressed quickly and used the extra few precious minutes of privacy to tuck my vials into the belt and fasten it underneath the flowing fabric. It still seemed like a mistake they'd left me with my supplies. The two most valuable, the antidote and Long Isle Iced Tea, stayed in the belt, but I had to lighten my load a bit. So, the rest I stashed in my room, just in case. It didn't make sense that they'd take the vials now when they could've done it already. But it wouldn't hurt to tuck them out of sight.

Once they were hidden, I moved over to the window, glancing behind me to ensure the door was still locked and Belinda remained in the hall. The window, as it turned out, was a pair of French doors that led outside onto a grand balcony. With another check of the door to ensure privacy, I twisted the handles and found them unlocked.

Stepping outside, a thin wave of humidity hit me, as did the constant swirl of movement. A grim sense of satisfaction hung over me as I realized that I had been right. Horrifyingly right.

We were in Wishery.

Somehow, The Faction had turned wish magic against itself, and they'd turned the Wishery Castle into something black and dangerous. Not a star shone through in the sky, nor did a fresh breeze filter through the air. A hot gust of wind blew over me, angsty and claustrophobic.

I continued to the far edge of the balcony and peered down at the ground below. My knuckles clasped hard to the rail as my mind wandered, calculating how far it might be to jump.

"There you are," Belinda said, stepping behind me onto the patio. "Admiring the view?"

"Something like that," I said, turning slowly to face her. "What time is it?"

Instead of answering, she clasped her hands in front of her body and smiled broadly. "You look beautiful. I'm so pleased."

"Where are we going?"

"It's dinner time. Why else would you be dressed like that?"

"I don't normally wear gowns to dinner."

"Well, you'll be dining in his presence."

"If it's only just dinner time..." I gestured behind me. "How is it pitch-black already?"

The first signs of nervousness displaced Belinda's otherwise positive attitude. "Honey, it's always night in Wishery. Now, that's enough with the questions. If you're late, he won't be pleased."

"I don't care."

"Come along," she said gently. "Because there is no other alternative."

"At least you're not lying anymore," I said, sounding sharp even to my own ears. "You're treating me like a guest, but I am most certainly not here voluntarily. I am a prisoner."

She shifted from one foot to the other in discomfort. "Just give him a chance."

"I don't know what spell he's got you under, but this?" I gestured to the eternal night outside. "Is not natural. It's black magic, and I know you can feel it. We all can."

"Miss Locke—"

"Forget it," I said, taking one last, long glance at the sprawling city limits.

If I squinted hard enough, it was almost as if I could see the pin-pricks of stars battling to burst through the swirling black clouds. I knew it was useless, but I focused on those shards of light and wished. I wished just as hard as I could, wished to replace my previous wish.

Opening my eyes, I caught Belinda watching with unabashed curiosity. At my gaze on hers, she startled and cleared her throat. "What was that?"

"Nothing," I said feeling hollow inside. "Take me to him."

Chapter 27

THE DINING TABLE SAT in a cavernous room lined with antique photographs of unsmiling individuals and images of a beautiful, bright city. Wishery in its glory days, most likely.

Thin gold lining reached every surface, giving the room a hazy, shimmering sort of glow, thanks in part to the flicker of the pillar-style candles on every shelf. The table itself was heavy and thick, covered by a deep red cloth and decorated with only two place settings, one on either end of the long table.

Belinda waited by the door as I studied the décor, the intimate formality to it. She stood next to me, twitching in what looked like excitement, until a faint bell rang in the background, and she turned one last meaningful look on me.

"Give him a chance," she begged. "Please."

"Why? I am a prisoner, what don't you underst..." I stopped, realizing she'd disappeared through the opposite door.

"I apologize for bringing you here like a prisoner." That now-familiar, gravelly voice spoke from behind me. "If there had been another way to entice you to visit, I would have done so. You seemed disenchanted with the idea of me, however, so I used other measures."

I hesitated, taking a deep breath before rotating to face him. "You can't expect me to forgive you for—"

The sight of him cut me off mid-sentence. It was the first I'd ever seen of *him*. The faceless shadow. The man who made the calla lily in my storeroom bloom and burn, bloom and burn, bloom and burn...in a fiery cycle of life. The man who, without a doubt, shared my genes.

"She kept a secret from both of us," he murmured, his face and voice softening as our eyes connected. "I can see that you know it, too."

I merely shook my head and continued to stare. Lucian had dressed in a suit of the finest materials, a blood-red swatch of fabric in his pocket. He wore no tie, kept the top button undone, and looked every bit the distinguished aristocrat.

There was no mistaking his handsomeness, whatever my thoughts on the rest of him. His eyes burned brown, a richness there lined with amusement. Sharp lines formed from the corners of his gaze and the sides of his mouth—laugh lines, or something worse. Something harder, something broken.

"I have waited so long to see you." He took a step further into the room, squinting at me. "I should've know you'd be beautiful; you look just like her."

A cleverness rested in his gaze, an intelligence that intimidated more than his size or stature. He reached for my chin and took it in his hand, leaning so close I could smell his breath. Sharp and clean, just like the rest of him.

I froze, staring into a reflection just vaguely familiar—a shadow of my own.

"You are her daughter," he said, his breath catching in his throat. "And mine."

My reaction was visceral, unconscious, as my hand flew from my side, slapping him across the cheek with enough force to unsettle him. The sharpness rang out in the air, suspended like a bell's reverberations.

He stepped back, blinking in surprise.

I couldn't believe what I'd done either. My breath came in heavy waves, bursting from my chest with fury as he rubbed his jaw. "You don't know me, and you don't know her."

"I know her better than you ever did," he said as an angry red mark in the shape of my hand bloomed on his cheek. "Can you tell me what her laugh sounded like? How the brush of her lips felt against your cheek as she kissed you goodnight? How the starlight flickered like lava in her eyes?"

Disorientation struck once more, and I spiraled to understand. "Why am I here?"

"Sit," he commanded.

"I want my questions answered," I growled, my fingers curling into balls. "I'm not a puppet you can jerk around. Answer my questions, let me go, or bind my hands so I don't slap you again. Do *something*, but whatever it is, don't pretend you care anything about me."

"I'm not pretending anything." He circled the table with sure footsteps. "I'm acknowledging we're related. Now, sit."

I hesitated, waiting until he reached the opposite end of the table. When his fingers gripped the edge of the chair, his gaze slipped from me, and that's when I made my move.

Darting for the door, I ducked the first spell that he murmured and blocked the second. I reached the doorway and slipped through. I hadn't had time to formulate a plan; all I knew was that I wouldn't be controlled. I wouldn't be treated like a puppet, wouldn't be—

My limbs froze. My body jerked once, and then my memory began to scramble, my thoughts coming more slowly, like being pulled through molasses. As my head fogged and my speech clouded, I began to lose track of everything. *Why had I run in the first place*? I only needed to sit down, and dinner would be served.

The voice was polite, commanding.

So, I sat.

By the time the fog lifted, a full meal rested on the table, and I perched daintily on the edge of my chair. I shook my head, fighting off the disorientation. I retraced my steps, struggling to figure out how I'd ended up with a fork in my hand.

With shaking fingers, I rested the fork on the table, my stomach roiling. A round of nausea overtook me, and I ducked under the table, breathing heavily until the threat of losing what little I'd eaten before arriving in Wishery had passed.

"Apologies for that," Lucian said, once I pulled my head back above the table. "But isn't this much nicer? We're two civilized individuals, and I believe we should act as such."

My stomach had cramped, but my brain had been working at double speed. I recognized this feeling, the sensation, the signs. I'd felt this before, heard those murmurs in my own head—obeyed someone while disagreeing with my very own voice of reason.

"Civilized?" I spat the question. "Since when is using blood magic on another person *civilized*?"

"You're my daughter, and you were being unreasonable. I need you to listen, to hear my point of view." He chewed slowly, unruffled by his use of an illegal magic against his own flesh. "Please, don't try to escape. It's not only impossible, it is disappointingly rude."

"We're far beyond manners here."

"You're my daughter, and you will—"

"I'm not your daughter," I snarled. "You might technically be my father, but that's where it ends. On a technicality. I am many things, but I'd prefer to be alone than to be related to you."

"There are others who know." He tilted his head to one side. "Who did your mother tell? Was it Hettie? They always were close."

My blood boiled, my fingers clenching the knife closer and closer as I sliced through my steak. I wasn't hungry, but if I didn't do something, I'd lose control. Losing control was not the answer; he was stronger and more knowledgeable in this place. He knew its spells and defenses, and more importantly, he would use blood magic against me again.

To escape, I'd need cleverness, strategy, and a lot of luck on my side. Until I had a plan, I forced myself to appear calm. The more I learned from him and about him, the more I could use against him.

"It doesn't work like that," he murmured, almost as if reading my mind. "It is impossible to escape. Surely you've already pieced together a simple fact: nobody is leaving this city until I say so."

"This city doesn't belong to you. It belongs to the people of Wishery."

"It did, until they donated it to our cause."

"Donated." I snorted. "Right."

"They came around at the end and evacuated. It's a beautiful place and perfect for our needs. I'm just pleased they could see my side of things."

"Oh, does it *please* you," I drawled, "to kick hundreds of people out of their homes?"

"I didn't—"

"Does it *please* you to kidnap islanders and take them from their families and friends?"

"Lily—"

"Does it *please* you to know your own daughter hates the idea of—"

"*Silence*." The volume of his command wasn't loud, but the implications resounded as if he'd roared. His eyes blazed in fury, and the underlying hint of danger behind his eyes bled into the room. "I will not be questioned in my own home. If you refuse to work with me, I will have no use for you any longer."

He could get rid of me with the snap of a finger; I had no doubt. I couldn't let that happen. Not before I found Poppy, Peter, Manuel, and the rest of the islanders. I needed to watch my tongue. If not for me, for them.

"I'm sorry," I said, gritting out the apology.

"Very good," he said. "I know you don't mean it, but at the very least you're smart enough to understand."

I looked to my food, the steak covered with onions and mushrooms, the dainty salad off to the side, and I pushed some of it around. Blood ran like lava through my veins, hungry for nothing except freedom.

"Don't worry. You'll come around." His voice returned to a conversational tone. "Please try your steak. It really is delicious."

I forced myself to take a bite, if for no reason but strength. I had no clue when I would eat again. The memory of the calla lily came back in a rush, the burst of sweetness dispelling any appetite I'd pretended to have. "Why did you kidnap me?"

"You wouldn't have talked to me otherwise."

"If you'd approached me during daylight without threatening me, I would've listened." I surprised myself with my answer. "Don't you think I'd want to know my father?"

He chewed, appearing at a loss for words. "I had no idea you existed until recently. If I had, things might be..."

"Different?" I gestured to the castle around us. "How? Have you always been like this, or—"

"Of course not," he snapped. "One does not choose a life of vengeance, they're forced into it. You'll understand someday."

"Vengeance?" I set my fork down, genuinely intrigued. "This is about vengeance?"

He, too, set his fork down and matched my gaze. "Do you know who we are?"

"The Faction? Yes."

"Do you know why we exist?"

I raised my eyebrows. "Because you believe that paranormals and humans can't co-exist, and you'd prefer to eradicate the humans instead of figuring out ways to cohabitate peacefully."

"Harsh."

"Am I wrong?"

"You're not correct."

"Then explain to me where I've misunderstood."

"It's more complicated than that." He twirled his fork before returning it to his napkin. "It's not that I dislike humans...or, at least, the idea of them."

I made noise in my throat but refrained from commenting.

"I dislike the way they *act*. They persecute our kind; for years they've driven us into hiding."

"Maybe some, but not all. Not all humans are bad, just like not all paranormals are good."

"Look at us." He gave a wry smile and raised a hand, circling his wrist to gesture the world around us. "We hide on islands, in magicked buildings forced to blend into human structures. We stay within our boundaries and go to great lengths to stay hidden. It wasn't always like this."

"I was raised a human. I've lived as a human more of my life than I haven't. Not all of them are interested in persecuting paranormals."

"And since you've moved to The Isle, how many of your friends from your *human* days have you talked to?"

I didn't respond—couldn't. I'd never stopped to think. Once I'd found my family, everything else—my entire life from the mainland had faded away.

"You're kind and funny, Lily. So why haven't you kept up with your friends? Or was it that you didn't actually have any?"

"You don't know me."

"No, but I knew your mother, and I imagine you're a lot like her. You have her spirit, that's for certain."

I inhaled a breath, hating that I was torn between two terrible options. I wanted to learn more about her from this man, but I was terrified to ask. Even more frightening: *how had my mother fallen for someone like him*?

"I wasn't like this back then." He answered my unvoiced question. "You asked how I got to be here, and that, Lily, is what I will explain."

"I don't want to hear it," I said, but it was a lie.

I needed to know, and he understood that as well as I did.

"You were raised under a lie, my daughter, and you want to know why. And more than your own past, you want to know how your mother—a woman much like yourself—could fall in love with a monster like me."

I could only sit in silence.

"Finally, we agree." He sat back, taking a few deep breaths. "When I met Delilah, it was an instantaneous sort of love. A whirlwind summer, a magical period in both of our lives. We spent every possible second together, and I only left once school beckoned in the fall. I swore I'd return for her."

"But you didn't. The fire..."

"I was chosen."

"She came to see you the night of the fire."

His eyes darkened. "Lies."

"She had found out she was pregnant, and she traveled to Cretan to tell you, to see if you'd come back and start a life with her on The Isle."

A quiet rage simmered, bubbling up, the pressure rising. If I said one wrong word, he might very well lose control.

"She arrived to find all evidence pointing to your death. So, she returned to the island and began to set up a life for herself there, surrounded by her family."

He slammed his fist on the table, rattling the silverware, cracking a plate. A piece of glassware tipped off-balance, and then shattered against the floor.

It was one move, a single motion, but it said everything. I'd drained him of all expression, all control. His emotions—every last one—came out with that punch of his fist. Even the chandelier on the ceiling shuddered with trepidation.

I forced my eyes to meet his gaze. "Then I was born, and she learned her daughter was the next Mixologist. People—*paranormals*—were after me. Us. We weren't safe, even on The Isle, so she took steps to protect me."

"She put an enchantment on you and sent you to the mainland."

"It worked for twenty-six years. Nobody knew my whereabouts, not even my family."

"Not even me."

Silence hung between us like a thin wire, a golden strand that would shatter with a breath.

Eventually, he cleared his throat. "What if I told you that's not the full story?" He leaned in, fingers steepled over the table. "As you have discovered by now, I lead The Faction."

My body tensed as I waited for him to continue.

"The Faction is not, as you suggest, a tool to kill off an entire species. It was formed to return paranormals to their place in the world as it once was. We are a race to be respected, to be proud of—all the paranormal species. The vampires, the witches and warlocks, the faeries. Shifters and gnomes, giants and mermaids. We've all gone into hiding."

"It's better than starting a war against innocent people."

"Innocent people who lead witch hunts, breed vampire hunters, and otherwise conspire to eliminate our races?"

"There has to be a different way. We can all live together."

He laughed, quiet. "A noble thought, one I'd expect from the Mixologist. Your mother would've said the same thing."

"But you didn't listen to her."

"I would've listened, but I wasn't given the chance."

"Because you chose The Faction."

"I didn't choose it. They chose me."

My shoulders straightened, my back rigid. "I don't believe you."

"I figured as much. That's why I kept this." Lucian reached into the pocket of his shirt and gently withdrew a small object. His fingers wrapped around it lovingly as he shielded it from view and admired it in private. "Here. I had this made for her the day before the fire. I wasn't planning to leave, Lily."

Lucian dropped a tiny, cold object into my palm. I flinched when the cool metal landed against my skin, and then I drew it closer. I studied the jeweled ring, not comprehending.

"What is this?" I held up the tiny, dainty thin band with a beautiful ruby fastened to the center. "What is it?"

"All I wanted was to earn a diploma in order to provide a life for my family, and then return to The Isle. To be with her."

"With..."

"Your mother. I selected this ring the day before the fire and have carried it with me ever since. I'd planned to propose the next time I returned to The Isle, preferably over her birthday."

My breath locked in my chest, straining to escape. "But you chose The Faction."

"Don't you understand?!" He stood, and with the motion came a piercing, guttural cry. "She was my life! I would never have chosen The Faction over her."

His hands fixed on the edge of the table, bringing the slab of wood with him as he stood. The dishware, the food, the candles—all of it clattered to the floor, broken and burned.

A candle brought fire to the rug, a puff of smoke rising where it'd singed the fabric. A strange man—staff of the castle, based on his attire—scurried in and began dabbing at the fire. He stopped once he caught the look on Lucian's face and retreated out of sight.

We stood, just Lucian and I, staring at one another. His hands hung at his sides while I'd just barely managed to clasp the ring in mine before he'd torn the room apart.

When he spoke, it was with the blade of a knife on his tongue. "There would be no Ghost if it weren't for her."

"Ghost?"

"The Ghost. That's the name they've given me." He laughed, dry and humorless. "The dead man living. The dead man brought to life for the sole purpose of carrying The Faction forward."

"Yet you continue to do the job," I said, papery thin in my response. "You could've walked away. I would die before I joined you."

"Would you?" He squinted, an almost forgiving look in his eyes. "Put yourself in my shoes, and—"

"I don't need to. I'm there now."

With supreme patience, he gave a tight smile and reached into his pocket yet again. This time, he withdrew a thin piece of newspaper. His face changed as he read the words several times before looking up at me with pain in his eyes. He extended the paper with trembling fingers.

I took it, watching his face as I flipped the article around. However, instead of a sheet of words like I'd expected, there was merely a caption underneath a photograph of a woman.

A beautiful woman, plain-faced and smiling. She had features that reflected a familiar face—my own face, I realized with a start. "This is her?"

"Read it. It's a human newspaper from Minneapolis."

I bit my lip, holding back the shock and fear battling to take over. At once there was sadness and joy—seeing a photo of her, holding a piece of her in my hands.

The words, however, were an obituary.

"They called it a mugging gone wrong," he said, breaking the silence. "She had human identification on her as Millie Banks—obviously fake."

"But..."

"She died on the mainland. It must've been just after she'd dropped you in protective custody—likely, she tried to return home, but one of them..." he hesitated, flinching. "One of the humans got to her first."

"You believe that?"

"The gun fired, from what I can tell, when it wasn't supposed to be loaded. I uncovered the police report. The rest of it is a mystery. A case never solved."

"The timeline here doesn't add up." I pressed my fingers to my forehead. "You were going to propose to her the next time you saw her, but then they took you...but that was over a year before my mother died. So why are you still here?"

"Tell me, my daughter. Can you escape from this?"

"From *what*?" I frowned in confusion, but the next moment, my mind turned hazy and foggy once more. An almost peaceful delirium, a path with no resistance. All that mattered was the voice in my head and following his instructions.

When he asked questions, I answered.

When he instructed me to move, I moved.

When he righted my chair and asked me to sit, I sat.

"I still don't understand."

"They kept me sedated for over a year. Under the influence of blood magic and other spells. Keeping me disoriented, washing me with their plans, their intentions, and my duty to fulfill them. When I re-surfaced to the world, your mother was...gone. I couldn't contact your family as our relationship had been a secret. I didn't know you existed. Delilah, my world, was taken from me, and I had nothing left."

"And now you're on a vendetta."

"No, I'm out to set the balance of this world right, and I'd like you to join me."

"I will not. What happened to her..." I gave one last look at the paper, then stepped across the room and handed it back. "Was all The Faction's doing. They killed my mother. They killed the woman you loved, the one person that would keep you from joining their cause. You think I've been lied to? Why do you think you were kept sedated until after her death?"

"Lily, no—"

"This place. How did you do it?" I asked, changing the subject and marching toward the curtains on the far window. "Wish magic can only be used for good."

I pushed one curtain back, fighting the urge to cry. I couldn't afford to cry. I also couldn't run, couldn't hide, couldn't make this disappear, so I needed to learn and understand and focus on those to whom I could still be of service. Poppy, Peter, Manuel...the image of Sophie, a hand on her stomach, appeared in a rush and bolstered my resolve.

The darkness swirled outside, trapping us within the castle walls. It might protect, but it also encased us all in a lightless cage.

"There are rarely black and white decisions in this world," my father said, his tone that of a schoolteacher. "What is wish magic?"

"Three requirements," I murmured. "It cannot be selfish, it can do no harm, and it must inspire a sense of wonder."

"Very good," he said. "Is there anything about good or evil?"

"It can *do no harm,*" I said. "It can't hurt anyone."

"It's insinuated that wishes will be for the good of people, but nowhere is it a requirement. Then again, who's to say what's best for the people? You believe in your fight, and I believe in my cause. We each believe strongly that we are right. Neither of us are hurting others."

"Maybe not *physically*. An unfortunate loophole."

"I'm not debating; I am explaining," he said sharply. "Using those three things, wish magic can be very powerful. A form of magic unlike anything this world has ever seen."

"Except in blood magic."

"Yes, it does have that raw, pure sort of magic to it, doesn't it?" Lucian lifted his nose upward, his profile powerful and sharp, and then he studied me. "What are you thinking?" he asked in the ensuing quiet. "I am here for you, Lily. I want to get to know you."

"Most fathers don't have to kidnap their daughters to get to know them."

"You're not *most* daughters. You're special."

As much as I'd waited to hear those words, as much as I'd wanted to know just one of my parents, the moment was bittersweet. The words were there, but they spewed from the mouth of the enemy.

"There will be a gala tomorrow night," he said, changing the subject. "And I would like to introduce you as my second in command."

"No."

"You can volunteer willingly," he said. "Or..."

"I thought you wouldn't use blood magic on me again."

"I hope it won't be necessary."

My heart constricted, sinking further. "You will do whatever it takes, won't you?" I turned from the window and shook my head, eyes glistening with tears of rage. "I will never be your daughter, nor will I be your second in command."

Then I turned, stormed from the dining room, into the kitchen, bursting past Belinda and the kitchen staff, all of whom rapidly tucked guilty expressions into cleaning up the dishes.

"Let me help you to your room," Belinda said, scurrying behind me. "I think the dress was a success, don't you?"

I strode through the castle, lost and not caring where my feet pulled me. Belinda hurried behind, struggling to keep up.

"Miss Locke, your room is the other way! Let me help you. I can explain. He can come off harsh."

"Don't," I said, turning to face her. I pointed away, anywhere, as my mouth curved into an ugly frown. "Don't follow me."

"But—"

"Leave me *alone*!"

I raised my hands, anger sizzling around the edges of my fingers like lightning. My magic brimmed within me, struggling to emerge with a burst of untamed emotion.

I had no intention of using any magic at all on Belinda, but it worked. She disappeared down a hallway, leaving me alone.

Alone.

As I'd always been and would always be.

I had Poppy, I had Zin, Mimsey, X, Gus, Hettie and the rest.

But as I wandered the hallways all by my lonesome, I wondered how on earth they'd continue to love me...knowing I'd come from a man such as *him.*

Chapter 28

BELINDA FOUND ME HOURS later.

I'd stumbled through the castle for some time, feeling eyes on me everywhere I went, watching as I moved through the dimly lit hallways. I pushed back curtains, tried doorknobs, and hadn't found anything of interest.

Whoever was watching me had most likely also been guiding me, and the doors I'd tested that were locked hadn't been on accident. Someone was letting me think that I was in control when really, I was no better off than a hamster in a maze of LEGOS.

Eventually, I found a balcony at the end of a hallway and planted myself there, waiting for someone to collect me and take me back to my room. I'd wanted fresh air, which was ironic since none of the air in Wishery was fresh at all.

They lived in a bubble, the swirls keeping us hidden and holding us captive all at once. I breathed deeply, but it didn't make a difference. My mind flew, crunching through the information I'd learned this evening, my chest tight.

"He really does want to get to know you," Belinda said once she found me. "May I join you out here?"

I gave a one shoulder shrug from my place in a chaise lounge overlooking Wishery. Quaint little homes, cute streets, and bright shops lined the roads below, now overshadowed by the very magic that'd built this place.

"For what it's worth, he truly believes nobody he loves is safe so long as the humans roam free. The technology they've invented—guns, weapons, everything else—they are as strong as us now, if not deadlier. They are more dangerous to us than ever before," Belinda continued. "Paranormals are a peaceful people by nature."

"How can you say that? Look around us. The Faction wasn't exactly peaceful when stealing Wishery from its people. You can't support what they do and believe that paranormals are peaceful."

"I've been born into this business," Belinda said. "My parents served The Faction leader before him, and I never left. For me, there is no other way of life."

Belinda stepped further out onto the balcony, glancing behind her as if worried she'd been followed. Eventually, she shut the doors and joined me against the ledge.

"What's it like out there?" she murmured. "Beyond the walls."

"You haven't been here your entire life," I said. "Wishery has only fallen in recent days."

"If not here, it's somewhere else. The magic, the spells are different—always different, but also the same. Nobody in and nobody out."

"If you wanted to leave, could you?"

She pinched her lips together. "I'm happy to be here serving the cause."

"Sounds a lot like brainwashing to me."

"I've never been touched by his magic."

I started, glancing at her. "You're talking about blood magic? You really believe he's never used it on you?"

"There are others who don't obey him as much as me. *They* require his discipline." She shook her head. "*He* is our leader now. Before it was another. There is always someone to lead the fight."

"Against what? Humans?"

"To bring the world back to the way it used to be."

"Hasn't anyone ever considered that the glory days might be gone? That all that's left is to adapt or die? We can coexist with the humans, I'm sure of it. There has to be another way besides war."

Belinda fell silent, obviously unwilling to speak ill of her leader. But in her eyes gleamed curiosity. I latched onto that, inched closer.

"I promise you, some of my closest friends live with the humans, work with them. For the majority of my life, I lived and worked as a human. I can tell you that for every non-paranormal who wants to hurt us, there are a hundred, or even a thousand, who would defend us."

"That's not what he tells us. He says they killed the woman he was to marry for no reason at all."

"Why does he use mind bending, then? Maybe you've been influenced, Belinda, and you don't even know it."

"Impossible."

"Until a few days ago, it was impossible to use wish magic for anything except Wishery." I gestured around us. "One of the purest forms of magic to ever exist has been tainted."

At this, she bowed her head. "I'm sorry."

"Sorry for what?"

"I will tell you, only if you promise me one thing." Her eyes flashed up at me. "Take me with you."

"With me, where? I'm trapped here."

"I can help you," she whispered, her voice as quiet as a breeze. "I don't want to be here any longer."

"How do I know this isn't a trap?"

"I need to see what it's like," she pleaded. "Out there. I need to know if there's more to this world, if there's a life for me beyond these walls."

She seemed earnest enough, but I hesitated. Belinda had gone from supporting Lucian to wanting to escape in a matter of minutes. If I was going to get out of here, however, I'd need help, and I had the feeling that would be hard to find in this place. It was a risk to trust Belinda, but one I'd have to take.

"Do you know where he's keeping the islanders?" I asked, watching her reaction carefully.

> "There's a ten-minute window between guard shifts. I can take you there and show you. I'm sorry, but that's all I can offer."

"Is my cousin there? Poppy?"

"That useless vamp?"

"She's not useless."

"She can't eat blood!"

"That doesn't make her *useless*!"

"Either way, she's there. I can show you if you'll follow me." She glanced at my gown. "Don't let that drag along the floor."

"WE'LL NEED YOUR HELP to give us a fighting chance of getting out," I said, as we crept through the corridors. "If you bring me to Poppy and the others and they're *safe,* I'll take you with me, I promise."

"Fine. It's the least I can do."

"What do you mean," I pressed, following her through a maze of corridors, "that it's the least you can do?"

She glanced at the artwork on the walls as if it could speak. Eventually, she cleared her throat, waiting until we'd reached a shadowy portion of the hall. "Obviously, it took a powerful spell to turn this wish magic inside out. *He* couldn't do it alone. He used us, all of us, to funnel power into the spell."

"You helped to create this place? The place that used to be Wishery?"

"No. Well, yes, but no. We didn't know what we were doing at the time; he used us as sheer power, nothing more."

"Why the change of heart now?"

A few steps further down the hallway, she hesitated and shifted her eyes toward the floor. "I think he's going too far."

"Are you not free to leave?"

"He says we are, but..." she paused, glancing around. Nobody was there, yet the feeling of being watched intensified. "We're all chained here because of this spell. We're tied to it in a way that can't be unlocked by anyone except *him* or you...or so they say."

"So *who* says?"

"Everyone. You're the Mixologist."

"Okay. Say I believe all of this. Why do you *really* want to break away from here? After all these years, why now?"

A small pool of tears formed in her eyes, and she shook her head. "I just do."

"Convince me that I should believe you."

"I have—*had*—a baby boy. His father was a human. I met his father when we were moving between locations, and we dated for some months. It's the only contact I've ever had with a human, and he was wonderful."

"Why didn't you stay with him?"

"*He* caught me when I tried to escape. And since my baby had human blood, *he* didn't let me keep him." Tears pricked at her eyes as her voice shook. "I left without telling them goodbye. My baby needs his mother."

"I'm sorry, Belinda."

"I've been debating *how* to leave since that day, but..." She peeked around once more, and then gestured to her arms. Thin strips of vines had begun to circle her forearms. "He has a charm so that any time one of us gets the urge to leave, to flee, it reminds us of our *ties* to The

Faction. It's not a matter of wanting to leave; this might be the first time I'm *able*."

"We'll get you out of here," I promised. "And your son will know you."

Belinda stopped, looking thoughtfully out the window at the swirling clouds. We'd reached the end of a long corridor. Suits of armor along the edges stood bare, save for the torches beaming from the walls.

"We are all part of this curse," she said hollowly, reaching for a torch. She gestured to the skies beyond. "That blackness. We are all tied to the dark magic—I can feel it in my bones. The destruction, the terror, the unrest. We created *that*."

Beyond the window the smoke puffed and chugged through the sky, circling us, tightening, constricting the very air inside. I rested an arm on Belinda's where the vines had slowly begun to retreat.

"It's not your fault," I said. "But I need you to think back; this next question is incredibly important."

An idea had popped into my head, a dangerous, risky one. Stupid, even, but I needed to find out the answer to my theory. "Did he tell you how wish magic works?"

"No. He never explains himself."

"You're sure you're linked to the spell?" I twirled her around to face me, demanding her answer. "You're positive?"

She raised her hands and stared at her fingers. "It shot through me like an electrical shock, jolted me, locked into place. We all felt it; we were all holding hands in a big circle."

Which meant, I realized, that she was bound by the rules of wish magic, just as Lucian would be. When a witch performed a spell, he or she had to obey the rules that went with it. I'd learned that in Basic Witchcraft 101.

The more *uncommon* knowledge was that wish magic took three factors: Do no harm, seek not for selfish purposes, and inspire a sense of wonder. I stood back, contemplating as Belinda watched.

"He *must* abide by these laws. He's the stakeholder in the spell," I muttered, pacing in circles. "Which means he must believe so fully in his cause that the wish wasn't selfish."

"What are you talking about?"

I waved her off, muttering under my breath. "He clearly had a sense of wonder for wish magic, or it wouldn't have worked. And lastly, he must have made the wish truly believing he wouldn't cause harm to another being."

"I don't understand."

"If the laws of magic are true," I said, my voice giddy with excitement. "That means anyone with a stake in the spell is bound by the same rules."

"Including me?"

"That's what I'm thinking." I blinked, running through the logic once more before nodding to confirm it. "If the spell cannot cause harm to anyone by the sheer nature of its being, then anyone bound to it cannot cause harm within its bounds."

"I'm sorry, Miss Locke, you're going to have to explain—"

"Take your torch and press it to my hand," I instructed Belinda. "Please."

"No!" She recoiled, bringing the torch closer to her. "I don't want to hurt you!"

"You won't! I don't have time to explain. If you want to help, this is how you can help." I reached for the arm that held the torch, lowering it close enough to my palm to feel the heat. "I'm going to let go, and you must touch my hand with the fire."

"But—"

"Do you trust me to get you out of here?"

A troubled gleam bounced in her eye. Then, a quiet *yes*.

Belinda gritted her teeth, clearly unhappy with the turn of events. She met my gaze and her face changed, probably at the determination in my own. We both inhaled at the same time, and then she plunged the torch toward me.

It should've burned, it should've singed; my flesh should've bubbled and boiled under the heat of the flame, and I should've passed out from the pain. I should've screamed with all the air in my lungs.

Yet somehow, I didn't even flinch. The torch felt like a warm, tender caress on my palm, as if I'd submerged my arm in bathwater.

"Why aren't you—" she yanked the torch away at the sound of footsteps.

I'd barely processed my theory, the realization sending a surge of hope to my core. *Anyone with a stake in the spell can't hurt me.* They couldn't hurt *us.* Not, at least, if we were within the bounds of Wishery.

That umbrella of a black cloud, the black magic, had turned from my captor into my savior. We would be protected by the sheer nature of wish magic. Nobody, including Lucian, could hurt us... *physically.*

"Good evening, Belinda," Lucian stepped from a door nearby, giving neither of us time to move, to hide, to react. Her face read guilty, while mine had settled in awe. "We're quite far from Lily's room, aren't we?"

"Tour," Belinda murmured, still looking surprised. "Took her on a tour."

I latched onto her dazed expression and stepped forward. "Leave her out of this. We both know what happened here. I'm looking for a way out and forced Belinda to show me around."

For a moment, Lucian angered, then eased. He glanced at Belinda, and then at me, as my insinuation set into place. "I see you *are* my daughter. I didn't think you'd allow yourself to use mind bending."

I kept my mouth shut, letting him carry the conversation from here. I knew he'd believe that I'd used blood magic to get Belinda here. Of course he'd believe me because it was the very same thing *he* would've done.

He'd never consider there was another way to ask for her help, and that was my advantage over him. *There is always another way,* I thought. If only he could understand that, we might not be here in the first place.

"No sign of Poppy?" he asked. "I assume that's who you're looking for. You won't leave without her. Hence the reason I needed to *bring* her here in the first place."

"Where is she?" I snarled. "I will stay if you let Poppy go."

"Get on to your quarters, Belinda," Lucian said, turning slightly to speak to his staff. "I'll take Lily from here."

Belinda's honest shock saved her. Mumbling, she stumbled away from me, swinging the torch like a drunken sailor. She scurried away down the hall, stopping every few feet to turn and stare at me.

Once she was gone, a wave of relief washed through my body. Until he spoke.

"Clever girl, aren't you?" His voice rang out clearly. "Once, I would've done that too."

"Done what?" My pulse raced. I strained for a glimpse of Belinda, but she'd rounded a corner and moved from sight. "What are you talking about?"

He pursed his lips, but didn't respond. Instead, almost in answer, a shrill scream sounded from around the bend, and I knew it belonged to Belinda.

"Let her go," I rasped. "This is between me and you. Don't get her involved."

The screams silenced, and he shook his head. "She already involved herself when she offered to help you. Don't worry, she's alive," he said. "Unharmed. It was just a warning."

Belinda appeared then, eyes vacant. "As you wish, sir," she intoned. "I am sorry."

"Belinda will see you to your room," my father said. "And she will lock you inside. Good evening, Lily. If you'd like to keep her free from mind bending, I suggest you leave her uninvolved in your attempts to escape."

"Wait!" I yelled after him. "You're just leaving me with her?"

He turned, smiling, as if it pleased him I'd asked the question. "I have no fear about leaving you with her, Lily. Your mind bending abilities, though inherited from me, are untrained and wild. You will not break Belinda no matter how hard you try."

"But—"

"Ah, I know you believe that you can outthink me, but that's where you're mistaken. See, I have two perspectives, Lily; I was like you *once*." He raised long, slender fingers to his lips and rested them there. "But I've seen more. I've been broken, and I've risen to new heights from it—heights I'd never have achieved otherwise."

"New heights? No," I said, my fingers clenching into fists. "You've fallen to new lows."

He grimaced, displeased at my response. "You might reconsider when you learn of the human ways. The filthy humans who murdered your mother. The woman I loved more than anything, the woman who loved you, I'm sure, more than life itself. She risked her life to save you, and..." He shook his head. "The humans took it from her. She was protecting you from the paranormals, but she couldn't keep herself safe from *them*."

"You don't know anything about it."

"I knew her longer than you. But alas, that's neither here nor there. I'm simply urging you to remember that I know the way you think, but that you can never know the way I think. So, if you decide to try another plan to escape, someone will suffer. Isn't that right, Belinda?"

I watched in horror as Belinda nodded, eyes blank, and then screamed. Her face, expressionless, was more eerie than the sounds she was making—she gave no sign of pain, save for a blood curdling wail that boiled my skin.

"Good evening," he said, dismissing me with a nod.

"Come, Lily," Belinda intoned, then began marching in that robotic movement signature of mind bending.

I watched the walls as we walked, every window and doorway. His magic was stronger than I'd thought; he could use blood magic for so long, and from such a distance.

Luckily, there were other ways to break the spell. It had worked on Zin, just minutes before she'd attempted to poison our own grandmother.

"Belinda, listen," I said as we walked. "It's me, Lily."

"Lily, we are walking to your room."

"Yes! I'm going to save you, remember? We're going to be free, I promise you."

"I serve at the pleasure of The Faction."

I walked behind her, struggling to make this conversation more personal. To force her to latch onto a piece of information that would jolt her free from the fingers of blood magic my father kept pressed to her. Something—a word, a memory, a phrase—that would help her remember herself, to pull her from the depths of the fog.

We stopped outside my bedroom door a few minutes later. Nothing I'd said, nothing I'd promised, made even an inkling of a difference.

"Belinda, wait," I said. "Please, focus on what I'm saying. *Listen* to my voice."

"I am listening to your voice," she agreed, monotone. "We have reached our destination. Please step inside the room."

"Belinda—" I repeated her name, praying for any sign of recognition, but she stopped me mid-sentence as she raised both hands in a stiff motion and rested them on my shoulders.

I glanced down, seconds before she gave me a shove that had me hurtling across the room. I hadn't been prepared for her to use force, and I'd especially not been prepared for the power behind it. Therefore, I hadn't braced myself whatsoever, and I crashed into the corner of the desk before sliding to the ground.

I stayed down, pleading with Belinda. My eyes, my words, everything I could think of, yet it didn't make a difference. She'd been under the influence too long; the spell was too difficult to break.

"Belinda, for your son," I begged. "Please, focus."

"I have no son."

"You do," I said, climbing to my feet. I inched across the room. "You have a son, and he'd love to meet you. A baby boy, a little boy now, out in the world. You want to find him."

Belinda blinked, watching me with rapt attention. "A son?"

"A son. A child. You wanted me to bring you to him, and I promised. You'll get to see him soon, okay?"

A flash of understanding appeared, and I latched onto it, grasping at her hands and squeezing. Unfortunately, my touch had the opposite effect, and instead, she raised a hand and slapped me across the cheek.

"I have no son," she said.

Then she turned and slammed the door shut so hard the entire room shuddered.

Footsteps carried her away, the sting of my cheek nothing compared to the pain lodged in my heart.

Chapter 29

THE NEXT DAY IN WISHERY was spent in a cave of my own thoughts: I worried about Poppy and the others, fretted over Belinda, dreamed of Ranger X, wondered what Gus might be thinking, or Trinket and Mimsey and Hettie. I worried about what would come this evening, and I worried if I would be prepared.

Around lunchtime, the worry faded and the hunger set in its place. I didn't dare ask for food, but the gnawing in my stomach grew worse, and by the time late afternoon rolled around I was starving.

Focusing instead on organizing my vials and potions, I used a simple Shielding Spell, an incantation designed to blur my movements from anyone watching, while I worked. Testing bits of potions, perfecting them, I combined the ingredients for the spell that would break the black magic and hopefully dissolve the dark dome over Wishery.

Once combined, I studied the vial of antidote, and I knew that there wasn't enough of it. For starters, the silver hadn't been left to absorb sunlight for three days, soaking up the light to strengthen its properties. It'd be too weak to break the curse once and for all.

Worse, there was just too little of it. Too little antidote to make a difference for an entire village. I'd need a vat, a cauldron fully brewed, to make any sort of dent in the city limits.

Once I'd prepared both potions—one to break Wishery's curse and the Long Isle Iced Tea for Poppy's party—I developed another plan. Slipping into the closet, I located the dress that Belinda had set aside for the evening's gala.

I surveyed it from a distance first, stepping as far back in the walk-in closet as possible. A shade of light blue in color, it boasted soft, flowing fabrics and a bit of volume in the skirt. A truly beautiful ball gown. Only the circumstances dictated the unease that went along with wearing it.

However, this dress would work perfectly for my plan. From within the confines of the closet, I set to work with a bit of magic and the sewing kit I'd found in one of the drawers. I pricked my fingers a few times, but managed to stumble through a skill I'd never taken the time to learn. I was going for function, not artistry.

Eventually, I stepped back and surveyed my work with pride. *It would do.*

I debated slipping into the dress to try it on and test my handiwork, but before I could do any such thing, the door flew open and someone from within yelled a *hello*.

I stepped from the closet, tucking the sewing kit behind my back, and came face to face with a strikingly peculiar man. His hair had been shaved on one side, and he wore skinny leather pants with a bright yellow tank top. Enough eyeliner caked his eyes to give him the haunting look of a raccoon.

"You must be Lily," he said, sticking out a thin arm. "It's a pleasure to meet you. I'm Bartholomew, and I will be helping you get ready for the gala tonight."

"Thanks," I said, offering a confused smile, "but I'm not really in need of help. I'm just planning on popping into the ball gown."

"Pop!" His eyes widened, and he giggled. "Just popping in, you're hilarious!" He chortled then, watching my face for a sign I was kidding. "*Pop! Pop! Pop*!"

I couldn't quite bring myself to laugh since I didn't see anything funny about it. "I'd prefer not to go at all."

"Oh, honey. You're serious."

"Of course I'm serious. I'm a prisoner. I have nobody to impress."

Bartholomew clucked his tongue. "Doesn't mean you can't look fabulous," he said, *popping* over to me and pinching the sides of my clothing. I still had on my street attire from the day before because it was the only thing here that belonged to me aside from my potions. There was a comfort to wearing them. "You have an excellent figure. You'll make my job easy."

"Who are you?"

"I am Bartholomew the Great," he said. "The paranormals call me Bartholomew, the humans prefer Bart. Who knows why? I don't mind either way. I still work the same magic on all of my clients."

"Who sent you here?"

"Belinda."

"But Belinda is..." I stopped, wondering for the millionth time today where she'd gone. "Where is Belinda?"

"She's downstairs preparing the food. She makes an excellent chocolate truffle."

"Do you work for The Faction?"

"I work for whomever pays me," he said, pulling out a comb from thin air and beginning to pluck at my hair.

"Are you helping with anyone else?"

"Just you, my dear. You're the guest of honor, yes? Belinda thought you might like a helping hand."

"But—"

"Hush now, and let me work."

After an hour of hair tugging, eyebrow tweezing, and lip painting, I looked like a new woman. Bartholomew had talked the entire time, yammering on about one client or another.

"You work with humans, yet you're here, employed by The Faction? Don't you take issue with that?"

"What am I doing wrong? Helping a beautiful woman *pop* into her dress? The only agenda I have is making the world beautiful. Politics bore me."

"I need you to help me."

"Oh, honey, I can't. My boyfriend and I are traveling to Hawaii the human way—on an airplane. My boyfriend's idea—*hilarious*, isn't he? We'll have to get going just as soon as I get out of here."

"No, Bartholomew, I mean it. I need your help. Something bad has happened to Belinda."

His flawless face turned downward in a frown. "But I just saw her."

"Last night. She's being controlled by the leader of The Faction."

"Oh, dear." Bartholomew took out a perfume bottle. "I was hoping you'd stop talking about this, but since I can't seem to keep you quiet...I'm sorry, Lily."

"Sorry for what?"

Raising a hand, he extended a pink colored bottle and spritzed once in my face. By the time he spritzed a second time, the room swirled, and I spiraled into the darkness.

"YOU'VE GOT TWELVE MINUTES." A voice hissed in my ear. "Move. *Quickly*."

Groggily, I rolled over and pulled myself to my feet. "What? Where am I?"

Belinda's face hovered above mine. Behind her, an odd-looking man stood near her shoulder.

"We've got you twelve minutes," Belinda said, eyeing me with urgency. "Bartholomew had to spritz you to keep you from talking. We *both* need to get out of here. There's no time to explain further—we need to move."

"Hurry *where*?" I couldn't get my brain to process correctly. My head slumped into my hands. "I'm so foggy."

"I shouldn't have spritzed a second time," Bartholomew said. "Sorry about that."

"Wait a minute..." I looked at him. "You *lied* to me?"

"Through my teeth," he said, eyes flashing as he glanced behind him. "I've been captured, too. I need to get away; my human clients need me. I have a *wedding* to get to for crying out loud."

"Why didn't you say anything before?"

"They were listening!" Bartholomew waved his hands. "I've been working with Belinda this whole time. We'll answer the rest of your questions later."

"I'm not leaving without my cousin and the others."

"Where do you think we brought you?" Bartholomew asked, gesturing toward an empty food trolley. "Sorry we had to knock you out, but you didn't seem to want to stop talking, and we couldn't wander openly with you through the halls."

"So, you stashed me in a food tray?"

"We couldn't take any risks," Belinda said. "We know where he's keeping your cousin. If you follow this passageway, you'll find the prison cells."

"You have ten minutes before the guards will begin their next rounds," Bartholomew added. "You must hurry."

"You're not coming with me?"

"I'm sorry." Belinda pursed her lips. "We can't. We're risking detection already by coming to this part of the castle. We need to go, Lily. Will you be okay?"

"Yes," I gargled, but they were already rushing away.

Still foggy from Bartholomew's spritz, I stumbled through the door they'd indicated and down a dim hallway, the walls damp with moisture, the floor covered in a thin layer of grime and dirt.

I located a torch on the wall and brought it with me, pressing onward despite my confusion.

As the fog evaporated and my task solidified in my head, I quickened my pace, rounding one corner after another, the quiet drip, drip of condensation on the walls leaving me with eerie tingles shimmering down my spine.

I rounded a curve, then came face to face with a stone wall. The material was a grimy yellow, almost golden brown, and had no keyhole. There was, however, an outline in the shape of a door and magic shimmering along the outside. I leaned in, feeling for any hint of spell, any familiarity that might help me to crack it.

The spell itself felt harmless, not a touch of dark magic inside of it. Frowning, I rested my hands against the door, waiting for any sort of pushback. Nothing.

In fact, the slight crunch of stone against stone sounded, and the door gradually slid open to reveal another passage. Stepping through, I glanced behind me as the door began to close. That's when I understood—the spell wasn't dangerous...unless I was on the inside. It was a one-way portal, and I'd just entered a passage with no return.

It hadn't locked yet, and as it began to swing closed, I pulled my sweater off and shoved it between the door and its frame. I could feel the spell sizzling with heat. Hopefully, it'd give me enough of an opening to latch onto during my return journey.

Then, because I had no other choice, I marched onward.

The hallway grew narrower, darker, smaller. By the time light shone in the distance, I could barely squeeze through the passageway. Claustrophobia set in, and it took every piece of willpower to control my breathing.

The light in the distance grew nearer—three feet away, and then two. *One foot from the light.* Suddenly, I reached it. The bright little halo danced at my feet, the result of an opening in the stone above my head just barely as wide as my shoulders.

I had two choices. I was either going up and toward the light, or back the way I'd come. There was no other way forward. The thought of going *up* had my chest constricting in fear. If I got stuck, nobody would find me. Yet, if I wanted to locate Poppy, there was no other choice.

Holding my breath, I reached one arm up through the hole toward the light, and then the other. My hands grasped for traction on a sandy surface.

I pulled up to my elbows, then backed down. I wouldn't be able to fit through there. Not unless I turned into a gymnast and lost half of my body weight.

But one more try wouldn't hurt before giving up, I figured, so I reached my hands up again. This time, my head made it through, then my shoulders. Pulling myself up, I inched my body into the opening, struggling to keep my breath from spiraling out of control and my heart from racing.

Another inch up. Then another.

Then, a touch froze me in place.

A hand on my ankle, cold and firm. The fingers were rough, and the strength with which the figure pulled had me thinking it was a man.

"Don't scream," he warned, confirming my theory. "Don't you dare make a sound, Lily."

He yanked harder as I struggled against him, but my balance was completely off, and in two tugs, my body fell through to the grimy floor of the cave.

I collapsed as a hand clasped over my mouth, silencing my screams.

The figure—most definitely a man—dragged me out of the sunlight and knelt next to me in the darkness of the cave. To my surprise, he murmured an apology in my ear.

"Did I hurt you?" he asked, running a hand along my shoulders as if checking for injuries.

I sat up, taking in the scratches along my arms and legs from the rough rock edges. My body stung, my heart pulsed, and yet, a sense of calm fell over me. I blinked as a shadow of his face came into view. Then I squinted, realizing I recognized the man. "*Peter*?"

I leaned closer, repeating his name quietly as I studied his face in the dim light. Familiar features came slowly into focus, and sure enough, he nodded.

"I'm sorry to be so rough on you, but I couldn't have you yelling. He might hear you."

"Peter, I'm so sorry!" My breath came in ragged gulps, my fear, my hate of this dark and grimy cave coming out in a hiss. "I should've believed you. I should've listened, and now...you're here."

"You came for me, for us."

"Is everyone else here, too?" A niggling sensation in the back of my head pestered until Zin's theory came rushing to me, and I briefly wondered if I'd misinterpreted Peter; if he could be involved in this whole thing. "You're not part of this, are you?"

"Of The Faction? No, of course not," he said, quickly. The excitement in his eyes was too true to fake. "But can you imagine the story I'll have when I return to The Isle? A first-person account! I couldn't have asked for a better end to this story. I predicted my own kidnapping, and I was *right.* Nobody can ever doubt me again."

"Let's focus on getting everyone home. Where's Poppy? Manuel? Jonathon—"

"We're all kept in the cells," he said. "Mine has a loose bar, so I can slip in and out. We heard you creeping by. The cells are right here."

Peter raised a hand and knocked on the rock wall.

"Cells? As in, jail cells?"

"Most of us are unharmed—"

"*All* of you should be unharmed," I corrected. "I discovered that the curse protects us from any of *them*. The Faction, the people who secured the curse over Wishery."

"Unharmed *physically*, maybe."

"Physically? What is that supposed to mean?"

"Come with me. Quietly. I'll bring you to Manuel. He's been here longer than me. Jonathon will want to talk to you, too, and Drew. Jon's been working on a plan."

"And Poppy?"

He hesitated. "She's..."

"Where's Poppy?" My hands linked onto his shoulders as I shook him hard. "Where is she?"

"She's here, too. Come and see for yourself."

Dread filled me, my stomach, every inch of my limbs as we crawled and hobbled our way through a different side path. I had missed the pitch-black opening on my first pass through the tunnel, and only now with the help of the guide, could I make out the edges of the entrance.

"Are any of *them* around?" I asked. "Guards on duty, or anything?"

"They're all getting ready for the gala. We have at least ten minutes. I don't know how much longer they'll give us before they retrieve us. We're required to attend the gala."

"Aren't you prisoners?"

"Of course, but we have to honor him...and *you*." He glanced over at me. "Speaking of which, I'd *really* love an exclusive interview after this is all over."

"First, let's get out of here. Alive."

"Here we are," he said, rounding a corner. "Poppy's in a different wing with Magdalena—men and women separated. Jonathon, Drew, Manuel? Lily's here."

"The Mixologist?" Manuel asked. "Lily Locke?"

"I told you she'd come," Peter said sounding cross. "Why does nobody ever believe me?"

"Because you report on UFOs," Jonathon said with a wry smile. "Hi, I'm Jon. Pleasure to meet you."

Jon reached a hand through the bars of his cell. The entire hallway had been carved from stone, the individual alcoves chiseled out with blunt force. It'd take powerful magic to break out of here.

I clasped Jon's hand and shook it. I sized him up, pairing him with the image of his mother, who'd very clearly seen Jon as the ugly duckling of the family. From my assessment, they couldn't be more different from one another.

He'd been locked up the longest, and it showed. He had an unkempt beard, straggly hair, and a ruddy complexion despite his wiry frame. Underneath the grime, however, his smile shone bright.

"I would've cleaned up had I known you were coming," he said, teasing with another grin. "By the way, Peter has been talking about you nonstop. We thought for a minute that he had a thing for you."

"I *told* you she was the only one with any hope of finding us!" Peter growled, his face turning red. He whirled to face me. "You got the map from Sophie?"

"You could've hidden the key in an easier spot," I said, with a grudging smile. "But we figured it out, and now we need to break you out of here."

"We have the start of a plan," Jon said, after Manuel and the others had introduced themselves. "But we're missing a few things."

"What sort of things?"

"A map," Jon said. "The route out of this place. We were all brought here with no memory of how we arrived. Then, if we make it out of this place, we'll need a way to get home."

"*When* we make it out of this place," I said. "What about the rest of the plan?"

"That's all we've got." Manuel shook his head. "They've taken everything from us. And we're the best-off out of everyone."

"The best-off? Where is Poppy? What's wrong with her?!"

"Lily," Peter said. "Focus on our plan. Do you have any thoughts on how to get us out of here?"

I hesitated, took a breath. "I do have one idea that could work, but we would have to act now. Today. At the gala. If we can cause a distraction, I will provide a way out of this city when its time. It's risky, but it's the only chance we've got."

"It's not enough time," Manuel said. "We don't have—"

"I agree with Lily," Peter said. "We're moving today with one caveat."

I turned to face him. "What?"

"I won't be leaving."

The rest of the men studied him with disbelief. Someone murmured, "Excuse me?"

"There are more people here than we can rescue in one day," Peter explained. "The Isle disappearances are just a fraction of the folks they have captured. We can't rescue everyone today. I'm going to stay behind with the others. Just promise you'll come back for us."

"No." I gave a hard shake of my head. "I'm not leaving anyone behind."

"You must," Peter said. "But you'll come back for us. Spread the word. Bring the Rangers, MAGIC, Inc. Everyone. Whatever you do, don't stay back, Lily. The Isle needs you there more than we do here."

"But—"

"There's no hope for the rest of us if you stay," he said firmly. "I'm volunteering to stay behind. Look at it this way—there is *no* way you can wipe out The Faction alone. So, let me stay, and you'll have an inside source. Work with the rest of the teams once you return, and formulate a plan to end everything—for good."

I swallowed, struggling to find a way to convince Peter his plan couldn't work.

"About that distraction," Peter said. "I have an idea."

Peter waited until the rest of us studied one another, silently taking a poll on his plan. One by one, we grudgingly turned our attention back to Peter. Jonathon was last.

"Well?" Jon said finally. "Let's hear it."

Chapter 30

PETER LAID OUT HIS surprisingly well-developed plan. As I thought about it, I found myself nodding along with him. Manuel agreed, too, then Jonathon and Drew.

"This might work," Jonathon said, tapping his fingers against the bars of his cell. "I think we have what we need. I'm looking forward to seeing you on the outside, Lily."

"Thank you," Manuel said, while Drew nodded in agreement. "We owe you, Peter."

I cleared my throat, still struggling with the idea of willingly leaving Peter behind in enemy territory. "Where is Poppy?"

"There's no time. The guards will be returning," Peter said. "We'll get her to you outside, I promise."

"Now," I said. "Or this plan isn't happening."

Jonathon nodded at Peter, who bowed his head in agreement. After a round of goodbyes with the men, I followed Peter to another wing of the underground tunnels.

We continued forward, rounding a bend, keeping quiet and low to the ground. When I finally stood and faced the next hallway, I exhaled, tears pricking my eyes.

"Poppy," I whispered, relieved to see her unharmed. "It's me. We're going to get you out of there. I'm so sorry about everything. I just—"

Poppy turned to me, her eyes wide, a curious smile on her lips. "Hello," she said, a lyrical lilt to her voice. "Who are you?"

I turned to Peter. My blood boiled. Lava coursed in my veins as my eyes narrowed on him. "What has happened to her?"

"Go!" Peter hissed urgently. "They're coming. They *can't* find you here. You have to leave."

"But Poppy!"

"You *have* to go. We'll get Poppy home."

The cat and mouse chase had begun. With a gut-wrenching ache, I let Peter pull me away from Poppy, my fingers lingering behind on the bars of her cage. Her disposition was polite and bubbly as usual, but the love in her eyes was gone. She hadn't recognized me.

Peter led me through a series of tunnels. He knew his way around, and I assumed he'd been combing through these passages since he'd been held here. He paused now and again to help me through difficult places, knowing exactly where boulders had fallen and ceilings hung low.

Footsteps gained on us, and we continued moving deeper into the castle. Every time we'd seem to get ahead, however, there'd be a moment of silence, and then...the pounding of feet, closer and closer.

"What happened to Poppy?" I demanded as we hurtled through a black tunnel in silence, save for our gasps of air. "Why was she talking like that? Why'd she ask who I am?"

"That's what I was trying to tell you." Peter extended a hand, hauling me around a tight curve. "Something happened. Her memory is wiped completely."

I stilled. "How could that have happened?"

"Lily, we can't stop. They're coming for us. We have to get you to safety."

"But Poppy—"

"I don't *know*. It happened before I arrived here, and I'm assuming it's a reaction to strong blood magic. There are a few other prisoners here with memory issues, and most say it's because they rebelled somehow, fought back against *him*."

"Poppy isn't susceptible to blood magic. She's a vampire."

The footsteps grew closer. "He is very powerful. Maybe she didn't fall under the spell of blood magic, but it scrambled her mind. Come on, Lily. *Move.*"

"We can't leave her here."

"We'll all be trapped if you don't move. Go," he said, glancing behind him. "They're catching up. I'm going to let them find me."

"You can't, Peter! We need you later at the gala! What about the distraction?"

"I'll escape."

"You won't be able to escape once they find you free! Come with me."

He shook his head, a thin glint of resignation in his eyes. "You need to get to the door up there. The guard password is *Open Sesame.*"

"You're joking."

"Go."

"Wait!" I fished around in my travel belt for one of the vials of Long Isle Iced Tea that I'd tucked there, and I pushed it into Peter's hands.

"What is this?" Peter asked as he clasped the vial. "I don't have time—"

"During the distraction at the gala. Make sure everyone takes a tiny sip."

"Is there enough in here for everyone?"

"It will have to be enough. One sip of this, and it'll change its user into a costume they most desire," I said. "Have everyone picture the image of a castle guard."

"We'll be costumed as a guard, and that will get everyone out faster," Peter said. "I knew you'd have the solution, Lily Locke."

"It'll have to work for now. It's not ideal, and with this small amount of potion, it will wear off quickly."

"Understood. Will you please take this?" Peter thrust a dirty scrap of paper into my hands and accompanied it with a pleading expression. "Make sure it's printed. Do it for me."

"We're going to get you out of here," I said, folding the paper and tucking it into my pocket. "You can print it yourself. We're coming right back for you."

Peter, in response, gave me a push that had me stumbling toward the end of the tunnel into a cavernous room. Thankfully, this one was tall enough for me to stand up straight, allowing me a full breath of air.

I let my hands glide over the rocky wall, finally landing on a place where the very thinnest glow appeared in the shape of a large half-moon door. This was a different way out than the entrance I'd come through. My sweater would be left behind, a clue that I'd been to see the prisoners. Hopefully, nobody would notice until it was too late. With any luck, we wouldn't be here much longer.

I rested my hands on the stone, but before I could murmur the password, a commotion began in the tunnel behind me. One of the guards had tripped, judging by his curses.

"Sorry," Peter said. "You caught on my leg there."

"What are you doing out here?"

"Getting some exercise," he said, glibly. "It's not working so well, is it? You guys managed to catch me, and you're not especially fast."

"Who's with you?" the guard growled. "I heard talking."

"Nobody."

"We heard voices."

"You heard *my* voice." Peter launched into a humming melody, somewhere between a song and a chant. "It's my exercise music."

"Where is he?"

"Who?" Peter's voice grew in volume and in urgency. "There is nowhere to go. You're welcome to look around."

There was a slap, a roar, and I heard a body crumple to the floor. *Peter.*

I hesitated, torn between going back for him and pressing onward. My fingers brushed the crumpled paper in my pocket, however, and it gave me the burst I needed to push all feelings, thoughts, worries away. Everyone's safety depended on me not getting caught.

The footsteps began pounding toward my direction, and I made my move. Resting my hands on the door, I whispered, "Open Sesame."

It swung open, exposing a dark cavern beyond. I moved through, following a pinprick of light from within. As the stone rolled open, however, it crunched—rock against rock—with enough force that the guards had to have heard it.

I pushed the door closed and sealed the entrance with a quick locking charm. It wouldn't hold for more than a few minutes, but it would hopefully be enough time for me to find my way out of here.

Glancing around, I got my bearings and realized I was in a quiet wing of the castle. It would be impossible for me to find Bartholomew and Belinda; I'd been unconscious when they'd brought me to the entrance, and this was an entirely different exit.

The only thing left to do was find my way back to my room as inconspicuously as possible and wait there. They'd return, sooner or later.

No sooner had I taken two steps than a voice called out from the opposite end of the hallway, a voice that made me freeze in my tracks.

"Lily, there you are." Lucian stepped from a doorway. "Good evening."

"I...I got lost." I hated how he had an uncanny way of appearing in the right places at all the wrong times. "Just looking for a way back to my room."

He closed the distance between us. "I'd be happy to walk you back."

"No, it's fine. Just a point in the right direction and—"

My response was interrupted by a door opening behind me. I turned, rigid with surprise, to find two men in guard uniforms standing behind me. Peter was hunched over between them, one of the men holding him by the collar of his shirt.

My mouth fell open at the first sight of Peter in full light. It'd been just a few days since he'd been taken, but already his skin had a yellowish, grimy tinge from living in utter darkness, and his clothes—a standard-issue baggy white shirt and pants—had browned with grime.

"Sir, we found him escaped from his cell," one of the guards said, spotting me out of the corner of his eye as he spoke. "Who is she? We have a reason to believe he had a partner with him. His partner is missing."

Peter and I made eye contact. I forced myself to look away before the pain on my face made our connection obvious.

"I don't see anyone around here who qualifies," Lucian said, his voice thin as he chastised the guard. "Do you?"

"Who is *she*?" the second guard asked, pointing at me. His eyes turned darkly suspicious, but before he could continue, Lucian silenced him.

Physically.

He extended a hand and pinched the air. The guard's body slumped limp to the ground.

"Stop!" I yelled, rushing toward the guard. "You can't throw around blood magic like that!"

Kneeling over him, I checked for breathing. The guard wasn't hurt, wasn't even unconscious. He sat up almost at once, pushing me away. He opened his mouth to talk, but nothing came out. His eyes widened, he spoke again, and still...*nothing.*

"What did you do?" I turned to my father. "Give him his voice back."

"As you wish," Lucian said with another flick of his wrist. He sounded almost annoyed. "He's unharmed."

"That's not the point." I brushed myself off and backed away. "That's no way to lead."

"You will not talk about my daughter like that again," Lucian said to the guard, ignoring me. "Understood?"

The guard nodded, then bowed. "Apologies, Sir. Ma'am."

"I'm not—" I started, but Lucian waved the guards away.

I watched as the guards dragged Peter off, my soul cringing as I was forced to stand by and watch. But it was as Peter wanted. I gripped the paper in my pocket for strength.

"Let us talk," Lucian said, stepping to my side. "Walk with me. I'll return you to your room."

We began moving in silence. Once the guards had disappeared, his eyes flicked over at me, curious. I didn't meet his gaze.

His voice turned icy as he spoke. "This gala is in honor of you, Lily. I expect proper behavior at it. And let me be clear, I'm *not* asking politely."

"You've no right to demand anything of me."

"Did you find your cousin?" he asked, changing the subject. He studied my face and found his answer there. "Good. Then you've seen she's still alive. But if you want that vampire to live, you'll behave this evening."

My blood ran cold. "Are you threatening me?"

"Never you, darling." He reached out and tucked a hair behind my ear. "Never you."

My body went into shock at the touch of his hand. I couldn't move, couldn't push him away. The thoughts of poor Poppy, locked alone in her cell with no memory of how she'd gotten there—no memories at all—stilled my desire to recoil away from him.

Stick to the plan, I told myself. However, a voice in the back of my head niggled there, haunting me. The plan may be broken now that

Peter had been discovered—I couldn't imagine the guards would let him attend the gala after his stunt. Without Peter, our distraction was gone, and without a distraction, we'd be at a major disadvantage.

"Get away from me," I said, finally finding my voice and stepping back. "I will never respect you."

We'd reached a now-familiar corridor, and I fled toward my room.

"Maybe not yet," he said, following me to my door as I forced it open. "But until you do, you can fear me."

Chapter 31

I SPENT THE FIRST MINUTES of my father's absence fuming. I paced around my room in circles until the anger had burned to a simmer, and finally, I was able to redirect my frustrations to a proactive task.

I first secured the travel belt against my waist, then slipped the gala dress over my head. I made sure to arrange it so that the tiny pockets I'd sewed earlier into the skirt allowed access to my supplies. As a knock sounded on the door, I added the note from Peter into a pocket, too.

"Did you find them?" Belinda asked after she and Bartholomew slipped inside. "What happened? We waited for you for ages."

"He was here." Bartholomew glanced around, sniffed, and shook his head. "His magic is all over this room. That, and you look incredibly upset."

"He...spared me," I said. "I mean, I guess. He knows I found Poppy."

"Here, darling, let me help." Bartholomew moved to his makeup displays on the table and grabbed some lipstick and a few brushes. He set to work on my face without waiting for permission. "Belinda, the hair."

Belinda came around, sympathy in her eyes, and plucked through my hair until it twisted into a stunning up-do. Bartholomew performed a near-miracle in transforming my face into something soft and gentle, reflecting emotions that could never exist in my current state of unrest.

When they finished, I studied myself in the mirror. Quite possibly, this was the most beautiful I had ever looked. Quite possibly, I'd never felt worse.

"Thank you," I said. "I'm sorry, I need a minute." Throwing the balcony doors open, I stepped into the darkness outside. Although it should've been sunset, nothing but the dead of night—pitch black, not even the glimmer of stars or the glow of the moon—encompassed the land.

My knuckles tightened around the railing as I looked over the destruction below. My mind swam with every item that could go wrong during the gala, everything that could implode and make all of this worse.

"You are doing your best," Belinda said, easing through the French doors to stand next to me. "You can't put all of this pressure on yourself; you're just one person. We're here to help you. Use us, trust us."

I bit my lip, tears pricking at my eyes. The weight felt crushing, cutting off my breath, but I had to take action. With a nod, I reached into my skirt to withdraw a tiny vial of Long Isle Iced Tea.

Handing it to Belinda, I nodded for Bartholomew to listen, too. "Stick together and drink this when you see...things happening."

"What will it do?"

I explained the qualities of the potion, leaving most of the plan in shadows. It would be best if fewer details were public knowledge.

"Will there be a distraction?" Belinda asked. "How will we know when to drink it?"

"I'm working on it," I said. "My first plan fell apart. I'm coming up with a backup plan."

"I can help," Belinda said. "If you need me, I will help. I can stay behind if you promise to come back for me."

"No, Belinda," I looked into her eyes and saw only strength there. "I made a promise to you, and I will keep it. We're getting you both out of here."

"What went wrong in there?" she asked, curious. "Something with your plan is off—what is it?"

"They captured the man who volunteered to create a distraction," I said, a surge of guilt washing over me. "His name is Peter, and he sacrificed himself so that I could get away from the guards."

"Let me take care of it," Belinda said, squeezing my hand. "Just promise you'll come back for me."

"Belinda—"

"It's time to go," she said briskly. "And, Lily..." She scanned me over, blinking too quickly. "You really do look beautiful."

Bartholomew nodded in agreement, and it was on a somber note that we left the room. A guard greeted me outside. It wasn't the same one, thankfully, who'd been in the tunnel and would've recognized me. This one arrived dressed in an impeccable suit, a stern expression, and a posture more rigid than a concrete wall.

"Thank you," I said to Bartholomew and Belinda as he led me away. "For everything."

We marched in silence, my gown making gentle swishing noises over the ground. The guard's shoes squeaked against the polished floors, and together we made our way toward a soft symphony of sounds.

"Where is the gala?" I asked. "Is *he* meeting us there?"

The guard didn't answer, instead opening a door before me to a new wing. We stepped through into a small chamber, subtly glamorous with its rich red curtains, decorative rugs, and golden-lined accessories.

Statues stood in corners of the room and artwork hung from the walls. A small drink cart sat in the corner, holding crystal goblets and a selection of beverages.

"Something to drink?" Another man in a suit, a butler of some sort, waited expectantly for my answer to his question.

I shook my head. "No, thank you."

The guard who'd accompanied me stood at the door we'd entered, and I hovered somewhere near an oversized chair in the corner. Another door sat along the far side of these chambers, and from behind it, I could hear the rustles of a large crowd.

"Where are we?" I asked again. "Is the stage behind that door?"

The butler, thankfully, was chattier than the guard. "We're in the small chambers behind the gathering space. Through that door is the stage where your father will be presenting you to the masses. I'd be happy to fix you a beverage to calm your nerves, Miss Locke."

"No, thank you," I said again. "Where is Lucian?"

The butler flinched at my use of his first name. "He is in a meeting, Miss Locke. He shall arrive shortly."

As if on cue, two male voices rang out from down the hallway. The butler let out a smile and set to preparing two beverages.

"That'll be him," he chirped, once the two goblets had been filled with liquid, one full of wine, the other of an amber-colored cocktail. "You'll likely meet Mr. Liam, as well."

"Mr.—" I couldn't process, couldn't register anything before the two men stepped into the room.

If I thought my blood had gone cold before, I'd been wrong.

"No," I breathed, my blood turning to ice at the sight of him standing too close to my father. "*Liam*?"

The men had been speaking to one another in almost pleasant tones, and judging by the way my father leaned toward Liam and mumbled into his ear, they appeared to be close. Close enough to share confidences.

Liam looked up, shock registering on his face, and he, too, stilled. The rest of the room faded away, save for the sight of the two men conspiring with one another.

After all of this, after all my frustrations, fears, and doubts... then *this.* One of the men I trusted the most had been a traitor the whole time I'd known him.

"I trusted you," I said, my voice a hoarse whisper. "I confided in you."

"She wasn't supposed to be here." Liam turned to my father, his voice rough. "Why is she here?"

"What's the problem?" Lucian turned a bright smile between us, and I had the sneaking suspicion he'd orchestrated this whole event. "It looks like we're all friends already. We can skip the introductions."

"No, we can't," I said. "Who is he?"

"Lily, I can explain—" Liam began, but my father cut him off.

"My oldest friend and confidant," Lucian said. "The first, and only one, to figure out that I was still alive. Save for your mother, I suppose."

"No." I shook my head, backing into the wall. Instead of the wall, however, my legs hit the oversized chair, and I collapsed into it. "No, no, no. Out of everyone on The Isle, Liam, I trusted you. Gus trusted you, and Ranger X."

"That is the beauty of it all," Lucian said. "That's what sacrifice is about."

"Shut up," Liam snarled at Lucian, and even the butler stilled. "Why is she *here*?"

"It doesn't matter," I snapped. "You're willing to sacrifice everything?! What is this about? Ilinia?" My eyes smarted as I looked at him, searching, praying for understanding.

"Lily, please." Liam crossed the room and took a knee before the chair. "You have got to listen."

I sat up, disappointment ringing through every bone in my body. "I need to listen to nothing. Let's get this over with." I spoke over him, facing my father. "Is everything ready? Let's do what needs to be done. Now. Start the gala."

"You have to understand," Liam said. "I wasn't doing this to hurt anyone."

"Well, you did." I looked into his eyes, saw too much there, and had to direct my glance elsewhere. "Get away from me."

"Please—" He reached for my hand, but I shoved it away and jumped to my feet.

"Stay away from me," I snarled. "Do not touch me."

Silence encompassed the room until the butler cleared his throat. "The stage is prepared, sir."

"Lily," Lucian said. "Let us begin our journey together."

I followed my father through the door, hardly able to comprehend everything that was happening. I couldn't meet Liam's gaze, couldn't look back at him. He made no move to explain, no further apology.

As I moved behind my father, the world around me faded to a dull buzz. We stepped on stage, and a sea of people filled the banquet hall. Standing room only, hands thrust in the air, deafening shrieks of excitement surrounded us. There were hundreds, maybe even thousands of them. People hanging onto Lucian's every word.

All of it was a haze. I could feel nothing, see nothing.

When my father clasped my hand, raised it, and forced me to wave to the crowd, I couldn't stop him. I couldn't process any of it.

The only thing I could see was Liam, watching from the wings, a heavy sorrow in his eyes.

Then my father launched into his speech, and I was guided to sit down by one of the many guards on stage. I sat, tucking the dress around me, struggling to remember the plan. The escape. I'd formulated a backup plan for a distraction. It would be risky, but it was better than staying here another night.

Lucian spoke about this being a proud moment for him, a moment in which he could bring his daughter by his side to help with the cause. Then, he asked if I would say a few words.

I moved forward, almost sedated by shock. There were no words for me to say, nothing that would make this moment go away. Nothing.

I stepped up to the microphone, a sea of bright, anticipating faces waiting for me to speak high praises of my father. Clearing my throat, I fought back a wave of nausea. All I could think of was the hurt and pain that misunderstandings had caused—secrets buried, lives taken. Then my thoughts turned to Belinda offering herself in place of Peter, who'd already offered himself—for *me*. For something larger than himself.

The tiniest flame began to burn again, the foundations of everything I believed still there, albeit shaken. Looking out over the crowd, I sought for a familiar face, just one, but there were none. Until I saw Liam, still waiting, watching from the wings—a man I'd considered my friend, now the right hand of the enemy.

"Tonight," I said, taking a deep, shuddering breath. "I came here—"

A low, distant rumble began. I hesitated, cast a glance behind me, but nobody else seemed to notice. They were too focused on the speech, too caught up in the excitement.

A thrill ran through me. I couldn't explain why, but something was happening. Belinda had pulled through. I knew it. I just had to stall, until—

The rumbling grew louder, and a murmur of unease rose through the crowd. Mere seconds later, the room began to shake, regal marble columns near the back began to topple, and screams of fear replaced those of excitement.

Curtains tore, statues tumbled, artwork shuddered and slipped from the wall.

The distraction had arrived.

For the first breath, everyone stopped, watching the surroundings crumble around us.

And then, the room melted into chaos.

"Lily!" Liam yelled through it all.

I glanced behind me, saw understanding in my father's eyes as terror rose through the congregation, and I made my move. Slipping one hand into my dress I pulled out the vial for Poppy's potion and took a sip, willing myself to be a guard.

At the same time, I leapt from the stage and into the pandemonium below.

The time had come for escape.

Chapter 32

A SUGARY SWEETNESS slipped down my throat and into my stomach as the potion began its work. A sizzling sensation, and then the morphing of my clothing to resemble that of the guards.

Unfortunately, I had yet to see a female guard, so my clothing resembled a man's outfit—black pants, black shirt. Thankfully, they wore hats, which allowed me to hide my hair and shield part of my face underneath the rim.

Nobody noticed the change—everyone in the crowd scrambled for exits, clawing past one another to be first from the building. A few cries of help came my way as people pleaded for answers from the guards.

I didn't listen to any of them. I moved swiftly toward the right side of the room as we'd first planned. Belinda must've come up with a distraction, and I hoped she'd managed a way to join the escape.

For now, though, we were all on our own. We were each responsible for making it to the meeting place. Anyone who didn't make it would be left behind.

In the panic, I was jostled left and right, received an elbow to the gut, and a stomp on the foot. It was nearly impossible to follow a straight line, and my trajectory ended up curved and jagged.

"Guard," a voice murmured quietly. "Guard, *help*."

My eyes flashed to my right toward the sound of the voice. It was Manuel, and he had a half-smile on his face.

"That way's the exit," I murmured. "Are the other *guards* coming?"

"We're all en route," he said, then chanced a wink through the chaos. "Nice work, Mixologist."

We separated, moving in the same direction, ducking and dodging the rest of the chaos as the rumbling grew louder still, and chunks of the gorgeously painted ceiling began to crumble.

Whoever had launched the distraction should be proud; it had worked better than anticipated. We were close, so close...close enough to see the door.

My heart pumped, and I wondered if possibly, maybe, this would work. I rested my hands at my waist to feel the comfort of the vials. The travel belt had remained secure when my dress had morphed into the guard costume.

Our time, however, was running out. The guard costumes would only work for another few minutes. I hadn't had enough potion to go around to last any longer, so we needed to move.

The door loomed before me, just paces away.

Jonathon appeared to my left, another cheeky wink coming from his direction as he spoke. "The guards are gathering outside. You're the last one. Let's move, Locke."

A sense of relief seeped through my veins as I nodded. "Good."

He ducked through the door first. I hung back one last second, glancing toward the stage. Lucian was nowhere to be seen, and neither was Liam. Pandemonium raged onward as a chandelier swung back and forth from the ceiling before crashing to the floor in the center of the room.

Turning from the chaos, I stepped outside of the castle.

"Lily." A hand grasped my wrist firmly and pulled me to the side. "Wait."

I blinked, heart racing, to find Liam standing before me. He looked ragged. Concern lined his face.

"Get away," I whispered. "I trusted you."

"I can explain."

"I don't have time," I said, a slight tingling starting at the back of my scalp signaling the potion leaving my blood. "You don't have to explain, just...leave me alone."

"I'm here to help you," he said, his voice flat. He neither pleaded nor begged, simply spoke. "You have to trust me. This is for the best."

"What's best is for you to let go of me."

Liam's eyebrows knitted together, his face, normally handsome and assured, struggled to stay calm. His hand gripped mine tightly and squeezed harder. He opened his mouth to say something, then closed it and backed away, letting my hand drop.

I allowed myself a single look back at him, and then I turned and pressed onward. Fighting not to glance over my shoulder, I moved quickly to the meeting place Manuel had suggested, a small garden near the side of the building that was shielded by rows of tall, thick pines. I stepped under the trellis, pushed through hanging vines, and found a group of ten individuals waiting for me.

Manuel stepped forward and gestured to the group around us. I recognized Poppy, Magdalena Sprite, Jonathon, Drew, Bartholomew, and Belinda. A wave of relief came at the sight of these familiar faces. Three others had joined them, all wearing the traditional prisoner garb.

Absent, of course, was Peter.

"Belinda, how did you...?"

"The distraction wasn't mine," she said with a shake of her head. "I had prepared something, not to this effect, but before I could set off my plan...this happened."

"Then who set off the bomb?"

The group looked around at one another, but nobody had an answer.

"We'll figure it out later," I said. "Everyone ready? This is the riskiest part. Just remember: *they can't hurt you*."

One by one, the guard outfits began to fade. I'd already lost my hat, and my uniform was slowly turning a faint blue shade that meant it was well on its way to returning to its original ball gown state.

"Everyone remember their routes?" Jonathon asked, the strategist behind this piece of the journey. "Stay the course, no matter what. If anyone doesn't make it...just keep going. We'll meet at the designated location. Lily, do you have everything you need?"

I brushed my hand against my waist, feeling the vial with the antidote that would hopefully give us just enough juice to break the curse. We only needed time and space for the ten of us to slip through; it *should* be enough, but we wouldn't know until we tried.

"I don't want to leave Peter behind," I said, feeling a pull to go back to the castle. "The others."

"We'll need to come back," Manuel said. "Stay the course, Lily. The only way to help them is to get out of here, and then come back. Returning to the castle will not help anything. The islanders need you there."

"Who's Lily?" Poppy asked, dazed as she stared around the circle. "Is that my name?"

My heart twisted. "Poppy," I said. "Your name is Poppy. I'm your cousin, Lily."

She chewed on it for a moment, but not a slice of recognition passed through her eyes.

"I've altered the routes to fit the updated distraction," Jonathon said. "Manuel is the strongest, so he'll go with Poppy. We must move before the costumes disappear. The farther we get before they revert, the better."

I swallowed and nodded, then I moved to Poppy and asked her for a hug. With a confused, loopy grin, she smiled and put her arms around me. I blinked away tears, savoring the familiar moment.

Then, I stepped back and surveyed the group. "Let's go."

One by one, we spread to the edges of the garden. We all had different routes to take through the castle grounds, all of them emerging at a discreet corner of the city limits where the curse met the land. The place where, if my antidote worked correctly, we would escape.

On Jonathon's signal, the mass exodus began. First Bartholomew and Belinda, then Manuel and Poppy.

Two by two, pairs left the garden and started on their paths, hunched to keep out of sight for as long as possible. Jonathon had created all the routes and designed them to spread the guards of the castle as thin as possible.

If we all made it, it would be close to a miracle.

"Ready?" Jonathon raised his eyebrow, having paired himself with me. "We're due to get there first. It should give you a few minutes to prepare the potion before the others arrive."

I nodded as my costume slowly bled from black to blue. I'd be running in a dress in minutes. "Wait." I kicked off my shoes, which would soon transform back into high heels. "Okay, now we can go."

Jonathon gave a grim smile, but a layer of excitement twinkled in his eyes. Underneath the severity of all this, there was a hint of adventure, of risk, of challenge that he was obviously thriving on.

"Right this way, Miss Locke." He pushed two small trees apart and stuck his head through. When he determined the coast was clear, he waved for me to follow. "Stay close. If anything happens—"

"Go," I interrupted. "We'll talk later."

He laughed. "I like having you around, Miss Locke."

"Lily."

He hesitated just before stepping through and extended a hand. "Lily."

We shook, but I watched him in confusion. "Is everything okay?"

"It's been a pleasure to know you during our short time together."

"Jonathon—"

"The guards are heading to the garden, right on schedule," he said, then snapped his fingers. "Damn, I'm a good strategist. Follow closely."

I did as he said, staying close behind as Jonathon weaved his way through gorgeously manicured castle grounds. Under a sparkling sun, this place would dazzle. Under the darkness of curses, it spooked.

As we moved from the castle grounds to the city surrounding it, the town created to support Wishery, I hesitated for a glimpse back. Made from glass the pale blue of Cinderella's slipper, the castle glistened and winked, even under the raging black shadows. Cute cottages, quaint shops, little parks and bakeries and flower gardens lined every street. The view filled me with wonder.

We made our way in and out of the abandoned homes and shops. It hadn't taken long for this place to go from a bustling, charming space to a ghost town filled with whispers, shadows, something darker lurking behind every nook and cranny.

"We're a bit ahead of schedule," Jonathon said, looking up at the skies as he picked the lock to an abandoned Sweet Shop. "The rest of the guards will be getting called to the castle now, and our path will open up in just a second..."

"Jonathon. Why'd you pair yourself with me?"

He glanced in my direction. "I made the plan; I knew it best. Figured I should be with the Mixologist."

"In case of what?" I shook my head. "Everyone's getting out of here. If you have some other plan underneath this, I forbid it. I won't let it happen."

"You'd make for a great gamer yourself," he said with a wink. "No time to talk. Let's move. After these next few blocks, we'll be at the rendezvous point."

"Jonathon—"

He grabbed my wrist, pulled me through the back of the candy store, swiping a stick of licorice along the way. "Energy," he said by way of explanation.

We exited through the back, snaking through a confusing series of alleys and continuing until the city center gave way to a more rolling countryside where houses were scattered fewer and farther between.

"See that line of trees?" Jonathon asked. "That's it, just behind them. It'll provide a bit of protection, hopefully long enough to get everything set up."

I nodded, palms slick with sweat.

"The second we leave here," Jonathon said, gesturing to the bale of hay we'd taken shelter behind, "the situation becomes a ticking clock. You have no more than seven minutes to get your potion working and everyone through that hole."

"Understood."

"Lily?" Jonathon waited until I met his gaze, and then smiled. "Good luck."

Before I could respond, he bolted, and I had no choice but to follow. I sprinted as fast as my legs could carry me, tumbling once into a hole. Jonathon didn't hesitate, stopping to haul me out of the divot before continuing on his way.

My uniform had faded back to the ball gown now, and it whipped in the breeze along with my hair. The wind picked up, the storm cracking around us with the curse close enough to touch. My skirt was ripped into shreds, my face heated, and I had scratches on my arms from snaking behind buildings and stumbling through trees.

"Here," Jonathon breathed. "Go."

We slipped behind a row of evergreens as what remained of my skirt billowed around me. It took all my might to control my clothes as I fished for the vials tucked into my travel belt.

Pulling them loose, I called for Jonathon to hold the first one.

He shook his head, not hearing. The wind whisked around us, screeching, screaming, turning and churning as wisps of black hurtled through the air. I hadn't anticipated a tornado, and these gale force winds wreaked havoc as I tried to pour the silver into the rest of the potion.

"Come on," I whispered as a tiny fleck escaped and landed on the ground. I couldn't waste so much as a breath, or everything would fall apart. "Come on...*there*. It's mixed."

Jonathon couldn't hear a word I said, but he caught the look on my face as I held up the vial. At the same time, Belinda and Bartholomew arrived, hand in hand, their faces red and chests puffing from exertion.

"Are we first?" Bartholomew yelled.

I couldn't hear him, but I could read his lips, and I nodded. Then I gestured for him to stand back as I approached the edge of the Wishery magic, the angry dome over the city, and set down the vial. I whispered the words to invoke the antidote, then pushed it closer to the blackness. An inch closer, and then it began.

The potion invoked with a curl of smoke, purplish in color, and began to wind its way upward. Magdalena Sprite and Drew arrived next, eyes glowing as they pointed toward the vial and watched in awe as it began to work.

The smoke grew and grew as another pair arrived. With eight of us present, the only pair missing was Poppy and Manuel. Meanwhile, the purple smoke rose like a snake, coiled, and eventually spread to the blackness around it.

Little puffs of white followed wherever the purple contacted the black, the antidote absorbing bits and pieces, little by little, of the curse.

"Where's Poppy?" I asked, yelling into Jonathon's ear. "She was supposed to arrive after Magdalena!"

He thumbed over his shoulder where, in the far distance, Poppy hobbled against Manuel's shoulder. "I'm going to help them. Get everyone else through."

By now, the antidote had opened a hole in the curse the size of a small circle. I gestured wildly for the others to approach and gathered them into a line.

I waited, counting under my breath for the moment it would be safe to press through. Finally, I reached the count of seven and, true to plan, the hole in the curse was large enough.

"Belinda, you're first!" I waved her through. "When you're on the other side—listen to me, Belinda—"

Belinda's lips trembled, but she nodded.

"Make a wish," I said, my voice nearly a shout. "A true wish on the first star you see. Wish harder than anything you've ever wished for, and ask for help from Wishery. Specifically, ask for Lizzie and Ainsley. Got it? Wish on a star, Belinda."

She nodded again, bit her lip, and squeezed my hand. Then, she took one step through and vanished to the other side. The air shimmered, bounced back like a bubble, and then righted itself.

The vial continued to smoke on the ground, already halfway gone. I nudged it closer to the curse with my foot. "We've got to move faster! Bartholomew, you're up."

The makeup artist went through next, then Magdalena and Drew. The other pair was just disappearing as the vial began to splutter.

I squinted past the trees and found Poppy, Manuel, and Jonathon in my sights. They were making their way at a steady pace, but not fast enough. I began to yell for them to hurry, but my words were eaten by a gust of wind and drowned by the voice behind me.

"So, it's come to this."

I whirled and came face to face with my father.

He gestured to the hole in his curse. "I should've known...if anyone could break this magic, it would be my daughter."

"Don't call me that."

"It's impossible to deny. You and I, we share DNA."

"That's all we'll ever be—shared DNA," I said, catching a glimpse of Poppy out of the corner of my eye. "That doesn't make a family."

He caught my glance toward Poppy and nodded in understanding. "Here's my proposal. I'll let them through, but you stay with me."

"I'll stay with you, but you'll have to kill me before I ever agree to join you."

We were close enough that our voices could just be heard over the roar of the wind, but neither Jonathon nor Manuel had spotted Lucian yet. They'd focused all their attention on Poppy, pulling her behind the trees.

"Here they are," Lucian said, stepping into the shadows and out of sight from Jonathon. "I'll let you make your choice. I will wait out of sight, so the others don't have to see me. But if you disobey me, I will make my presence known."

My mouth snapped shut as I watched my father melt into the shadows. At the last second, I jumped to attention and hurried to help Manuel with Poppy.

"Let's get her through," I said, trying to be nonchalant—hoping it'd be enough to distract the rest of the group from the shadowy figure lingering just behind the trees. "The vial's almost out."

Manuel nodded, clambering toward the opening in the curse. Nobody looked back; an air of excitement had hit with the thought that maybe we'd all make it out alive.

"Poppy first," I instructed. "Manuel, you follow her."

"But—" Manuel glanced at me.

"Go to Sophie," I said. "Thank her for helping us."

Jonathon leaned closer to me as Manuel climbed through just after Poppy. "That sounded like a goodbye."

"Nope," I said, pursing my lips. "You go next because I have to close the curse."

He glanced over my shoulder. I tried to block his view, but it didn't work. Jonathon looked at me in confusion as he caught sight of the shadowy figure behind the trees.

"Lily!" His eyes grew in understanding at what I'd planned to do, but it was too late.

"I'm sorry," I said, just as I bit my lip and shoved him with all my might, sending Jonathon through the opening and beyond Wishery.

"Very good," Lucian said, stepping out of the darkness. "Now, close the vial."

I glanced down at the antidote, now puffing little clouds of smoke. It had less than ten seconds on it. I debated for a second, diving through the opening, but I couldn't. I couldn't risk it for their sakes. If Belinda had done as I'd asked, wishing upon a star, it might appear on Lizzie's radar and the MAGIC, Inc. folks would surely rescue them.

Reaching for the cap, I picked up the vial, but before my fingers grazed it, an arm shot through the opening and yanked. I began to tumble head first, skidding into the grass on the other side as my eyes made contact with Jonathon's.

The opening in the curse began to close, shrinking rapidly. Manuel reached for me and pulled me, dragging me away from Wishery and into the fields beyond the curse. I screamed as a spell shot through, expanding the hole for one last minute.

It hit Jonathon in the chest, and he cried out, no longer safe underneath the dome of blackness. The spell that'd both kept him captive and protected him from physical harm ceased to exist outside of Wishery.

Crumbling forward, he landed on his knees as the spell pulled him forward.

I yelled out, reaching for him as Manuel lunged, too, but we were too far away. Jonathon, eyes blank and unseeing, fell toward the rapidly closing portal, his breathing halted.

I had a snap decision to make my move. *Now or never, and I choose now.*

Closing my eyes, I concentrated and reached for the black magic circling the city. I'd spent so much time studying the darkness that I'd become strangely in tune with it. As I could manipulate potions, I discovered, so could I manipulate their evil counterparts.

Channeling a pillar of black smoke, I sent it spiraling past Jonathon and directly at Lucian. His eyes widened, seeing the attack, his hands too full with Jonathon to deflect it. The curse bowled into his shoulder, a neat, sharp little spiral that burned through his flesh and pulled a scream from him that shattered a piece of myself. He crumpled to his knees, too weak to fight back.

Do Good. That was my one task as the Mixologist.

No matter what Lucian had done, it didn't matter.

I'd broken my promise. I'd *caused harm.*

From Lucian's perch on the ground, his eyes turned black, smoky with the curse that'd permeated his body. He lashed out one final time, sending poison green flames to lick the edges of the portal.

Manuel yelped, forced to pull back. By the time I'd unfrozen and lunged to help, the flames were too strong, the opening too small. We'd failed.

As the portal shrunk, Jonathon's eyes met mine, a reluctant smile frozen on his face as he knelt at the feet of my father.

Then, with a final pop, the curse sealed.

Wishery had closed once again.

Chapter 33

THEY PUT ME IN A ROOM to wait.

So, I waited, hands curled into my lap for what felt like hours.

Finally, the door to the sterile conference room burst open and Ranger X appeared there, his hair a mess, his clothes more rugged in appearance than usual. His breath came out a gasp.

"Lily."

I opened my mouth to greet him, but only a sigh escaped. With a concerned expression, he glanced over his shoulder at Ainsley, who'd opened the door for him. She nodded.

X crossed the room in three steps, pulling me from my chair and crushing me into a hug. He nuzzled his head to my neck, and I'm certain my feet left the floor as his arms crunched the wind from my lungs.

"What happened?" he demanded, as Ainsley quietly backed out of the room and closed the door. "I'm so sorry we didn't arrive sooner; I knew something was wrong when you weren't at the bungalow, but..."

"Lucian came to visit me," I said, gritting my teeth. "It wasn't the family reunion I'd dreamed of."

"Did he hurt you?"

"I'm fine, but others aren't. People were left behind in Wishery," I said. "We have to go back."

"Ainsley told me you rescued eight people."

"Sure. But how many are still waiting?"

A glimmer of dismay flickered in X's eyes. "You are safe. That's what's most important."

A burst of fury rose inside me, and I stepped back from him, my hands balled into tight little fists. "How can you say that?! I still *failed.* You know it, too. If the situation were reversed, you would be saying the same thing."

Despite the heated reaction, my stomach plummeted as I looked up into those eyes, the expression that'd shown me the meaning of falling for another, of getting lost in a gaze so deeply I didn't care to look away.

I saw in his expression a pain there, a worry that sliced deeper through him than anything he'd felt before; I could say this with confidence because I knew, had the situation been reversed, that I would've felt the exact same way. It was only this knowledge that eased the fire skimming through my veins.

Subdued, I reached a hand out and rested it on his chest, over the heart that had taught me to love, to love so strongly it pained me to see him hurt. Then I stepped into the arms that'd taught me to trust, to lean on another when the world on my shoulders became too heavy to bear alone.

My cheek pressed into his chest, and his hands stroked my hair. My arms circled his back, held him close. My nails dug into his skin as I clawed at him. He didn't say anything, not a sound, as I let a silent stream of tears wet his chest.

Everything—the adrenaline, the complications, the discoveries—was too much. I crumbled against him, every piece shattering as he carefully, gently, gathered me back together.

"Come here, sweetheart." He sat on a black armchair in the corner of the room, and pulled me onto his lap.

My arms looped over his neck, and I leaned my face against his forehead as I curled in close. "I'm sorry. I love you, and I'm sorry about everything else."

"I've been *so worried* about you. I've been going insane trying to get you back, and nothing seemed to be working."

"I'm back, I'm okay," I whispered. "I promise; I'm here now."

"What if you hadn't come back?" He asked this with a tentative hitch in his voice, a tender turn of words. "What then, Lily? How could I have gone on without you?"

"You don't have to," I said, running a hand over his back. "I am fine."

"But without you..." Ranger X's hands came up to my shoulders, pulling me far enough back for him to study me, to drink in my features as if he'd thirsted for this moment. "I don't know how to *be* without you."

Cupping his chin in my palm, I brought his face to mine and kissed him. His lips met mine, sweet and sure, as his hands trailed over my body. My hips, my legs, my back.

"Lily," he said. "I've been thinking, and—"

At that moment, Ainsley re-opened the door, studied our position—too close for innocence—and apologized. "I'm really sorry, Lily," she said. "But someone's here to see you."

"I'm sorry," I said to X. "Can we finish this later?"

Struggling to get ahold of his expression, he gave a nod that wasn't entirely convincing.

Neither of us had a choice to continue the conversation, however, because at that moment, a thump against the floor signaled Gus's arrival. "I thought you said ten minutes would be long enough," he groaned, his face turning red as he stepped through the door. "They're still going at it."

"Give them some space," Hettie whispered to Gus, as if we couldn't hear them in the doorway to the conference room. "We'll come back when you're ready."

"Come in," I said on a sigh. "Consider the moment ruined."

Hettie shuffled in first, her gray hair showing hints of teal today. The purple tracksuit was back, and her shimmering sequins made a tittering sound as they brushed against Gus's cane when she pushed into the room.

"It's great to see you, Lily," my grandmother said, sounding proud. "I knew you'd get out of there; that's the West Isle Witch blood in you working its magic. And stubbornness. But why on earth are you dressed like *that*?"

"How do I put this..." I squinted. "Imagine if Cinderella lost both of her shoes, confronted a curse, and spent the night running through an abandoned town. That's why I'm dressed like this."

Behind Gus came Ainsley, and then Harpin. I surveyed the crowd with confusion, then turned a questioning glance on X. "Why is everyone here?" I asked. "I don't understand."

Hettie spoke first. "I called a meeting of The Core once you'd been confirmed missing."

"After the way I left things?" I frowned. "I didn't exactly leave the last meeting on a positive note."

"You had a reason for storming out," Hettie continued. "We were acting irresponsible and selfish, and for that, we're sorry."

Gus nodded in agreement.

"But," Hettie continued. "We'd never let one of our own disappear without fighting to bring him or her back."

"By the time we'd formulated any sort of plan," Ainsley said, "Lizzie had received a Wish Alert asking from help at Wishery's borders. Seems you broke free without us."

Hettie offered a grin. "That's my granddaughter."

"Yet you're still here," I said, sensing there was something they'd still not told me. I glanced around the group, none of them offering an explanation. Finally, it dawned on me. "You want to go back."

Hettie raised a finger. "We know *you* want to go back, and we're not letting you go at it alone."

"But—"

"We're a team," Hettie said, sounding more stern than usual. "And it's useless to argue. If you go back, we all go back."

Ranger X grimaced. "I don't like this idea. I don't think we should put Lily back in harm's way when she's just escaped. It's too risky."

"I'm sorry," Ainsley said, sounding truly apologetic. "But there's no other way. We need Lily to break the magic surrounding the castle. Gus, did you bring everything she'll need?"

Gus nodded. "The ingredients are being held in the lab."

"All the supplies?" I asked, then listed them off one by one. "Especially the silver?"

"All of it," Gus confirmed. "It's prepped and ready to be Mixed, which you can do on location."

"At least give her some time to recover," X argued, cinching me closer to his side. "She hasn't even caught her breath."

"I'm fine," I said. "The others, the ones still trapped in Wishery, are far worse off than me."

"I wouldn't ask if it wasn't of the *utmost* importance," Ainsley said, almost pleading as she focused her attention on X. "But the clock is ticking. We need to disperse the magic if we have any hopes of catching Lucian and his crew in the act."

"And Liam," I said.

Ranger X frowned, then faced me. "Liam?"

"He was at the gala," I whispered. "He seemed to be friends with my father."

Ranger X digested this, but eventually shook his head. "Impossible."

"I thought so too, but he was there and surprised to see me."

"Liam?!" Hettie crossed her arms. "What else have we missed?"

I took a brief moment to give the group a condensed version of my stay at the castle. I included everything, including Poppy's lack of memory. "Peter's still there," I added. "And Jonathon."

"And if we wait any longer," Ainsley said, "there's no telling what they might do. Our only hope is returning now and capitalizing on the pandemonium."

"You would do it for your men," I said, squeezing X's hand. "I'm not leaving anyone behind if I can help it."

"The only way to properly do this as a group is to vote." Hettie stepped into the center of the room and raised a hand. "All those who think we should follow Ainsley into battle, say aye."

"I didn't say battle," Ainsley said. "But *aye*."

I raised a hand, as did Gus. Harpin frowned, then raised his, too.

Eventually, all eyes turned to X. He rubbed his hand over his forehead, then added his hand to the raised pile. "Aye."

"Unanimous," Ainsley said with a tight smile. "Fabulous. Let me find us some brooms, and we'll be on our way."

"You"—X reached for my arm and pulled me close— "are staying next to me. Until this is over, you're not to leave my sight. Understood?"

"It'd be my pleasure to stand next to you," I said, sidling up beside him. "But don't think you get to tell me what to do."

"That's right," Hettie said. "Happy wife, happy life!"

X and I stopped dead in our tracks and turned to stare at Hettie. She covered her mouth with her hand, then turned and left the room with red cheeks.

"She didn't mean anything by it," I said after a pause.

At that moment, Gus re-entered the room with his arms full of vials and sacks brimming with supplies and spared us from further discomfort.

"Is this everything?" Gus asked. The rest of the ingredients were tucked into a series of vials fitted tightly into a suitcase. "I tried to travel light, but these ingredients are damn heavy."

"Looks good," I said to Gus, still distracted.

"Here are the sticks," Ainsley said, returning to pass out brooms. "Our plan is to fly to Wishery, set up shop so Lily can disperse the antidote, and then swoop in to free the prisoners. Anything—or anyone—else is extra."

All of us climbed to the flight deck and perched over the brooms as we stared out beyond the ledge, looking down at the miniature civilization below.

"It's nice to be back in business," Hettie said with a broad smile at the lineup of Core members. "I missed this group. And my broomstick. Remind me file a petition to allow these bad boys back onto The Isle."

"And now," Ainsley said, a grim set to her smile. "We fly."

Chapter 34

WE LANDED SOME THIRTY minutes later outside of Wishery city limits, stopping behind a well-covered, tree-lined street belonging to the humans.

The black cloud spiraled in front of us, angrier than ever, whipping so loudly it was difficult to speak. My dress fluttered around my ankles as we reached the place where we'd take a stand.

"Ready?" X asked. "You're up, Lily."

Kneeling, my hands fluttered over the ingredients, gathering and Mixing them until I'd filled several beakers. The Core stood around me in a tightly wound circle.

"I'm going to Mix more as we go," I said. "I think we should get started. This won't destroy the curse, but it'll dent it enough for us to get a view of what's happening inside. By the time they realize we're here, I'll have punctured enough holes to make the curse a sieve."

"I don't think that's the best route—" Harpin began, but was silenced by X's glare.

"You heard her," X said. "We're going with Lily's plan. Everyone ready?"

We'd carried the broomsticks with us, and one by one, we mounted them, rising into the air and keeping the circle intact. The potion had been dispersed, one vial to each person. I had more ingredients to Mix, but that would have to come later.

"It will hit the curse harder if we drop these at different locations. Harpin and Ainsley, you two take the far side. Hettie and X take the middle. Gus and I will stay here, so we can use this up and create more."

X nodded. "After we release the potions, then what?"

"Return here, so I can distribute the next round. The first opening large enough to fly through, let the rest of us know," I said, meeting everyone's gaze in turn. "Nobody's going in alone."

"On the count of ten," Hettie began. "Ten..."

The broomsticks began to separate as everyone spread to their posts. We each counted in our heads until the clock wound down to one.

On *zero,* all six broomsticks nosedived toward the ground, releasing the antidote as we swerved toward the black cloud. Gus and I were first, since we were the closest, and as soon as we'd hit the black magic, we pulled back to the ground and set to work on creating the next round of antidotes.

Hettie was the first of the others to return. "I got a peek inside—all seemed quiet."

X came back next. "Looked empty from where I was flying. Evacuated."

Harpin and Ainsley returned after, both confirming what X and Hettie had reported. "The streets were abandoned," Ainsley said. "If anyone's there still, they've retreated to the castle."

"Let's get another round in," I said, handing out another series of vials. "X, take this antidote and go—"

I never did tell him where to go because at that moment, arrows sailed at us. One of them struck Harpin on the arm, a black mark tearing at his skin as he clawed at his robes with a death-defying shriek.

"The arrows are *enchanted,*" X growled, pulling Harpin's arm toward him as he examined the wound. "Fall back!"

"The silver!" I cried, reaching for the bag of it. "I need..."

Even as I spoke, another arrow sailed toward the bag of silver, this one with a flaming tip. It hit the bag, sending the material up in smoke.

"No!" I lunged for it. "We need to destroy the black magic. We *need* the silver."

A pull on my arm held me back. I could only watch, mesmerized, as X's hands glowed gold, and he rose from the ground on his broomstick. The rest of us followed suit, Hettie shouting orders as we formed a tight, protective circle around X.

His eyes went all black, unseeing, and his face fell slack. Eventually, his fingers began to pluck at the air as if he played a silent instrument that nobody else could see or hear.

"Uncap your vials!" I yelled, as I threw the cork from mine to the ground.

Everyone followed along, understanding dawning as X's powers began to reveal his plan. Bit by bit, he pulled at imaginary strings on an atomic level, purple puffs of antidote dancing through the air as if he were sewing, puncturing the dome and piercing the black magic from every angle.

He was using his power, his Uniqueness—the telekinesis he had yet to master—to spread the antidote thin and cover every inch of the cloud. It just might work. If we could weaken the storm enough, we'd be able to reclaim Wishery once and for all.

"Protect him!" I screamed above the wail of the tornado-like winds. With a jolt, I remembered X's words, his fears. Using his power meant he was at his strongest...while also the most vulnerable. "Whatever you do, he can't get hurt."

"Nobody gets hurt," Ainsley snapped back. "Stay in a circle, keep your backs to one another. X in the middle."

X didn't respond, his gaze focused, almost trance-like as he pushed and pulled the remaining antidote in spirals around the black magic. He weaved it through, creating fissures that hissed and smoked as if pierced by a knife.

Meanwhile, enchanted arrows with glistening red tips sailed at us, cursed and intending to kill. Showers of sparks trailed behind, flames curling away in all directions.

Harpin grunted with pain, using only his good arm as the attack raged on. He maneuvered pillars of black ink extending from his fingers, moving them like the arms of an octopus and slashing through any arrows coming in his direction.

Ainsley hurtled MAGIC, Inc. spells, flinging them back toward the archers while Gus pulled the emergency vials he kept strapped to his chest, sending hexes in all directions.

I couldn't be sure what Hettie had planned, but she was screaming like a tribal warrior and sending flames from both fists towards the origins of the arrows. It seemed effective, so I let her be and focused, invoking a force-field like protective spell I'd learned from Zin.

"How much longer?" I shouted toward X. "Can you sense it?"

"The foundations are beginning to crack," he said, his voice almost musical. "Just a little longer."

"Nice job on the antidote, Lily," Hettie whooped. "That's my granddaughter!"

Harpin growled, ducking as a barrage of arrows leapt toward him. He swiped most of them away with the twitch of an inky arm, but it was Gus who sent a fire ball that singed the one closest to Harpin's head and quite possibly saved his life.

"Thanks," Harpin muttered.

"Shut up," Gus said. "Fight."

"I'm happy to see my boys working together," Hettie said with a high-pitched yip. "If we hold out a little longer, we'll wear them down."

"Stay tight," Ainsley yelled. "X is getting tired, and not an arrow gets through us."

Her last words rang out over a silent attack. The world rolled to a slow freeze, and we all waited as the flood of arrows dripped to nothing. Complete silence, save for the crackling of Ranger X's magic as he continued to thread the antidote through the strongest points of the dome holding Wishery captive.

"I don't like this," Ainsley whispered, her hands poised in front of her face. "It's too quiet."

I nodded in agreement, my breath coming in heaves. "This isn't over."

Gus held a purple cloud in one palm while Harpin let the black extensions of his arms wave in the slight breeze. Hettie shot a few fireballs into the sky while Ainsley's fingers sizzled with electricity.

"Where are you? Come out, come out, wherever you are..." Ainsley murmured. "They're preparing for the final att—"

Her last word became a screech as arrows sailed from every direction, circling us, pummeling our tight circle of defense. A flaming arrow sliced through my sleeve, setting it ablaze as it sailed past.

Ainsley slapped the flame out as Harpin covered us, wiping away a sheet of arrows sailing toward us. He nodded when I murmured a thank-you, and Ainsley grunted in agreement.

"Almost..." X said. "Done."

The next cry came from Hettie, a guttural screech that sent shivers down my spine. I stopped mid-toss of an enchantment, turning to find an arrow sticking out of my grandmother's shoulder. Its entrance was surrounded with black, the curse already spreading through her clothes and into her skin.

"No!" I yelled, as she began to tip from her broom. "Hettie!"

I launched into a nosedive as Hettie fell over and spiraled to the ground, her broomstick hovering in the sky. Arrows whistled past my ears. Harpin extended his inky arms on either side of me as I sailed toward Hettie, beating back the onslaught of an attack.

I landed on the ground just seconds before Hettie, tumbling off my broomstick and catching her in a weak embrace. We both crumbled to the ground, my body a pillow for Hettie's.

I ripped off a swatch of my dress and used it to press against Hettie's shoulder. "I'm sorry, but you're going to have to hold on through the pain. I can't remove the arrow or the curse will spread faster."

Arrows whistled above us. "Get up there," Hettie whispered. "Fight."

"I'm not leaving you." I removed Aloe Ale from my belt, a simple pain reliever that traveled everywhere with me, and pressed it to the site of the wound. "This will hold you off for now. I'm not leaving your side."

"You need to protect..." Hettie rasped for breath. "X. I know how his magic works; he's at great risk."

"But—"

"Go," Hettie said, her eyes blinking more slowly as the curse began to take hold of her veins. "I've got thirty minutes before the damage is irreparable. So, end things *quickly.*"

"I'm not leaving you. We'll get you back in no time. Just breathe, Hettie. Breathe."

"Your grandfather would've loved this. The Core, watching you up there..." Hettie forced a smile, her face going pale. "You're just like him, you know."

My lips tightened to return her smile.

"You're prettier, though," she said with a weak snort of laughter. "He had charm, but you've got the beauty."

"Hettie, stop. You're going to be fine."

"I know," she said, her voice a mere whisper in the swirling winds. "Look..."

I followed her shaking finger to watch above as X, face streaked with sweat and blood, a ferocious look in his eyes, waved both arms and sent a spiraling drill of golden energy straight toward the center of the black dome.

It flowed from him, into the black magic now rife with brilliantly clear air, and shattered it. The blackness dispersed with a piercingly high-pitched whine, puffing into clouds of purple, then white, and then finally...*nothing*.

Nothing.

No arrows, no blackness, no storming mass of evil, no curse.

The Core looked at one another from above, then carefully guided their broomsticks to the ground. As they did so, a transformation began. One by one, we looked to the sky and watched.

For the first time since its invasion, rays of sun hit the light-deprived city, spreading from street to street with a warming glow. The city shimmered with fresh air, and the castle beamed and glistened with a light so bright I had to look away.

When I finally turned my gaze back on the city, shimmering gold sunshine battled back the last of the black clouds, revealing a stunning, beautiful city in its wake.

Wishery.

I leaned against X as Harpin collapsed onto Gus. The old man, looking surprised, lent Harpin his walking cane as Ainsley crouched next to Hettie.

Harpin examined his arm, gave a shake of his head. "Lucky," he muttered, pulling back his clothing. "Just grazed the surface. Curse didn't get into the bloodstream."

"You're going to be fine," Ainsley said to him, and then turned to Hettie. "You are, too. Don't give up on me now, old woman."

"Who you calling old?" Hettie gasped. "I'm not...*old*."

Ainsley smiled. "We've got Curse Control on standby at MAGIC, Inc. Let's get you back."

X wrapped his arms around me, holding my weight against him even as he shook, drained from the effort of sustaining his magic for so long.

"I'm proud of you," X whispered against my hair. "That antidote was something else."

"It wouldn't have worked without all of us." I looked around at the group. Bruised, battered, exhausted. My limbs trembled with relief, with exhaustion. "Thank you all for not giving up on us."

"Amen," Hettie mumbled. "I like The Core."

"Can we get this woman some help?" Gus croaked. "I want to learn how she pulled that fireball trick."

"I'll carry her on my broomstick," I volunteered. "Hettie—"

"No." Hettie gave a barely perceptible shake of her head. "You and X stay behind."

"But—"

"There's something you need to do."

I looked up at X, who gave no signal either way. Reaching for Hettie's hand, I squeezed. "Are you sure you'll be okay?"

"Are you kidding? They're gonna have to work harder than this to kill me." Hettie plucked at her shirt. "If this is their best shot, I'm feeling pretty confident about our odds."

The group lifted Hettie into the air and carried her away, balanced on Ainsley's broomstick. Gus rode on one side, and Harpin on the other.

I took a deep breath and leaned against X. "My grandmother is a nut."

"Tough nut to crack." X put his hand on my shoulder. "So, what is it Hettie wants us to do?"

I slid my arm around his waist. "I have unfinished business in the castle. I don't want to go alone."

X leaned against me, his lips held against my forehead. "You won't be alone ever again," he said against my ear. "Not so long as I'm alive."

Chapter 35

I'D SPENT MORE THAN enough time inside Wishery, but as X and I returned, I didn't recognize a piece of it.

Where black clouds had contained the city, now blue skies expanded its reach to the ends of the earth. The buildings, though still abandoned, now shone with glimmers of life, of personality, of quirky decorations and broad windows. Wildlife rustled and chirped in the hedges, and store signs glittered against the sunlight. The castle itself gleamed as the opaque centerpiece of the city.

"What are we looking for?" X asked. "Or, should I ask, who?"

"Anyone. Survivors, prisoners...anyone left behind."

We perused the city as quickly as possible, poking our noses into shops and houses with unlocked doors. It quickly became clear, even as we worked our way to the castle, that Wishery remained empty of all inhabitants.

"Why don't we send in the Rangers to clean up? With more manpower, they'll be able to search this place faster. We're only two, Lily. You'll want to be next to your grandmother over the next few hours. It won't be pleasant for her."

"Two of us is enough. We're going into the castle; we didn't fight for nothing."

Into the castle we went, entering the crumbled ballroom still in disarray. We pressed on through the back room where I'd first glimpsed Liam's traitorous self, then moved down the halls and into the main branches of the castle.

Only silence greeted us. Absolute stillness.

"Where..."—X cleared his throat—"did they keep you?"

I gestured for him to follow me and, somehow, wound my way to the bedroom where I'd met Belinda and Bartholomew. We walked into the room, past the four poster bed, and up to the French doors that overlooked the city.

"The others had it worse," I explained, as the elegant room surrounded us.

"They kidnapped you."

"They gave me a bed," I said. "The others..."

X followed as I left the room, thankfully refraining from comment. A sense of relief had set in at the sight of the city below, the gorgeous greens and vibrant yellows returning the city to its former brightness.

"To the cells," I directed him. "Peter and Jonathon might still be here."

And Liam, I thought. But I didn't say that aloud.

I managed to find my way to the rocky caves where they'd kept Poppy, Manuel, and the others, but they were empty. All empty.

"It's time to go home," X said, his voice cracking with thirst. "We need to go home."

My throat was dry, too. We'd been searching for hours and found absolutely nothing. Except for the crumbled ballroom, everything looked to be in place.

"But—"

"Lily." X put his arms around me and held on so tight I couldn't breathe. "You have to let it go. We'll find them, bring them home, but they are no longer here. We need to regroup and expand our search."

I fastened my arms around his back, tears of frustration staining his shirt. "I can't believe it. He took them all away—again."

"How many more were there?"

"I don't know."

"A handful." A new voice spoke from the depths of the caves. "Ranger X is right—they're gone."

I looked up, pulled my face away from X's chest. It was dark, but not so dark I couldn't make out the features of the man who'd sacrificed himself to get me away from Wishery.

"Jonathon!" I cried. "You're okay!"

"I'm fine," he agreed with a smile. "But Ranger X is correct. It's no use searching any further; they're all gone."

"To where?" I asked, still registering. "And how did you..."

"Get out?" he grinned. "Walk with me. This place is empty. I've already checked."

X took my hand as we followed Jonathon out into the gardens where I'd first gathered with the group of escapees. He sat on a bench, and I sat next to X across from him.

"After you left, The Faction moved quickly to break everything down. They gathered all their things, their supplies, their prisoners. Then, they took off."

"And how did you manage to stay behind?"

"I was in line with the rest of the prisoners, the last in line, when someone grabbed my arm," Jonathon said, a look of confusion knitting his eyebrows together. "I didn't recognize him."

"What did he say?"

"He didn't give us a name." Jonathon squinted at us. "I'd put him at older than you, slightly graying hair, but still handsome. Well dressed."

My voice caught in the back of my throat. "Liam."

"Like I said, he didn't give a name, but he did cut Peter and I free."

"Peter's here?!" I looked over Jonathon's shoulder, as if expecting to find the reporter hovering in the bushes. "Where?"

"He chose to stay with the group."

"Why would he do that?" X growled. "He chose to remain a prisoner?"

"He's going for the big story," Jonathon said. "Peter Knope—he will do *anything* to get a front-page headline."

"Including staying inside enemy lines?" X shot back. "I don't think so."

"You'd do anything for your job," Jonathon said. "Why shouldn't he?"

"Because he writes articles out of left field for the newspaper. Nobody believes him."

"We'll believe him this time," Jonathon said, eyeing X. "He's the only one who'll have these insights. I wouldn't put it past the man to risk his life for his job. The best ones do."

X glanced over at me and slowly nodded before turning back to Jonathon. "Fine. And you? What's your story?"

"This guy—Liam, I suppose—told me to find you," Jonathon said, fixing his gaze on me. "He asked me to relay a message."

"I don't want to hear it."

"He asked me to tell you to give him a chance. To hear him out."

I tightened my lips. "I'm not sure I can do that. He was standing right next to my father, conversing as if they were friends."

"Maybe there's more to the story," Jonathon said. "He didn't have to free me. Peter said he let him go earlier, too. Apparently, Peter had been captured in the tunnels, and Liam orchestrated his release."

"The distraction..." I glanced at the destroyed ballroom behind us. "*Peter* caused the distraction."

Jonathon nodded. "It went according to plan, after all. Then once I broke free, I waited here and watched as they took off carrying everything they could hold."

"Where did they go?"

"I imagine they haven't told anyone," Jonathon said. "I certainly don't know."

I shook my head. "They're gone. The question is for how long?"

"I have something more for you." Jonathon reached into his pocket and handed me a crumpled sheet of paper. "It's from Peter."

I scanned it quickly, and gave a soft laugh. "Another article."

Jonathon stood. "He also asked me to let you know he's still expecting an exclusive when this is all over."

"Exclusive?" X asked.

"An interview." I shook my head. "For the paper."

"Did the others make it?" Jonathon stretched, looking into the blue shades of sky. "Is it too much to ask for a ride out of here?"

"I'll ride with X," I said to Jonathon. "You can take my broomstick. We should be getting back."

"Poppy?" he asked. "Is she...?"

I couldn't meet his eyes. "She's still the same."

"I'm sorry, Lily."

"It's not your fault," I said. "Let's get out of here."

Chapter 36

THE JOURNEY BACK TO MAGIC, Inc. was a fast one.

Jonathon, X, and I returned the broomsticks, then waited around as the medical team performed a quick full body scan. They finally declared all of us clean to head back to The Isle and arranged for transportation. The others had already gone before us.

By the time the bungalow loomed into view, we were all weary and exhausted.

"Do you need a place to stay tonight?" I asked Jonathon, "You could always stay here, and I could go with X."

"No, thank you," Jonathon said. "I'm going to head home. Not that my mother will notice, but my friends might. Thanks again for everything."

"Thank you." I gave him a hug, and then stepped back as Ranger X shook his hand. "If you think about it," I added. "Swing by next week for Poppy's birthday party. I'm sure she'd like to see you."

The caveat remained unspoken. *If* she remembered him.

I climbed the front stairs, leaning heavily on X as we did so. "Do you feel like staying here tonight?" I asked, then came to an abrupt stop as I entered the storeroom. "What are you guys doing here?"

Gus, Hettie, and Poppy sat before a roaring fire, the former two cupping mugs of tea in their hands, the latter humming a nonsensical tune as she examined every jar and vial in the place as if she'd just seen it for the first time.

"They couldn't find anything wrong with her," Hettie explained, nodding toward her granddaughter. "They scanned her for everything from human medical issues to magical malfunctions." She shook her head. "The only thing the MAGIC, Inc. doctors suggested is that the blood magic scrambled with her brain."

"She's a vampire," Gus said. "That magic ain't made for vamps."

"This magic was stronger than I've ever seen." I moved across the room and rested a hand on Poppy's shoulder. "How are you? Do you remember me?"

Poppy squinted for a moment, then gave a gleeful smile. "Hello, I'm Poppy. Have we met?"

"She's needs an anchor." I straightened, shaking Poppy's extended hand while speaking to Gus and Hettie. "Something from her past, something so strong that when she sees it, or remembers it, she'll have no choice but to slip back into reality. She's not lost, I know it. She's..."

"Scrambled," Gus said. "Scrambled like eggs in there."

Hettie elbowed him. "Be sensitive."

"I'm just saying," Gus said. "Lily, isn't there a way you can...unscramble her?"

Another elbow from Hettie and a grunt from Gus.

"I don't know." I shook my head, my lips in a thin line. "When we pulled Zin out of the mind bending trance, it was an accident. It wasn't something I tried to do."

"Well, we have to figure something out," Gus said, crossing his arms. "Her mother can't see her like this."

"We need an anchor," I repeated, thumbing through my supplies. "Or maybe there's a better way. Maybe I can create some sort of Mix, something familiar that will trigger her memories to return."

"You can't reverse an antidote," Gus said. "That'd just be the original spell."

"I know that," I snapped. "But I can take piece of it, and...*here* we go, Poppy. Poppy? Can you do me a favor?"

Poppy balanced precariously on a stepstool, climbing to reach for a glass jar of frog legs near the top shelf. "A favor?"

"Come on down from there," I coaxed. "I need you to try something for me."

She climbed down, giving one last, longing glance at the frog legs. "Try what?"

I brought a few jars to the middle of the storeroom and began combing Dust of the Devil into small piles. I had nearly completed Poppy's latest batch of Vamp Vites before my unexpected visit to Wishery.

"Take a sip of this," I said, extending her a glass of water. "And then have a seat. We're going to put something together to make you feel better."

"But I feel fine."

"Who am I?" I asked her pointedly.

She frowned, but didn't answer.

"Exactly," I muttered to myself. I struggled to keep the nerves at bay, to push away the fear that Poppy's damage had become permanent. "Not even a flicker of remembrance."

"How are we going to keep her away from Mimsey?" Gus asked, looking perplexed. "She'll ask about Poppy the second I see her, and I can't lie."

"We're all staying here until we get to the bottom of this," Hettie said. "Let's get working. No sneaking out on us, Gus."

"I don't sneak over to Mimsey's," Gus retorted. "We're both adults. Hell, we're old folks."

"If you're old, what does that make me?" Hettie snapped, then gripped Gus's ear and gave it a good shake. "Watch your mouth. Don't forget, you date my daughter, and I don't care if she's ninety-two years old, she's my baby."

"She's not..." Gus hesitated. "Ninety-two?"

Hettie just crossed her arms and gave Gus the death stare when, as if on cue, Ranger X stiffened just a second before the door burst open. There, framed with the darkness behind her, stood Mimsey, panting with exertion.

"You're back?!" Mimsey puffed, her eyes streaked black with mascara and rimmed in red. "Why did nobody tell me—" She stopped dead at the sight of her daughter, her eyes widening. "Poppy!"

Poppy had her back to her mother, sorting through a few more jars on the shelves. She'd returned to humming, pausing only to ask, "Who are you?" as she turned.

"Poppy..." Mimsey's voice froze in her throat as her daughter stopped moving and faced her. "Poppy, I'm so sorry about everything. I've been trying to explain, but you went away, and I couldn't find you. I promise that I can explain everything."

Mimsey halted her speech, the rest of the group bowing their heads. I took a step back, desperate to leave the room and give the mother and daughter their privacy.

However, Poppy's new phrase of *Hello, I'm Poppy,* never came.

After a painstakingly long wait, I glanced up and watched in awe as Poppy took a step closer to her mother.

"What's wrong with her?" Mimsey asked to the general audience. "Why is she acting strange? Is it me? Do you still hate me, Poppy? I promise, I love you more than anything."

"I love you," Poppy parroted, a weak sounding voice as she took another step closer. "Mom?"

"Of course it's me, honey," Mimsey murmured. "I've never gone anywhere. I've always been your mother, I promise you."

"Mom, I don't know..." Poppy stilled, then turned in a slow circle. "Lily? And X? Why am I here? What happened?"

Hettie shrieked in excitement. "Do me! Do me next! What's my name, Poppy?"

"Stop it, Hettie," Poppy said, wincing as she covered her ears with her palms. "You're bursting my eardrums. Will someone please explain why you all are staring at me like I'm one of Lily's weird Mixes?"

"What did they do to you?" Mimsey asked, still struggling to comprehend. "Why can't you remember how you got here?"

"Mimsey, until you walked in, she couldn't remember a thing," I said, stepping forward. "She couldn't seem to remember my name, even after I'd told her several times. All from a blood magic spell gone bad."

"But—" Mimsey spluttered. "That's impossible. She knows who I am."

"What the hell was in that cup of water you gave her?" Gus asked me in a whisper. "I want some of that potion if my mind ever starts to go."

"It wasn't a potion," I argued. "It was water."

"Water is a potion?" Mimsey asked. "What are you all talking about?"

"The Faction had attempted to use blood magic on Poppy, and..."

"They can't do that," Mimsey interrupted me with a sharp inhalation. "She's a vampire. It either won't work, or it will..."

"Scramble her," I said, for lack of better words. "It completely wiped her memory."

"But..." Mimsey squinted. "Is it back?"

"She needed some sort of anchor to her previous life, something so strong it couldn't possibly let her forget," I explained. "It's you, Mimsey. You are her anchor—her mother. You brought her back."

Poppy had been listening, too, her mouth hanging open in surprise. "How long have I been wandering around clueless?"

"Too long," Mimsey said, her gaze fixed on me. "Is she fine, otherwise?"

"Fit as a fiddle," Hettie said. "They did a full scan on her at MAG-IC, Inc. They just couldn't figure out why she struggled with memory loss. They worried it might be irreversible."

"Do you remember...?" Mimsey asked, her voice hushed. "The conversation we had just before you left?"

Poppy frowned, thinking hard, and then stilled. The moment it clicked, there was a visible slump to her shoulders. "Yes, mom, I'm so sorry...I'd meant—"

"I'm sorry, honey," Mimsey said. "I'm sorry that I kept it from you for so long."

"I'm sorry I ran off," Poppy said. "I'd only meant to grab a breath of fresh air, maybe talk to Zin and Lily about it...I'd never meant to disappear."

"I thought you wanted nothing to do with me." Mimsey's lips quivered, her entire body shaking with terror and relief. "My darling, I love you more than anything in this world, and I just want you to know that whether you're my blood or not...I'm yours. I'm here for you, if you want me as a mother."

Poppy collapsed against Mimsey, her arms reaching around and latching on from behind. "Of course you're my mother! I've never doubted that, mom, I was just processing. It's a surprise, you know?"

"Of course," Mimsey said, half giggling with hysteria, half crying. "B-but I thought maybe I wouldn't be good enough for you any-more."

"You're the only mother I've ever had, ever needed, and will ever need," Poppy said. "If anything, we're lucky. People don't get to choose their families, but we...I guess we sort of did."

"No," Mimsey said, wrapping her daughter into her arms. "There was never a choice. You were always mine."

Chapter 37

"SO, WHAT YOU'RE SAYING is..." Poppy began, leaning toward the group with a smile on her face. "We should celebrate my birthday more often?"

"How do you figure that?" Zin asked. "You practically passed out from thinking we hadn't planned anything."

"But you *had* planned something," Poppy corrected. "And if Lily hadn't created the Long Isle Iced Tea, you wouldn't have gotten into the uniforms and out of the castle. Speaking of parties, is mine still on?"

The whole lot of us who'd returned from Wishery, along with Zin, sat around a crackling fire in the bungalow. We'd spent the last few hours talking, eating our fill, and generally enjoying the feel of home.

"Of course your party is still on," I said. "Sorry it's no longer a surprise, though."

Poppy waved a hand. "I've had enough surprises."

"Well," Hettie said. "I'm ready for a hot shower and my bed. These muscles aren't what they used to be. What do you say we break for now and regroup later?"

"Poppy," I said, as everyone stood. "Can I talk to you for a second?"

"Sure, Lil." She followed me off to the side of the room, concern inching her eyebrows together. "What is it?"

"Did they..." I paused to clear my throat. "Did anyone ever tell you why they took you?"

"It doesn't matter anymore," she said. "I'm back, and—"

"It might matter. He's still out there."

Poppy's bright eyes faded some, and her shoulder sagged. "It was to keep you there," she said. "He told me himself. Said it was a way to keep you around without having to lock you in a room."

"Poppy, I'm so sorry."

"It's my fault," she said. "If it were Zin or Ranger X, they'd probably have been able to get themselves out of the mess, but me..."

I wrapped my hand around her wrist and pulled Poppy close. "No, of course not. It's because we're family," I told her. "It has nothing to do with anything else. In fact, speaking of family..."

"Yes?"

"There's something I need to tell you. There's a reason he came after you to get to me."

"Right, because you're the Mixologist."

"No, it's more than that," I said, twisting my fingers in front of my body. "I'm...he's my father."

Poppy's eyes widened, and then her face crumpled into an expression of pure sympathy. In true Poppy form, she didn't ask questions or press for more. She simply opened her arms, pulled me to her, and held me for a long moment.

Eventually, we parted and Poppy rejoined her mother's side as she took off with Mimsey and Hettie. The sun had begun to rise in the distance, glinting off the shimmering surface of the water. The only people to linger behind were Ranger X and Zin.

"So, how do you feel about me sticking around for a bit?" Zin asked. "Not to move in permanently, but maybe for a couple of days? It's just—"

I raised a hand to stop her. "Pick your favorite room."

As Zin climbed the stairs, I sank against Ranger X and watched the glow across the lake.

"When did you know I was gone?" I asked him, quiet. "I wanted to give you a warning, but Lucian didn't give me time."

"I suppose I knew right away. There was this uneasiness in the air," X said, his voice a soothing rumble in the early morning sunlight. "Gus and I arrived at the bungalow at the same time. He'd come back from dealing with the shipment of supplies, and I'd felt...I'd felt a need to check on you. When we both realized we hadn't heard from you, we knew something was wrong."

I squeezed his arm to me. "This isn't over, I suppose. Wishery. The Faction."

"It's never over," X agreed. "But we'll find Peter and the rest of the prisoners; the Rangers are already on it. I briefed them while you were in testing at MAGIC, Inc."

"I just wish—"

"Be careful what you wish for," X said, turning to face me. "Wishes are powerful."

I remembered the wish I'd made just a few days ago. Then, I looked into the skies and said a tiny thank-you to Lizzie and her team at Wishery.

Having my family around me tonight—everyone tucked safely back home—came very close to perfect.

"HAPPY BIRTHDAY DEAR Poppy..." we all chorused. "Happy birthday to you."

She smiled, blinking back tears, and then raised a glass of Long Isle Iced Tea. "Thank you to everyone who put this party together. It's the best surprise yet. Now, drink up and show me your costumes!"

I'd offered to host the party at Magic & Mixology, the bar area just outside the bungalow, so the festivities could sprawl across the beach.

Torches burned along the edges of the grounds, giving the air a flickering, almost tribal sort of feel. Underneath the sky dotted with stars, we all began to sip the cocktail that'd transform us into the costume we most desired. Poppy went first, and with a soft pop turned into a princess. Her outfit came complete with a pretty pink dress, a tiara, and white gloves up to her elbows. She twittered with happiness.

Ranger X approached me, and I turned to him, startled. "I thought you said you'd be late!" I opened my arms, but he didn't lean in for a hug. "Is something wrong? Is it work?"

"Something is seriously wrong," Ranger X said, but it wasn't Ranger X's voice. "Lily, it's *me*. Something went wrong when I drank the potion, and I turned into...*this*! Save me!"

I squinted. The voice was familiar and, now that I looked, the shape of X was all wrong. Far too feminine. Under the darkness of night, however, I couldn't trust my judgement. "Who is it?"

"It's me! Zin!" She pulled me to the side. "You need to reverse this before the real Ranger X arrives. How *embarrassing*."

I covered my mouth with my hand. "You're saying you drank the potion, and it turned you into Ranger X? That's your costume?"

"I kept thinking in my head I just wanted to be a Ranger. And, well..." She shrugged helplessly. "This happened."

"I guess he's made an impression on you."

"Real funny, Lily. Now, fix me before it's too..." She trailed off as a shadow appeared behind her. "It's too late, isn't it?"

A throat cleared behind Zin.

"Oh, um, hello," I said, as the real Ranger X appeared under the flickering torch light. "How are you?"

X didn't respond, staring down at his Mini Me. "Who is that?"

"Nobody," I said, spinning the real Ranger X around and sending him off with a little shove. "Go wish Poppy a happy birthday."

"I already did."

"Go, again."

He began to march away, still shooting confused glances over his shoulder.

"What do I do?" Zin squeaked. "This is mortifying! He can't know that it was me."

"Go into the kitchen—there's a bright yellow jug in the fridge. Looks and tastes like lemonade. It'll take care of all of..." I hesitated, running a hand in circles before her. "This."

Zin whimpered. "Even you can't stop smiling."

"I'm not smiling," I said, with a huge smile on my face. "It's not a smile."

Zin threw her hands up, shoved around me, and marched toward the kitchen. Ainsley tottered over after her, dressed like a flamingo. Then, a procession began with Hettie, dressed as a motorcycle mama, then Mimsey, a bird watcher, and Trinket...who looked to have no costume at all.

The sisters were already back to arguing over whether the hor d'oeuvres had been served too early or too late, too crispy or too soft. Hettie didn't seem to care either way, since I'd watched her dump two plates of them straight into her purse.

The party had been a hit. I had yet to drink the potion, and I wasn't sure if I planned on it. Someone had to make sure the supplies didn't run out and the drinks stayed fresh. My party, my job.

"Y'all think you're getting out of this costume party, but you're not," Poppy said, shuffling over with two drinks in hand. Behind her trailed Ranger X, as if on a leash. "Even Chuck over there is getting into the spirit. His spirit animal is an elephant."

I glanced at the gnome who, with a disgruntled look on his face, was examining a trunk that extended longer than his arms.

"Come on," Poppy said. "Drink up."

"I will if you will," I said, raising a glass to X.

He wrinkled his nose. "I don't think so. Best if I stay on duty."

"Uh, I work dispatch," Poppy said. "I see the schedule, and there are plenty of people on duty. Drink up."

I took his hand, urged him on with a big smile. "Please?"

Reluctantly, he clinked his glass against mine, then downed it in a few gulps. I followed suit.

"What's wrong with him?" Poppy watched Ranger X. "And what is your costume, Lily?"

I'd felt the tingle of the potion changing me, but I couldn't tell what I'd become. Glancing at Ranger X, I, too, couldn't see a change. "Did you grab the right potion?"

"Oh, wait," Poppy said with a short laugh. "I see X's change. But you, Lily...I don't understand."

"What's X's change?" I demanded. "Have you figured out what mine is?"

"You'll figure it out!" Poppy linked her arm through mine. "Lily, come with me. X, can you give us a minute? Why don't you hang out here while I borrow Lily, and you can..." She paused, looking coy. "*Ring* in my birthday!"

"What are you doing?" I asked, once she pulled me into the storeroom and we'd gained a bit of privacy. "What's so important you're not outside enjoying your own party?"

She opened her mouth to respond, but Zin stumbled in then, her Ranger X costume shrinking rapidly. Poppy watched, her mouth hanging open, until Zin returned to her normal black clothing.

"What was that?" Poppy asked, stifling a giggle as she looked to me. "Was she dressed as Ranger—"

"Shut up," Zin snapped. "I need to talk to you both about something."

"Okay, go ahead, then." Poppy paused as Gus stumbled into the storeroom dressed as a pirate. He barely glanced our way. "Unless it's private."

"It's private."

"Who are you?" Zin asked, surveying my costume change.

"I don't know," I confessed. "None of us do."

"Follow me." Poppy drew the three of us outside, pointing herself toward the edge of the lake as we huddled near one of the bonfires set into the sand. "Okay, Zin. What is it?"

"I'm not going to be staying with you anymore," Zin said. "I'm sorry."

"But I thought—"

"Lily, I love you," Zin said, "and I appreciate you giving me a place to crash the last few days. But after everything with Poppy, I did some thinking. I'm going to help my mom out for the summer with the kids, and then I'll look for my own place. I'd like to have some peace and quiet in my off time, and Lily, the bungalow is anything but peaceful!"

Poppy nodded. "Same goes for me. Who knows? I'm trying to get Zin to ask the Witch of the Woods if we can move into her old place."

"Of course that's fine, but you're always welcome with me. Just promise you'll ask for help before camping out in some abandoned shack."

"What?" Poppy asked. "Who did that?"

"Never mind," Zin said. "And I promise."

"Now it's my turn to share the news," Poppy said. "Well, actually, it's Lily's news. Did you ever figure out X's change?"

"I haven't even figured out my *own* change."

"Well..." She winked, then raised her left hand. "Someone had a ring. On his ring finger."

I shook my head. "What are you saying?"

"I'm saying that what he desires most is to be with you forever! To get married, Lily," Poppy said on a huge, dramatic sigh. "Just think. He's spent all these years—most of his life—being told he *can't*. He can't have ties, can't have a relationship, can't fall in love. So, it's not that far-fetched to imagine that the one thing he'd desire above all else is a permanent commitment."

"I don't know," I said, though my face heated at the thought. "Don't you think it's too soon to be thinking about forever?"

"He seems like a man who knows what he wants and goes for it," Poppy said. "I don't think there's any such thing as *too soon*."

"I don't know, I mean..." My heart pounded against my chest. *Was it true? Is that what X wanted above* all *else*? "He just gave me a key. He can't be thinking about permanent attachments yet."

Zin snorted. "Ranger X handing out a key is the *equivalent* of a permanent attachment.

Suddenly, I couldn't breathe. I'd barely come to terms with the fact that I had magical powers, that West Isle Witch blood ran through my veins. I loved Ranger X, absolutely, but the thought of marriage—it seemed, somehow, too soon.

I tried to catch my breath while the party carried on merrily without us. Sophie and Manuel snuck out early, holding hands and so very madly in love. *They* were ready to be married—*not* me.

Jonathon, Drew, and Magdalena Sprite had all come as well, checking on Poppy as soon as they arrived. The group had truly bonded during their time in Wishery. Even Belinda had made an appearance, smiling and introducing everyone to her son. It seemed she had already found her life outside the confines of The Faction.

"Our family is so strange," Poppy muttered as Hettie started a conga line. "She's almost ninety. Shouldn't she be playing bridge or something?"

"She's having fun," Zin said, a smile on her face. "I like our weird family."

"Me too," Poppy said. "And I also like the way Jonathon is looking tonight. Do you think he'll mind if I hop in the conga line behind him?"

"I've gotta see this," Zin said.

The two girls rejoined the party, Poppy sliding in line behind Jonathon while Zin pulled several of her siblings to the dance floor. I hung back, not quite ready to participate, as Poppy's words came flooding back.

Had she been right? Was Ranger X ready to get married *now*? The thought sent my heart skittering in every direction.

The sound of soft footsteps approached from the side. Whoever made them was unsure, hesitant. Sucked into a daydream, I watched the party, the dancing and eating and drinking, waiting for my visitor to speak.

"Lily?" The voice belonged to Trinket, though it wasn't her usual snappy tone. "Is that—"

I began to turn toward her, and she reacted instantly. Flailing her arms, stumbling backward, Trinket collapsed to the ground. She tried to struggle, but her smart gray pantsuit restricted her movements as she scrambled away from me, as if she'd seen a ghost.

"Trinket, it's me," I told her, reaching out a hand. "Calm down. What's wrong?"

She stared at my hand as if it were cursed, stumbling to her feet without my help. "It's—you're...*her*."

"Who?"

At my question, Trinket's face crumpled, her eyes pooling with tears. "Lily, how can you not know?"

Finally, Trinket rested her hands on my shoulders and gently guided me forward. She brought me to the edge of the lake and urged me to peer into it. Into the pure water at our feet, reflecting the night sky, the stars behind us, and...my face. The face that *should* be mine, rather, and now belonged to another.

"Delilah," Trinket said, raising a hand to touch my cheek. "Oh, Lily, you look just like her."

"But my wish..." I hesitated. "I wasn't *supposed* to change. When I drank the Long Isle Iced Tea, I wished only to be surrounded by my family—I wished for us all to be happy and healthy and safe. I didn't *want* to change, and I didn't try to."

Trinket's face flickered, revealing a light behind her eyes that I hadn't seen before. "You are truly incredible, Lily. Your potion must be stronger than you'd ever imagined. It must read the contents of your heart, the wishes, the questions that you can't hide."

"What good does *that* do? I wanted it to be a fun party trick not..." I kicked at the water, sending my mother's reflection scattering in every direction. "I didn't want *this*."

Trinket took my hand and knelt down. I went with her, and together we stared at my new face—*her* face—in the water. It moved with every ripple, every breath of the tide, but the similarities were there; we had the same eyes, the same curve of smile, but her hair was curlier than mine, and lighter. She had been beautiful.

"She was beautiful," Trinket echoed, as if reading my mind. "Just like you."

"But *why*?"

"We don't *really* know how we lost her," Trinket said. "And Lily—"

I froze at the sharp inhalation of Trinket's voice. "What is it?"

She stopped abruptly, reaching for my neck. Before, I'd been wearing a heart locket that had been passed down from my mother—a locket meant to protect me from harm. Normally it shone gold, but now, it glowed blue.

"A prophesy," she breathed. "Lily, I think...I think it's trying to tell you something."

"But *what*?!"

Trinket reached for my neck, her fingers grasping for the glowing blue locket. She swiped, but instead of connecting with the chain around my neck, her hand sailed right through it. The illusion was severed. It broke into a million pieces, fragments of diamonds sending mirages of color in every direction of the lake's reflection. By the time Trinket recoiled her hand, the transformation was over.

I had returned to Lily, and my mother, once again, was gone.

"I think it was trying to tell you something," Trinket whispered. "Drink another round of the potion. Let me see her again."

"I—I don't think that's a good idea."

"Lily, I need to *see* her. It's been so long."

"Not *now*. I don't think it's a good idea. The potion isn't meant to be used continually for too long. A person can start...losing themselves if that's the case."

"But—"

"Tonight is about Poppy," I reminded her. "And family. And being together. Go back to the party, Trinket. I think we should keep this to ourselves—at least, for now. We don't know that it means anything. Maybe it's just my missing her, my curiosity, my not knowing that slipped out."

"I don't think so."

But Trinket didn't argue. Shaky, she backed away with only a slight nod of agreement. As she stumbled back toward the party, she turned, glancing back once, and then twice, then a third time, before she realized Delilah was gone for good.

"Making a wish?" A deep voice spoke in a hushed tone behind me. Ranger X came to stand next to me, not yet touching, just looking at the sky. "I didn't believe your little chant, at first."

"And now?"

"Now..." A crooked smile tilted his lips upward. "I guess we'll see."

Still reeling from the shock of discovering my mother's face in my reflection, I couldn't respond with my normal light-hearted banter.

Ranger X seemed to sense this and took my hand, leading me further away from the rowdy conga line behind us. Our bare feet kicked up the sugar-white sand on the beach, sending sprays of powder in a soft *puff* before us.

He stopped near the edge of the water, just beyond the waves threatening to inch over our toes. The bright night reflected against the lake, casting a magical sort of glow around us. Away from the party, silence encased us.

The kiss came from nowhere. My eyes had been fixed on the starlight dancing in the water when X's lips, soft and sweet, met mine. It lasted longer than I'd expected, his touches tender, sugary sweet, and tasting of Long Isle Iced Tea.

When he finally pulled away, he left me wobbly against him. I couldn't help but grin sleepily. "That was nice."

Ranger X murmured an agreement, tucking me to his side as we listened to the steady beats from the party mixed with the underlying pulse of the water. "What'd you wish for this time?"

"I wasn't making a wish," I said, leaning against his chest. My fingers traced a pattern over his white shirt, feeling the firm muscles underneath. "I don't *need* a wish right now, so I didn't make one. I left them for someone else, someone who needs one more than I do."

"I shouldn't be surprised," he said, a flicker of understanding passing in a shadow across his face. "Is there nothing more that you want?"

My arms linked around his body as I thought hard, but I couldn't come up with anything I needed. *Wanted,* maybe, but not needed. I *wanted* to find out what the glowing orb around my neck had been, and *why* I'd transformed into my mother, but I didn't *need* to know. Not now, at least, not yet.

So, I shook my head. "I'm happy. My family is safe and together, you and I are here—what more is there?"

"You don't sound very happy."

"I'm sorry," I said, leaning my head against him. "I'm confused."

His expression pinched, and he cinched his fingers tighter to my waist. "What's wrong?"

Startled, I found tears pricking the backs of my eyes, and I blinked, fighting them back. Ranger X's eyes, dark and serious, landed on mine in concern.

I looked up at this man who I'd seen face the worst of evils without so much as flinching, yet now, here he stood with fear in his eyes.

"Are you worried about...*this*?" He raised a hand, the ring still sparkling there. "You don't need to be—I don't need...I *do* need you, Lily, but I'm not going to rush you into anything."

"Why did we drink the potion?" I asked my voice hoarse. "It made everything more complicated. I changed into my mother, X. I didn't get a ring. I'm sorry."

"Don't apologize. All this means is that when they took you from me, it made everything perfectly clear," Ranger X said, speaking in a gravelly voice. "I didn't know how to...to understand it. To deal with it, all of it—*us,* our lives having become so entwined, my happiness so linked to yours."

"Cannon, it's okay. We'll figure it out together, and—"

"I know," he said, his gaze steady as he met mine. "I knew I loved you before, Lily, but I didn't know how much. When I realized there was a chance you might never come back..."

He hesitated, and my heart constricted for him as he struggled to find the words. Even after he coughed and started again, the hoarseness lingered.

"I love you more than this world, more than this life," he said. "I never imagined that I would *think* of marriage—with anyone."

My limbs shook. Every inch of my body tensed as he stepped away, glancing down at his feet before returning those dark chocolate eyes to mine.

"I know what I want, what I need, and the truth is..." His eyes gleamed with certainty. When he spoke next, it was with the utmost confidence. "I *can't* live without you."

The tears pricking my eyes turned into small pools, and I trembled under his gaze. "You don't want to marry me," I told him, a sob scratching at my throat. "You don't—you *can't* want to. Not after what happened with Lucian."

Ranger X's eyes opened in alarm. "What are you talking about?"

"You didn't hear his scream." I closed my eyes, hearing the cry as if my father was kneeling before me, breaking a piece of my soul off with his pain. "I *hurt* someone, and I hurt him badly. Do you not know what I do? What I *am*?"

"Of course, Lily—"

"I'm the *Mixologist*," I cried. "The *only* rule I have is to *Do Good.* I didn't do anything *good* back there, X, I hurt my own father!"

"You stood up to a man who is causing an entire civilization harm. Sometimes, to protect those we love," he said, speaking from a place that knew this struggle well, "we have to do things we aren't proud of."

"That's *your* job. Mine is to *Do Good.* To protect the world, to make it better. If I start using my powers to hurt others..." I gasped, my chest tightening with pain. "I'm no better than *him.*"

Ranger X held me, my shoulders wracked with sobs as my worst fears were realized—that my father and I shared more than simple DNA. That I would be like *him,* the enemy I'd sworn to defeat.

"You are *not* like him," Ranger X said, tilting my chin upward. "You are mine, you belong to this island, and you are good."

My breath died as he locked his lips on mine with a ferocity that told me he'd never let go. My heart thudded against his, and I let my arms wrap around his sturdy back.

"Someday, Lily Locke," Ranger X whispered against my hair. "I'm going to ask you to marry me. And when I do, I'm going to tell you that you make me the happiest man alive. That you are the brightest star in the darkest sky, and that you're the only truly good part of *me.*"

He hesitated, stroking my hair, holding me close.

"And then," he continued. "I'll make my final wish—a wish I can't tell you because *I need* it to come true."

"Cannon..."

"Once I have you forever, I will need nothing else."

My throat parched from pain, and my eyes red from crying, didn't seem to bother X. He leaned in, pressing another kiss to my lips that stopped my heart. When he finally pulled away, I raised a hand to my chest and gripped the locket that'd been passed down to me from my mother. It was warm to the touch.

"I know she would've liked you," I whispered. "If only she could have met you."

"If only." X reached for my hand, held it to his side. "Shall I take you home?"

"Tell me one thing." I didn't want to ask, but the question had been burning a hole in me. "How long will you wait? For me?"

Ranger X smiled. Then he reached over and brushed my wild hair away from my face. "Until the world ends, Lily Locke."

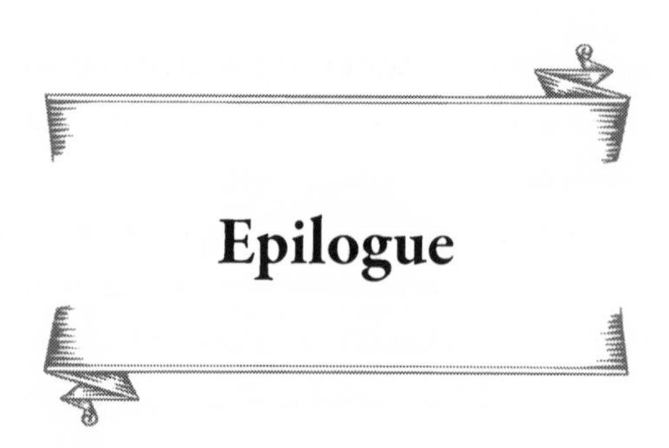

Epilogue

ONE WEEK LATER

"Make it stop," I instructed, lounging against a wall of blankets. "All the way."

X stood on the edge of the cave deep in The Forest. Ranger X extended his hands, glowing gold, and brought the waterfall before us to a complete stop.

"Now make it change directions and flow the other way," I said.

He let his hands drop, giving me a cheeky smile as he turned and let the water return to its normal flow. "You know that'd take every last ounce of my strength, right? You don't want that."

"Oh really?!" I shrieked as his hands reached for me, plucking me from the blankets and moving me onto his lap. "And what might you need energy for?"

I curled against him in our makeshift camp, the cozy little nook where we'd set up a bed and bonfire for the evening. We'd returned to our date spot from just before the mess of Wishery had begun, deeming it a secluded portion of this island reserved just for us.

It was here that we'd decided to travel together once a month. Ranger X could hone his powers under my tutelage, or my bossiness. He'd prevent another bout of Lumiette from happening, and as a bonus, we now had a standing date together once a month. An escape, a private getaway, for just the two of us.

Especially after the excitement from our previous week, we'd needed a break—a break from people, from reporters, from my family. From the thoughts and dreams that plagued me—the ones where I looked into the mirror to find my mother with a locket glowing bright around her neck.

Once here, we'd been able to finally relax. This evening, Ranger X wore nothing except a pair of shorts. He'd been working with the waterfall, practicing his telekinesis, and doused his only shirt. I certainly didn't mind; my hands trailed over his shoulders, so strong, so defined. His back, his chest, his waist.

Meanwhile, he laid back, easing me against him into the little crook in his arm where I fit snugly, like I belonged. He took one of my hands and laced his fingers through mine.

"Thank you," he murmured between kisses along my cheek, my neck, my shoulders. "For coming out here with me."

"No need to thank me," I chirped. "I'm having a fabulous time."

He laid me down beside him, then rolled over so he was on top of me. The way he'd moved, he had me pinned to the blankets.

Those dark, chocolate eyes warmed as he watched me, studied every millimeter of my face. Now and forever, I was his, and his alone.

"What are you thinking?" I whispered.

A pop in the distance sounded, and in an instant, my tender, sensual Cannon vanished as he coiled into Ranger X, and we lost all train of thought. Creeping along the edge of the cave, he huddled against the ledge and gestured for me to shrink back and stay quiet.

I didn't argue since I didn't have all that much clothing on myself. So, I pulled the blankets up to my chest and watched through my fingers.

Ranger X listened, almost catlike in his stance, as another sound crackled, and then another. It didn't make sense; we had told nobody where we'd gone. Even if we had, the journey to reach this location was a difficult one. It would have to be someone familiar with The Forest, familiar with X, with The Isle, with—

A gargling sound matched the exact moment Ranger X stretched his hand out, a beam of concentrated light shooting straight ahead and pulling a body from the shadows. Much like the night of The Core meeting when he'd first exposed his powers on Harpin, a man now dangled from thin air just feet before the cave.

"Liam!" I wrapped the blankets around me like a toga and stumbled into a standing position. "What are you doing here?"

Though he hung off a cliff, suspended by nothing but Ranger X's mental power, he didn't flinch. Liam's face remained passive, and his figure limp. Not an ounce of fight in him.

"I'm sorry to interrupt," he said, gasping for air. "But I couldn't risk anyone finding out about my visit."

"Because you're working with *him*!" Ranger X's concentration was funneled entirely toward keeping Liam suspended, so I did all the talking. "You traitor! To think I trusted you. We trusted you."

"I did what I had to do. I've been in talks with your father for years, Lily, and without me, you wouldn't have escaped," he said. "Jonathon and Peter—who do you think set them free?"

"You're doing what's best for yourself, not for *us*," I spat. "Maybe you let them go, but only after I caught you there. You're scrambling, Liam, and I'm not falling for it."

"Don't believe me then. I will prove myself to you. I know where they've gone."

"How do we know it's not a trap?"

"You... don't." His breath became more ragged as Ranger X cinched tighter. "But I'll tell you, anyway."

"Then *speak*."

"They're in transit now," Liam gasped. "If you can get to them in the next two weeks, the rest of the prisoners will be freed."

Ranger X twisted his hands, bringing Liam's feet to rest against the edge of the cliff. X approached him slowly, cautiously, and when he spoke, his words were edged with the hint of death. "I don't have to tell you what will happen if this offer isn't genuine."

Liam shook himself off. "Of course not, and I'd expect nothing less from you, Cannon."

We both froze at Liam's use of Ranger X's name.

"I know more than the two of you could ever imagine," Liam said as an explanation. "And believe it or not, this visit has nothing to do with The Faction or its prisoners."

"Then why did you come?" I asked.

"I need your help. We need your help," Liam said. "The entire *world* needs your help."

"My help?"

"There are things at play here bigger than The Faction. Bigger than your father, bigger than you and me. Lily, there are things I wish I could tell you, but..." Liam swallowed, looking to be in excruciating pain as he struggled with his next words. "I can't," he gasped, the pain seemingly physical. "You don't have to trust me now, but listen. Give me a chance."

"Why did he take me? Is it because I'm his *daughter*?"

Liam's face contorted in a new form of pain, a form that told me it wasn't inflected externally. "No."

"You once said that you have a vested interested in me," I said. "Why me?"

"There's a prophecy," Liam said. "And you, Lily, are the key to it."

"Lily?" Ranger X snapped. "What does Lily have to do with any of this?"

"It's not Lily *herself,* but someone very close to her." Liam closed his eyes. "I can't say anything more on it."

"This prophecy," I said. "*That's* why he went through all of this to bring me to him? To try and make me see his side?"

"Let me put it this way: when this prophecy comes true," Liam groaned, forcing the words out as if it seared his throat to speak. "Whoever is on *your* side will rule this world."

"That's impossible," I said. "Who came up with this nonsense?"

"I cannot..." he gasped, his voice whistling, as if there were something preventing him from saying more. His face crumpled, his skin red with the effort of speaking. "*Please*."

"When can you tell me more?"

He merely shook his head. "I can't..."

"Lily," Ranger X said, his eyes lighting in recognition. "He *can't*. A curse, an enchantment—something. Liam, if you can't tell us more, what *can* you tell us?"

"The Master of Magic," Liam said, his voice raspy. "He is the next target. And if the Master of Magic—the master of all things paranormal, the one responsible for every thread of magic in this universe—is...*disrupted*, everything will perish. This is the reason Lucian reinstated the SINGLES program to begin with—to prepare for the battle that will destroy magic as we know it. Wishery was just the beginning, a stop along the way. I'm asking for your help."

"I need more information," I said. "This Master of Magic—"

"Is real," Ranger X confirmed. "Also known as the creator of magic, maker of magic..."

"And without this person..." I looked to X. "What would happen?"

"Our world would crumble."

"He's correct." Liam gave a terse smile. "Will you help us?"

Ranger X nodded toward me, his face pale. "It's your decision, Lily."

I took a long, shuddering breath, then raised my eyes to meet Liam's gaze. "Where do we start?"

The End

Author's Note

ISLANDERS,

Thank you for reading! I had so much fun writing this story, and I hope you enjoyed returning to the world of The Isle! Stay tuned for the next installment coming soon. To be notified when it releases, please sign up for my newsletter at www.ginalamanna.com.

Happy reading!

Love,

Gina

Thank you...

To all my readers, especially those of you who have stuck with me from the beginning.

By now, I'm sure you all know how important reviews are for Indie authors, so if you have a moment and enjoyed the story, please consider leaving an honest review on Amazon or Goodreads. I know you are all very busy people and writing a review takes time out of your day—but just know that I appreciate every single one I receive. Reviews help make promotions possible, help with visibility on large retailers and most importantly, help other potential readers decide if they would like to try the book.

I wouldn't be here without all of you, so once again—*thank you.*

See other books by Gina here:

List of Gina's Books![1]

Gina LaManna is the USA TODAY bestselling author of the Magic & Mixology series, the Lacey Luzzi Mafia Mysteries, The Little Things romantic suspense series, and the Misty Newman books.

List of Gina LaManna's other books:

Lola Pink Mystery Series:
Shades of Pink

Magic & Mixology Mysteries:
Hex on the Beach
Witchy Sour
Jinx & Tonic
Long Isle Iced Tea

MAGIC, Inc. Mysteries:
The Undercover Witch
Spies & Spellbooks (*short story coming soon*)

Reading Order for Lacey Luzzi:
Lacey Luzzi: Scooped
Lacey Luzzi: Sprinkled
Lacey Luzzi: Sparkled
Lacey Luzzi: Salted
Lacey Luzzi: Sauced
Lacey Luzzi: S'mored
Lacey Luzzi: Spooked
Lacey Luzzi: Seasoned
Lacey Luzzi: Spiced

---

1. http://www.amazon.com/Gina-LaManna/e/B00RPQD-NPG/?tag=ginlamaut-20

Lacey Luzzi: Suckered
Lacey Luzzi: Sugared
The Little Things Mystery Series:
One Little Wish
Two Little Lies
Misty Newman:
Teased to Death
Short Story in Killer Beach Reads
Chick Lit:
Girl Tripping
Gina also writes books for kids under the Pen Name Libby LaManna:
Mini Pie the Spy!

Made in the USA
Middletown, DE
04 January 2019